FALSE FRIENDS

STEPHEN LEATHER

ISIS
LARGE PRINT
Oxford

Copyright © Stephen Leather, 2012

First published in Great Britain 2012
by
Hodder & Stoughton

Published in Large Print 2013 by ISIS Publishing Ltd.,
7 Centremead, Osney Mead, Oxford OX2 0ES
by arrangement with
Hodder & Stoughton
an Hachette UK Company

All rights reserved

The moral right of the author has been asserted

British Library Cataloguing in Publication Data
Leather, Stephen.
  False friends.
  1. Shepherd, Dan (Fictitious character) - - Fiction.
  2. Suspense fiction.
  3. Large type books.
  I. Title
  823.9'2–dc23

ISBN 978–0–7531–9076–0 (hb)
ISBN 978–0–7531–9077–7 (pb)

Printed and bound in Great Britain by
T. J. International Ltd., Padstow, Cornwall

For Sam

Seal Alpha stood up, bracing himself against the fuselage. "Lock and load!" he shouted. "Five minutes and counting." His name was Adam Croft and he was the ranking non-commissioned officer and leader of the mission, a ten-year veteran of the Navy Seals who had spent half of those years serving in Iraq and Afghanistan. There were thirteen Navy Seals sitting on the floor of the UH-60 Black Hawk helicopter. All the seats had been stripped out to keep the payload to a minimum. The Seals weren't in any way superstitious and thirteen was the maximum number that could be squeezed into the belly of the helicopter. All thirteen had been hand-picked by Croft.

The Seals started chambering rounds as Croft and the Black Hawk crew chief readied the four ropes that they would be using to abseil down into the courtyard close to the main house. They were all dressed in the same desert camouflage fatigues and bulletproof vests but their headwear varied. Some favoured Kevlar helmets, others wore scarves or floppy hats. Their weapons varied too. Most cradled M4 rifles fitted with noise suppressors but there were several Heckler & Koch MP7 carbines and one pump-action shotgun.

They all wore noise-cancelling headsets to neutralise the roar of the Black Hawk's two General Electric T700 turboshaft engines.

The co-pilot waved again. Three fingers. "Three minutes, guys!" shouted Croft. He peered through a window. They were flying over houses and roads, but there were no street lights and almost all the homes were in darkness. Abbottabad didn't have much in the way of nightlife and it was now almost one o'clock in the morning. He couldn't see the second helicopter but he knew it would be close by, somewhere to starboard.

The helicopters were in full stealth mode, their engines quietened, their bodies covered with a radar-dampening fabric coating, their tail sections modified, including extra blades on the tail rotors. Pakistan was supposedly America's ally in the war against terrorism, but no one in the White House took that alliance seriously and the Pakistani authorities had not been informed of the mission.

The turbines powered down and the nose pitched up as the helicopter transitioned into a hover.

"This is it, guys — go to night vision!" shouted Croft.

The men removed their noise-cancelling headsets and pulled on their night-vision goggles, pressing the button on the right-hand side that activated them. Croft pulled on his own and blinked as they flicked on, casting everything in a green hue. The Seals were from the Naval Special Warfare Development Group but everyone knew them as Team Six. So far as US special forces went, they were the best of the best. They had been training for the mission for more than six weeks in North Carolina followed by another three weeks at Camp Alpha, a highly secure area of Bagram Air Base in Afghanistan.

The Black Hawk hovered about a hundred feet above the building. It was a manoeuvre the pilot had practised a hundred times over a mock-up of the compound at Camp Alpha. Contractors had built a replica of the compound and the three-storey building, complete with contents. He eased back on the power and the helicopter began to descend. He scanned the instruments but he was flying by feel, as if the helicopter was an extension of his own body.

"One hundred feet," said his co-pilot.

The helicopter slowly dropped, the backwash kicking up dust in the compound below.

"Ninety feet," said the co-pilot.

The pilot smiled to himself. He didn't need the verbal reminder of how high they were; he could do this bit with his eyes closed.

"Eighty feet," said the co-pilot. "All good."

The pilot grinned. He knew it was all good. Compared to some of the missions he'd been on in Iraq this was a piece of cake. At least no one was firing missiles at him.

The helicopter began to shudder and he had to fight the pedals to keep it from swinging around.

"What's the problem?" asked the co-pilot.

The nose pitched down and then just as quickly reared up. Both men scanned the instruments, trying to see if there was a technical problem, but everything seemed to be working perfectly; it was just that the helicopter was refusing to respond. It began to spin to the left as it continued to descend, faster now.

"Seventy feet," said the co-pilot.

The juddering intensified and the pilot felt the rudder pedals banging up and down, beating a rapid tattoo on the soles of his feet. "I'm losing it," he said. "We're going to have to abort."

The helicopter continued to spin and the pilot pulled on the collective to increase power, then pushed the cyclic forward trying to get the helicopter moving forward.

"We're going down!" shouted the co-pilot.

The pilot gritted his teeth as he fought to regain control of the helicopter but nothing seemed to be working. It bucked and tossed like a living thing and his hands were aching from the strain of gripping the controls. "Help me with the cyclic!" he shouted. "I'm losing it."

The co-pilot grabbed at the cyclic between his legs but it was too late: the helicopter was spinning out of control and losing height rapidly.

The pilot twisted round in his seat. "We're going down!" he shouted. "Brace, brace, brace!"

His words were lost in the roar of the turbines but the Seals knew that they were in trouble and they grabbed on to whatever support they could find.

The pilot turned back to the instruments but realised immediately that there was no point: if they were going to survive he'd have to fly by instinct alone. The helicopter was spinning in an anticlockwise direction so he pushed the cyclic to the right to try to counteract it and pulled the collective up to full power. They were going to hit the ground, he was sure of that, so all he could do was try to lessen the impact.

Out of the corner of his eye he caught a glimpse of the other Black Hawk. It was hovering just outside the northeast corner of the compound. He yanked the cyclic, trying to push the spinning helicopter away to the west. If he collided with the other helicopter it would all be over.

"Thirty feet!" shouted the co-pilot.

They were still over the compound, spinning crazily. The perimeter wall was eighteen feet high.

"Brace for impact!" the pilot screamed, though he knew that no one would hear him over the noise of the engines.

He saw the house flash by and realised that he was too far away to hit it but he still had to worry about the wall. The power was on full and the turbines were screaming but the rotor blades just didn't seem to be generating any lift.

"Twenty feet!"

Below him was the wall and then they were over it, but as he struggled to stop the spinning there was the sound of tortured metal and the helicopter lurched to the left. The tail rotor had slammed into the wall and almost certainly disintegrated in the impact.

The pilot reacted instantly, thrusting the cyclic forward so that the Black Hawk would hit the ground nose first. If they hit side on the main rotor would slam into the ground and the resulting crash would destroy the rotor blades and send lethal shrapnel through the cabin. He saw the ground rushing up at him and then they hit, hard, the cockpit shattering and the harness biting into his shoulders with such force that his right collarbone snapped. He could hear panicked shouts from behind him and then everything went black.

"Go left, left, left!" shouted the co-pilot of Helo Two but the pilot was already pushing the cyclic to the left to get it away from Helo One. He was also pulling the collective up so that they gained height. He concentrated on the instrument panel, which meant that he lost sight of the other helicopter, but the way that it had been spinning left him in no doubt that it had crashed.

A Seal appeared behind him. "What's happening?" screamed the Seal but the pilot ignored him and concentrated on flying the helicopter. The crew chief grabbed the Seal's arm and pushed him down to the floor, then pointed a warning finger at the man. While they were in the air the aircrew were in charge and the last thing they needed was soldiers in full combat gear moving about when they weren't supposed to.

The Black Hawk gained altitude and the pilot put it into a hover outside the compound, then turned it round so that he could see what was happening to Helo One.

"They're piling out," said the co-pilot.

"Any sign of fire?" asked the pilot.

"They look okay. The rear rotor is smashed and the tail's broken but that's it. The main rotor isn't even damaged. They were lucky."

"If they were lucky they wouldn't have crashed in the first place. You have control."

The co-pilot gripped the cyclic and tested the rudders. "I have control," he said and he took over the flying while the pilot clicked on his mic so that he could speak to the Seal in command behind him. "Helo One is down," he said. "What do you want to do?"

Chief Petty Officer Guy Henderson cursed under his breath. He peered out of one of the side windows but couldn't see the downed helicopter. "They okay?"

"There's no fire and they're getting out. But they're outside the compound."

"Can you patch me through to Seal Alpha?"

"I can talk to the pilot and co-pilot but they look like they're busy right now. It has to be your call, unless you want to talk to command centre."

"Negative that," said Henderson. His mind raced. In all the rehearsals they'd carried out in North Carolina and Afghanistan they hadn't once considered that one of the helicopters would crash. There was no contingency plan for what had just happened and he knew that if the decision as to what to do next was left up to the top brass then the mission would probably be aborted. There were simply too many chiefs: the President was in ultimate control in the White House but he wasn't a soldier, so it would be up to his military advisors to make the call. That meant taking the views of the command centres in CIA headquarters at

Langley Virginia, the Navy Seals' command centre in Afghanistan and the command centre in the American Embassy in Islamabad. By the time a consensus had been reached Pakistani jets would have been scrambled and be on their way.

"Clock's ticking," said the pilot. "You're going to have to make a decision here. Do we continue or do we go into rescue mode?"

Henderson held up a gloved hand. By now Helo One should have been in position over the courtyard and the Seals dropping down on ropes before storming the house. Helo Two should have been dropping four of its Seals outside the compound to secure the perimeter and then Henderson and the rest of the team were to be dropped on to the roof of the main building to gain access from there. But that clearly wasn't going to happen now. When the CIA had first been told who was living in the compound President Obama had considered demolishing the building using B2 stealth bombers, and then had discussed using armed drones with Hellfire missiles; but he had been advised that neither offered a cast-iron guarantee of success. The only way to be sure was to send in a team of Seals, which is when they had begun to plan Operation Neptune's Spear. Two pilotless drones fitted with high-resolution infrared cameras were already three miles above the compound and sending back live visual feeds to the other side of the world, where the President and his staff were gathered in the White House's situation room.

The fact that the President was watching made Henderson's head spin but he forced himself to concentrate on his options. They could change the plan completely and all go to the roof, but the element of surprise had gone and the occupants might well start shooting. They could drop down into the compound and take the role of the Helo One strike team and storm the building through the front door, but they hadn't rehearsed that and they'd be using only half the number of men they'd used in training.

Henderson jerked his thumb down. "Take her down, outside the compound," he said. "Let's see what Adam says."

Croft made sure that all his men were out safely, then he hurried over to the cockpit. The pilot was slumped forward but seemed to be breathing. The co-pilot had unbuckled his harness and taken off his helmet but was having trouble opening his door, which had buckled in the crash. Croft ran round to it, and using all his strength he managed to yank it open.

"Is everyone okay?" asked the co-pilot.

"Shaken but nothing broken," said Croft. "What about the helo? Will she blow?"

The co-pilot shook his head. "All the electrics are off and the fuel tanks haven't ruptured, so no, she won't burn."

The pilot groaned and the co-pilot and Croft opened the door, unbuckled his harness and helped him out. He was conscious but groggy and they sat him down next to a concrete wall. They'd landed in an animal compound, close to a feeding pen filled with grain. A small herd of scrawny cows had bolted when the helicopter crashed but were now standing a hundred feet away, watching what was going on, their tails swishing from side to side.

Croft looked across the street. The second Black Hawk was hovering a few feet above a field. It landed gently and the Seals on board piled out, bent double to keep their heads away from the spinning rotor blades.

The leader of the Helo Two Seals rushed over to Seal Alpha. "You okay, Adam?"

"I've been better," said Croft.

"Do we abort?" asked Henderson.

"Hell no," said Croft. "We've no injuries so all we've got to do is go through the main gate. But get your pilot to radio for a Chinook to get us out of here."

"Roger that," said Henderson, and he ran back to the Black Hawk.

The co-pilot gestured at the wrecked helicopter behind them. "We're going to have to destroy the electronics and then burn the ship," he said.

"Wait until we're out," said Croft. He waved at his team. "Let's get into the compound," he said. "The clock's ticking." He jogged over to the compound wall and examined the gate. It was metal with wheels on the bottom so that it could be pushed to the side. He tried to move it, but it was obviously locked on the inside. He kicked it hard, several times, and it rattled but remained obstinately closed.

All the Seals from Helo Two had moved some distance away because the main rotor was still turning.

Henderson leaned into the belly of Helo Two and briefed the crew chief.

When he'd finished talking a soldier holding a Heckler & Koch put a hand on his arm. "What's happening, Guy?"

The soldier was English, the only non-American on the team, and although he was there as an observer he had been issued with a Glock pistol and Heckler & Koch MP5 carbine complete with suppressor.

"We're going ahead, but through the gate," said Henderson. "We can't risk losing the second helo."

The crew chief appeared at the Black Hawk's side door. "Chinook's on its way. ETA five-zero minutes."

"Roger that," said Henderson. He nodded at the Englishman. His name was Dan Shepherd and he worked for MI5, the British intelligence agency. It was MI5 who had provided much of the intelligence on the interior of the compound and they had insisted that they were represented on the mission. Shepherd had been chosen because he had a special forces background with the Special Air Service, the nearest thing the Brits had to the Seals. "I've got to talk to Adam, stick with me."

Henderson jogged over to Croft with Shepherd following closely behind. Croft looked up as they reached him. "What's the story?" he asked.

"Chinook's on its way, ETA fifty minutes. What's the plan, Adam?"

"We breach the compound," said Croft. "Then in through the front door."

"What about my team?"

"Four men to secure the perimeter; you and the rest follow me." He waved at a short, squat Seal who was standing looking at the downed helicopter. "Get the C4 out, Tommy," he said. "Blow this fucking gate in."

Tommy was the leader of the unit's three-man demolition team and they hurried over to the gate and started unpacking C4 charges from their backpacks.

"You think it's a good idea to take everyone in through the front?" asked Shepherd.

"We can't risk crashing the second helo so rope drops are out," said Croft. They were all wearing night-vision goggles so it was impossible to read their faces, but it was clear from Croft's tone that he wasn't happy about having his orders questioned.

"Let's move, Dan," said Henderson, turning towards his team.

Shepherd stood where he was, staring at Croft. "I get that, but do you think it's smart to send everyone in through the gate?" he said. "They'll know we're coming and if they start shooting it'll be a massacre."

"We can take fire," said Croft.

"I hear you, but the smart thing to do would be to move in on two fronts."

"I only see the one gate, and we're not using the helo. Now get out of my face and let me get to work."

"Come on, Dan . . ." said Henderson, putting his hand on Shepherd's shoulder. He tried to move Shepherd away from Croft but Shepherd wouldn't budge.

"You could send a team over the wall at the side," said Shepherd. "If you go through the main gate you only get to the first courtyard by the guest house. You still have to get into the courtyard where the main building is. That's going to slow you down. But if you send men over the west wall they'll drop straight into the main courtyard and they could move around the west side of the house. If you come under fire they could deal with it."

Croft took out a small laminated map of the compound and realised that Shepherd was right. But he still didn't appreciate having his orders questioned. "Last time I looked that wall's eighteen feet high," said Croft.

"There's a stack of oil drums over there by the cowshed and we can pull down some of the planks of wood. That and the ropes from the helo should get us over."

"That would work, Adam," said Henderson.

The two Seals stared at each other, looking for all the world like two giant insects about to attack each other, then Croft nodded. "Let's do it," he said. "Leave four men watching the perimeter but take the rest over the west wall. And stay in radio contact; we don't want any surprises in there."

"Roger that," said Henderson. He nodded at Shepherd and the two men ran back to the Black Hawk.

Croft paced up and down outside the gate. The ground was rough red dirt that had turned to mud in recent rain and it sucked at his rubber-soled boots. Tommy and his team had finished attaching four charges the size of cigarette packs at the four corners of the gate.

"Ready when you are," said Tommy, running wires from the charges to a safe distance. Croft crouched down on one knee and turned his head away. "Fire in the hole!" shouted Tommy, and he blew the charges. The gate fell inwards and slammed into the muddy ground.

Croft led the way, his boots thudding over the gate. His men followed. There was an alleyway some twenty feet long with another locked metal gate at the end.

Croft pointed at Tommy, and then at the gate. Tommy nodded and went forward with his demolition team. As they fixed charges to the second gate, Croft looked at his watch. It had been seven minutes since the Black Hawk had crashed. According to their game plan they should have been inside the house already. As it was they were still outside the residential part of the compound and whoever was inside would know that they were under attack.

There were two explosions and the second gate was down. "We're almost at the outer courtyard," Croft said into his radio mic.

"Roger that," said Henderson. "We're just about to go over the wall."

Croft led his team over the second gate into a courtyard. There was a small building to the left. It was a guest house, used by a fifty-year-old man and his family. At the far end of the courtyard was another metal gate. Croft's heart was pounding and sweat was dripping down his forehead. He wiped it away with the back of his left hand. He was finding it hard to visualise the layout of the compound. All the training had started with him doing a fast rope drop directly into the residential compound and then storming the building. Everything they'd done since the helicopter had crashed was totally new and unplanned. He reached into the top pocket of his tunic and pulled out the laminated map again. He stared at it, trying to get his bearings. According to the map, the third gate led to the inner courtyard and the house.

A three-man team headed by Seal Golf peeled off to secure the guest house as Croft waved at Tommy and pointed at the third gate. "Last one and then we're in, Tommy."

Tommy and his team rushed forward and started attaching C4 charges.

Henderson and Shepherd studied the platform that the Seals had built against the perimeter wall using oil barrels and planks taken from the animal compound. There were three barrels at the bottom with planks on top, then two more barrels on top of that. Standing on the top barrels they'd have to jump only a few feet before scrambling over the top.

"They're just about to access the inner compound so we need to go now," said Henderson.

"I'll go first," said Shepherd.

"You're here to observe," said Henderson.

Shepherd tied a rope round his waist. "It was my idea so it's the least I can do," he said. He handed the other end of the rope to Henderson. "Just be gentle with me," he said. "Eighteen feet isn't that big a drop but I don't want to go breaking an ankle at this stage."

Another Seal was also getting ready to go over the wall but Shepherd slung his MP5 on his back and beat him to it, clambering up on to the wooden planks and then carefully climbing on to one of the barrels. He reached up to the top of the wall, grabbed it with his gloved hands and dragged himself up with a grunt.

Henderson played the rope out between his fingers, keeping a careful eye on the Englishman as he straddled the wall and dropped down into the courtyard. Shepherd's knees scraped against the concrete wall as Henderson lowered him down. As soon as Shepherd's feet touched the ground he turned and reached for his MP5, checking that the immediate area was clear.

A small cat with a broken tail ran away but other than that the courtyard was deserted.

The Seal dropped down next to Shepherd, unhooked the rope from his waist and pulled it twice to let the man on the other side of the wall know that he was down. Shepherd did the same and the two ropes snaked back over the top.

The rest of the Seals came over the wall in pairs, with Henderson bringing up the rear.

"We're in the compound," Henderson said into his mic.

There was a burst of static then he heard Croft. "About to blow the third gate and then we're in."

Henderson motioned for his team to move forward.

"Fire in the hole!" shouted Tommy and the four charges attached to the third gate blew. The gate buckled but remained in place so Tommy and one of his team rushed forward and finished the job with two hard kicks.

The gate went down and the Seals stormed through into the inner courtyard.

A man appeared at a doorway, holding an AK-47. He was short, portly and bearded, wearing a long nightshirt. It was the courier, Croft realised, recognising him from the dozens of surveillance photographs they'd studied in North Carolina. Three red dots from the laser sights of the M4 carbines danced on the man's chest then three shots rang out and the courier fell back, the AK-47 tumbling to the ground. There were screams from a woman and children inside the house as four Seals stormed in, stamping over the body in the hallway.

Croft looked round, checked that the rest of the Seals were ready, and pointed at the main house. "Here we go," he said. "Home stretch."

As they approached the main house a heavyset man with a thick moustache appeared on the patio. Next to him was a middle-aged woman in a nightdress. The man was holding an AK-47 in one hand, and he was holding up his other hand as if telling the soldiers to stop where they were. The three-man unit to Croft's left fired as one and three bullets slammed into the man's chest. He slumped to the ground and almost immediately the woman's face imploded as she was hit.

Even with the suppressors the noise of the shots echoed off the courtyard walls as dull thuds.

Three small children ran out of the house screaming. The soldiers let them go, keeping their weapons trained on the entrance to the house.

Croft waved his men forward. "In we go," he said.

Henderson flinched at the sound of shots. "They're taking fire," he said, ducking down into a crouch.

"All suppressed M4s," said Shepherd. "And they weren't from the house."

They came round the corner just in time to see Croft and his men burst through the front door.

Shepherd looked up at the upper levels of the building. All the windows were in darkness. If the occupants had any intention of fighting back the best time would have been when the Seals moved into the compound. Then they'd have been firing from cover and with the advantage of the high ground. Now that the Seals were moving inside the advantage switched to the Americans. They were highly trained in close-quarter combat and the night-vision goggles gave them an extra edge.

Shepherd moved forward but Henderson held him back. "They go in first," said Henderson. "You're an observer, remember?"

Seal Alpha moved through the hallway with his team, using their weapons to cover all the angles. They had spent hours practising clearing the mock-up house in Afghanistan, and the exercises had always included dealing with booby traps — tripwires, alarms and explosives. But the fact that there were children in the house suggested that it hadn't been booby-trapped, which would make their life easier.

There was a metal cage around the staircase that led to the upper floors and the three-man demolition team hurried over to it and began attaching charges while the rest of the Seals cleared the ground floor. There were four rooms including a kitchen and a bathroom, a sitting room with an old-fashioned television and karaoke machine, a bedroom with single beds. The Seals were thorough, opening all the cupboards and overturning the mattresses.

When they were satisfied that the ground floor was clear they moved to the far end of the hallway while the demolition team finished attaching the explosive charges.

Shepherd walked up to the house with Henderson in tow. Behind them Henderson's team fanned out, covering the upper floors of the house with their M4s. Shepherd stared down at the dead man and woman on the patio. Blood was still pooling around the woman's chest as she lay face down on the tiles. "We're shooting women now, are we?" he asked.

Henderson gestured at the AK-47 by the dead man's feet. "What do you call that?"

"You've been around as long as I have, Guy," said Shepherd. "The only shots we've heard have been fired by suppressed M4s. No AK-47s have been fired."

"Maybe that's because we got our defence in first."

"Yeah, well, that doesn't explain the woman. When did Seals start killing women?"

"We can't take any chances — under those baggy clothes she's wearing she could be rigged up with a suicide vest."

"It's a nightdress," said Shepherd scornfully. "It's well after midnight. They were in bed and they came out to see what was going on."

"With an AK-47?"

"Guy, mate, you're from Texas. I'm betting you'd have a gun in your hand if you heard noises in your garden late at night. We've just crashed a bloody helicopter in theirs."

They heard two dull thuds from inside the house, small explosive charges. Shepherd looked across at Guy, wondering if he'd been right about the suicide vest.

Henderson read his mind and shook his head. "That's C4. Our guys are blowing the staircase cage."

Shepherd nodded. "Let's go," he said, and he headed inside. Henderson hurried after him.

Croft pulled open the mangled mesh cage and led the charge up the stairs. As he got to the halfway point he saw a man peering round the corner at the top and he pulled the trigger of his M4, sending a bullet smashing into the wall inches away from the man's ear.

The man jerked back. Croft had recognised him from the photographs they'd studied back in the States. It was Bin Laden's twenty-three-year-old son. He'd been seen in the compound most mornings lifting weights and doing push-ups.

Croft ran up the stairs just in time to see the man reach the end of the hallway. He fired again as the man turned but his shot went wide. Croft cursed, then he flinched as a gun went off behind him, two shots in quick succession. Seal Bravo. Both shots hit the man in the chest, just above the heart, and he fell backwards, hit a wall and then slid down it, his eyes wide and staring as blood spurted from the two wounds. He was one of four adult males that the Americans knew were living in the compound. Now three of them were dead.

The Seals piled up the stairs and began clearing the rooms. There were four, including a foul-smelling bathroom. They found two women hiding under a double bed in one of the bedrooms and roughly patted them down for explosives before one of the Seals hurried them out and down the stairs. They screamed and cursed and spat at him every step of the way.

The stairway leading up to the top floor was caged too and the demolition team went to work, attaching charges to the metal frame.

Shepherd ducked as he heard the shots, then smiled ruefully as he realised that it was his instincts that had taken over. The gunfire was upstairs. Then he heard rapid shouts and Arabic cursing and saw two middle-aged women being pushed down the stairs by one of the Seals. The women were both in their fifties, with weathered skin and bad teeth and hooked noses peppered with blackheads. Their faces were contorted with hatred and one of them spat at Shepherd as she went by, then screamed something at him in Arabic.

"Nice," said Henderson. "Something about your mother."

"Hearts and minds," said Shepherd sarcastically as he wiped away the phlegm with the back of his hand.

"We tend to find shock and awe works better," said Henderson. "We don't have time for please and thank you and tea and crumpets. And don't think for one moment that those bitches wouldn't blow you away in a heartbeat if they were the ones with the guns."

They went up the stairs to where Croft was watching the demolition team attach their charges.

"You guys get down the hallway," said Croft. "We're just about to blow the cage."

Henderson put a hand on Shepherd's shoulder. "Come on, we need to get away from the charges." He pushed Shepherd down the hallway. They almost stumbled over the dead man lying there. Fresh blood glistened greenly through Shepherd's goggles, a slightly darker green than the man's T-shirt. Two black dots showed where the bullets had struck home. Shepherd looked around the floor but there was no sign of a weapon.

He ducked involuntarily as the explosive charges went off.

The charges had wreaked havoc on the cage around the stairway, mangling the metal frame and twisting the hinges, but it was still in place and blocking the stairs. Tommy and his number two on the demolition team grabbed it and pulled hard. It came away from the wall and they dragged it into the hallway.

Croft led the charge up the final staircase. As his feet pounded on the concrete steps a door opened on the top floor. Croft caught a glimpse of a bearded man and then the door slammed shut.

He reached the top floor, hurried along to the bedroom door and paused for a second for the rest of his team to join him. He stepped to the side and Seal Delta kicked the door hard, just below the handle. The jamb splintered and the door crashed open.

Croft went in first, just as they'd rehearsed, bent forward to keep his centre of gravity low, his carbine sweeping the room. One step into the room then a quick shuffle to the right so that the next man had a clear view.

There were three targets in the room. There was a man standing by the bed. A craggy face with a long straggly beard. Two women, both wearing long cotton nightgowns.

The women began screaming in Arabic. The younger one took a step towards the Seals, her hands curved into claws, her face contorted with hatred. "*Neek Hallak!*" she screamed. Croft knew enough Arabic to know that she was telling them to go fuck themselves.

The older woman stepped to the side, putting herself between the soldiers and the old man. Her husband. They were both his wives, and both would die to protect him.

Seal Charlie shouted at the younger woman. "Shut the fuck up, bitch!"

The woman continued to scream at the Americans in Arabic, shaking her fist, her eyes blazing. Then suddenly she charged at Seal Bravo, wailing like a banshee. Seal Bravo lowered his aim and shot the woman in the left calf. Her leg collapsed and she staggered against the wall, her screams of anger turning into howls of pain.

The older wife grabbed hold of the injured woman and she too began to curse. Seal Charlie let his weapon fall on its sling and he dashed forward, shoving the two women against the wall.

Croft brought his gun to bear on the man, who was still standing next to the bed, a look of quiet serenity on his face. There was no fear, no anger, just blankness as if he couldn't comprehend what was going on around him. Croft raised his weapon, his finger tightening on the trigger.

Off to his left, the injured woman had slumped to the floor, blood streaming from the wound in her leg, and the second woman was trying to stem the flow with her nightdress. Croft was barely aware of the women; he was totally focused on the man in front of him. Two more Seals moved into the room, their M4s sweeping left and right.

The man was still raising his arms, and now he stood almost as if he was crucified, his palms open, fingers extended. His eyes stared blankly at the soldier and a smile slowly spread across his face. It was the smile of a man at peace with himself. Croft pulled the trigger and a small dark-green rose blossomed in the centre of the man's chest and his whole body shuddered, and even

24

before he began to fall Croft fired again, this time at the man's face. The bullet blew away most of the man's skull above the eyeline, splattering blood, brain and bone over the wall behind him. The target fell backwards on to the bed, his arms still outstretched.

Three more Seals piled into the room. They began whooping when they saw the dead man on the bed. Croft clicked on his radio mic. "For God and country — Geronimo, Geronimo." His breath came in ragged gasps, the adrenaline still coursing through his system. He took a deep breath to steady himself before clicking the mic again. "Geronimo EKIA."

EKIA. Enemy killed in action. The most hunted man in the world was dead.

Croft turned to look at his colleagues and punched his fist in the air. "You do not fuck with Navy Seals!" he shouted. "Who do you not fuck with?"

"Navy Seals!" they chorused, then began whooping and pumping the air with their fists.

Shepherd stood in the doorway, his Heckler & Koch cradled in his arms as he watched the Seals cheering and slapping each other on the back. Henderson came up behind him and put a gloved hand on his shoulder. "We should go, Dan. It's over."

The woman who hadn't been shot tried to get over to the dead man but Seal Bravo pushed her back down on the floor. "Stay where you are, bitch, or I'll shoot you too!"

"Stand down!" shouted Croft. "I want the place searched from top to bottom. We want computers, papers, photos . . . Anything that looks like intel we take. And let's get his body into a bag." He saw Shepherd looking at him.

Shepherd took off his night-vision goggles. There were thin curtains over the windows and there was enough moonlight filtering in for him to see. There was a big-screen television on a table in one corner of the room, along with a video recorder and a stack of tapes.

"What's your problem?" asked Croft.

"Dan, come on," said Henderson, trying to pull Shepherd out of the room. Shepherd shrugged off Henderson's hand.

"What the fuck did you do?" shouted Shepherd.

Two Seals pushed by Shepherd and headed for a cupboard on which there was a laptop computer and a stack of DVDs. They knelt down and took off their backpacks.

Croft pushed his goggles to the top of his head. "What do you think happened?" he growled at Shepherd.

"I think you shot an unarmed man, that's what I think."

Croft pointed at an AK-47 leaning against the wall by the bed. "What do you call that?"

"I call it murder. He didn't make a move for the weapon and yet you double-tapped him."

"Yeah, well, I wanted to make sure he was dead. That bastard was responsible for Nine-Eleven. He deserved what he got."

26

Seal Delta appeared in the doorway, with Seal Echo close behind him. Seal Echo was holding a tube of rolled-up white plastic. "Got the body bag," he said.

"You and Pete put the body in it," said Croft. He nodded at Seal Delta. "Are they searching the rooms downstairs?"

"We're on it," said Seal Delta. "They've already found a stack of porn."

"Make sure they take it with us. We need to show what degenerates these bastards are," said Croft.

Seal Delta disappeared out of the doorway and thudded downstairs. Seal Echo and Seal Charlie went over to the bed and unrolled the body bag.

Croft realised that Shepherd was still staring at him. "What the fuck are you looking at?" he said.

"I'm here to observe, remember?" said Shepherd. "That's what I'm doing. Observing."

"Get back to the chopper," said Croft. He pointed at Henderson. "You're supposed to keep him out of trouble, Guy, and at the moment you're not doing a great job."

"This isn't over," said Shepherd. "No one told me this was a kill mission. I was told that we were here to capture and remove for interrogation."

"Yeah, well, maybe you weren't in the loop," said Croft. "Now get back to the chopper. We're leaving as soon as the body's bagged."

"Who authorised you to kill him?"

Seal Bravo came up behind Shepherd. He elbowed Henderson out of the way and jabbed the barrel of his weapon against the side of Shepherd's neck. "Do as he

27

says and get the fuck out of here," he growled. "You won't be the first Brit to get caught in friendly fire."

Shepherd slowly turned to face Seal Bravo and stared at him with unblinking eyes. "If you want to pull the trigger then you go right ahead," he said. "But, just in case you're wondering, that hard thing pressing against your leg isn't my cock, it's my Glock, and if you do shoot me my gun's going to go off and blow away your nuts. To be honest, I'd rather be dead than live the rest of my life with no balls, but maybe you're okay with that."

Seal Bravo took a step back. Shepherd's MP5 was hanging on its sling and he'd taken his Glock out of its nylon holster and it was now pointing at the soldier's groin. Shepherd's finger was tightening on the trigger.

"Stand down!" shouted Henderson. "Both of you."

"Tell him to take his gun away from my neck or I will shoot him," said Shepherd.

"Eddie, stand down," said Henderson.

Seal Bravo snarled at Shepherd, but he took another step back and lowered his weapon.

"Shepherd, if you've got a problem with what happened, you take it up with your bosses," said Croft. "You've no jurisdiction here. You're an observer, you observed, now get back to the chopper or so help me God I'll leave you here for the Pakistanis to find."

Shepherd holstered his Glock and walked out of the room.

Henderson followed him. "Dan, you've got to watch it with these guys. In a war zone they're a law unto themselves."

28

"So they can get away with murder? Is that what you're saying?"

"I'm saying this is their mission; you're a passenger. If you've got a problem with anything you'd better stow it until you're back home."

"What's his fucking problem?" growled Seal Bravo. "I thought the SAS were special forces, but he's behaving like a crybaby."

"He's an observer, that's all," said Croft. "The Brits insisted he was on the team because they supplied the intel. I told them it would be like mixing oil and water but the top brass said he was in so he's in. Doesn't mean we have to like it." He looked at his watch. It had been just thirty-four minutes since they had entered the compound. In all the rehearsals they'd done in North Carolina and Afghanistan they'd been in the air and on their way home within thirty minutes.

Seal Echo rolled Bin Laden's body into the body bag and zipped it up.

"Take it down to the helo," said Croft. Seal Echo and Seal Charlie picked up the body and carried it out.

The Seals by the television had stashed the laptop and the DVDs in their backpacks and were working their way through a stack of magazines and newspapers they'd found in the wooden cupboard.

"Take it all," said Croft. "They'll want to know what he was reading; it'll give a clue to what he was planning." He nodded at Seal Bravo. "Five more minutes and we're out of here," he said, then hurried down the stairs.

More Seals were searching the bedrooms. The walls were all concrete and the floors were tiled, which cut down the number of possible hiding places, but they tapped everything with the stocks of the M4s to be sure. They smashed cupboards and tables and used their knives to rip open mattresses.

"Come on guys, the clock is ticking, move it!" he shouted before hurrying down the stairs to the ground floor, with Seal Bravo hard on his heels.

Shepherd stood and watched as four Seals brought half a dozen children out of the compound. They were all barefoot and wearing shabby nightgowns and their hands had been tied behind their backs with flex cuffs. Two of the children were girls who couldn't have been more than six years old and they were crying uncontrollably. "They're just kids," said Shepherd.

"Kids are as dangerous as adults in this part of the world," said Henderson. "We have to make sure they're not a threat."

The Seals pushed the kids along the perimeter wall to where a group of women and children were sitting. One of the women tried to get up but a Seal pushed her back down with the barrel of his weapon. "Stay on the ground!" he yelled.

The woman screamed at him in Arabic and the Seal prodded her again.

The children ran towards her and sat down around her. The younger ones were crying but one of the boys, barely a teenager, glared sullenly at the Seals. Even though he was standing fifty feet away Shepherd could feel the hatred pouring out of the boy.

Off in the distance, to the west, Shepherd heard the twin rotors of a Chinook helicopter. "Cavalry's on the way," he said.

He pulled his night-vision goggles back over his eyes and scanned the night sky. The Chinook was half a mile away, flying low. It was a much bigger helicopter than the Black Hawk and able to carry four times as many troops. It was only slightly slower than the Black Hawk but it didn't have the Black Hawk's stealth capabilities and was an easy target, hence the pilot's decision to fly as low as possible.

The Chinook transitioned into a hover and came in to land about a hundred feet away from the compound. Immediately six Seals jumped out and took up position around the helicopter, guns at the ready.

Four Seals came out of the compound, carrying a white body bag. They were jogging and breathing heavily from the exertion, their faces glistening with sweat.

As they headed towards the Chinook, Croft appeared, followed by half a dozen of his men. They were all carrying black bags stuffed with whatever they'd taken from the building.

The Seals with the body bag dumped it on the ground at the rear of the Chinook as the ramp slowly descended and banged on to the ground.

A medic ran down the ramp and hurried over to the body bag. He unzipped it and then took out a medical kit from a pouch on his belt. He rolled the body over and pulled up the shirt, then stabbed a hypodermic into the base of the spine and carefully extracted more than fifty centilitres of spinal fluid. He put the hypodermic into a plastic case and handed it to a Seal, who jogged over to the Chinook and climbed on board.

Croft and his men hurried up the ramp with their black bags as the medic took another hypodermic and withdrew a second sample of bone marrow, which he put into a plastic case before hurrying back into the rear of the helicopter. The two Seals zipped up the body bag and carried it up the ramp after him. Croft came out of the Chinook and headed back to the entrance of the compound, looking at his watch.

"Why the two samples?" asked Shepherd.

"We're not home and dry yet," said Henderson. "Taking two samples gives us twice the chance of getting the DNA back home."

"Did you know this was a kill mission, Guy?" asked Shepherd. Henderson ignored him. "What, are you deaf as well as blind?" said Shepherd.

Henderson shook his head and sighed. "You just won't let it go, will you?"

"Let it go? We've just assassinated five people, and from what I've seen only one of them was holding a gun and that gun wasn't fired. We killed an unarmed woman and shot another in the leg."

"You're just an observer, remember? No one here wanted you to come in the first place."

"Yeah, well, if my bosses had known this was going to be a kill mission I don't see that they'd have sent

32

me," said Shepherd. "So I'm asking you again, did you know they were going to kill him?"

Henderson turned to look at him. "We rehearsed dozens of scenarios. We tried it with booby traps, with return fire, with grenades — they ran us through anything that we might come across, and yes, in a lot of scenarios the targets ended up dead."

"And what about rehearsing what just happened? Where not a single shot is fired and Bin Laden is standing unarmed with his hands up?"

"There was an AK-47 in the bedroom. You saw it."

"He wasn't holding it, Guy. And he didn't even make a move towards it. He wasn't resisting. And he was shot twice. A double tap. One in the chest, one in the head. You only do that when you want to be sure of a kill. If Croft was worried about return fire one shot to the arm or leg would have done the trick."

"Dan, with the greatest of respect, you weren't in the room. It was dark, there was a lot going on, they had no reason to know that they weren't under fire. Plus, you had those screaming women, who could easily have been hiding bombs under their clothes."

"That's bullshit and you know it."

The twin rotors of the Chinook started to pick up speed.

"You're asking me if I knew that they weren't going to take him alive. I didn't. That's God's truth."

"They had a body bag ready, Guy. And a kit to take spinal fluid for a DNA test. They wouldn't have needed either if he was alive."

The demolition team came out of the compound. Croft shouted over at Tommy and pointed at the crashed Black Hawk. Tommy flashed him an "OK" sign and ran over to the helicopter with his men close behind.

The co-pilot was already in the cockpit using a hammer to smash the radio and the instrument panel, and any other equipment that the military regarded as classified. America was years ahead of the rest of the world when it came to helicopter technology and the Pakistanis would happily sell anything they found to the highest bidder.

As the co-pilot continued to smash up the cockpit, the three demolition Seals began attaching C4 charges around the Black Hawk, paying particular attention to the engine, the avionics and the rotor head. Tommy shouted for the co-pilot to get clear as the Seals placed the final charges around the undercarriage.

Tommy shouted, "Fire in the hole!" and tossed two thermite grenades inside the belly of the Black Hawk. The Seals all pushed up their night-vision goggles as the helicopter erupted in a ball of flame.

Croft ran over to Henderson. "We'll use the Chinook," he said. "You and your girlfriend take the Black Hawk. You'll probably have to refuel over the border."

Henderson nodded. Croft looked at Shepherd as if he was about to say something but then he appeared to have a change of heart and just shook his head contemptuously before running over to the Chinook.

He stood at the rear of the helicopter counting off his men as they approached.

As the final Seal ran up the ramp, Croft clapped him on the shoulder, then he stopped to look at Shepherd. He mouthed an obscenity and gave him the finger, then turned and jogged into the bowels of the helicopter. The ramp at the back slowly rose into place then the turbines roared and the Chinook rose a few feet off the ground. It turned to the east and then sprang forward and leaped into the air.

The remaining Seals were hurrying towards the Black Hawk, bent low as its rotors began to blur.

"Come on, Dan, I've got the feeling that they wouldn't be heartbroken if we got left behind." Henderson slapped Shepherd on the back and the two men ran towards the helicopter, cradling their weapons.

Chaudhry hefted his bike on his shoulder and carried it to his second-floor flat taking care not to mark the wallpaper. There was more than enough room to leave it in the hallway but one of the residents had taken to pushing pins into the tyres of any bike left there overnight as a way of registering displeasure. It was probably the little old lady who lived on the fourth floor. Her name was Mrs Wilkinson and no matter what the time of year she wrapped herself up in a tartan coat and a fur hat. On the rare occasions that she passed him on the stairs she glared at him with open hostility and once he was fairly sure that he'd heard her mutter "Paki bastard". Chaudhry didn't care; he was twenty-four and over the years he'd heard much worse.

35

Besides, she was in her eighties, born in an era when Britannia truly did rule the waves. He put the bike down in front of the door and fumbled for his keys, but before he could open the lock the door opened. His flatmate, Malik, was standing there, his eyes blazing.

"Where the hell have you been?" said Malik.

"Lectures," said Chaudhry. "Where do you think?"

Malik stepped to the side and Chaudhry wheeled his bike inside. "I've been calling you all afternoon."

"Yeah, well, I turn my mobile off in lectures," said Chaudhry, steering his bike through the narrow hallway. There was a small balcony at the far end of their poky kitchen where they left their bikes.

"You haven't heard, have you? You've no idea what's happened?" Malik was bobbing from side to side like an excited toddler. His first name was Harveer but like many British-born Pakistanis he had adopted a nickname that was easier to remember and everyone other than his immediate family called him Harvey. Chaudhry's own true name was Manraj, which meant "the heart's king", but he'd been known as Raj ever since primary school.

"Heard what?" said Chaudhry, taking off his safety helmet and putting it on the kitchen table.

"He's dead," said Malik. "He's fucking well dead. The Sheik. The Americans have killed him. It's been on the TV all day."

"No way!" said Chaudhry. He took off his grey duffel coat and dropped it on to the back of a wooden chair.

"Total bloody way," said Malik. "On every channel, pretty much."

Chaudhry hurried into their sitting room and dropped down on to the sofa in front of the TV. A blonde newsreader was on the screen. Behind her was a head-and-shoulders photograph of the man himself, his eyes blank, his straggly brown beard streaked with grey, a white skullcap on top of his head: the most hated man in the western world.

"Navy Seals blew him away," said Malik. "Shot one of his wives and maybe one of his kids — they're not sure."

Chaudhry shook his head in disbelief. "It can't be," he said.

"It's on all the channels," said Malik. "Why would they say it if it wasn't true?"

"When?"

"I don't know. Today. Last night. But he's dead, Raj. They bloody well killed him."

"And it was at the house? The house in Abbottabad?"

Malik nodded enthusiastically. "They went in with helicopters. Stormed the compound."

Chaudhry stared at the television. His whole body was trembling and he clenched his fists, trying to steady himself. "That's not what John said would happen. He said they'd take him out with a Predator. Shoot him from the sky. That's what John said."

"Yeah, well, John's a British spook and it was the American military who killed him so maybe the left hand doesn't know what the right hand's doing."

Malik's eyes blazed with a fierce excitement. "You know what this means, Raj? We did it. You and me. We killed Bin Laden."

Chaudhry folded his arms to try to stop them trembling.

"Don't you get it, Raj? We're bloody heroes."

Chaudhry turned and glared at his flatmate. "Are you crazy? Talk like this is going to get us killed."

"There's only you and me here," said Malik. "What's crawled up your arse and died?"

"Have you any idea of the danger we're in? What if anyone finds out it was us?"

"How would they find out? On TV the Yanks are claiming the credit for the whole thing."

"Then let's leave it that way. No more cracks about heroes, okay? If anyone asks then it's Americans murdering Muslims and we need to stand up to them blah blah blah. You got that?"

Malik nodded. "I hear you, brother."

"Where's the remote? I want to check the other channels. Let's see what the BBC are saying."

Malik groped under a cushion, pulled out the remote and tossed it to Chaudhry. "You think we should call John?"

"Let's wait until he gets in touch with us," said Chaudhry, flicking through the channels.

Shepherd's BlackBerry rang when he was in a black cab a mile from his rented flat in Hampstead. It was Charlotte Button. He took the call.

"You're back, then?" she said.

"Almost home," he said. "I'm in a cab."

"We need to talk, obviously."

"Yeah. Obviously."

"Do you want to do it tonight? I can swing by your place."

"It's a mess," said Shepherd. "But yes, we need to discuss a few things and the sooner the better."

"I didn't know what was going to happen," said Button. "You know that if I had known I'd have told you."

"Yeah, I'm not sure that the fact they kept you in the dark inspires me with confidence," said Shepherd, as the taxi pulled up at a red light.

"Be with you as soon as I can," said Button, ending the call.

Shepherd's flat had been supplied by MI5 as part of his cover. He was a freelance journalist and the flat was in keeping with a journalist's lifestyle: a cramped one-bedroom flat in a side road off Hampstead High Street. The taxi dropped him outside and Shepherd paid the driver. The taxi drove off just as Shepherd realised that he hadn't asked for a receipt and he cursed under his breath.

The flat was in a block built during the sixties to fill the gap left when two mews houses were demolished by a stray German bomb during the Second World War. Shepherd's flat was on the second floor with a small sitting room overlooking the street, a bedroom at the back, a small shower room and a kitchen that wasn't much bigger than the shower room.

He let himself in, tapped in the burglar alarm code and then dropped his kitbag behind the sofa before taking a quick shower.

He was combing his still-damp hair when the intercom rang and he buzzed Button in. He had the door open for her when she came up the stairs, and as always there was the briefest hesitation when it came to greeting her. A handshake always seemed too formal but she was his boss and a kiss on the cheek always seemed somehow wrong. She made the decision for him, putting her right hand on his arm and pecking him just once on the cheek.

"Good to see you back in one piece, Spider," she said, moving past him into the hallway. She was wearing a black suit and black heels and her chestnut hair was loose, cut short so that it barely touched her shoulders.

"I've got wine," said Shepherd, closing the door. "Or are you driving?"

"I'm being driven," said Button. "One of the perks. So anything white would be good, preferably without bubbles."

Shepherd went into the kitchen and opened the fridge. "I've got Frascati."

"No Pinot Grigio?" asked Button.

"Sadly, no. I'm a freelance journo, remember?"

"Then Frascati it is."

"Screw top, I'm afraid."

Button laughed. "Corks are overrated." She took off her jacket and sat down in an armchair. It and the two-seater sofa were the only places to sit and there was no dining table. "Cosy, isn't it?" she said as he walked in from the cubbyhole of a kitchen.

"It's close to the Heath so I get to run whenever I want to. And it's close enough to Stoke Newington so that I can be over there in a hurry if necessary."

"Have you fixed up a meet with them?"

"I will do," said Shepherd, sitting down on the sofa with the bottle of wine and two glasses. "So, you had no idea that they were going to kill him?" asked Shepherd. "No hint? No clue?"

"How can you even ask that?" said Button. "I was as much in the dark as you were. All I was told was that we could have one operative on the team. My understanding was that providing Bin Laden wasn't armed he was to be held for interrogation and eventual trial."

"He was unarmed," said Shepherd. "They all were."

"There was no firefight? The Americans are saying they came under fire."

"The only shots fired were fired by the Yanks," said Shepherd as he poured wine into the two glasses. "They shot one of his wives and then they shot him. A double tap to make sure. Then they all cheered and did that stupid whooping thing. They shot an unarmed man and then act like they're bloody heroes. Twats."

"I'm sorry it worked out that way, Spider."

"You know, it seems to me that whenever the Americans come up against someone who can shoot back they fall apart. The only time they come off best is against an unarmed opponent." He shook his head and sneered in disgust.

"At least you're back in one piece."

"Yeah, well, no thanks to the Yanks. You heard about the helicopter they crashed, right?"

Button nodded.

Shepherd tapped his chest. "Well, I nearly bought it when it came close to crashing into the chopper I was in. Missed us by feet. I tell you, if it had hit us it would have been thank you and good night."

"What happened?" She picked up her glass, sniffed the wine, then sipped it.

"The pilot got too close to the compound wall and the rotor blast got deflected back. Instant loss of lift and down they went. Lucky no one was hurt. I tell you, Charlie, from start to finish it was a disaster. The plan was to lower us by rope inside the compound. The chopper crashes so we're on the wrong side of the wall. They tried to break down the gate and when that didn't work they had to use C4 to blow it. By the time we got into the compound every man and his dog for miles must have heard us." He shrugged. "Sorry. It just pisses me off how badly organised they are. And after all that they still start shooting unarmed men and women. They killed Bin Laden's son and he didn't even have a gun. For all I know he could have been surrendering. It was an assassination, nothing less."

"There are those that might say it's better they didn't take him alive. Can you imagine what al-Qaeda might have done to try to force the Americans to give him back? At least this way that's not an option."

"Yeah? You think there won't be repercussions? Because I'll take any bet you want to place. If Bin

Laden had come out firing an AK-47 there might have been an argument for shooting him, but he was unarmed and they put a bullet in his chest and one in his head." He forced a smile. "At least they didn't shoot me. I guess I should be thankful for small mercies." He toyed with his wine glass. "So what now?"

"Business as usual," said Button. "I need you to hand-hold Chaudhry and Malik. Especially after what's happened."

"I'll check in by phone tonight and arrange a meeting."

"How do you think they'll react?"

Shepherd grimaced. "They'll be pleased he's dead; they both hated him for what he'd done. But they'll wonder why I didn't give them a heads-up about what was going to happen."

"Smooth their feathers," she said. "Say whatever's necessary to keep them on track."

"I'm not going to lie to them, Charlie."

She swirled her wine around the glass. "No one's asking you to lie, or even bend the truth. But they're amateurs doing a very dangerous job and they need the kid-gloves treatment. For instance, probably best not to tell them you were in Pakistan."

"I wasn't planning to," said Shepherd. "They don't know about my SAS background."

"That's the way to play it," she said. "You're a regular MI5 intelligence officer with undercover experience pretending to be a freelance journalist," she said. "Anything else will just overcomplicate it."

"Let me ask you something," said Shepherd. "Do you think killing Bin Laden makes it more likely now that Raj and Harvey are going to be put into play?"

"They were already in play. They've been trained in Pakistan; they met with Bin Laden; they've been groomed to commit a major terrorist atrocity. It has always been a matter of when and not if. I'm surprised it's taken as long as it has."

Shepherd sipped the last of his wine and then refilled their glasses. "I just can't help thinking that killing Bin Laden is like a red rag to a bull. Especially the way they did it. Shooting him in cold blood and dumping his body at sea. If I was a radical Muslim I'd be getting ready to make my point."

"But as the Americans are taking the credit, they'll be the ones suffering the consequences," said Button. "No one knows of our involvement and the Americans certainly won't be publicising that you were with the Seal team."

"But if al-Qaeda does lash out at the UK, Raj and Harvey could be at the forefront."

"We'll be listening for chatter and the Border Agency is on alert," said Button. "I think if anything it'll subdue al-Qaeda for a while. They'll retrench and regroup."

"Would you like a bet on that?"

"I never gamble, Spider. You know that." She raised her glass to him. "And seriously, I'm glad you're okay. I was never convinced that sending you to Pakistan was a good idea but my bosses wanted one of ours on the team. Word had come down from Number Ten."

"What, to demonstrate that the special relationship is still there?"

"Who knows how our masters think?" said Button. "It was probably just to get one over on the French." She sipped her wine again. "While we're waiting for Chaudhry and Malik to be put into play there's another job coming up, if you're interested."

"I get a choice?" said Shepherd. "That's a change."

"It means a secondment to the Met."

Shepherd's eyes narrowed. "I'm not investigating cops again," he said. "I told you after the last time, that's not what I'm about."

"Heard and understood," said Button. "No, it's run-of-the-mill bad guys being targeted. And it'll mean you meeting up with someone from your past. Sam Hargrove."

It was the last name that Shepherd had expected to hear and he raised his eyebrows.

"Sam's found a home in the Met's Covert Operations Group and needs a hand on an undercover job," continued Button. "He's a DCS now. He was still a superintendent when you were with his unit, right?"

"Yeah," said Shepherd. "Good to see him doing so well. Did he ask for me specifically?"

Button shook her head. "The Met is stretched, SOCA's in disarray and the head of Covert Policing Command knows my boss at Five so I think it got discussed over lunch at the Garrick and I was asked to put someone forward. With your police background you were the obvious choice."

"Okay," said Shepherd hesitantly.

"Problem?"

"No, it's not that. It's just, you know, the past is a different country. You can't go back, can you? I left the Met to join SOCA and left SOCA to go to Five. It's going to feel strange going back to where I started."

"It wasn't that long ago. But if you've any reservations, any reservations at all, let me know."

"No, it's all good." He nodded. "Really. It'll be interesting to see how the Met's been getting on without me." Shepherd smiled. He wasn't worried about working with Sam Hargrove again. In fact he was looking forward to it. He'd enjoyed working for Hargrove in the Met's undercover unit in the days before it had been taken over by SOCA, and there had several times over the past few years when he'd considered giving his former boss a call.

"Why don't you sleep on it and if you're not keen you can let me know tomorrow?"

"I don't need to," said Shepherd. "It'll be fine. It's not as if I'm rushed off my feet, is it?"

"There's a lot of waiting, that's true," said Button. "But I've made it clear to Sam that if you are co-opted your Five work takes absolute precedence. If Chaudhry or Malik need you, you drop everything."

Shepherd nodded and sipped his wine, watching her over the top of his glass. She almost always referred to the men by their family names, almost never as Raj and Harvey. He wondered if it was deliberate and that she was distancing herself from them. And that made him wonder how she referred to him when he wasn't around. Was he Dan? Or Spider? Or Shepherd?

"What?" she said, and he realised that he must have been staring.

He grinned. "Nothing, I was just wondering if Jimmy Sharpe would be involved. I haven't seen him for months but the last I heard was that he was doing some undercover work with the Met."

"Well, if he is, give him my best." She looked at her watch. "I'd better be going, I've a stack of emails that need answering and I've a conference call with Langley in a couple of hours."

Shepherd slapped his forehead. "Damn, I knew I'd forgotten something. I was supposed to Skype Liam." He groaned. "They're not allowed to use their laptops after eight. I'll have to call him tomorrow."

"How's he getting on at boarding school?"

"Loves it," said Shepherd. "His grades are improving and he's really into all the sports. He's started rock climbing, and that's something I used to do as a kid so hopefully we'll get in a few climbs together at some point."

"It's funny how quickly they adapt," said Button. "My daughter always wanted to go to boarding school. There were a few tears the first week she was away, but these days she can't wait to get back. It's a teenage thing, I guess; they'd rather be with their friends."

"It works out really well for me," said Shepherd. "I can take him out any weekend if I want and they're very relaxed about midweek visits. I try to Skype him every evening but this whole Pakistan thing has meant that I haven't spoken to him for a week."

"What did you tell him?"

"I spoke to him just before I went away, but obviously I didn't say where I was going, just that I was working and that I probably wouldn't be able to use my phone or computer. The Yanks were so paranoid they took everything off me as soon as I got to their airbase. They didn't give me my phone back until I was boarding my plane this morning and by then the battery was dead."

"He'll be okay. He's used to your absences."

"It's not him I'm worried about," said Shepherd. "I'm the one that misses him, not the other way round." He drained his glass. "At least I don't have to nag him to do his homework; the school's doing a better job of that than I ever did."

He stood up and showed Button to the door.

"I'll get Sam to call you, then," she said, heading downstairs before he had time to worry about whether to shake her hand or accept a peck on the cheek.

Shepherd watched the battered black Golf GTI pull into the car park and drive slowly around before parking in the bay furthest away from the M1 motorway. London Gateway services, between junctions two and four north of the capital, was perfect for clandestine meetings. It was a place full of transients: everyone was a stranger and everyone was on the way to somewhere else. London Gateway was just a stopping-off point for a coffee, a toilet break or an expensive and badly cooked meal. Businessmen with mobile phones glued to their ears, chav housewives shepherding unruly broods towards the bathrooms, bald-headed white-van drivers chewing gum and knocking back cans of Red Bull, they all remained the centre of their own universes and showed little if any interest in the people around them.

Miles to the south, moored on the Thames in the centre of the city, was the museum warship HMS *Belfast*. Shepherd had read somewhere that the warship's guns were aimed so that their shells, if fired, would fall directly on to the service centre. It was a nugget of information that his perfect memory kept locked away for ever, but for the life of him he had no idea why the centre had been targeted, and could only assume it was a comment on the drab architecture. Or maybe someone had once eaten a bad sausage roll there.

Shepherd climbed out of the Volvo, a three-year-old model from the office pool. He locked the door and walked over to the Golf, whistling softly to himself. He had a baseball cap pulled low over his eyes and he kept his head down. He tapped on the rear window of the car and the two men inside jumped as if they'd been stung, then they relaxed as they recognised him.

Shepherd opened the rear door and got in. "Harvey, when are you going to get yourself a decent motor?" he asked, clapping the driver on the back.

"This, it's a classic, innit?" said Malik. It was cold in the car and both men were bundled up, Chaudhry in his duffel coat and Malik in his green parka jacket.

Shepherd pulled on the handle to close the door and it threatened to come away in his hand. "It's a piece of shit," he said.

"So how about your bosses pay for a new motor, then?" said Chaudhry. "There was a reward for Bin Laden, wasn't there? Twenty-five million bucks. How about sending some of that our way, John?"

John Whitehill was Shepherd's cover name. It was the only name they would ever know him by. "I'll ask, but the Yanks are taking the credit," he said.

"Yeah, but they know the information came from us, right?" said Malik, twisting round in his seat.

"What do you think, Harvey? You think we've been shouting your names from the rooftops?"

"No, of course not," said Malik, his cheeks reddening. "But Obama knows, right?"

"Of course Obama doesn't bloody well know," said Shepherd. He ran a hand through his hair, trying not to lose his temper. He forced himself to smile. "If the President knew then at least a dozen other people would know, and Washington leaks like a bloody sieve. All the politicians are hand in glove with the media so it wouldn't take long for the info to go public and then the two of you would be well fucked. I presume you don't want your names splashed across the *New York Times*."

"But someone knows, right?" said Malik. "We get the credit, right?"

"We know, Harvey. That's what matters."

"And who is 'we', exactly?" pressed Malik.

Shepherd's eyes narrowed. "Are you okay?" he asked quietly.

"I'm fine," said Malik. "I just want some reassurance here that someone else isn't taking credit for what we

50

did. We found Bin Laden. We found the man the whole world was looking for. And we told you and then the Americans went in and killed him. And nowhere do I hear that it was anything other than an American operation."

"Which is what we want. That sort of disinformation keeps you safe. What do you want, Harvey? You want to go and shake hands with Obama in the White House and have him tell you how proud he is?"

"What I want, John, is a piece of the twenty-five-million reward that the Americans promised."

"That was up to twenty-five million," said Shepherd. "If they do pay it then it'll be split among everyone involved."

"Including the Seals?" asked Malik.

"Maybe. I don't know."

"You know the Yanks paid thirty million dollars to one informant who gave up Hussein's kids," said Chaudhry. "Uday and Qusay. Remember? The Yanks went in and blew them away too. And like I said, they handed over thirty million dollars to one man."

"How do you know that?" asked Shepherd.

"Google," said Raj. "It ain't rocket science."

"So do we get a piece of the reward, or not?" asked Malik.

"I'll put out some feelers, Harvey."

"Yeah, well, make sure you do. I just worry that what me and Raj did is going to get lost in all that Yank back-slapping."

"What you did won't be forgotten, you have my word."

"That and a quid'll get me on a bus," said Malik, his voice loaded with sarcasm.

"You're not saying you're doing it for the money, are you?"

"Fuck you, John!" spat Malik. "Fuck you and fuck MI5. We put our lives on the line, Raj and me. We spent three months in Pakistan and if we'd put a foot wrong they'd have killed us without blinking an eye. But we went into the lion's den and we walked out and now it's like we don't fucking exist." He grunted and pounded his fists against the dashboard.

"Bloody hell, Harvey. Steady, mate, or you'll set off the airbag," said Shepherd.

Malik grunted again but then began to chuckle. He shook his head as he laughed.

"You okay, brother?" asked Chaudhry anxiously.

Malik nodded. "Aye, brother, I'm fine." He looked over his shoulder. "I'm fine. It's been a bit stressful, you know?"

Shepherd patted him on the shoulder. "Mate, more than anyone I know what you guys went through and as far as I'm concerned the sun shines out of your arses."

Chaudhry gestured at the service centre. "Can we go and get something to eat? I'm starving."

"Not with me," said Shepherd. "Can't take the risk."

"No one knows us this far out of London," said Malik.

"That's why we're here," said Shepherd. "We need to keep our heads down for the next few days. Everyone's going to be ultra-sensitive so I don't want anyone spotting us together in a coffee shop or on the Heath."

"So we have to drive out here whenever we want to meet?" asked Malik.

"Here or somewhere just as safe," said Shepherd. "Just for the next week or so until it dies down. Look, it's Sod's Law: the time you think you're safest is the time when you bump into someone who recognises you. So we'll stay right where we are and you can go and have a coffee when I've gone."

"Why don't you get us a safe house?" asked Malik. "You people always use safe houses, don't you?"

"Horses for courses," said Shepherd. "But if you were seen going into a strange address then you'd be screwed. This way is best. Not much can go wrong in a service station car park." He tapped the side of his head. "Touch wood."

"You know what? I'd really like to see inside the MI5 building," said Chaudhry. "What's it called again? The one by the Thames?"

"That's MI6's HQ," said Shepherd. "Vauxhall Bridge. MI5 is at Thames House, in Millbank. It's not as impressive. Why would you want to look round it?"

Chaudhry shrugged. "Dunno. Just be interested to see what the place is like, that's all."

"It's easily arranged," said Shepherd. "But best to wait until this is over."

"And what happens then?" asked Malik. "When we're done with this?"

"What do you mean?"

Malik looked at Chaudhry, then back at Shepherd. "What happens to us? We get the reward, right? Do we get new identities? Witness protection?"

"Have you two been discussing this?" asked Shepherd.

"We were wondering what you'd got planned," said Chaudhry.

"What do you want to happen, Raj?"

"Other than the reward, you mean?" Chaudhry smiled. "I'm joking. I just want this to be over, John. I want be a doctor; I want to help people."

"You should think about joining MI5," said Shepherd. "Or the police. Once this is over you could write your own ticket."

"Be a professional liar? Because that's what I've been doing for the last twelve months. I'm sick of it. Sick of the lies, sick of playing a part. I want my life back." He grinned. "And the reward, of course."

"You'll get your life back, I can promise you that," said Shepherd. "But that's why we have to keep you both deep undercover at the moment. Once the operation's over we pull you out, you move on and do whatever you want to do. But no one must ever know."

"That's for sure," said Malik. "If anyone at the mosque knew about us they'd hack off our heads with a blunt knife."

"That's not going to happen, Harvey," said Shepherd. "And most of the guys at your mosque would be as appalled as anyone about what's being planned."

"Yeah, but they'd see us as traitors for spying on our own."

Shepherd didn't like the way the conversation was going. It was vital that the two men concentrated on what they were doing and not on what the possible repercussions were. The more they considered the downside, the more likely it was that they would become nervous and make mistakes. "Guys, you're doing a great job and we're on the home stretch. What you're doing is going to save a lot of people."

"But no one can ever know, right?" said Malik.

"The people who matter will know," said Shepherd. "And afterwards, doors are going to be opened for you. Like I said, you'll be able to write your own ticket. If you want a job within the security services I doubt that'd be a problem. They'd bite your hand off."

"I don't wanna be no spy," said Malik.

"Brother, you've already crossed that bridge," said Chaudhry. He laughed and squeezed his shoulder. "That's what we've been doing for the last year. But go on, tell John what it is you want out of life."

Malik shook his hand away. "Stop taking the piss."

"Harvey wants his own restaurant."

"Seriously?" said Shepherd.

Malik nodded enthusiastically. "Japanese. I love sushi, the whole raw-fish thing. I was telling Raj that if we get the reward for Bin Laden I'm going to open one up. Fly in the best chefs from Japan, really go upmarket. You like sushi, John?"

"It's okay. I prefer my food cooked, though. I like that thing the Japanese do, cooking the stuff in front of you with the flashing knives. Food and theatre combined."

"Teppanyaki," said Malik. "Yeah, I thought I'd do that too, concentrating on seafood. Lobster, prawns."

"You've given a lot of thought to it," said Shepherd.

"My plan was to get my master's then try to get a job with one of the big restaurant groups, but now I'm thinking about my own restaurant. That would be something, right?"

"It'd be great," agreed Shepherd. A white Transit van pulled up close by and parked with its engine running. Shepherd sat back and looked over at the driver. He was shaven-headed with a mobile phone pressed to his ear and as Shepherd watched he pulled out a copy of the *Sun* and spread it across the steering wheel. Shepherd relaxed. "So what was the buzz after everyone heard what had happened in Pakistan?" he asked.

"In the mosque?" said Chaudhry. "Mostly they thought it was a lie. They don't believe anything the Americans say these days. I kept hearing that it was all bullshit and that Bin Laden's been dead for years."

"What?"

"I shit you not. The Americans have been caught out lying too many times. And, to be honest, until I met the man I thought he was a myth too. I figured that he'd died in the caves in Afghanistan years ago. But it's not like I can tell the brothers in the mosque that, is it? So they reckon that the Americans had been using Bin Laden as an excuse to invade Muslim countries and now that they're pulling out of Iraq and Afghanistan they don't need the myth any more. So they tell the world that he's dead and that they buried the body at sea."

"It's a nice story," said Shepherd. "Most conspiracy theories are."

56

"The same brothers don't believe that Bin Laden was behind Nine-Eleven either," said Malik. "They say it was all an American-Zionist plot."

"There're plenty of Americans who believe that too," said Shepherd. "But why would the Americans kill their own people?"

"For oil," said Malik. "You think they care about their own people? How many of their soldiers have died in Iraq? Five thousand or so, right? Plus how many Iraqis? A million? You think with numbers like that they'd worry about how many were in the Twin Towers? And you know that at first Bin Laden denied having anything to do with Nine-Eleven, right?"

"There was a lot of confusion in the early days," said Shepherd. "But I don't think there's much doubt now. You should have asked the man himself when you had the chance."

Malik snorted. "We weren't allowed to ask anything," he said. "They were very clear on that before they took us in to see him. No questions, no speaking unless he spoke to us, minimum eye contact, never contradict him."

"He knows that, Harvey," said Chaudhry. "He debriefed us, remember?" He turned round to look at Shepherd. "There are those who don't believe that Bin Laden died in that raid, but there are others who see it as yet another American attack on Islam. And the Pakistani brothers are the most fired up because of the way they flew in without telling anybody. Some of them are talking about it as if it was an invasion."

"Which it bloody well was," said Malik.

"But you can see why it had to be done that way," said Chaudhry, turning back in his seat. "If they'd told the Pakistanis then someone would have tipped off Bin Laden."

"But if they'd done an air strike or something it wouldn't have looked so bad," said Malik. "Flying in troops was like invading the country, wasn't it?" He looked over his shoulder. "Do you know why they didn't do an air strike, John?"

Shepherd laughed. "Mate, that's well above my pay grade," he said.

"Yeah, but you must have an opinion. Why would they piss around with helicopters and guns and that? Why not use one of them Predator things?"

"Maybe they wanted to make sure," said Shepherd. It was something he'd asked Charlotte Button when she'd first told him that he would be going on the mission as an observer. Usually the Americans preferred to strike from the sky using the unmanned drones that were piloted from the other side of the world. Malik had referred to the Predator but the American military's death-dealer of choice was now the Reaper, bigger and faster than the Predator and able to stay in the air for more than twelve hours before firing its fourteen Hellfire missiles. Button had explained that the Americans wanted to collect DNA evidence to make absolutely sure that they had the right man, but that hadn't made sense to Shepherd, especially when the Seals had gone and buried the body at sea. A body was proof of death, a DNA sample wasn't. "Also they're saying that there were women and children in buildings nearby."

"That's never worried them before, has it?" said Malik.

"You know, the Americans are a law unto themselves," said Shepherd. "The important thing is that he's dead. And the fact that he's dead makes it much more likely that they'll do something with you guys, sooner rather than later."

"You think?" asked Chaudhry.

"Al-Qaeda will want revenge, there's no question of that," said Shepherd. "And you guys are in place."

"At what point do you arrest them?" asked Chaudhry.

"That's above my pay grade too," said Shepherd.

"But they'll stop them before anyone gets hurt, won't they?"

"I'm sure they will," said Shepherd.

"What about if we wore a wire or something?" said Malik.

"Wouldn't that help? We could record Khalid talking about what he wanted us to do — that would be conspiracy, wouldn't it?"

"And what if they found the wire?" said Chaudhry.

"Why would they find it?" He looked at Shepherd. "They're really small, aren't they? They can put them in buttons, can't they? Cameras too."

"Raj is right," said Shepherd. "You'd be taking too much of a risk. And Khalid is very unlikely to start revealing his plans all of a sudden; he's only ever going to tell you what you need to know. He'll give you the mushroom treatment."

Malik frowned. "Mushroom treatment? What's that?"

Chaudhry laughed. "It's when they keep you in the dark and feed you bullshit," he said. "And John's right. That's how terrorist cells work: the upper echelons restrict the information that goes to the individual cells. That way the damage is limited if a cell is blown." He nodded at Shepherd. "Right?"

"I couldn't have put it better myself, Raj," said Shepherd. "But even a tape of Khalid saying what he wants to do isn't enough. He could claim to be a fantasist, he could say that he was joking, or that you were acting as an agent provocateur. We need him with weapons, or bombs — hard evidence that no jury can ignore. So we just carry on playing the waiting game."

"And you have him under surveillance all the time, right?" said Malik.

"Best you don't know about the operational details," said Shepherd.

"Now who's treating us like mushrooms?" said Malik.

"There's a difference, Harvey," said Shepherd. "I'm doing it because I've got your best interests at heart. I'm on your side. Khalid just wants to use you."

Even as the words were leaving his lips, Shepherd wondered just how truthful he was being. Yes, he was looking out for the two men and didn't want them in harm's way, but he was also being very selective about what he was telling them and in that respect he wasn't much different from the men planning to use them as terrorists.

"You're doing a great job, and I'm watching your backs every step of the way," he said, smiling confidently.

Chaudhry and Malik joined the queue of men, mainly Pakistani, waiting to enter the Musallaa An-noorthe mosque in Dynevor Road. It was close to where they lived and catered for mainly Pakistani Muslims, with room for about a hundred worshippers at any one time. They nodded to those that they recognised but didn't talk to anyone. The man in front of them was in his seventies, wearing a grey dishdash and a crocheted skullcap. He flicked a cigarette butt into the street before heading through the door at the side of a run-down sportswear shop. Chaudhry and Malik went down the stairs after him, keeping their hands on the walls either side for balance. At the bottom of the stairs they slipped off their shoes and put them in one of the wooden racks by the door. They were both dressed comfortably but respectfully in long-sleeved shirts and trousers and they were wearing ties. It had been drummed into Chaudhry as a child that the mosque was a place where men went to commune with Allah and that it was important to dress accordingly. But as he looked around he could see that most of the Muslims who had come to pray had not had the same upbringing. There were men in grimy sweatshirts and loose tracksuit bottoms, loose shirts and baggy jeans, stained overalls; there were even two teenagers wearing football shirts and shorts who were obviously on their way to a match. They were both chewing gum, and Chaudhry considered going over to them and admonishing them but he knew that it wasn't his place to do that. He was there to pray, not to get into arguments with Muslims who should know better.

At just after sunset it was time for the Maghrib prayers, the fourth of five formal daily prayers that every good Muslim carries out. The man standing directly in front of Chaudhry rolled up his jeans to make it easier to kneel when praying, but he did it casually, one leg rolled right up to the knee, the other to mid-calf, and when he did kneel the jeans rode down and revealed his underwear. Chaudhry shook his head at the lack of respect.

He looked over at Malik and nodded at the uneven trousers of the man in front of them. Malik grinned. Like Chaudhry he had been born in Britain to hard-working middle-class Pakistani parents and had been brought up to respect the sanctity of the mosque.

The man's toenails were long and yellowing and there was dirt under them. Chaudhry shuddered. He could never understand why people who followed a religion where shoes were always being removed didn't make more of an effort to take care of their feet. It didn't take much to clip nails and to wash before heading to the mosque. He took a deep breath and looked away. There was no point in worrying about the personal grooming habits of others.

He knelt down and began to pray. As his face got close to the prayer mat the stench of sweat and tobacco hit him and his stomach lurched. Whoever had last been on the mat had obviously been a heavy smoker and hadn't been overzealous on the personal-hygiene front. He sat back on his heels and sighed.

"What's wrong?" asked Malik.

"The mat stinks," said Chaudhry. "What's wrong with people? Why can't they shower before they come to pray? Or at least spray on some cologne."

"Do you want to move? There are spaces at the back."

Chaudhry looked over his shoulder. The mosque was busy and moving would mean threading their way through the rows and even then he couldn't see two places together. "I'll put up with it," he said. "But I don't understand why the imams don't say something."

"I think they're more worried about numbers than hygiene," whispered Malik. "Come on, let's finish and get out."

Chaudhry nodded and began to pray, as always forcing himself to concentrate on the words even though he had said them tens of thousands of times before. He knew that many of the men around him were simply going through the motions, their lips moving on autopilot while their minds were elsewhere, their thoughts on their work, on their families, or more likely on what they were missing on television or on what they would be eating for dinner. That wasn't how Chaudhry had been brought up to pray. Prayer was the time when one communed with Allah and to do it half-heartedly was worse than not doing it at all. Not that he found it a chore. In fact he relished the inner peace that came with focused prayer, the way that all extraneous thoughts were pushed away, all worries, all concerns, all fears. All that mattered were the prayers, and once he had begun he wasn't even aware of the stench of stale sweat and cigarette smoke.

When they finished they made their way out and slipped on their shoes. They headed up the stairs and out into Dynevor Road. It was a cold day and Malik pulled up the fur-lined hood of his parka as they turned right towards their flat, but they stopped when they heard a voice behind them.

"Hello, brothers."

They turned round. It was Kamran Khalid, their friend and mentor. And the man who had sent them to Pakistan for al-Qaeda training. Khalid was tall, just over six feet, and stick-thin. He had a close-cropped beard and a hooked nose between piercing eyes that rarely seemed to blink.

"Brother," said Chaudhry, and Khalid stepped forward and hugged him, kissing him softly on both cheeks. He did the same with Malik.

Khalid claimed to be from Karachi but never spoke about his family or schooling in Pakistan. He spoke good English, albeit with a thick accent, but Chaudhry had also heard him talking in Arabic on several occasions. As far as the authorities were concerned, Khalid was an Afghan, a refugee from the Taliban. He had claimed that his family had been massacred by Taliban tribesmen and that had been enough to get him refugee status and eventually citizenship, but Chaudhry doubted that he was an Afghan. On the few occasions that he'd talked to Khalid about his background, the man had been vague rather than evasive and had smoothly changed the subject.

"All is well?" asked Khalid, addressing them both.

Chaudhry and Malik nodded. "We are all in mourning for what happened," said Chaudhry, keeping his voice low.

Khalid smiled tightly. "At least we know that The Sheik is in Paradise reaping the rewards of a holy life. And how lucky were you to be blessed by the man himself."

"There will be retribution, won't there?" asked Chaudhry.

Khalid smiled easily, showing abnormally large teeth that were gleaming white and almost square. "Not here, brothers," he whispered. "Walk with me."

He took them along to Stoke Newington High Street and into a Turkish-run coffee shop. The Turks ran most of the restaurants and shops in the area and they guarded their territory jealously, which was why none of the major chains were represented. It was clammy and hot inside the shop and Malik and Chaudhry took off their coats. Khalid waited until a young Turkish boy had set down three espressos on their table and gone back to the cash register before leaning across the table and addressing them in a hushed voice. "The Americans will pay, the British will pay, they will all pay," he said.

Chaudhry could see the irony in the fact that all three of them were British citizens, but it was clearly lost on Khalid. No matter how long he lived in the UK,

Khalid would never think of himself as British. The British, like the Americans, were the enemy.

"Do you know what happened, brother?"

"I know that The Sheik died bravely with the name of Allah on his lips," said Khalid. "And that the kafir that killed him will burn in hell for all eternity."

"How did they know where he was?" asked Malik.

"They are saying that a courier led them to the compound, but who knows? The Americans always lie. And they have satellites in the sky that can read a number plate. Or it could have been the Pakistani military who betrayed him."

"You think they knew he was there?"

"How could they not, brother? He was not in London, where strangers are ignored. People would see who came and went. Do you think they would not ask who was living behind such high walls?"

"But why would they betray him?"

Khalid shrugged. "For money. For influence. Who knows?"

"May they also burn in hell," said Malik.

"Inshallah," agreed Khalid. God willing.

Chaudhry stirred two heaped spoonfuls of sugar into his coffee. "And what about us, brother?" he asked. "How much longer must we wait?"

"Not much longer," said Khalid. "Your impatience is understandable but you are resources that must not be squandered. You will not be used until the time is right."

"And how will we be used?" asked Malik. "Can you at least tell us that?"

"When I know, you will know," said Khalid.

"All the training we did, and yet now it's as if it never happened," said Malik. "I had assumed that by this time we'd . . ." He shrugged and left the sentence unfinished.

"Brother, I understand your frustration. But we cannot rush. We never do. That is why we are so successful. We watch, we wait, we bide our time and only when we are sure of victory do we strike. We could give you arms now and tell you to storm the American Embassy and you might kill a few kafirs and it would be a news story for a couple of days, but then life would go on and you would soon be forgotten. That's not what we are about, brothers. What we want is another Nine-Eleven."

Malik frowned. "Planes, you mean? We're going to crash planes?"

Khalid looked around as if he feared they were being overheard, then he shook his head. "No, brothers. This is not about planes. Nor do we plan to make you martyrs. You are no shahid. You are warriors, warriors who will strike again and again." He reached across the table and held each of them by the hand, his nails digging into their flesh. "What we are planning, brothers, will change the world for ever, you have my word on that."

"When?" asked Malik.

"All in good time," said Khalid. "We will strike when the time is right and not before."

It was early September when Sam Hargrove called. Shepherd had spent the weekend in Hereford and was on his way back to London when his mobile rang and he took the call using his hands-free. "Can you talk?" asked Hargrove. He spoke with no introduction because he had no way of knowing if Shepherd was alone.

"I'm driving, but yes, go ahead," said Shepherd. "Charlie told me back in May that you might be calling."

"The operation I'm working on has taken longer than I expected," said Hargrove. "It's just about coming together now. Are you in London? Be handy to have a chat."

"I'm here most of the time at the moment, so whenever works for you is fine," said Shepherd.

"Sooner rather than later," said Hargrove. "I don't suppose I could persuade you to swing by Broadway?"

Broadway was where New Scotland Yard was based, just down the road from St James's Park tube station.

"I'd rather not," said Shepherd. "The job I'm on is local and I'm keeping a low profile."

"Where's your base?"

"Hampstead."

"Anywhere near the King William? A colleague told me that's a good place for a meet."

"No problem. It's just round the corner from my flat."

"We can catch up over a drink," said Hargrove. "How's an hour from now for you?"

"Traffic's not great," said Shepherd, "but yeah, I should be able to make it."

Shepherd ended the call. The traffic wasn't as bad as he'd thought and he had more than enough time to find a resident's parking space close to his flat and to grab a Jameson's and soda and a corner table before Hargrove arrived.

Hargrove seemed a bit heavier since Shepherd had last seen him and his overcoat was a little tighter round his midriff. As he walked into the pub he undid the buttons of his coat and revealed a dark-blue pinstriped suit, a crisp white shirt and a tie with light and dark blue stripes. He looked around, saw Shepherd at the table and waved. He ran a hand through his greying hair as he walked over, and when they shook hands his cuff edged out of his jacket sleeve revealing a gold cufflink in the shape of a cricket bat.

"You're looking well," said Hargrove.

"You too," said Shepherd. He grinned over at his former boss. "You know this is the oldest gay bar in London?"

"I didn't know that," said Hargrove, looking around. There were no women in the pub, although that wasn't especially unusual for London. But the clientele was mainly under thirty, well groomed and with a fashion sense that was definitely a cut above that found in the average London hostelry. Hargrove chuckled. "I see what you mean."

"It's not called the Willie for nothing," said Shepherd. "It's been an openly gay venue since the 1930s, back in the day when they sent you down for being gay. But they're not prejudiced, they'll serve anyone. So what can I get you?"

Hargrove rubbed his stomach. "I've had to give up the beer," he said. "Cutting back on the calories. Gin and slimline tonic will be fine. Ice and a slice."

He took off his coat, draped it over the back of a chair and sat down. He was adjusting the creases of his trousers when Shepherd returned with his drink.

"Still running?" asked Hargrove.

"I'm on the Heath every day, pretty much."

"You still doing that thing with a rucksack full of bricks?"

"Builds stamina," said Shepherd. He clinked his glass against Hargrove's. "Anyway, good to see you."

"And you," said Hargrove. The two men drank. Hargrove smacked his lips and put down his glass. He patted his stomach again. "I'm going to have to start doing something."

"Running is good," said Shepherd. "With or without the bricks."

"It's the wife that's the problem," said Hargrove, stretching out his legs. "She's been watching all those cooking shows. Loves Gordon Ramsay. Anyway, she started cooking herself and went on a few courses and I have to say she's brilliant. She was always a good cook but this last year she's moved up to a whole new level. Can't remember the last time I ate out. It's like having my own Michelin-starred restaurant. But I hate to think what my cholesterol levels are like." He sipped his gin and tonic. "So how are things with the fragrant Charlotte Button?"

"We have our ups and downs, but generally it's good," said Shepherd. "The last year I've been hand-holding a couple of guys who are undercover. They're amateurs so I have to watch them every step of the way."

"That'll be a change for you, seeing life from the other side."

"Tell me about it. I hadn't realised just how much ego-stroking had to be done."

"You never needed much," said Hargrove. "I nearly gave you a call when I heard you were leaving SOCA but then you decided to go with her to Five and I figured it would be disrespectful to poke my nose in."

"I'm happy enough," said Shepherd. "It's a bigger canvas and a lot less PC." He grinned. "And not much in the way of paperwork."

"Yeah, that's more than fifty per cent of the job these days," agreed Hargrove. "Ticking boxes and meeting targets. But I have more freedom than most."

"Still undercover operations, right?"

"I head up the Covert Operations Group," said Hargrove. "COG. We form part of the Covert Policing Command which is the old Criminal Intelligence Branch. Basically my task is to control all undercover operations throughout the Met. Any of the boroughs can call on us, though all requests are dealt with through SCD. Recently they've been subcontracting us out to other Forces and between you and me I think the long-term aim is to make the COG a national unit but controlled by the Met. Basically to do the job that SOCA was supposed to do."

"SOCA was a total waste of time," said Shepherd. "I should never have joined."

"To be honest, you weren't given much of a choice," said Hargrove, adjusting his immaculate cuffs. "Still, what's done is done. I hear you're doing great things at Five. And Charlotte seems well pleased with you."

Shepherd shrugged. "They keep me busy," he said.

"And they let you out of the country."

Shepherd steepled his fingers under his chin as he studied Hargrove. He knew the policeman well, trusted him without question, but working for MI5 brought with it a whole new degree of security. He didn't know what Hargrove's clearance was and until he did there was no way he could talk about any MI5 operations, past or present. "I've been getting around," he said.

"How's your boy? He must be — what, thirteen now?"

"He's fine. He wanted to go to boarding school so it's all worked out well." He sat back in his chair.

"You still living in Ealing?"

Shepherd shook his head. "We moved to Hereford a few years ago."

"To be near the Regiment?"

Shepherd laughed. "No, that's where Liam's grandparents live. It made more sense to be closer to them."

"So you commute, back and forth?"

"Depends on the job. Most of the work involves deep undercover roles and they usually come with accommodation. Now that Liam's boarding it's less of an issue."

"Well, you'll be glad to hear that the operation I need help with is a bit closer to home. Birmingham, in fact. That's only fifty miles or so from Hereford."

"The job I'm on is in London. Did Charlie explain that if I need to get back at short notice I'll have to drop everything?"

"She made that clear. I don't see that as a problem, if all goes to plan you'll only have to put in a couple of appearances. A cameo, you might say."

"The problem I have is that I never know when it might kick off. It's very much a long-term thing but when it does start to go it'll probably do so very quickly."

"We can work around that," said Hargrove. "What is it, terrorism?"

Shepherd nodded. "Couple of guys in a London mosque were recruited into an al-Qaeda cell. I was drafted in early on because they are total virgins. They've been groomed and trained and done the Pakistan training camp bit but since then they've been put into cold storage. To be honest, I'm starting to wonder if they've been rumbled. But until we know either way we're just watching and waiting." He smiled ruefully. "Truth be told, I've been on more exciting jobs so I'm more than happy to work with you. What's the story?"

"Simple enough," said Hargrove. "You've heard of the English Defence League, right? There're a couple of guys in an EDL offshoot in Birmingham looking to buy guns. We've got an inside track and need someone to play the part of the arms dealer. It's a role you've played before with some success."

"I remember," said Shepherd.

"We don't need much in the way of a legend," said Hargrove. "You'll be brought in as a London arms dealer through the contact we already have in place. I thought we might pull in your teammate Jimmy Sharpe."

"Razor? He's working for you?"

"Joined my team three months ago," said Hargrove. "Since he left SOCA he's been rattling around the Met and no one really knew what to do with him. They offered him a retirement package but he turned that down and then they sent him to me."

"He's a good operator," said Shepherd.

"One of the best. It's just that he's old school and the world has changed." He drained his glass.

"You're prospering," said Shepherd.

"I'm management so it's easier for me. I follow the rules, see which way the political wind is blowing and go with it, and I make sure that all my boxes are ticked. If I don't screw up I could go up another rung before retirement, maybe two. That'll do me, Spider. I already have my cottage in Norfolk and my flat near Lords and a Cordon Bleu cook to wait on me hand and foot, so all's right with the world."

"It'll be good to work with Razor again."

"Well, he's the perfect fit for this job. The guy we have in place is young but experienced. He's involved in the long-term penetration of right-wing groups. To be honest, he's been undercover too long and wants out so he can probably appear in court to give evidence, which gives us a huge advantage."

"Sounds like a plan," said Shepherd.

"I'll put you together with Razor and we'll see what we can put together by way of samples. Then the inside man can fix up a meeting with the buyers and we'll take it from there." Hargrove grinned. "It's good to be working with you again, Spider. The old team back in harness."

Shepherd grinned back. "I was just thinking exactly the same thing," he said. He held up his empty glass. "One for the road?"

Hargrove looked at his watch. "Would love to but I have to get back. The wife is doing something special with duck tonight." He stood and picked up his coat. "I'll be heading up to Birmingham in a couple of days and it'd be handy if you could come with me. Bit of a briefing with the locals and it'll give you a chance to have a sit-down with Razor."

A young man in a leather jacket smiled at Hargrove and raised his martini glass.

Hargrove smiled and nodded, then he patted Shepherd on the shoulder. "Next time I'll let you suggest the venue."

"I still don't see why Mohammed can't come to the mountain," said Sharpe as he walked out of Starbucks and onto Hampstead High Street. It was Friday morning and the sky overhead was threatening rain.

"Now what are you moaning about?" said Shepherd.

They were both carrying coffees. Hargrove had sent Shepherd a text saying that he was on his way and Shepherd was holding two coffees, a regular for himself and a latte for the chief superintendent.

"Why are we having to schlep up to Birmingham?" said Sharpe. "There're three of us; why can't the undercover guy come down to London?"

"To be honest, I don't want to be going into New Scotland Yard unless I have to," said Shepherd. "And Hargrove said that the West Midland cops don't want any of their intel leaving their office."

"That doesn't make any sense," said Sharpe. He sipped his coffee and looked at his wristwatch, a cheap Casio. "What are they saying? They don't trust the Met?"

"It's that whole right-wing thing," said Shepherd. "It's not unknown for cops to be supportive of organisations like the BNP and EDL. From what Hargrove was saying, it looks as if they're not even putting their intel on to the computer."

"So have they checked us out, do you think? To make sure we haven't got any right-wing sympathies."

"Clearly not," said Shepherd, "or they wouldn't be letting you loose on their precious operation."

"I resent that remark," said Sharpe. He grinned. "Anyway, I'm a changed man, haven't you heard? I've been on all the diversity courses going and passed with flying colours. I fully understand the role that the police service of the twenty-first century has in maintaining productive and respectful relationships with the various ethnic components of the community." He laughed.

"Load of bollocks." He was about to say more when Hargrove's black Vauxhall Vectra appeared at the end of the road.

"Here we go," said Shepherd.

"I thought he'd have a driver," said Sharpe.

"I think the days of drivers for senior officers are long gone," said Shepherd.

The car pulled up next to them. Shepherd climbed into the front while Sharpe got into the back. Hargrove was wearing a dark-blue suit and had put the jacket on a hanger on the hook at the rear passenger side. "Good morning, gentlemen," he said.

Shepherd gave Hargrove his coffee and he slotted it into a cup-holder before putting the car into gear and pulling away from the kerb. The drive from London to Birmingham took just under two hours, during which time Hargrove briefed them on the West Midlands operation, which had been codenamed Excalibur. The Major Investigations Unit had targeted a dozen right-wing activists in Birmingham, most of whom were members of the English Defence League. The investigation had begun in 2010 and had initially been little more than low-level intelligence gathering. But following the countrywide riots and looting the activists had started talking about arming themselves. Several had already acquired handguns but at least two of the men under investigation were now looking to buy more serious weaponry. According to the undercover cop that Hargrove had in place, they wanted AK-47s.

"Why would anyone want an AK-47?" asked Shepherd.

"Birmingham is right up there with London and Manchester when it comes to guns on the streets," said Hargrove. "Most of the illegal guns are in the hands of gang members and there are already plenty of AK-47s, Uzis and Ingrams knocking around."

"So what do you think's going on? Are these guys planning to take on the gangs, is that it?"

"Our man doesn't know why they want the guns. Self-protection, maybe. Could be they just want to pose for pictures on their Facebook pages. Hopefully when we throw you into the mix we'll be able to find out what their intentions are."

They turned off the A41 and arrived at Lloyd House, the headquarters of West Midlands Police. Hargrove's car had been approved for secure parking and they went through a rear door from the car park and along a corridor to a main reception area, where Hargrove showed his warrant card. Ten minutes later they were in a fourth-floor meeting room drinking watery coffee with a uniformed superintendent and a plainclothes sergeant in a grey suit that appeared to be two sizes too large for him. They made uncomfortable small talk while they waited for the undercover officer to arrive. The superintendent, Richard Warner, was in his early fifties, grey-haired and wearing thick-lensed spectacles.

They were halfway through the coffee, and the small talk had pretty much dried up, when the door to the meeting room opened. Jimmy Sharpe grinned and cursed under his breath when he recognised the new arrival. "Ray Fenby," he said. "Bloody hell, it's a small world."

He stood up and embraced the man. Fenby, in his early twenties, was wearing a brown leather bomber jacket and camouflage cargo pants. His head was shaved and as he hugged Sharpe, Shepherd saw that he had MILL tattooed on the knuckles of his right hand and WALL on the left.

"How's it going, Razor?" said Fenby.

"I didn't realise you knew each other," said Hargrove.

"We worked on a SOCA case two years ago," said Sharpe, releasing his grip on the younger man. "Just after he left school."

Fenby chuckled and ran a hand over his shaved head. "I'm twenty-four," he said.

Sharpe grabbed him by the back of the neck and gave him a good-natured shake. "He was wearing his school blazer the first time we met."

"We were in a pub," said Fenby. "And the way I remember it, you didn't even buy a round." Fenby glanced shame-facedly at the uniformed superintendent. "Sorry, sir."

The superintendent smiled amiably. "Take a seat, Ray," he said. Fenby shook hands with Shepherd and introduced himself.

"Ray was one of a group of officers in training who were pulled out of Hendon and seconded to the Football Intelligence Unit," Hargrove explained to Shepherd. "We've drafted him into the Covert Operations Group and he's been part of Operation Excalibur from the start." Hargrove smiled at the uniformed superintendent. "Over to you, Superintendent."

Superintendent Warner nodded and reached for an open laptop that was connected to a projector. He launched a PowerPoint presentation and clicked on the first slide. Two surveillance photographs filled the screen. "Simon Kettering and Paul Thompson. They were big wheels in the EDL, especially on the fundraising side. They're not your usual right-wing extremist thug. They wear suits, they drive nice cars, they're well spoken, they have no criminal records. In fact if it wasn't for Ray here they wouldn't even be on our radar. They always maintained a low profile when they were with the EDL but they now appear to be heading up their own splinter group. And before anyone asks, it doesn't seem to have a name. It's just a group of like-minded people who get together from time to time. Ray has spent some time penetrating this group, and it looks as if he has been accepted. And last week he came to us with the news that two of the men want to buy weapons. Serious weapons. They have been talking about AK-47s and Uzis."

He tapped the keypad and another picture flashed on to the screen. Kettering and Thompson sitting outside a wine bar with a bottle of champagne in an ice bucket. Both men were smoking large cigars.

"To any outside observer the two of them seem to be nothing more than a couple of yuppies."

He clicked the mouse several times and they looked at a succession of photographs, mostly taken with a long lens. Kettering getting into a Porsche. Thompson getting out of a Mini Cooper. The two of them at a football match, shouting and punching the air.

"But there is a darker side to them," said the superintendent. He clicked the mouse again and a photograph that had been taken from CCTV footage popped up. It was grey and grainy, almost as if it had been taken in thick fog. It showed two men in suits kicking a man on the ground. "We are fairly sure that this is the two of them attacking an Asian teenager three months ago. The CPS say the footage we have isn't good enough for a positive identification but they were heard boasting about the attack."

Another click of the mouse brought up a montage of sixteen photographs of young men — all of them white and aged between twenty and forty. More than half had shaved heads.

"We have identified these sixteen men as being close to Kettering and Thompson. Between them they have more than fifty convictions for assault, racial abuse and threatening behaviour, mainly against members of the Asian community. Most have been photographed at BNP and EDL demonstrations and are regular posters on anti-Islamic and anti-Asian internet forums. I should make it clear at this point that neither Kettering nor Thompson has ever been charged or convicted of any offence and so we don't have fingerprints or DNA on file. We think that's because they're smarter than the average right-wing thug."

He clicked the mouse for a final time. The logo of West Midlands Police filled the screen along with the motto, "Serving our communities, protecting them from harm."

Sharpe put a hand up to scratch his cheek as he attempted to suppress a grin and Shepherd turned away so that he didn't have eye contact because he was sure that Sharpe was about to wink at him. Shepherd knew that Sharpe had nothing but contempt for cops who thought that their job was to serve. In Sharpe's view, the police were there to catch criminals and everything else should be left to Social Services.

"So as of today we have a total of eighteen suspects under investigation here in the West Midlands. As regards the sixteen faces I showed you, the CPS is satisfied that we have enough evidence to charge them with conspiracy to commit various illegal acts, including assault and arson. But we don't have anything yet to pin on Kettering and Thompson and until we do I'm reluctant to charge anybody. Once we start making arrests they're going to realise that we've had a man on the inside so the investigation will have to come to an end. So we need to make sure that we have enough to convict Kettering and Thompson." He smiled at Hargrove. "Which is hopefully where your team comes in."

Hargrove nodded. "Happy to help," he said.

"On several occasions Kettering and Thompson have talked about buying a high-powered weapon and if we can get them in possession then we can put them behind bars for a few years at least. And once we have them in custody we hope to turn one of their friends and get evidence of their involvement in the racial attack." The superintendent gestured at Fenby. "Ray has let them know that he has contacts in London who

82

have access to guns. Kettering and Thompson have expressed interest but want a good look at any weapons on offer. But let the man himself do the talking." He nodded at Fenby.

The undercover officer cleared his throat nervously. "They want big stuff, AK-47s, and they keep talking about the guns that the armed cops use, the Heckler & Koch MP5."

"And have they said what they want to do with the weapons?" asked Hargrove.

"They keep their cards close to their chest," said Fenby. "Kettering and Thompson are tight. They might even be partners, in a sexual sense. They're not overtly gay and I've seen them with girls but there's something weird about the two of them when they're together. They finish each other's sentences; they mimic each other's body language." He shrugged. "Like I said, it's weird. It's taken me months to get close to them but they're still cagey when I'm around. Those faces you saw represent most of the group that they hang around with, but there's a lot of coming and going. I'm in pretty tight with three guys I met through football but they're not much closer to Kettering and Thompson than I am. They seem to keep everyone at a distance."

"How did Kettering and Thompson come to know that you had arms-dealer connections?" asked Hargrove.

"The guys I was hanging with started talking about guns. They wanted to know how to get their hands on some and I thought they meant handguns so I began to tell them a few stories about south London, how you could go into a pub and buy a gun for a century, and their ears pricked up. A couple of days later I was in a club and Kettering pulls me to one side and asks me if I know anyone who can supply guns and I took it from there."

"And where do you stand at the moment?"

"I've said I know a couple of guys in London and that I'll see if I can get some prices."

"You're okay with that?" asked Shepherd. "Might be safer if you make us friends of friends, that way you don't have to know our shoe sizes and dates of birth."

"I don't think they'll go with complete outsiders," said Fenby. "I'll have to vouch for you personally."

"They'll trust you with this?" asked Shepherd.

Fenby shrugged again. "They've no reason to doubt me. I've proved myself often enough."

The superintendent tapped a pen on the table and flashed Fenby a warning look.

Fenby looked pained. "You know what it's like undercover. I'm one of the lads. We talk the same language, walk the same walk. I haven't put a foot wrong so far."

"The problem is that we don't have a large undercover squad," said the superintendent. "And those that we do have are more used to drugs work than weapons."

Hargrove nodded. "I think we can put something together," he said.

"That's good to hear," said the superintendent. "How do we move it forward?"

"We need to arrange a meeting, through Ray here. Put Kettering and Thompson together with Jimmy and Dan. Get them to spell out what they want."

"And you'll have the guns?"

"Not at the first meeting," said Hargrove. "Arms dealers are like drug dealers; they're not comfortable selling to people they don't know. You might be able to buy a cheap handgun from a stranger in Brixton, but the big stuff is too sensitive. No dealer would sell guns on the first meeting. And any sale would be done in very controlled circumstances."

"Can we do that here? In Birmingham?"

Hargrove wrinkled his nose. "Any dealer worth his salt is going to expect the buyer to come to him. At least in the first instance. If we appear too keen it's going to look suspicious."

"So London?"

"Home turf, yes. For the initial meeting. We'll get a sense of what they want and decide how to run it."

"And what about surveillance?"

"For the first meeting I'd suggest a totally hands-off approach. Everyone tends to be on edge."

The superintendent nodded but didn't look happy. "You're the expert," he said. "Obviously we'll follow your lead."

"We'll give you a full report of what happens in London and we'll arrange for the sale to take place up here," said Hargrove. He looked at his wristwatch. "Before we head back, I'd like Dan and Jimmy here to be given full access to the investigation files that you have."

"I can't let you take anything out of the building," said the superintendent quickly. "We've kept all our files off the mainframe. Everything is either on paper under lock and key, or on two laptops." He tapped his computer. "This is one. They're under lock and key too and never leave the building."

"That's not a problem." Hargrove nodded at Shepherd. "Dan has a photographic memory so he won't even have to take notes."

"Useful skill," said the superintendent.

"It's stood me in good stead so far," said Shepherd.

Hargrove, Shepherd and Sharpe reached the outskirts of London at nine o'clock in the evening. Hargrove dropped them in Hampstead High Street, not far from the Starbucks where he'd picked them up. Shepherd and Sharpe waved as Hargrove drove away.

"Like the good old days," said Sharpe.

"What do you mean, us standing out in the cold while he drives off in a warm car?"

"You know what I mean," said Sharpe, punching him on the shoulder. "We were a bloody good team." He looked around. "Is there a half-decent pub near here?"

"I quite like Ye Olde White Bear."

"Do ye now?" laughed Sharpe. "Then lead on, McDuff."

Shepherd took him towards the Heath and into the pub. Sharpe pulled out his wallet and bought a pint of lager for himself and a Jameson's, ice and soda for Shepherd. A football game was playing on an overhead screen.

"So what's it like, being at the Met?" asked Shepherd after they had clinked glasses.

Sharpe pulled a face as if he had a bad taste in his mouth. "The whole multicultural-community bollocks gets on my nerves, but at least with Hargrove I get to do real police work and put some real villains behind bars. You know what he's like; he protects you from the shit that comes running downhill." He sipped his lager. "That whole SOCA nonsense — bloody waste of time from the get-go."

"No arguments here," said Shepherd.

"They should have left us with the Met instead of forcing us to work with Customs officers and tax inspectors. Whoever thought that was a good idea should be put up against a wall and shot. SOCA turned into the worst sort of bureaucracy and didn't put away a single high-profile villain. And what did it cost? Billions? All of it money down the drain."

"Water under the bridge now, Razor."

"Maybe, but one of the reasons that the cops are so under-resourced is because so much was put into SOCA. Like the bloody NHS: too many chiefs and not enough Indians." He took another drink of lager. "What about Five? What's it like there?"

"Can't tell you, Razor. Official Secrets Act and all that."

"Screw you."

Shepherd grinned. "It's okay. It's not as bureaucratic as SOCA and money never seems to be an issue."

"And the lovely Charlotte?"

"She's a good boss, Razor, no matter what you think."

Sharpe put down his glass and raised his hands in surrender. "I didn't say anything."

"Put your bloody hands down, you idiot. Charlie's like Hargrove — she takes any flak that's flying about."

"And tells you the bare minimum."

"It's the Security Service, Razor. Most of what goes on is on a need-to-know basis."

"Yeah? Well, I like to know exactly why I'm putting my balls on the line. I can't abide all that secret squirrel stuff." He picked up his glass again.

"Yeah, maybe I'm not totally in the loop but the money makes up for that," said Shepherd. "Do you want to talk pay grades? You went back into the Met as a DS?"

"Detective Inspector," said Sharpe, squaring his shoulders. "Hargrove pushed through a promotion."

"Yeah, well, DIs don't get overtime, and trust me, I'm paid a shedload more than you."

Sharpe chuckled. "Next round's on you, then." He drained his glass and banged it down on the counter. "Whenever you're ready." Shepherd ordered another round of drinks as Sharpe looked around the pub. "So what's with you and Hampstead?" he said. "Full of TV producers and poncy writers and lesbians, isn't it?"

"Part of my legend," said Shepherd. "And just in case we bump into anyone who knows me, I'm John Whitehill and I'm a freelance journalist."

"Yeah? I'm DI Jimmy Sharpe with the Covert Operations Group."

"Very funny, Razor."

"This job you're on, terrorism-related?"

"Pretty much everything Five does at the moment is," said Shepherd.

"The world's gone mad," said Sharpe. "You know that, right? The number of people killed in acts of terror in the UK is a small fraction of the number stabbed and shot every year on our streets. Yet how often do you see cops walking the beat?"

"Flashing back to your days in Glasgow, huh?"

"Take the piss all you want, Spider. At least we could still give a teenager a clip round the ear without being hauled up on charges. I don't know why anyone joins the police these days. It's all PC bullshit and paperwork, and you're as likely to be grassed up by a colleague as you are to be dropped in the shit by a member of the public."

"Sounds like you're ready to quit."

"Retire, you mean? I've thought about it. But what would I do? Too young for a pipe and slippers." He took a long pull on his pint. "So Button isn't worried that Hargrove is going to poach you?"

"Why would she think that? Hargrove was looking for someone and she figured I'd be the best bet because I've worked with Hargrove before."

Sharpe grinned. "Is that what she said? Naughty Charlie. Hargrove asked for you specifically. Because you've worked with him before, but also because of your experience with guns. I figure she didn't have any choice because the request was made at the top. Just like her to take the credit." He shook his head and took another pull on his pint. "Women, huh?"

"I don't think her sex has anything to do with it, Razor. Anyway, doesn't really matter whose idea it was. The important thing is that we pull it off."

"Piece of piss," said Sharpe. "How many times have we done this before?" He took a deep breath and stretched out his arms. "I feel like a curry," he said. "Any good Indians in this neck of the woods?"

Shepherd got back to his flat just after eleven-thirty. He'd taken Sharpe to the Meghna Tandoori in Heath Street, a short walk from the pub they'd been drinking in. The restaurant was much more upmarket than Sharpe was used to, with minimalist white decor and white high-backed chairs. But the food was terrific and they'd washed the meal down with several bottles of Kingfisher. After Shepherd's cracks about their relative salaries Sharpe had insisted that Shepherd paid, and then he'd left in a minicab.

Shepherd made himself a coffee before sitting down in front of the television and calling Major Allan Gannon, his former commanding officer in the SAS and a longtime friend.

"Spider, how the hell are you?" said the Major.

"All good, Boss. Can you talk?"

"The hind legs off a donkey. Where are you?"

"London. You?"

"Locked up in Stirling Lines," said the Major, referring to the SAS headquarters at Credenhill in Herefordshire.

"I need a favour," said Shepherd, and he ran through the undercover operation that Hargrove was planning.

"AK-47s aren't a problem; we've stacks of them here. But if you're playing at arms dealer why not go for the Yugo AK?"

"You've got some?"

The Yugo AK was manufactured by Zastava Arms, a Serbian company, and was the Yugoslavian People's Army's assault rifle of choice before the country was ripped apart by civil war. It was a good weapon and many soldiers thought it superior to the Russian Kalashnikov.

"Loads," said the Major. "We use it all the time in exercises. I'm pretty sure we've even got a few of the crates they came in."

"That would work," said Shepherd. "I'll run it by Hargrove, see if we can just use them. It'll make our cover seem more authentic."

"Damn right. There's a fair number of Yugos knocking around the UK. Former Serbian military types have been selling them to gang bangers. I tell you what, Spider, I've got some Zastava M88 pistols too."

"Better and better," said Shepherd. "And there's no problem you loaning them to us?"

"I'll sign it off as an exercise," said the Major. "You can pick them up from here, can you?"

"Sounds like a plan," said Shepherd.

"Let me know when you want them," said the Major. "Be good to have a chat. I've been hearing some very interesting stories about you."

"My ears are burning."

"They should be."

"So how are your studies, Manraj?" asked Chaudhry's father as he dropped down on to the sofa and stretched out his legs. His fiftieth birthday was fast approaching but he looked a good ten years younger, with not a single grey hair and only a few laughter lines at the corners of his eyes. He was a keen squash player, had been for more than thirty years, and it showed in his lean physique. On more than a few occasions people had assumed that he was Chaudhry's elder brother rather than his father.

It was Saturday afternoon and Chaudhry had cycled from Stoke Newington to his parents' house, a neat four-bedroom detached house in Stanmore. It was the house that he'd been brought up in and as he looked around it he felt as if he'd never left. At the far end of the room was the piano on which he and his brother had practised for half an hour every night; through the French windows he could see the garden where his father had taught him the finer points of spin bowling; he knew that at the top of the stairs was his bedroom, pretty much exactly as it was the day he'd left to go to university three years earlier. Leaving home had been symbolic rather than a necessity. He could have commuted back and forth from Stanmore but Chaudhry had wanted to be independent; plus, he'd become bored with life in the suburbs. His elder brother had studied for his degree at Exeter so it hadn't been too much of a struggle to persuade his parents to allow him to rent a place in Stoke Newington.

"It's getting harder, but you know what med school is like," said Chaudhry. His father was an oncologist at Watford General Hospital, and had been since before Chaudhry was born. "Third year was much better because we had the attachments, so you actually got to deal with patients. The fourth year is all bookwork and the supervised research project. It's a grind."

His father nodded sympathetically. "It's a grind all right, but we all go through it. Just take it one day at a time. Once it's done and you've passed the exams you get your degree and then you can really start to learn about medicine."

"Fourth year's the worst, right?"

"Every year's tough, Manraj; they're just tough in different ways. But it's when you start working as a junior doctor that the pressure really starts."

"The killing season, they call it at King's."

"They call it that everywhere," said his father. "Just don't ever let the patients hear you say that." He smiled over at his son. "I'm really proud of you, Manraj. I hope you know that."

Chaudhry nodded. He knew. And he could see it in his father's eyes.

"So, are you seeing anyone?"

Chaudhry frowned, not understanding what his father meant, then realisation dawned and he groaned. "Dad . . . Please . . ."

"I'm your father and you're my only unmarried son, so I'm entitled to ask."

"You have only two sons and Akram got married last year."

"I'm not getting any younger and I'd like to be able-bodied enough to play cricket with my grandchildren."

Chaudhry laughed and slapped his own thigh. "You're crazy. Now you want me to be a father and I haven't even graduated. What's the rush?"

"There's no rush, it's just that I've found what I think might be the perfect girl for you."

"Say what?"

His father looked at him over the top of his spectacles. "What's the problem? I thought you'd be pleased."

"You thought I'd be happy because you're fixing up an arranged marriage for me?"

"Who said anything about marriage? I was at an NHS conference last week and I met up with an old friend who works as a cardiologist in Glasgow. He was talking about his daughter — she's a second-year microbiology student at UCL — and I mentioned you were at King's . . ."

"And the next thing you know you've got us married off. Dad, I'm more than capable of finding my own girlfriend."

"Which is why I asked you if you were seeing anyone." He pushed his spectacles higher up his nose. "Her name's Jamila, and she's from a very good family. According to her father, she hasn't had a steady boyfriend. He was very impressed to hear that you're at King's."

"You didn't show him my CV, did you?"

94

"I might have mentioned a few of the highlights, yes. Look, no pressure, but why don't you at least get in touch, maybe ask her out?"

"It's not going to be one of those chaperoned things, is it? With half the family tagging along?"

His father laughed. "What century do you think you're living in?" he said. "She's on Facebook. She's been told to expect you to ask to be a Facebook friend, to chat online for a while and see if you get on."

"You've already told her about me?"

"Her father has, yes."

"How long have you been planning this?"

"We're not planning anything. I told you, I met her father at a conference and we got talking. You can at least get in touch on Facebook, can't you? I don't want her father to think that we're snubbing her."

Chaudhry sighed. "Okay, I suppose I can do that."

"Manraj, there's no pressure here, really. There's no need to make a big thing about it. It's not like when your mum and I were introduced. Back then they almost put a gun to my head."

"Seriously?"

His father laughed again. "Of course not seriously," he said. "But I was left in no doubt that I'd need a pretty good reason to turn her down. Things were very different back then and most marriages were arranged."

"And you were okay with that?"

"Your grandfather is a pussycat these days, but thirty years ago he was as tough as they come. He was born in Pakistan, remember. Or British India, as it was then. He came over with nothing and it wasn't like it is now, with benefits and handouts. The people in his village paid for him to come to the UK and when I was old enough to marry it was time for him to pay the piper."

Chaudhry leaned forward. "You never told me this before."

His father shrugged. "That's the way it worked. Your mother's grandparents helped pay for my father to come to this country. I had citizenship so if I married her then her parents and her grandparents could come too. Which is what happened, of course. Our marriage helped their family, and that was only fair because they'd helped my father."

"And what if you hadn't liked her?"

His father laughed out loud. "We'll never know," he said. "But I did have a few tense moments, I can tell you. They sent over a photograph but it was a group photograph and her face wasn't clear because she was wearing a headscarf. There was no Skype back then and no Facebook. We managed a few phone calls but she was shy and she didn't speak any English." He shrugged. "I tell you, I was bloody shaking when I got off the plane."

"You flew to Pakistan to meet her?"

"To marry her, Manraj. It was a done deal by the time I arrived in Pakistan."

Chaudhry's jaw dropped. "And that didn't worry you?"

"I understood that I had an obligation to my father. How could I have refused? It would have been a slap in the face for him and for everyone who had helped him get to England." He sat back on the sofa. "Anyway, all's well that ends well. We were met at the airport by her parents and they drove me to their village in this rickety old truck that seemed to be held together with string. The first time we met her whole family was there, so were my parents, and she had her face covered. The minutes before she took down her veil were the scariest in my life. Then she did and . . ." He grinned. "Wow. That's what I said. Wow. I remember how everyone laughed. She was a lovely girl, Manraj. Like a supermodel. Her hair was just amazing; it came down to her waist and was so soft and shiny. And her skin . . . I tell you, the first time I touched her arm I —"

"Dad, please," said Chaudhry, holding up his hands. "Enough. I get it."

"Get what?" said his mother, arriving with a tray of tea things and a plate of chocolate cake that she had baked specially for him. She put the tray down on the coffee table and sat next to her husband.

"I was just telling him about Jamila," said his father.

"Oh, isn't she lovely?" said his mother, picking up the teapot.

His mother wasn't supermodel fit any more, thought Chaudhry, but she was still a lovely woman. The woman he'd known had always been cuddly rather than fit but as he looked at her pouring tea he could see what had attracted his father. She had high cheekbones and flawless skin the colour of the milky tea that she handed him. Her eyes were wide, with impossibly long lashes, and her hair was still as lustrous as a model's in a shampoo advertisement. It was hard to imagine her as a simple village girl unable to speak English. His mother was always immaculately dressed, either in a traditional sari or in a western designer outfit, and she was always well made-up, even if she was just popping down to the local shops.

"How would I know? I haven't seen her," said Chaudhry.

Mrs Chaudhry looked over at her husband. "Didn't you show him the picture?"

"I haven't had the chance," said his father. He grunted as he pushed himself up off the sofa and walked over to a sideboard that was loaded with framed family photographs. He pulled open a drawer and rooted through the contents.

"She is gorgeous," said his mother. "And smart."

"Yeah, Dad said she was a microbiologist."

"And she's got such a good heart. She took a gap year to work in an orphanage in Pakistan. Like you did last year. You'll have so much to talk about."

"It wasn't an orphanage Manraj worked at, it was a hospital," said his father.

"It's the same thing, giving up your time to help others less fortunate." She smiled at Chaudhry in the way that only a proud mother can and Chaudhry's stomach lurched. He tried to cover his discomfort by sipping his tea.

He'd never lied to his parents before he started working for MI5 but there was no way he could have told them that he had gone to Pakistan to attend an al-Qaeda training camp, where he learned to strip and fire a whole range of weapons, construct explosive devices and manipulate biochemical agents. He'd told his parents that he was volunteering at a country medical centre during his Christmas break and he'd never felt more guilty than when his father had offered to pay for his ticket. The people at MI5 had told him that under no circumstances could he ever tell his parents what he was doing, that to do so would risk his life and theirs. So he had lied, and he hated himself for doing it.

"Are you okay, honey?" asked his mother.

Chaudhry forced a smile. "I've been studying too hard and not sleeping enough," he said.

"Why don't you stay for the weekend? I'll feed you up, you can lie in tomorrow and if you need to get some work done you can use your father's study."

"We've only just kicked him out of the nest. Don't say you want him back already," said his father. He held up a photograph. "Here it is." He walked back to the sofa and gave the picture to Chaudhry.

Chaudhry took it. He looked at it for several seconds and then looked back at his father, his eyebrows raised. "Wow," he said.

Shepherd woke up early on Monday morning, half an hour before his alarm was due to go off. He'd spent the weekend in Hereford and had arrived back in London late on Sunday night. His back was aching, probably from the long drive, so he did a few stretches before heading to the bathroom to clean his teeth. His back was still sore so he decided to go for a run to see if that would loosen it up. He pulled on an old sweatshirt and a pair of track-suit bottoms and went through to the kitchen, where he kept his army boots and weighted rucksack. He figured it best to forgo the rucksack and he went downstairs. He jogged to the Heath, then set off on his regular route: up North End Way and round the Hampstead Heath extension, a large open space to the north-west of the main Heath. In the past it had been farmland and while it wasn't as pretty as the rest of the Heath it was generally quieter and Shepherd always preferred to run alone. He did two circuits of the extension then cut around West Meadow and down to Parliament Hill Fields. Several running clubs used the Heath and as he got closer to the Parliament Hill athletics track he was overtaken by a group of serious runners, all in hi-tech trainers and Lycra shorts and vests. Several grinned as they overtook Shepherd and he heard one mutter something about Shepherd's choice of footwear. Shepherd always ran in boots. Running was a survival skill as well as a way of keeping fit and the heavy boots meant that he was able to push himself to his limits faster and more efficiently. He headed east to Dukes Field, skirted the secret garden and then headed north to Cohen's Fields, increasing the pace until he felt his calf muscles burn.

He reached Kenwood House, the spectacular white-stucco mansion built on the ridge that linked the villages of Hampstead and Highgate. Stopping at the duelling ground where grievances were settled with pistols during the eighteenth and nineteenth centuries, he dropped to the ground and did a hundred press-ups in four sets of twenty-five. Then he carried on running for another thirty minutes. He slowed to a jog as he headed back to his flat, picking up a copy of the *Daily Telegraph* and the *Daily Mail* and a carton of milk on the way.

Back in the flat he showered and shaved, changed into a clean shirt and chinos, then made himself a mug of coffee and flopped down on to the sofa. He sipped his coffee as he scanned the front page of the *Telegraph*, then turned to page two. His jaw tensed when he saw the headline of the lead story, then he began to curse as he read it. He was only halfway through when he picked up his BlackBerry and called Button.

"Have you seen the *Telegraph*?" he said as soon as she answered.

"About an hour ago," she said. "We're talking it through as we speak."

"And you didn't think it was worth talking to me?"

"I don't think this is the sort of conversation we should be having on an open line," she said. "Can you come to the office?"

"I'd prefer somewhere outside," said Shepherd.

"I've got an active investigation that means I have to be here all day," she replied.

"Give me an hour," he said and cut the connection. He read through the rest of the article and then picked up the *Mail*. The same story was on page seven.

Charlotte Button kept Shepherd waiting for half an hour in a conference room on the third floor of Thames House, but her apologies when she did finally arrive seemed genuine enough. Shepherd stood up out of politeness but she waved him to sit back down as she dropped into one of the high-backed executive chairs on the opposite side of the highly polished oval oak table. Shepherd had the *Telegraph* and *Mail* open in front of him. Button was holding a cup of tea and she placed it carefully on the table.

"How the hell could this have happened, Charlie? Whose side are the Pakistanis on?"

The thrust of the articles in both papers was the same: an unnamed spokesman for the Inter-Services Intelligence, Pakistan's premier intelligence agency, had announced that a hand-drawn map had been found in the compound where Bin Laden had been living, a map that could have been left only by the Seals. The map showed the layout of the compound and had floor plans of the main building, including the bedroom where Bin Laden was shot. The spokesman also said that the fact that the Americans had destroyed their own helicopter was a sign that they no longer trusted their Pakistani allies.

"Their noses were put out of joint because the Americans made them look stupid, or at best incompetent, so this is them getting their own back. They just want to show that the Americans make mistakes."

"Even if it means putting our guys in the firing line? And what about the bloody Yanks? What were they thinking? Are their memories so bloody poor that they can't commit a floor plan to memory?"

"Spider, you're blowing this out of all proportion," said Button calmly.

Shepherd's jaw dropped. "I'm what?"

"Look, you're right: a mistake was made. The Seals shouldn't have left the map behind, but Bin Laden's dead and what's done is done."

"You're not serious, are you?" said Shepherd. Button said nothing. She picked up her cup and sipped her tea. "Charlie, you don't need me to spell this out for you, do you?" Button continued to sip her tea. Shepherd leaned forward, his eyes locked on hers. "That piece of paper shows that the Yanks had intel on the inside of that building, intel that couldn't have come from surveillance or satellites. The only way they could know the layout of the inside of the building is if they'd spoken to someone who'd been inside."

"He had visitors. We know that," said Button, putting down her cup.

"Are you being deliberately obtuse?" asked Shepherd. "If anything had changed in that room, anything at all, then it would give them a timeline. If a chair had been brought in and that chair was shown on the plan then they'd know when the traitor had been there."

"You're assuming that the bad guys will get sight of the map," said Button.

"And you're not? It's the Pakistanis, for God's sake. Their intelligence services leak like a bloody sieve. They probably showed the map to al-Qaeda before they went public. And why go public with something like that in the first place? There's only one reason, and that's to embarrass the bloody Yanks. They're no allies of ours, that's for sure."

"And why has this map come forward now? Bin Laden was killed months ago. Why have the Pakistanis just released it?"

"We don't know," said Button. "Either they found it at the time and have been sitting on it, or they've only just found it. They're getting ready to demolish the building so they could have just swept through the building again and stumbled across it. The when doesn't really matter. All that matters is that they've gone public with it."

"Whose side are they on?"

"Supposedly ours," said Button. "But there are a lot of different factions within the Pakistani intelligence community. And some of those factions are close to al-Qaeda."

Shepherd cursed and shook his head.

"Spider, what are you worried about? That al-Qaeda is going to be looking for revenge?"

"You think they'll just let it go?"

"It's a terror organisation. They plant bombs and they crash planes. They're not geared up for individual assassinations. And who's going to be authorising and funding a revenge operation?"

"He had his supporters. Rich Saudis. They might want to prove a point."

Button sat back in her chair. "I think you're worrying about nothing," she said. "Even if someone in al-Qaeda realises that there was human intel behind the raid there's still nothing to point to our people."

"There's the timeline," said Shepherd. "How many visitors do you think he had during the five years he was in Pakistan? The Americans had the compound under surveillance for six weeks before the raid and in that time there were just three visitors, and one of them was his courier. So in a year, maybe twenty? Do you think they'd believe that the Americans would wait a year before taking him out? Six months, max. So they can probably pin it down to ten visitors, maybe a dozen."

"That's complete guesswork, Spider. Bin Laden wanted to brief our two guys personally, but he might have met hundreds of others."

"Our guys were special, that's what he said to them. He was taking a particular interest in them because he really wanted to hurt the UK."

"He probably said that to all the girls," said Button, then she quickly held up her hand as she saw the frown flash across Shepherd's face. "I'm sorry, misplaced flippancy. But my point is valid. He's not going to tell his people that they're disposable, is he? He's going to tell them all that they're vital to his organisation, that they're the centre of his universe. You make a shahid feel that he's the most important person on earth because that's the only way he's going to blow himself to kingdom come. My point is that Bin Laden will have had several visitors and I don't see that our guys are any more at risk than anyone else. And the Americans are already feeding the media with stories that it was Bin Laden's courier who led them to the house."

"And you're prepared to take that risk, are you?"

"It's a calculated risk. You've worked undercover and you know that there's always a risk."

"But I'm a professional. Our guys are amateurs. You brought me in to babysit them for exactly that reason. You needed a pro to hold their hands. Well, that's what I'm doing. They don't know the danger they're in right now so I'm the one who has to speak for them."

"And what do you want to do? Pull them out? Blow the whole operation?"

"Blow the whole operation?" repeated Shepherd incredulously. "They supplied the intel that led to Bin Laden being taken out. That operation is well and truly over."

"But what al-Qaeda are planning in the UK is ongoing," said Button. "What happened in Pakistan isn't going to put the brakes on what's happening here. If anything, Bin Laden's death makes it even more likely that they'll carry out attacks here and in the States. And pulling Chaudhry and Malik out at this late stage is going to make them appear as guilty as hell." She leaned forward. "You're over-thinking this, really. So far as the world is concerned, the Americans followed a courier to the compound based on intel they got from waterboarding. Now you and I know that's a fairy story, but the media's lapping it up and the Americans love it because it makes them look like heroes for once."

Shepherd nodded thoughtfully. "Okay, I'll buy that. But they're going to need more protection."

"Like what? You want to go Salman Rushdie on them and have them assigned round-the-clock Special Branch guards? You want them followed by unmarked cars? Helicopters?"

"Of course not," said Shepherd.

"What, then? I understand you're anxious about their safety. That's what happens to handlers. You get attached. You care."

Shepherd smiled tightly.

"And before you ask, yes, I care when I'm running you. Every handler does. You're not chess pieces that we move around as part of the greater game. What you're feeling is totally natural. A sort of reverse Stockholm Effect. Every handler goes through it. Which is why every handler in turn has a supervisor who can keep an eye on the bigger picture. And that's what I'm doing now. You're close to these guys. That goes with the territory. But I am taking a broader view, and I think you're worrying unnecessarily."

"What about bugging their flat? A tracker in Malik's car? Letting Amar work his magic on their mobile phones?"

"And what if any of that hi-tech stuff is discovered? Then they are in trouble. Big trouble."

Shepherd sighed. Button was right. She was telling him exactly what he'd said to Chaudhry and Malik. A GPS in the car or in their phones would be a dead giveaway. Chaudhry and Malik weren't professionals; they were just young men doing what they thought was right, and they'd never be able to lie their way out of trouble. When Shepherd worked undercover everything was a lie from his name onwards. Lying didn't exactly come naturally to him but he was proficient at it. The big advantage that Chaudhry and Malik had was that they were real. Everything about them was genuine. That was their strength — and their weakness.

"I hear you," he said.

"I know these guys too, don't forget. I'm not as close as you are, obviously, but I do care what happens to them. And there's no way I'd put them in the line of fire. I really do believe that increasing their security now would do more harm than good. At the moment the only link between them and us is you. And your legend as John Whitehill, freelance journalist, is watertight. Anyone who checks up on you will find a website, dozens of articles in magazines and journals, and a rented flat in Hampstead. The worst accusation that could be levelled against them is that they've talked to a journalist. But that all changes if anyone finds one of our gizmos."

"So we just leave things as they are?"

"Our friends over at GCHQ are listening for chatter," she said. "If we get any sense that there's a witch hunt going on then we can rethink. We'll put an extra watch at the borders, and check on the usual suspects here."

"Forgive me if that doesn't inspire me with confidence," said Shepherd. "Our borders still leak, we both know that. Known terrorists have walked into the country without anyone batting an eyelid."

"That's a bit harsh."

"And GCHQ listening for chatter didn't stop the London tube bombings."

"Exactly," said Button. "That's why what Chaudhry and Malik are doing is so important. They've got the inside track on a major terrorist attack that no one, absolutely no one, is aware of. We need them, Spider. We need their intel."

Shepherd nodded. "You're right."

Button grinned. "That's good to hear," she said. "Look, I understand your concerns, but I think the chance of anyone connecting them to what happened in Pakistan is remote. If it makes you feel better, why not give them a security briefing, give them some tips about what to watch out for. That's why I wanted you involved, to share your expertise. They're virgins at this and you've been around the block a few times."

"That's the truth," he said. "Okay, let's do that. But you really need to keep your ear to the ground, Charlie. Any intel at all that they might be at risk and we pull them out, right?"

"Absolutely," she said. "I wouldn't have it any other way."

After the meeting with Button, Shepherd went up to the sixth floor to talk to Damien Plant, one of MI5's top dressers. Plant was a one-stop shop for everything needed to back up a legend. He could supply any paperwork from a driving licence and passport to a utility bill or credit card, in any name and with any address and date of birth. His department also supplied homes and offices, vehicles, furniture, clothing and jewellery. There was almost nothing that Damien and his team couldn't provide.

Plant shook Shepherd's hand and waved him to a chair. He was in his early thirties, with sunbed-brown skin and a shaved head, and he was wearing a black linen jacket and blue Versace jeans. His desk was piled high with catalogues and fashion magazines and his walls were lined with reference books.

He sipped from a bottle of Evian and swung his feet up on to his desk. "You're not here to complain about your flat, are you?" he said. "I was working to a very tight budget and you can't blame me for that. And when we set it up we had no idea the operation would go on for as long as it has."

"It's fine," said Shepherd.

"I know, but there's barely enough room to swing a cat. If I'd known you were going to be there for a year I would have tried to fix up a bigger place. Within budget, of course."

"I've not been there much over the last few months, the operation had gone quiet," said Shepherd. "But on the plus side, it's great to be so near the Heath."

"I love Hampstead," said Plant. "Used to go cottaging there in my misspent youth."

Shepherd wasn't sure if Plant was joking or not. "Funnily enough I was in the Willie not that long ago," he said.

"You should have told me you were on the turn," said Plant, raising one eyebrow. "I could have taken you out and shown you the ropes."

"It'll be a cold day in hell before I go down that route," said Shepherd. "It was a business meeting. About this job, as it happens. Basically I'm an arms dealer, so pretty much none of the John Whitehill props

110

work, especially the clothing. The job's actually for the Met but Charlie's fixed it up so she'll sign off on it."

"I trust you, Spider," said Plant and he reached over to pick up a clipboard and pen. "Full wardrobe?" he asked, the camp act completely forgotten.

"I guess, but I'm probably going to be in character only a couple of times so no need to go overboard on the number of outfits."

"Suits?"

"One suit. A name. Whatever you think."

"Paul Smith should work. I'll see what I can get in the way of a leather jacket. Shirts? Ties?"

Shepherd sighed. He hated the feel of a tie round his neck but there were some times when it was necessary. "Maybe. What do you think?"

"We could do *Miami Vice* and put you in a T-shirt, show off your abs. Well-cut suit over it."

Shepherd grimaced. Given the choice between a tight T-shirt and a tie, on balance he'd prefer the tie. "Tie, I guess. And good shoes."

"Bally, I think," said Plant. "What about jewellery? That watch has to go, of course."

Shepherd held up his left hand. He was wearing a cheap Casio, which was the sort of watch that a freelance journalist would wear but it wouldn't do for an arms dealer with criminal connections. "I'll wear my own Submariner," he said.

Plant looked pained. "I'd advise against the Submariner," he said. "You've got the steel model, with the black bezel, right?"

Shepherd nodded. It was the watch that he'd worn ever since he'd been with the SAS.

"See, that screams military. You'd be stressing the action-man aspect when you're playing a villain. With villains it's all about show so I'd go for a gold Cartier. Or a Patek Philippe. Something that says you're wearing twenty or thirty grand on your wrist and you don't give a shit."

"Okay," said Shepherd.

"And I'm thinking a gold chain for your right wrist. Maybe a ring?"

"And a money clip," said Shepherd. "Something gold."

Plant scribbled on his clipboard again. "And what's your legend? English? London?"

"Yes. Former soldier; did some contracting work out in Iraq six or seven years ago, now self-employed."

"Car?"

"You know, I think we can leave that. There's no need to overcomplicate things. I'll be with a Met guy so he can take care of the transport."

"I do have a new Maserati that I'm trying to get a few miles on."

Shepherd laughed. "I'll pass, but if things change I'll definitely let you know."

"So we don't need accommodation?"

"It won't be an issue. I won't be having the bad guys round for drinks."

Plant scribbled on his clipboard. "Paperwork?"

"I doubt I'll be asked for ID but I might as well have a driving licence."

"Same date of birth but we'll knock a couple of years off," said Plant. "Name?"

"Garry Edwards. Double r."

Plant frowned. "In Edwards?"

"In Garry."

Plant looked at him over the top of his clipboard. "I have to say, I don't see you as a Garry."

"I've played the part before," said Shepherd. "No one's complained." Edwards was a former soldier who worked as a security contractor in Afghanistan and sold weapons on the side. The legend was one that he'd used once before when he'd worked for Hargrove's police undercover unit and it would withstand close scrutiny.

Plant passed a sheet of paper across the table and Shepherd scribbled a "Garry Edwards" signature and passed it back.

"Anything else?"

"I think we're good," said Plant. "What's the time frame?"

"No great rush, but as always the sooner the better."

Shepherd left Plant's office and headed for the agency's training department. He had something he needed to run by them.

Shepherd caught the tube to Hampstead and walked back to his flat, taking a circuitous route to make sure that he wasn't being followed. He had spent all afternoon with the training department arranging an exercise for Chaudhry and Malik. He let himself into the flat and tapped his security code into the burglar alarm console. He switched on the kettle and then called Chaudhry on his BlackBerry.

"Couple of questions for you, mate," said Shepherd. "Do you know anyone in Reading? Anyone at all?"

"Never been," said Chaudhry.

"And you don't know anyone from there? Anyone at the university?"

"Not that I know of. Why?"

"Something I want to do," said Shepherd. "What about Harvey?"

"He's here now. I'll ask him." Shepherd heard a muffled conversation and then Chaudhry came back on the line. "He says no. What's going on, John?"

"I want to run you through a training exercise, show you a few anti-surveillance techniques, and I want to do it in a place where no one knows you. What are you doing on Thursday?"

There was another short muffled conversation. "We've both got lectures but we can duck them. Why do we need to do this?"

"There're a few tricks of the trade I want to run by you, that's all," said Shepherd.

"Has something happened?" asked Chaudhry suspiciously.

"No, everything's good," lied Shepherd. "I just want to keep you both sharp. Here's what I want you to do. On Thursday morning I want you both to get the train from Paddington to Reading. The trains run throughout the day and the journey takes about half an hour."

"Be easier for Harvey to drive," said Chaudhry.

114

"This isn't about getting there, it's about knowing whether or not you've got a tail," said Shepherd. "I want you to get to Paddington, then get on the train. When you get to Reading, I want you to go to the Novotel. It's about half a mile from the station. Take whatever route you want. Once I'm in the room I'll give you the number so you can go straight up."

"That's it? What's the point?"

"The point is that I'll have you followed. The guys who'll be following you won't know your destination, so if you can throw them off and get to the Novotel without them following you, you'll get a gold star. If you can't throw them off then I want you to describe anyone you spot."

"And who are they? Who'll be following us?"

"Professionals," said Shepherd. "They do it for a living, for MI5."

"We're going to be followed by spies?"

"That's the plan. It'll be good experience."

"But why've we got to trek across London to Paddington?"

"Because I want you to get the feel of moving across the city knowing that you're being followed. Then I want you in Reading so that I can run you through a few exercises without any chance of you bumping into someone you know. Trust me, it'll be worth doing."

"If you say so. And you'll cover our expenses?"

"Of course," said Shepherd. "I'll have a brown envelope with me. See you on Thursday."

Shepherd ended the call. He'd bought half a dozen salads from Marks & Spencer and he took out a niçoise. He was about to make himself a coffee but then changed his mind and took a bottle of wine out of the fridge and poured himself a glass. He carried the salad and wine through to the sitting room and sat down opposite the television. It was five-thirty and he'd promised to call his son on Skype at six, so he switched on the television and watched the BBC rolling news as he ate his salad and drank his wine. At six o'clock he switched on his laptop and went through to his Skype program. Liam was already online.

Shepherd put through the call and almost immediately Liam appeared on screen, his tie at half-mast as usual, his hair unkempt. "You look like you've been dragged through a hedge backwards," Shepherd laughed.

Liam ran a hand over his hair but it didn't make any difference. "Rugby practice," he said. "We've got a big game on Saturday."

"How's the rugby going?"

"It's brilliant, Dad. I thought football was the best but I'm really into rugby now."

"I'll try to make it," said Shepherd.

"Cool," said Liam.

"And what about the climbing?"

"Yeah, that's good fun. I'm getting really good on the wall and next month the instructor's taking us out to some crag that's about a hundred feet high."

"Good luck with that. We'll have to do some climbing together some time." Shepherd sipped his wine.

"Are you drinking?" asked Liam.

"It's wine. With my dinner."

"It's a bit early to be drinking, isn't it?"

Shepherd laughed. "What are you, the alcohol police? I'm in for the night, I'm not driving anywhere, so let your old dad have a drink, why don't you?" He raised his glass. "Cheers."

"Where are you?" asked Liam. "You're not home, are you?"

"London still," said Shepherd.

"When are you seeing Katra again? Do you think she can come to the match?"

"Maybe," said Shepherd. "If I can get the timing right I can go to Hereford, pick her up and come to your school."

"Please try, Dad."

"I will. Of course I will."

"You're not going to sack her, are you?"

Shepherd put down his wine glass. "Why do you say that?"

Liam shrugged and looked away, embarrassed. "I don't know."

"Come on, spit it out."

Liam sighed. "You don't seem to be at home much. And I'm at school all the time. So maybe you'll decide that you don't need her."

"That's crazy," said Shepherd. "Someone still has to take care of the house. You're at home for the holidays. And I'll be back once this job is done and dusted. Trust me, I'm as fond of Katra as you are. As long as she wants to work for us, she can."

"Great," said Liam. He looked back at the screen, grinning broadly.

"And what about maths? How are you getting on? Didn't you have a test today?"

Liam's face fell. "Can't we talk about something else, Dad?"

Shepherd grinned. His son was still young enough to read like a book.

The Al Nakheel on the top floor of the Al Khozama Centre was generally regarded as the best restaurant in Riyadh. It certainly had the best view, and the tables on its panoramic terrace were almost always fully booked. Fully booked or not, Ahmed Al-Jaber was always guaranteed to be given a table. His connections to the Saudi royal family were second to none and, even in a country of billionaires, Al-Jaber's wealth was revered. Al-Jaber was sitting at his regular corner table when Bin Azim walked into the restaurant. The lunchtime clientele was almost exclusively male and dressed in either made-to-measure suits or the full-length white Saudi robes and checked shemagh head-dresses. Al-Jaber was a traditionalist and always wore a robe and shemagh, even when he was overseas. As always he was accompanied by bodyguards, large men in black suits and impenetrable sunglasses. Two of them stood at the far end of the terrace, hands clasped in front of their groins, and there were two more by the doors that led to the kitchen. Bin Azim walked over slowly, favouring his left leg. He would soon be turning seventy-five and the last five years had not been good to him. Diabetes, arthritis and a worrying tendency to forget people's names. Bin Azim preferred a well-cut suit to a flowing robe and he always found the shemagh an annoyance, but he wore them out of respect for Al-Jaber.

Al-Jaber smiled when he saw Bin Azim walking towards him. In terms of money and status Bin Azim was a pygmy compared to Al-Jaber, but he was ten years older and, out of respect for his age, Al-Jaber stood up and held out his hands in welcome. It was Bin Azim who initiated the kissing, a soft peck on each cheek, before they sat down.

"I'm not eating," said Al-Jaber. "But please order whatever you like."

"Coffee is fine," said Bin Azim, adjusting his robe around his legs. A hovering waiter asked him what sort of coffee he wanted and Bin Azim ordered an espresso. His doctor was constantly asking him to switch to tea but coffee was one of the few pleasures that Bin Azim had left in his life and he intended to enjoy it until his last breath.

"How was Karachi?" asked Al-Jaber.

"It there a worse place in the world?" said Bin Azim. "If there is I have yet to find it."

"Perhaps in Africa," said Al-Jaber. "But there is money to be made in Pakistan and the generals are easy to work with. Everything and everyone has a price there."

Bin Azim's hand moved slowly inside his robe. He was well known to Al-Jaber's bodyguards but they still stiffened and their hands moved to their concealed weapons. Bin Azim's hand reappeared holding a piece of paper and the bodyguards relaxed. He slid the piece of paper across the table.

"The Americans had help," said Bin Azim.

"From the Pakistanis?" There was a pair of gold-rimmed reading glasses on the table by Al-Jaber's right hand and he put them on.

"From someone," said Bin Azim. He nodded at the piece of paper. "That's the proof."

Al-Jaber unfolded the sheet of paper. It was a photocopy of a hand-drawn floor plan.

"It is a drawing of the compound and the buildings in it," said Bin Azim. "The walls and the exterior can be seen from satellites but, as you can see, the map shows the internal walls."

Al-Jaber studied the map for almost a full minute before looking up. "And it is accurate?"

"Absolutely. Every room."

"So it was drawn by someone who had visited the compound?"

"That is the only way to get that amount of detail. You see the doors? The way they are drawn open?"

Al-Jaber looked back at the map. "Yes, I see that."

"The hinges are all on the correct sides. If the door is hinged on the left, it is drawn that way. And the furniture. It is exactly as it was in the house. I checked with his family."

"The Americans are saying that they followed The Sheik's courier to the compound."

"Yes, I know."

"Is that a lie, then?"

"It might perhaps be how they found the compound. But the courier would never betray The Sheik."

"The map is definitely genuine?" asked Al-Jaber.

"I have no reason to doubt its veracity."

"They are duplicitous bastards, the Pakistanis. You shake a Pakistani's hand and you had better count your fingers afterwards."

Bin Azim laughed. "My contact is solid. He met with The Sheik himself, many years ago. And he has supplied us with top-grade intelligence in the past."

"Leopards can change their spots," said Al-Jaber. "Especially ones from Pakistan."

"I can vouch for him," said Bin Azim.

"My concern is that the Pakistanis might want to cause mischief for the Americans." He held up the piece of paper. "ISI could have made this map after the event. Then leaked it to you."

"Why would they do that? What is there to gain? Are we going to hate the Americans more because of this map? Of course not."

"And the timing is very suspicious. Why release it now?"

"It has only just been discovered. My contact says that they were clearing out one of the upstairs bedrooms and they found it under a mattress. The Americans were in there at night, the map must have been dropped in the confusion and the mattress tipped on top of it."

"So the Pakistanis didn't search the building after the attack?"

"Why would they? They would have assumed that the Americans had taken everything of importance." He held out his hand and Al-Jaber passed the map back.

"What about the Americans? Could they have wanted the Pakistanis to find the map? The Americans might want to sow dissent among our ranks. We start to suspect everybody. Once an organisation loses trust, it cannot function."

The waiter reappeared with Bin Azim's coffee and they waited until he had set the white porcelain cup down on the table and left before continuing their conversation.

"So that is the question we must ask ourselves," said Al-Jaber. "Did the Americans leave it to be found? Or do we have something that they would rather we didn't have?"

"The fact that ISI went public is an embarrassment to the Americans. It makes them look less than professional."

Al-Jaber chuckled. "Crashing their helicopter did that," he said. "My worry is that the Americans want us to act on this map. That they left it there for the Pakistanis to find, knowing that the Pakistanis would in turn pass it to us."

"If it was a plant it was very cleverly done. I am more inclined to believe that it was an error. These are the same Americans who crashed their helicopter, remember?"

Al-Jaber nodded slowly. "Then let us assume that the map is genuine and that the Americans made a mistake. What do we do?"

"We find out who betrayed The Sheik and we kill him. Such a betrayal cannot go unpunished."

"The Sheik is dead," said Al-Jaber. "Killing the betrayer will not bring him back. One must be careful

122

with revenge. Remember what the Koran says, old friend. 'If thou dost stretch thy hand against me, to slay me, it is not for me to stretch my hand against thee to slay thee: for I do fear Allah, the cherisher of the worlds.' Revenge is not for good Muslims; it's what the infidels do."

"Then not for revenge, but to make sure that it doesn't happen again. Whoever gave away The Sheik's location might be in a position to betray us in some other way. Who knows who else he might give up? We have to find out who the traitor is, find out what he knows, and then . . ." He shrugged. "I do not see that we have any choice." He sipped his coffee.

Al-Jaber stroked his chin. "How do we find this traitor?" he asked.

Bin Azim unfolded the map again and placed it on the table. He tapped a finger on one of the rooms. There were the outlines of a bed and a cupboard and what appeared to be a flat-screen television against one wall. "This is the room where The Sheik died," he said. "It is accurate: the furniture is correctly marked and the door opens with the hinges on the left." He tapped a second door, to the right of the bed. "This door leads to a bathroom. But last summer this door was not here. The room next door to the bedroom was used as another bedroom. But a builder was brought in to turn it into a bathroom and make a connecting door." He tapped the map again. "So prior to mid-August this door did not exist. Whoever drew this map could only have visited the compound between mid-August and when The Sheik was killed. That is a narrow time frame. Nine months."

"And what about the builder? Was he aware that The Sheik lived there?"

"I'm assured that he wasn't. The Sheik and his family were moved to another safe house while the work was carried out. Only when the building workers had gone did The Sheik move back."

"We would need to be sure that the builder is not the traitor," said Al-Jaber.

"Of course," said Bin Azim. "But if he is cleared we will then need to take a look at every visitor that The Sheik received over the nine months since the bathroom was installed."

"Do you have someone in mind for this?"

"I do, yes. A Palestinian who has handled interrogations for me before."

"And if the betrayer is found will this Palestinian be able to take care of things?"

"Absolutely," said Bin Azim.

"Then that's what we shall do," said Al-Jaber. "There is a problem, though. Of those that visited The Sheik, most were being readied for jihad in countries around the world. Do we allow them to go ahead, or do we stop them?"

"If we pull them out now questions will be asked and rumours will start. If we let it be known that we suspect we have a traitor then all trust will be shattered. Suspicions will spread like a cancer."

"So we tell no one? Only the Palestinian?"

Bin Azim nodded. "I think it is best. Only one apple is bad. The Palestinian will identify the bad apple and will remove it. But we will be watching all our operations carefully. If we so much as suspect that any have been compromised we will cauterise them immediately."

"I agree," said Al-Jaber. He looked at his watch, a diamond-encrusted gold Rolex. "I have to go soon; my wife wants to go shopping."

"Where are you heading?" asked Bin Azim.

"London," said Al-Jaber. "The weak pound makes their Harrods as cheap as a market bazaar. She has a shopping list that is longer than my arm."

Bin Azim knew that Al-Jaber had four wives, but he didn't have to ask which one was going on the shopping trip. Al-Jaber's first wife was in her sixties and was rarely seen outside the family compound. His second and third wives had borne Al-Jaber sixteen children between them. One was in a top American hospital being treated for bowel cancer and the other was rumoured to be in a Swiss facility being treated for depression following two failed suicide attempts. Al-Jaber's fourth wife was a third of his age, a stunning Lebanese girl. Bin Azim was one of the few non-family members who had ever seen her face. She only ever wore a full burka including a mesh veil that shielded her eyes when she went out. Even when she was overseas Al-Jaber insisted that she stayed covered. The women of Lebanon were more spirited than their Saudi sisters, but Al-Jaber's fourth wife knew better than to argue with her husband. The marriage had been arranged — she was the granddaughter of one of Al-Jaber's business associates — and the union had been financially beneficial to her family to the tune of tens of millions of dollars. In the grand scheme of things the burka was a small price to pay.

"I am using the large jet, but the Gulfstream is available for whoever you decide to use," said Al-Jaber. "My people can also arrange for diplomatic status and a passport."

"As always, you read my mind," said Bin Azim.

"Only Allah can see into our minds," said Al-Jaber, getting to his feet. "But I understand what needs to be done. And I am privileged to be able to offer the assistance that is within my gift."

Bin Azim stood up and kissed Al-Jaber on both cheeks. Al-Jaber's bodyguards were already moving towards the restaurant doors, and Bin Azim knew that, far below, more big men in dark suits would be standing by Al-Jaber's bombproof white Bentley.

Chaudhry looked at his watch, then over at Malik, who was sitting on the sofa with his feet up on the coffee table, watching football on the television. "We've got to go, Harvey," he said.

"This is bloody ridiculous," said Malik. "Did he say why we're going to Reading?"

"He wanted somewhere where nobody would know us."

"But Reading?" He slapped the arm of his sofa. "How do we even get there?"

"Trains run from Paddington all the time."

126

"Yeah, but getting to Paddington from Stokie is a pain."

"It's for our own good. It's a training exercise, so we'll know what to do if we're ever followed."

Malik's eyes narrowed. "See, that's what's worrying me, brother. Why would anyone be following us? They'd only do that if they suspected us, right? And if they even suspect that we're spies then we're dead."

Chaudhry walked over to the sofa and stood looking down at his friend. "We've been through this," he said. "Khalid might get someone to check us out. Or the cops might follow us. No one knows what we're doing, remember? And the cops are always looking at the mosque, you know that. Someone at the mosque passes our name on to the cops and they might take a look at us. John's putting us through this so we'll know what to look for."

"It's a waste of time, innit?" scowled Malik. "We're not doing anything wrong. Even if they follow us what are they going to see? We go to lectures, we eat, we sleep, we shit. You play squash. I play five-a-side. It's not like we're mixing explosives or scoping out targets. We're waiting, brother. That's all we've been doing for months now. If anyone follows us they'll be bored out of their skulls in a few days."

"Harvey, we have to do this."

"Brother, we don't have to do anything. We're not on staff, are we? Last time I looked MI5 weren't paying us a salary. In fact they're paying us fuck all, in spite of everything we did for them." He jabbed his finger at Chaudhry. "We killed The Sheik, you and me. We grassed him up and the Yanks blew him away and that's down to us. But instead of being heroes we're supposed to drag our arses all the way to Reading to prove a point?"

Chaudhry sat down next to Malik. "What's up with you?"

"It just feels like they're yanking our chain," said Malik.

Chaudhry grinned. "Are you not feeling loved, is that it?"

"Screw you," laughed Malik.

"We're not doing this to be loved, Harvey. We didn't go to MI5 because we wanted a medal or because we wanted money. We went to them because it's the right thing to do. This is our country and people like Khalid are trying to destroy it. It's up to us to help stop them."

"I get that. I'm not stupid."

"No one's saying you're stupid, but you sound like you're losing focus. We have to be committed to this. If we aren't you know what could happen?" Malik didn't say anything. He looked away, unwilling to meet Chaudhry's piercing gaze. "How will you feel, Harvey, if you do bail out and a few weeks down the line something bad happens and a lot of people die? How are you going to feel then, knowing that you could have stopped it?"

Malik shrugged. "Okay."

"Okay what?"

"I hear you." He nodded. "I'm just pissed off at all the waiting. It's doing my head in. Why won't Khalid just tell us what we're going to do?"

"Maybe he doesn't know himself. Maybe he's taking orders from someone else. All we can do is wait. As for John, he wants to help. He's not doing this to piss us around. It's to keep us sharp."

Malik threw his hands in the air. "Okay, fine, let's do it." He stood up. "But how the hell do we get to Paddington?"

"Tube."

"That'll take for ever," said Malik, picking up his jacket. "Can't we get a minicab?"

Chaudhry frowned. "I hadn't thought of that. I guess so."

"Let's do that, then. And John can reimburse us." He grinned. "You know what? We should just get the cab to take us to Reading. See if they can follow us. That'd serve them right."

"Yeah, okay. All John said was that we should go to Paddington," said Chaudhry. "I don't see why we can't get a cab to the station. But on the way we keep our eyes open because he's going to ask us if we saw anyone following us." He stood up. "It'll be fun," he said, punching his friend lightly on the shoulder.

They put on their coats, left the flat and walked along to Stoke Newington High Street. There was a minicab office in a side road, marked by a flashing yellow light above the door. Like most of the businesses it was run by Turks though the drivers were a smorgasbord of London's ethnic communities — Nigerian, Indian, Iranian, Polish, Somalian — and there was barely a country not represented on the company's roster.

The driver who took Chaudhry and Malik was an Iraqi who treated his ten-year-old manual Toyota as if it was an automatic, doing most of the journey in second gear. They chugged along at low speeds, the engine screaming whenever they went above thirty-five miles per hour. The car stank of garlic and stale vomit despite a Christmas tree-shaped air freshener hanging from the driving mirror. Arab music was blaring from the stereo and the driver was constantly drumming his fingers on the steering wheel in time to the beat.

Malik twisted round in his seat as they headed west.

"Can you see anyone?" asked Chaudhry.

"There's a woman in a hatchback who's been behind us for a while."

"Where?" said Chaudhry.

"Behind the van," said Malik. "The grey one."

Chaudhry saw the Volvo and he laughed. "There's a kid in the back seat," he said.

"So?"

"So no one takes a kid on a surveillance job," said Chaudhry. He slapped Malik on the leg. "There'll probably be two people in the car, both adults, and the car will be new or fairly new. A saloon, not an estate or a sports car or anything out of the ordinary. Maybe a van."

"And you know this how?"

"I read," said Chaudhry.

"Read what?"

"Books. It doesn't matter."

"Fiction," said Malik. "You're talking about those Andy McNab books you're always reading."

"He was in the SAS," said Chaudhry. "He knows his stuff."

The minicab lurched to the side to avoid a bus that had stopped suddenly and the driver screamed abuse in Arabic. "Fucking buses," he said over his shoulder. "You see that? You see that bastard?"

"Yeah, we saw him," said Chaudhry.

"Bet he doesn't have a licence. You know how many drivers don't have licences in London?"

Chaudhry ignored him and looked over his shoulder again. There was a motorcycle courier about twenty feet behind their minicab. He had a tinted visor and a fluorescent vest and Chaudhry frowned as he tried to remember whether he'd seen the same man in Stoke Newington. Then the bike indicated left and turned into a side street.

"I think we're okay," said Malik. "He would have thought we'd be going by tube so he probably just had a couple of people waiting for us on the pavement. I reckon they were fuming when we got into the cab. Serves John right, playing games like this. And don't forget the receipt. He's bloody well going to cover our expenses."

Chaudhry thought Malik was probably right: the traffic was heavy and he couldn't see how a car could be following them, especially considering how erratic their driver was.

When the cab dropped them at the station entrance Chaudhry paid the driver and took a receipt, then stood on the pavement looking around.

"What?" said Malik.

"Just checking," said Chaudhry. A minibus pulled up and five teenagers in sports gear piled out.

"It's pointless," said Malik. "He knows we're coming here so he's bound to have people waiting for us. Whatever we do they're going to see us. They're probably looking at us right now."

They looked towards the platforms. A man in a grey suit walked by, talking into a mobile and pulling a small wheeled suitcase. Two uniformed drivers were heading for the exit, deep in conversation. Two teenage girls in school uniforms were giggling as they shared an iPod, one earpiece each. A blond-haired young man with a large rucksack was studying a map. He looked up and made eye contact with Chaudhry, then he smiled and walked over to him.

"Bayswater?" he said. "You know Bayswater?" He had a Scandinavian accent and Chaudhry could smell alcohol on his breath.

Chaudhry pointed in the general direction of Bayswater and the young man thanked him and headed off, folding up his map.

"Do you think he was one of them?" asked Malik.

"They wouldn't talk to us," said Chaudhry. "Look, all we can do is go to Reading and tell John who we saw. It's not as if we can shake them off, even if we spot them. Come on."

They went over to the ticket machines and Chaudhry used his credit card to buy two return tickets to Reading. The next train was due to leave in ten minutes so they walked to the platform, boarded the train and found two window seats with a table between them.

There were already a dozen or so people in the carriage and a few more arrived before the train departed. Malik looked around, frowning.

"Could you make it more obvious?" asked Chaudhry, taking a Galaxy tablet from his pocket. He had stored several textbooks on the computer and he figured he'd get some revision done while on the train.

"What do you mean?"

"You're staring."

"I'm trying to see who might be following us."

"So you don't have to stare. They'll be with us all the way to Reading if they are following us. And don't forget that they know where we're going; they'll probably be waiting for us in Reading anyway. Why don't you make yourself useful and get us something to eat?" He pointed towards the front of the train. "There's a restaurant car down there. And get me a Coke or something."

"John'll pay us back, right?"

Chaudhry grinned. "Get a receipt."

As Malik headed out of the carriage, Chaudhry looked around. There were two suited businessmen working on laptops at one table, and an old couple sharing a bag of crisps directly behind them. Sitting at the rear of the carriage was a grey-haired man wearing dark glasses, which Chaudhry initially thought looked suspicious until he saw the seeing-eye dog, a golden retriever, sitting under the man's table.

He settled back in his seat and started reading an anatomy textbook.

Malik returned after ten minutes with two paper bags containing soft drinks, sandwiches and muffins. He sat down and handed a receipt to Chaudhry. "You're his mate so you can get the money from him."

"I wouldn't say he's a mate," said Chaudhry, slipping the receipt into his wallet.

"He chats to you more than to me, have you noticed that? And when he calls it's you that he phones."

"That's alphabetical," said Chaudhry, popping the tab of his Coke.

"What are you reading?" asked Malik.

"Anatomy," said Chaudhry.

"Got anything I can read?"

Chaudhry held up the tablet. "This is all I've got," he said. His mobile rang and he took it out and looked at the screen. "It's John."

"I told you he always calls you," said Malik, folding his arms.

Chaudhry pressed the green button to take the call. "How's the sandwich?"

"What?"

"The sandwich. Cheese, right?"

"Cheese salad," said Chaudhry. He looked over at Malik and pointed at the phone and then mouthed, "He knows what I'm eating."

"I just wanted you to know I'm in the Novotel, room 608. Come right up and knock on the door."

"Okay," said Chaudhry. "How do you know what sandwich I've got?"

"I know you've got a sandwich and a can of Coke and Harvey's got two chicken sandwiches and a muffin, and I also know that Harvey asked for a receipt because he probably thinks I'm going to reimburse you."

"Are you on the train?"

"I told you, I'm in the room. I'll see you when I see you." The line went dead and Chaudhry stared at the phone in amazement.

"What?" said Malik.

"He knows what we ordered. He knows you asked for a receipt. One of his people must have been in the restaurant car."

Malik sipped his Coke. "At least we know someone's watching out for us," he said. "But bloody hell, they must be good."

Shepherd opened the door to the hotel room just as Chaudhry was about to knock. Chaudhry froze with his mouth open in and his hand in mid-air.

"Hello, lads," said Shepherd.

"How did you know we were here?" said Malik. "We didn't talk to anyone at reception. We came right up."

"I got a call when you walked into the hotel," said Shepherd. "And I was told that you were walking here."

"We were followed from the station?" said Chaudhry.

"Every step of the way," said Shepherd, ushering them inside and closing the door. "They were on your tail from the moment you left the flat. Though they were surprised that you took a cab to Paddington."

Malik looked around the hotel room. "You haven't got cameras in here, have you?" he asked. Shepherd laughed. "I'm serious, man. You spooked us with that sandwich thing. There was someone in the restaurant car when I was buying them, right?" He took off his parka jacket and tossed it on to the bed.

"It was our man behind the counter," said Shepherd.

"The old guy?" said Malik. "How did you manage that?"

"We knew you'd be on a train to Reading, which was a bit of a cheat, so he had the uniform and was ready to go. Whichever train you got on, he'd get on."

"You can do that?" asked Chaudhry.

"It's MI5, Raj, they can do pretty much what they want. We had a British Transport Police guy primed to go and he arranged it. He flashes his ID and tells the staff to do as our guy says." There was a small sofa by the window and he waved at it. "You guys take the weight off your feet. We're going to be here for a while."

Chaudhry and Malik sat down.

"Do you want room service? Coffee? Water?"

"Coffee would good," said Chaudhry. Malik nodded. Shepherd picked up the phone and ordered three pots of coffee.

It was a large room with a double bed and a working area where a whiteboard had been placed on an easel. There was a connecting door to the adjoining room and as Shepherd put down the phone there was a soft knock on it. Shepherd opened the door and took a handful of photographs from a man in the next room.

"Who's that?" asked Chaudhry as Shepherd closed the door.

"One of the guys who followed you," said Shepherd. He handed the photographs to them and the two men started looking through them. There were pictures of them leaving their building, getting into the minicab, and walking through the station. There was a photograph of them buying their tickets, and another of them getting on to the train. One photograph of them sitting on their train even appeared to have been taken on a mobile phone.

Chaudhry looked up in amazement. "How many did you have following us?" he asked.

"There were two on the pavement outside your flat. We had two motorbikes just in case you went by bus or cab, which was lucky."

"Was one a courier?"

"They were both couriers," said Shepherd. He gathered up the photographs and put them on the desk.

"I think I saw one following the cab."

"Well done," said Shepherd. "I hope he wasn't too obvious. We had four at the station, plus the BTP officer and the guy ready to go in the restaurant car. And I cheated a little by having three at Reading station so that even if they missed you completely in London they could pick you up there."

"How come we didn't spot them?" asked Malik.

"Because they're professionals," said Shepherd. "They look totally normal. They blend in and they do absolutely nothing to attract attention to themselves. No one was going to get close enough to see what ticket you were buying, but that's not an issue. If they're professional then as soon as they know you're heading for the station they'll just buy tickets for all the main lines anyway. And our guys have British Transport IDs so they can just flash them to a ticket inspector." He showed them the picture of them boarding the train. "It's always best to board a train at the last moment. It gives anyone following less time to get sorted. You made it too easy."

"The guy in the suit," said Malik. "There was a businessman at Paddington. He kept looking at us."

"He was probably looking at you and wondering why you were staring at him. He wasn't one of ours. Our people would never look directly at you. And they'd never make eye contact with you. In fact that's one of the ways you can spot a close-up tail — they'll be avoiding eye contact even when you'd expect them to be looking at you."

"How do we spot them, then?" asked Malik.

"If they're doing their job properly you shouldn't be able to," said Shepherd.

"I looked at everyone in our carriage and I didn't think anyone was following us."

"There's a good chance that they wouldn't be in your carriage," said Shepherd. "That's the beauty of a train. There's no getting off anywhere other than at a station, so while the train's moving they don't even need to have you in sight. All that matters is that they see when you get off."

"So you check who gets off with you?" said Chaudhry.

"Not necessarily," said Shepherd. "If they're pros there'll be at least two on the train. One will stay put while you get off and radio or phone the other to say that you're on the move. So your tail could actually be ahead of you."

"It's impossible to tell you're being followed, is that what you're saying?"

Shepherd shook his head. "It's not impossible, but it takes practice. That's why we're here. This isn't about us showing off. It's about demonstrating what a good surveillance operation is like. What I want to do is to run a few exercises with you. And give you a few tips about what to look out for and what to do if you think you are being followed."

"Is something wrong, John?" asked Malik. "Has something happened?"

Shepherd smiled and shook his head. "Everything's fine," he said. "This is just a training exercise."

"Do you think someone might be following us?"

"No, this is just a precaution," said Shepherd. "But the closer we get to the operation, the more likely it is that they'll run a check on you. I don't want a panicky phone call from either of you in a week or so saying that you think you're being followed."

"Khalid, you mean?" asked Chaudhry.

Shepherd nodded. "There's every possibility that he'll have you checked out, just to see what you're up to. It might be nothing more than him getting someone to follow you for a day or two, but if it happens I want you to know it's happening and to act in the right way." He could see that both men were tense so he smiled, trying to put them at ease. "The good news is that today at least you were clean. We're sure that no one was following you today, other than our people. And in future, if at any time you are worried that someone is

139

following you, you can call me and I'll get you checked out."

There was a loud knock at the door and both men jumped.

Shepherd grinned. "Relax, guys. It's our coffee."

"Okay, there's one of ours now, within a hundred feet," said Shepherd. "See if you can spot him." He smiled. "Or her."

They were sitting on a bench in Forbury Gardens, close to Reading Town Hall. It was lunchtime and a lot of office workers were strolling around, many of them either smoking or eating sandwiches.

Chaudhry and Malik looked around.

"Try to be casual," said Shepherd. "Don't stare and try to avoid eye contact, but if you do make eye contact with anyone make it as natural as possible. If it's a pretty girl it's okay to say hello. The key is for every interaction to be exactly as it would normally be. So you'd normally want a prop like a newspaper or your mobile, something that you can keep looking at. Especially in a static situation like this. A guy sitting on his own doing nothing looks suspicious. Give him a newspaper and he's just a guy taking a break. Better still give him a pen so that he can do the Sudoku and no one will give him a second look." He held up the copy of the *Telegraph* that he was holding. "Also, just like in the movies, you can open it up and peer over the top of it."

"The woman with the pram has walked by us three times," said Malik.

140

"Yes, but the baby's crying. It's very rare for a watcher to bring family. Especially kids. If something goes wrong and a kid gets hurt there'd be hell to pay."

"Maybe it's not a real baby," said Malik. "Maybe it's a recording."

Shepherd laughed. "Fair enough," he said. "But no, it's not her."

A council employee in blue overalls and a fluorescent jacket was emptying a litter bin. He was bobbing his head in time to whatever music he was listening to through large black headphones atop a woollen hat.

"That guy," said Chaudhry, nodding at the man.

"Because?"

"Because when we walked by that bin it wasn't even half full."

Shepherd grinned. "Well spotted."

"Am I right?"

"Spot on," said Shepherd. "We'll often use people in uniforms because they tend to pass unnoticed; generally you'll see the uniform and not notice the face. The downside of uniforms is that if they're not in the right setting they show out. So he looks right in the park, or the street, but you'd notice him straight away in a shop or a bar." He took out his BlackBerry and tapped out a number. A few seconds later, the man who was emptying the litter bin straightened up and answered his phone. "All right, Tim, on to phase two."

"Phase two?" asked Malik.

Shepherd ended the call and put his phone away. The man in the fluorescent jacket pulled the rubbish-filled black bag out of the bin, fastened it and then walked away towards the town hall.

"Tim's going to walk behind the town hall. We're going to carry on with another exercise and I want you to tell me when you see him reappear."

"Check we can multitask, is that it?" asked Chaudhry.

"Sort of," said Shepherd. He stood up. "Let's just take a walk," he said. "But keep your eye on the town hall. As we walk around I want you to watch out for someone taking your photograph. There are plenty of buildings overlooking the park so you can easily be snapped with a telephoto lens."

They did a slow circuit of the park, with Chaudhry and Malik keeping a close eye on the town hall while also checking out the buildings around them. They walked slowly and Shepherd chatted to them both as they walked, explaining in detail how the surveillance team had followed them from their flat to the hotel in Reading.

When they got back to the bench a middle-aged man in a raincoat and trilby hat had taken their place. He was reading an iPad and chewing on a baguette.

"So first things first," said Shepherd. "Did you see Tim come back from behind the town hall?"

Chaudhry shook his head. "Definitely not," he said.

"Yeah," agreed Malik. "I saw him go behind the building but he never came back."

Shepherd grinned. "Well done, Tim," he said to the man on the bench. "They missed you completely and I only just made you."

The man with the iPad stood up and pushed back his trilby. Chaudhry and Malik groaned as they realised it was the man who had been emptying the litter bin.

"He changed his clothes," said Malik.

"Exactly," said Shepherd.

Tim nodded and walked away as Shepherd, Chaudhry and Malik went to sit on the bench.

"Here's the thing," said Shepherd. "Professional followers will always carry with them things that can change their profile. Hats. Jackets. Bags. Plus props. If you see a guy carrying a copy of the *Financial Times* you're more likely to notice the paper than the man's face. So if he drops the paper and carries a cup of coffee you won't remember him. If he goes into a shop wearing a baseball hat and comes out wearing a scarf there's a good chance you won't recognise him. It can help you lose a tail too. A reversible jacket can change your colour scheme completely, or take off your pullover and tie it round your waist, roll up your sleeves, develop a limp, put your arm in a sling. Glasses on, glasses off. Tim there was wearing a fluorescent jacket and carrying a black bag the first time you saw him. That's what you were looking for, so when he walked by you in a raincoat and carrying an iPad you didn't notice him."

"So what's the trick, what are you supposed to remember?" asked Malik.

"Try to get a good look at faces. If you can't see their faces look for body shape. And despite what I said about developing a limp, most people tend to move the same way. Look at the way people walk, how they move

143

their shoulders, the angle of their neck. And shoes. A watcher might have time to change his jacket but shoes are usually too much trouble."

Shepherd's BlackBerry buzzed and he took it out of his pocket. He looked at the screen and grinned. "Here's the first of the photographs," he said. He showed them the screen. There was a picture of Chaudhry and Malik, close up.

"You're shitting me," said Chaudhry. "Who took that?"

"One of the watchers. She walked right by us."

"Why didn't we see her?" asked Malik.

"Because you were looking at the buildings," said Shepherd. "You were concentrating on the distance so you didn't see what was right under your noses."

Shepherd's BlackBerry buzzed again as it received a second photograph. This one was of Chaudhry, side on. He showed it to Chaudhry, who shook his head in amazement.

"That was taken just feet away. From a phone, right?" Chaudhry said.

"No, that was taken by Jake, who had a camera in his hat. He can take a picture of anything he's looking at, and the shutter button is in his pocket. Even close up you'd never see the lens; it's not much bigger than a pin."

The phone buzzed once again. The third photograph was of the three of them, taken from some distance away. Shepherd showed it to Chaudhry and Malik. "This camera was in a briefcase."

144

"Okay, I get it," said Chaudhry. "Your guys are pros and we're the amateurs. But you didn't have to bring us all the way to Reading to tell us that."

Shepherd put the BlackBerry away. "You're absolutely right, Raj. So now we'll move on to the next stage."

"Sit down and try it out for size," said Shepherd. He had taken Chaudhry and Malik to the John Lewis department store, close to Reading station. They were in the sprawling furniture department on the fourth floor.

"Are you serious?" asked Malik.

"We're here to look at furniture, right? So sit."

Chaudhry and Malik dropped down on to the long leather sofa, a dark-brown Chesterfield. Shepherd sat in a matching armchair.

"The key to spotting a tail is to take them to an environment where they show out," said Shepherd. "Department stores are perfect. Look around, what do you see?"

The two men casually looked around. "Housewives," said Chaudhry. "And couples."

"Exactly. And not just housewives. Well-to-do housewives. Generally middle-aged and middle class. You don't see many young single men here. Or people in jogging clothes. Or businessmen with briefcases. Or anyone in a uniform. And if they were here they'd be the proverbial sore thumb. Choosing furniture takes time, so you can spend ten minutes or more here and no one will think anything about it."

He stood up. "Come on," he said. "Menswear next." He took them downstairs to the menswear department and through to the suits section. "Browse," he said. "And let me know what you see. Or don't see."

There were half a dozen men looking through the racks of men's clothes.

"No women," said Malik. "I get it."

"Yes, you rarely see women buying men's clothes," said Shepherd. "So a watcher who blends in in the furniture department won't fit in as well here."

"Could be a middle-aged guy," said Chaudhry. "He'd fit in in both places."

"So you'd then go to the lingerie department and do a walk-through there. Or the toy department. Or cosmetics. That's why department stores work so well. They have everything under one roof. And, because there are multiple entrances and exits, they have to stick with you. High street shops don't work so well. They can just wait outside."

"So what are you saying? That we have to go shopping every day to see if we're being followed?" asked Malik.

"What I'm saying is that if you suspect that you are being followed you head to John Lewis or Debenhams or House of Fraser and you make sure. You can do it without being obvious that you're looking for a tail."

A male shopping assistant in a dark suit was heading their way so Shepherd took them towards the escalators.

"And then what?" asked Chaudhry. "Then we lose them, right? We shake them off?"

Shepherd chuckled. "No, Raj. Then you call me."

"Look around and tell me what you see," said Shepherd. They were in the Oracle Centre, next door to the John Lewis store. There were ninety shops on three floors under a vaulted glass ceiling. Shepherd had taken them to the upper floor, from where they could look down on the crowds below.

"A lot of people," said Chaudhry.

"Exactly," said Shepherd. "People of all shapes and sizes, every ethnicity imaginable, men, women, young, old, rich, poor. In an environment like this there's no way of spotting a watcher by appearance alone. Plus, it's all open, so from here we can see pretty much everyone on the ground floor, and everyone up here. And they can see us. If you go into a shop all they have to do is wait for you to come out. The situation is similar in the high street. But there is a big advantage to a place like this." He turned around to face the shop that they were standing in front of. It was an Apple store, one of the busiest in the mall. Inside were dozens of customers playing with iPads, iPhones and Mac computers while black-shirted sales staff looked on.

"Reflections," said Shepherd. "If you look into a shop window your watchers will relax and tend to look at you directly. If you get the angles right you can see behind you and to the sides."

Chaudhry and Malik moved their heads from side to side. "So you stop, is that it?" said Chaudhry. "Then check in the reflection to see if anyone's looking. That works?"

"Like a charm," said Shepherd. "Chances are they'll look to see why you've stopped. But it's also a good way of checking if anyone across the road is watching you. The distance means that if you've got your back to them they'll feel they can look at you without any risk. Shop windows are also a good way of backtracking."

"Backtracking?" repeated Malik.

"I'll show you," said Shepherd. "I'll walk off down the mall and you two follow. Try to be casual, and if I look your way avoid eye contact. Okay?"

The two men nodded.

Shepherd grinned. "Don't look so serious," he said. He turned and walked towards Debenhams, then headed left towards Boots. He walked slowly, glancing in shop windows, his hands in his pockets.

Chaudhry and Malik followed about twenty paces behind. "Shall we walk together or split up?" asked Malik.

"I don't think it matters," said Chaudhry. They moved aside to let two young women with scraped-back ponytails push their buggies by.

Shepherd gazed at the computers in the window as he walked by PC World, then he paused at the entrance to allow a group of teenagers to walk out. He looked at his watch before carrying on towards Boots.

Chaudhry and Malik continued after him. But then Shepherd stopped, turned, and began walking back towards them. Malik made eye contact with Shepherd and froze; Chaudhry took a single step and then he stopped too.

Malik turned, bumping into Chaudhry and knocking him off balance. Chaudhry reached out to grab Malik's arm as Shepherd stopped and looked again at the computers in PC World's windows. He stood there for several seconds, rubbing his chin.

"What do we do?" asked Malik. "Do we walk by him?"

"It's too late," said Chaudhry. "He got us. Look at his reflection."

They looked at Shepherd's reflection in the shop window. He was grinning at them.

Shepherd carried the three coffees over to the corner table where Chaudhry and Malik were already sitting. He put the mugs on the table and sat down. They were in Caffè Nero on the ground floor of the Oracle Centre.

"What I've been showing you is how to spot if you have a tail," said Shepherd, keeping his voice low. "But here's the important thing: if you realise that you are being followed you mustn't let on that you know. You guys are just regular citizens. You're not spies and you're not criminals. You shouldn't be able to spot a tail, and you certainly shouldn't have the skills to shake one off." He sipped his coffee. "Villains are different. To them surveillance is one of the hazards of the job. If you're a career criminal then from time to time the cops will follow you. They know you're a villain and you know you're a villain, and giving the cops the slip is part of the game. But say we're looking at a guy who might be a spy. We put him under surveillance. If we become aware that he's spotted us then that's a red flag right there. The very fact that he knows he's being tailed almost certainly means he's a spy."

"I don't get it," said Malik.

"If you've got nothing to hide you'll never know that you're being followed. I could follow a civilian around all day and he'd never see me because most people are too wrapped up in their own lives. But someone with something to hide will be looking around. If someone does start following you, and they see you using anti-surveillance techniques, they'll know that something is wrong." He sipped his coffee again. "That technique I used, the backtrack? You can do that and make it look natural. Walk past a newsagent and then go back and buy a pack of gum. Walk past a newspaper seller and then go back and pick up a paper. Look at your watch and then change direction as if you'd forgotten you had to be somewhere. And you can use reflections. It doesn't have to be a shop window; you can use car mirrors, mirrors in shops. Anything, so long as it looks normal. But if you do spot someone following you the worst possible thing you can do is acknowledge it. You have to carry on as if nothing has happened."

"So what's the point?" asked Chaudhry.

"The point is that if you ever do think that someone's watching you, you let me know as soon as you can. I can then check it out, see if there is any surveillance and decide what to do about it."

"Just phone you, is that it?"

"Sure. Or text. Tell me your location and who you think is following you."

150

"And what will you do?"

"I'll get a team out and put them in counter-surveillance mode. There's always at least one team of watchers on standby at Thames House. They'll check you over and identify anyone who's following you, and they'll do it without the tail ever knowing. People carrying out surveillance are often the easiest to follow because they're usually so involved in what they're doing."

"And you think Khalid or one of his people might follow us?" asked Malik.

"It's possible," said Shepherd. "But that doesn't mean it'll be somebody you'll recognise. They're much more likely to bring in someone you don't know."

"This backtracking thing, do we do that every day? Every hour? Or what?"

"If you get the feeling you're being followed, at any time, give it a go. You don't want to be doing it all the time, that's for sure. But if I'm on my way to a meeting I'll usually do it at least once. And always when I'm on my way home."

"Why would anyone be following you?" asked Chaudhry.

"Any one of a dozen reasons. It would depend on whatever case I'm working on," said Shepherd. He leaned closer to them. "There's something else we need to set up. We need to agree an alarm code, a way of you letting me know that there's a problem without anyone else being aware of what's going on."

"Like a safe word?" said Malik.

"What's a safe word?" asked Chaudhry.

"If you're with a dominatrix you agree a safe word, so that if she's hurting you too much you say the word and she knows to stop."

Chaudhry laughed out loud and looked over at Shepherd. Shepherd grinned.

"Hey, I read it somewhere," protested Malik. "Oh, screw the two of you." He folded his arms and glared at Chaudhry. "Ha ha bloody ha."

"To be honest, he's right," Shepherd said to Chaudhry. "We need to agree a word or phrase that you can remember, and if you ever use it in conversation with me I'll know that you're in trouble."

"Like what?" asked Chaudhry.

"Something that's easy to remember but that you wouldn't ordinarily say. But it has to be a word or phrase that won't arouse suspicion."

Chaudhry smiled slyly at Malik. "What do dominatrixes use?" he asked.

Malik flashed him a tight smile. "You see, I know you're taking the piss but the whole point is that the submissive uses the safe word. That way he has the ultimate power even though the dominatrix is in control."

Chaudhry shook his head in mock sadness. "You know far too much about this domination stuff," he said.

"I was Googling something else and it came up," said Malik.

"Googling what? 'Naughty boys want their arses spanked'? I have to say, Harvey, this is a very worrying side to you. Now I'm scared that I might wake up one morning and find myself tied to the bed and you standing over me with a whip in your hand."

The mickey-taking was a good sign, Shepherd knew; it showed that they were relaxed. So he drank his coffee and let them get on with it.

"Do you see what I have to put up with?" Malik asked Shepherd.

"I don't know — I think he might have a point. You know that we do positive vetting, don't you? Something like that would definitely show up."

"Are you serious?" asked Malik, leaning forward, then he saw from the look on Shepherd's face that he wasn't. He sat back. "You're as bad as he is."

"All right, guys, let's get back to the matter in hand," said Shepherd. "A phrase that I've used in the past is 'like my grandfather always used to say'. You can start pretty much any sentence with that. How does that sound?"

"I never knew either of my grandfathers," said Malik.

"Grandmother?" asked Shepherd.

Malik nodded. "Yeah, that'll work."

Shepherd looked across at Chaudhry. "Works for me as well."

"Excellent," said Shepherd. "And it can work both ways too. If you hear me use that phrase it means there's a problem and you need to treat with suspicion anything that I say."

Chaudhry frowned. "Say what?"

"Suppose there's somebody listening in and I know they're there. I could use that phrase to tip you off. Or say I was being forced to arrange a meeting with you —

if I used that phrase you'd know right away that you're not to turn up."

"Are you saying that someone might be after you?" asked Chaudhry. "Is that what you mean?"

"It's just a safety net," said Shepherd. "It's standard in undercover work. There's another useful phrase I'll give you. If I call you I'll ask what the weather is like. If you say it's fine then I'll know that everything is okay. If you say it looks like rain or snow or anything negative then I'll know you've got a problem."

"Well, why haven't we needed it before now?" asked Chaudhry. "What's happened to bring this up?"

"Nothing's happened," said Shepherd. "It's just standard procedure. We're obviously getting close to the critical stage so we need to have all our ducks in a row. Show me your hands."

"What?"

"Just let me see your hands. Palms down." Chaudhry held out his hands and Shepherd studied the fingers. Then he nodded at Malik. "You too." Malik held out his hands and Shepherd looked at them. "Okay, neither of you is a nail-biter, so we can use that as a visual sign. If there's a problem, if you're in danger or there's something wrong, and we have visual contact but can't speak, then make a point of biting your nails."

Chaudhry frowned. "Now you've really lost me," he said.

"Suppose we arrange a meet. And you turn up and you're waiting for me. But then you realise that you're being watched. You might not have time to text me. I might be there already and walking towards you. If you

154

start biting your nails I'll immediately abort the meeting. Ditto if you're on your way to see me and I spot somebody who might know you. I see you, I bite my nails, you back off. Again, it's a safety net. You'll probably never have to use it but we have it in place, just in case."

"Okay," said Chaudhry, but Shepherd could hear the uncertainty in his voice.

"Trust me, we're just being cautious," said Shepherd. "Best to talk it through now rather than trying to put something together at short notice. I'll give you another one while we're at it. You both wear coats with hoods, right?"

"Now you're the fashion police?" said Malik.

"I'm just saying that you normally wear your parka and Raj has his duffel coat. Changing the hood can be a sign that there's a problem. Say it's up and you want to let me know there's a problem. If you're sure I'm watching you, you put your hood down. Or vice versa. If it's down you pull it up. It's a natural gesture but it can let me know that something's wrong. Got it?"

Chaudhry nodded. "Got it." He looked over at Malik and grinned. "Think that'll work with your dominatrix?"

Shepherd finished the last of his coffee. "Okay, let's run through a few exercises in the mall. There're a few more tricks I want to show you, then I'll put you on the train back to London."

Shepherd was half an hour from Hampstead in his Volvo when his mobile rang. He took a quick look at the screen. It was Hargrove. He took the call on hands-free.

"I've had Fenby on the phone. Good news and maybe not so good news," said Hargrove. "Kettering and Thompson are okay to meet you in London. But they want to see you at a charity boxing night."

"What?"

"They're down tomorrow for a charity do at a hotel in Russell Square. The Royal National Hotel. They've got a table and they want you there."

"That's not on, is it? What if I bump into someone I know? Is it a big event?"

"Four hundred-odd people, mainly from south London. The event's to raise money for a boxing club in Croydon. A couple of fighters that Kettering knows are coming down from Birmingham so Kettering has told Ray that he wants to kill two birds with one stone."

"We're not going to be able to arrange an arms deal at a table full of boxing fans," said Shepherd. "We're going to have to give this a body swerve."

"No can do," said Hargrove. "You've got to look at this from their point of view. They don't know you — you're Fenby's contact. So they want to meet you in a social context first."

"So we'll have a pint in a quiet pub somewhere off the beaten track. I've done God knows how many jobs south of the river and if anyone there recognises me I'll be blown."

"We can run a check on the guest list for you," said Hargrove. "Look, Ray has already tried to put them off but Kettering is insisting and if we start to make a fuss he's going to get suspicious. He just wants to sit down with you and get to know you."

Shepherd sighed. "If that's the way you want it I won't argue, but don't blame me if it goes tits up," he said.

"Your reservations are noted," said Hargrove. He cut the connection.

Shepherd phoned Damien Plant and asked him how he was getting on with the Garry Edwards legend.

"I put the finishing touches to it this morning," said Plant.

"I need it for tomorrow evening," said Shepherd. "The clothes and bling, anyway."

"Where are you?"

"On my way to Hampstead."

"I could drop it off on my way home," said Plant. "In an hour."

"Perfect," said Shepherd. "It'll give me time for a shower."

"Don't go to any trouble on my account," said Plant.

"I'll have coffee ready for you," said Shepherd. "How do you like it?"

"Same as I like my men," said Plant. "Black, sweet and with bulging forearms."

Shepherd laughed and ended the call.

The traffic was light heading into London and he had parked the car, showered and changed, and was stirring sugar into a mug of black coffee when his intercom buzzed. He pressed the button to open the downstairs door. Plant was wearing blue Armani jeans and a blue blazer over the sort of tight white T-shirt that he'd threatened to make Shepherd wear. He was carrying a blue nylon holdall in his left hand and three grey garment covers in his right.

Shepherd showed him through to the sitting room.

"I'd forgotten how cosy this place was," said Plant, looking around. He had chosen everything in the flat, from the furniture and LCD television to the books on the shelves and the pictures on the walls.

"Yeah, it's not exactly a cat-swinging room, is it?"

"Perfectly in keeping with a freelance journalist," said Plant. "Frankly we were lucky to get you into Hampstead the way rents are moving here."

He sat down and sipped his coffee as Shepherd opened the garment covers. There was a dark-blue single-breasted suit, several shirts, a black linen jacket not dissimilar to the one that Plant had been wearing at Thames House, and a brown leather jacket that zipped up the front.

"The leather jacket's Armani," said Plant. "I've scuffed it a bit to give it some character. I wouldn't mind it back when the job's finished; it's the sort of thing I can use again and again. The suit you can keep. The shirts too."

Inside the holdall was a padded manila envelope. Shepherd opened it and slid out a driving licence. It had his photograph and the name of Garry Edwards, with the signature that he'd given Plant in Thames House. Shepherd didn't recognise the address on the licence and he frowned at Plant. Plant smiled. "I've used an office address for you. They'll have the Edwards name on file so will field any enquiries."

"I doubt I'll be flashing it around," said Shepherd. Also inside the envelope was a gold Cartier wristwatch, a gold money clip and a heavy gold bracelet.

Plant took a sheet of paper from his jacket pocket and handed it and a slim gold pen to Shepherd. "The jewellery you'll have to sign for," he said. "It's fully insured but please take care of it."

"I'll do my best," said Shepherd, signing the form and giving it back to Plant.

"I'll love you and leave you," said Plant. He finished his coffee and stood up. "Thought I might swing by the Heath for old times' sake."

"Bloody hell, Damien, be careful."

Plant winked. "Not to worry, I'm loaded up with fake ID."

"I meant gay-bashers. It still goes on, you know."

Plant grinned. "I'm just off the close-combat course and there're a few new tricks that I'm dying to try out."

Shepherd opened the door for him. "Why would they send a dresser on the close-combat course?"

"Have you been to the Harrods January sales?" said Plant. "Middle-aged women with fur coats and umbrellas are bloody lethal." He laughed and headed down the stairs.

The black cab turned into Russell Square and joined a queue of cars and coaches heading towards the Royal National Hotel, a massive nondescript concrete building that looked more like an office block than a hotel. "I'm not happy about this, Razor," said Shepherd.

"What, because it's got only three stars?"

"No, because there're going to be more than four hundred people here including a fair sprinkling of south London villains, any one of whom might know you or me."

"Hargrove has checked the guest list, right?"

"Yeah, but most of the tables are in one name. I tell you, this could all turn to shit very quickly if someone recognises us."

"We could always grab a pair of gloves and sort it out in the ring," joked Sharpe.

"Why am I the only one worried here?"

Sharpe patted Shepherd's knee. "Because every day of our lives we run the risk of coming across someone who might recognise us. It can happen in the street, at a football match, at a restaurant. If you start worrying about it then you'll end up a basket case. What happens, happens. *Que sera, sera.*"

"Bloody hell, Razor, when did you go all Buddhist on me?"

The taxi pulled up in front of the hotel and Sharpe reached for the door handle. "If it happens, we'll deal with it," he said. "You can pay for the cab, right? You get better expenses than me and, as you love to point out, I'm not getting overtime." He got out of the taxi as Shepherd handed the driver a twenty-pound note. Shepherd told the driver to keep the change and asked for a receipt, then joined Sharpe on the pavement. To their right was a pub with more than two dozen men standing around drinking and smoking. Like Shepherd they were wearing lounge suits and ties but there was plenty of bling on show as well, expensive watches, gold chains and diamond rings. Shepherd scanned faces as the cab drove off but he didn't see anyone he recognised. A coach began disgorging its load of Chinese tourists, led by a middle-aged man in a rumpled suit holding a red flag above his head.

The reception area of the hotel was gloomy and despite the fact that it was almost eight o'clock there was a long line of guests waiting to check in. The Chinese tourists filed in, chattering excitedly.

"I hope it's boxing and not that kung fu bollocks," growled Sharpe.

A printed sign with an arrow pointing to the left showed them the way to the boxing. They went down a wood-panelled corridor to a large room with a bar packed with a couple of hundred men. Half a dozen bar staff in black T-shirts were working hard to keep up with the orders, with most of the drinkers paying with fifty-pound notes. Shepherd scanned faces again. His memory was near-photographic and he didn't see anyone that he'd ever met but he recognised at least twenty criminals whose records he'd seen and one face that the Met were looking for in connection with a Securicor van robbery two years earlier.

To the left of the room was a seating plan on an easel. They went over to it and found Kettering's table. It was number 21, close to the ring and just behind the judges' table.

"Drink?" asked Sharpe, nodding at the bar.

Shepherd looked at his watch. "Let's get to the table," he said.

They weaved their way through the bar to the entrance of the main hall. A boxing ring had been erected in the centre of the room underneath a massive dome-shaped chandelier. A long table had been erected on a podium against the far wall giving the organisers and VIP guests a clear view of the ring. There were another thirty tables around the ring, each seating a dozen people. Most of the tables were empty and a few Indian waiters were making last-minute adjustments to the cutlery and glasses.

"Remind me again who I am?" said Sharpe.

"Don't be a tosser all your life," said Shepherd. "Come on, let's sit down. Might as well get ourselves a good view of the door."

They were both using legends that they'd used before. Sharpe was James Gracie, a Scottish criminal who'd served time for armed robbery in the eighties before moving out to the Costa del Sol, from where he ran his arms business. The legend was rock-solid and even a check on the Police National Computer would come up with Gracie's record. He'd used it several times over the years.

Shepherd sat down at the table, choosing a seat that allowed him a clear view of the entrance. Sharpe sat a few seats away so that he was directly facing the ring.

There were unopened bottles of red and white wine on the table. Sharpe reached for one and sneered at the label. "Cheap plonk. Fancy champagne?"

"Let's wait until the guys get here," said Shepherd. "We can make a show of it."

Guests were moving into the hall and taking their places. A group headed for the VIP table, including a large black man wearing a floppy pink hat and what appeared to be a black mink coat, and a good-looking black man with a greying moustache, dressed in a sharp suit.

"That's John Conteh, isn't it?" said Sharpe, nodding at the man with the moustache.

"Yeah," said Shepherd. "What is he, sixty? I hope I look that good when I'm sixty."

"Do you think he runs marathons with a rucksack of bricks on his back?"

"I don't run marathons, you soft bastard."

The VIP table began to fill up. Sitting next to Conteh was a sharp-faced man in a beige suit. He was talking animatedly to the heavyweight boxer and demonstrating an uppercut to the chin. Like most of the guests on the top table his head was shaved.

Four stunningly pretty black girls, as tall and willowy as supermodels, walked to one table followed by four heavyset men in Italian suits. Shepherd recognised one of the men; he was a well-known drug dealer based in Beckenham, south London. He looked over at Sharpe to see if he'd spotted him and Sharpe nodded.

"Problem?" asked Sharpe.

Shepherd shook his head. He'd worked on a case involving the drug dealer but had never met him. Shepherd saw Kettering and Thompson at the doorway but kept his face blank. Edwards and Gracie had never met the two men so they had to wait until they'd been introduced. "Here we go," he whispered to Sharpe.

Then in a louder voice he began telling Sharpe a joke about a one-legged safecracker. He stopped when Kettering and Thompson arrived at their table.

Kettering grinned amiably. "You James and Garry?" he said.

Shepherd stood up. "I'm Garry," he said, and held out his hand. Kettering shook it. He had a firm grip and Shepherd squeezed back hard.

"Simon," Kettering said. He shook hands with Sharpe, and then introduced Thompson. "This is Paul." Thompson shook hands with them both and then they took their seats. Kettering sat on Shepherd's left and Thompson sat between Shepherd and Sharpe. "Well, Ian speaks very highly of you two." Ian Parton was the cover name that Fenby was using.

"Yeah, he's a riot is Ian," said Shepherd. "He's not here?"

"Nah, don't think he's much of a boxing fan," said Kettering. "Football's his game." He winked at Shepherd. "You a boxing fan, Garry?"

"I like a good punch-up," said Shepherd. He nodded at Sharpe. "James is the pugilist. That accounts for his battered face."

Sharpe laughed. "Yeah, I boxed a bit when I was a kid," he said. "What brings you down to the Big Smoke?" he asked Thompson.

"We've got a couple of fighters here," said Thompson. "We support a youth club in Birmingham and Harry was looking for some fighters who weren't local so we said we'd bring our boys down."

"Harry?" said Shepherd.

"Harry's organised tonight," Thompson said. "It's a fundraiser for his club. Next time we have a fundraiser in Birmingham he'll repay the favour."

More people were arriving and the room was echoing with conversation and laughter. The guests were mainly men and the few women who were there looked as if they could well be charging by the hour.

Sharpe waved a waiter over. "Get me a bottle of Bollinger, will you?" he said. He pointed at the bottles of wine on the table. "I can't drink this crap."

Kettering saw what he was doing. "What's the problem, James?"

"No problem," said Sharpe. "Just fancy a drop of bubbly. I'll pay for it."

"You bloody won't," said Kettering. "Tonight's on me." He pointed a finger at the waiter. "What champagne have you got? Got any Cristal?"

"Bollinger and Moët," said the waiter.

"Two bottles of Bollinger," said Kettering. "And the bill comes to me, right?"

"Yes, sir," said the waiter, and he headed for the bar.

Two men appeared at their table. Big men with weight-lifters' forearms and bulging necks that suggested years of steroid use. Kettering stood up, walked round the table and hugged them both, then introduced them to Shepherd and Sharpe. "Terry and Tony," he said. The two men sat down and started chatting to Thompson.

"They're brothers," Kettering said to Shepherd. "Kickboxing champions, both of them."

"Who else is on our table?" asked Shepherd.

"Couple of pals of Harry's, and three or four of my mates, assuming they can make it," said Kettering. "Don't worry, you're among friends."

"I'm not worried," said Shepherd. "I'm just not sure it's the most secure place for a meeting."

Kettering laughed. "We're just here to watch some boxing and have a bite to eat," he said. He leaned towards Shepherd, so close that Shepherd could smell the man's aftershave, sweet with the scent of lime. "The thing is, Garry, we need to trust each other. Am I right? You don't know us and we don't know you but this way we get to feel each other out. See how the land lies."

"Point taken," said Shepherd. "But I hope at some point we can talk business."

Kettering nodded enthusiastically. "You can count on it," he said.

The waiter returned with two bottles of champagne in individual ice buckets. He was followed by another waiter who was carrying a tray of champagne flutes. The first waiter popped the cork of one of the bottles while his colleague placed the glasses on the table. Two more men arrived at the table: one, obese, in a dark-blue suit, his hands festooned with gold rings, the other tall and thin with a shaved head and a large diamond stud in one ear. Kettering introduced them to everyone else at the table. The fat man was Davie, a scrap-metal merchant; the thin man was Ricky, a property developer.

Once all their glasses were filled, Kettering clinked his against Shepherd's. "Here's to swimming with bow-legged women," he said.

Shepherd sipped his champagne and smacked his lips appreciatively, even though he didn't really like the taste. "I love a drop of bubbly," he said.

"Big fan of Cristal, myself," said Kettering.

"Yeah, you can't beat Cristal," said Shepherd. He raised his glass to Sharpe. "Me and James, we knocked back half a case one night, remember?"

"I remember the bloody hangover, that's about all," laughed Sharpe. He leaned over and clinked his glass against Shepherd's.

"Then it couldn't have been Cristal because you never get a hangover from Cristal," said Kettering. "You get what you pay for." He touched his glass against Shepherd's again. "Anyway, great to finally meet you. Ian tells me good things."

"I hope he's not told you too much," said Shepherd. "Wouldn't want my name being taken in vain in Brummie-land."

The doors to the kitchen burst open and a dozen waiters filed out carrying trays. The first course was a prawn cocktail served in stainless-steel bowls, followed by roast beef, Yorkshire puddings, roast potatoes and vegetables. Kettering made small talk with Shepherd while they ate.

As the plates were being taken away, Kettering ordered another two bottles of champagne, then he patted Shepherd on the arm. "You smoke, Garry?"

"Not really," said Shepherd.

Kettering slid a brown leather cigar case from his jacket pocket. "I've got some nice Cubans."

"I'll take a cigar, yeah," said Shepherd.

"Come on, then. Let's give dessert a swerve and we'll have a chat outside." He stood up and gestured with his chin at Thompson. Shepherd caught Sharpe's eye and nodded at the door and the four men threaded their way through the tables to the doorway. They headed along the corridor and over to the pub. "Hey, Paul, get us some brandies," said Kettering. "The good stuff."

Thompson went inside the pub while Kettering handed cigars to Shepherd and Sharpe and then lit them with matches. The three men blew smoke up at the stars.

"So, Ian says you're the go-to guys," said Kettering.

Shepherd leaned towards Kettering and lowered his voice. "What is it you want?"

Kettering looked around, then bent his head towards Shepherd. "AK-47s. Can you get them?"

"I can get you anything, mate. The question is, have you got the money?"

"We've got money," said Kettering. "Money isn't a problem. So what would an AK-47 cost?"

"Depends on how many you want," said Shepherd.

Kettering shrugged. "Forty?"

Shepherd laughed. "Forty AK-47s? What are you planning, a war?" He continued to laugh but his mind was racing because Kettering had caught him by surprise. He had been expecting the man to want to buy two or three, or maybe half a dozen. But forty was a totally different ball game. As he laughed he looked over at Sharpe and could see that his partner's eyes had also hardened with the realisation that their investigation had moved up to a whole new level.

"Can you get us forty or not?" asked Kettering.

Shepherd forced himself to appear relaxed. "I can get you four hundred. Give me a month and I could probably get you four thousand." He took a pull on his cigar and held the smoke in his mouth rather than inhaling before blowing it out. "A grand each. So forty grand."

"Pounds?"

Shepherd frowned. "Of course, pounds. What do you think I meant? Roubles? Rupees?"

"A grand each, though," said Kettering. "That's more than we thought."

Thompson returned with four brandy glasses and he handed them out.

"Garry here says a grand each," Kettering said to Thompson.

"Fuck me," said Thompson. "That's about three times what we thought we'd have to pay."

"What, Googled it, did you?" Shepherd chuckled. "It's like buying bubbly, mate. You get what you pay for. If you want Bolly or Cristal you pay top price. If you want a bottle of fizzy white wine then you piss off down to Tesco with a tenner in your hot little hand."

"You can get a second-hand Romanian knock-off for a couple of hundred quid," said Sharpe. "But it won't be new and you won't know whether or not it's going to blow up in your hands. We've got the real thing, brand new and still in their boxes, never been fired."

Shepherd nodded in agreement. "We only sell good gear," he said. "No one has ever complained about our product." He sipped his brandy.

"But a grand," said Kettering. "That's steep."

"Plus the ammunition," said Shepherd.

"How much?"

"Again, depends on how much you want. We can do you a good deal if you want to bulk buy."

"We do," said Thompson. "The more the merrier."

"And these guns, where do you get them from?"

"Not thinking about trying to cut out the middleman, are you?" asked Shepherd. "Because that's a dangerous game to be playing in this business."

"That's not what I meant," said Kettering. "Jeez, you're a suspicious bugger. I just meant where do they come from? Russia? China?" He flicked ash into the street.

"I wouldn't sell you a Chinese gun," said Shepherd. "Pile of crap, they are. As bad as the Romanians. No, mate, we've got the Rolls-Royce of the AK. Made in the former Yugoslavia. Serbia. Google the Yugo and you'll see what I mean. Everybody loves them."

"The Yugo's a car, isn't it?"

"Yeah, but I'm sure you'll be able to tell the difference," said Shepherd. "Our Yugos are the ones that go bang."

"I thought the best AK-47s were the originals, the Russian ones," said Thompson.

"Nah, the Yugo's better, no question," said Shepherd.

"And you can get us forty?" asked Kettering.

"Like I said, forty or four thousand."

"What, you get them from the factory?"

"Where I get them from isn't the issue, mate," said Shepherd. "The issue is you paying for them."

"Cash?"

Shepherd laughed. "No, mate, Amex will do nicely." His face went hard. "Of course, cash. But if you've got krugerrands I'll take them."

"Krugerrands?"

"Gold," said Shepherd.

"We can get the cash," said Thompson.

"Glad to hear it," said Shepherd. "So we're agreed on forty? For forty grand?"

Kettering nodded. "And the ammo."

"I can let you have the ammo for £50 a box."

"And how many bullets in a box?" asked Thompson.

"We call them rounds," said Shepherd. "Or cartridges. And there's a hundred in a box."

"So a bullet — I mean a round — costs fifty pence?"

"I guess you were good at maths at school," said Sharpe. He grinned over at Shepherd and they both laughed.

"Yeah, fifty pence each," said Shepherd.

"That's bloody expensive," said Kettering.

A couple went by, a man in a cashmere coat walking arm in arm with his fur-coat-wearing wife, and the men stopped speaking until the couple were out of earshot.

"Yeah, well, it's not as if you can drop into B&Q and buy a few boxes, is it?" said Shepherd. "It all has to be brought in from the Continent and there are risks and costs. Plus, you need special rounds, 7.62 by 39 millimetre. They're not easy to come by in this country. Most of the ammo you'll be offered is nine mill or .22 so it's pretty much a seller's market for the AK-47 ammo." He shrugged. "You're welcome to see if anyone else can get you the rounds cheaper but I can tell you now you'll be wasting your time."

"Plus, there are quality-control issues," said Sharpe. "We've got a saying. Guns don't jam; ammunition jams. It doesn't matter how good the gun is, if you start using it to fire crap ammo then your weapon is going to jam. And that can ruin your whole day."

Kettering nodded thoughtfully. "We'll need about twenty thousand rounds," he said. "So two hundred boxes."

Shepherd's jaw dropped. "Two hundred boxes? That's five hundred rounds per gun, right?"

"Is that a problem?"

Shepherd looked across at Sharpe. The same thought was obviously going through his partner's mind. Why would anyone want to buy twenty thousand rounds?

"If you've got the ten grand it's no problem at all." Shepherd took a long pull on his cigar.

"What about a discount?" asked Thompson.

"As you're such a good customer, you can have the ammo for eight grand," said Shepherd. "We're looking at a total of forty-eight grand."

"How about we split the difference and call it forty-five?" said Kettering. "Seeing as how I'm buying the Bolly?"

"Forty-five it is," said Shepherd. "But, mate, what are you going to be doing with twenty thousand rounds?"

"Self-protection," said Kettering.

"From what? The bloody army?"

172

"Look, you said the ammunition was hard to get hold of. I don't want to be coming back to you for more."

"You know the magazine only holds thirty rounds?" said Sharpe.

"So?" said Kettering.

"Just thought I'd mention it. I mean, twenty thousand rounds is a lot of ammo. Are you planning to fire them at the same time?"

Kettering shrugged. "Why?"

"Because it takes time to reload," said Sharpe. "You can fire thirty rounds with one pull of the trigger if you're on fully automatic. Then you've got to start slotting in fresh rounds one at a time."

"What he means is that if you're planning to fire off a lot of rounds you're better off with pre-loaded magazines," said Shepherd.

Kettering nodded slowly. "Okay," he said. "I get it. You mean we put the rounds in magazines and then just shove in a new one when the old one's empty."

"Click, clack," said Sharpe. "It's as easy as that."

"We can do you polymer magazines at thirty quid a pop," said Shepherd.

Kettering looked over at Thompson. Thompson pulled a face.

"What if we wanted ten magazines for each gun?" said Kettering.

"Sure. Four hundred magazines. We can do that."

"But that would be twelve grand," said Thompson. "That's a bit bloody steep for magazines."

"But you can give us a discount, right?" Kettering said to Shepherd. "They're only plastic."

"Polymer," said Shepherd. "As good as the metal ones and lighter. But that's what they cost. How about we say four hundred for ten grand? So all in, guns, ammo and clips, fifty-five grand."

"Fifty for cash?" said Kettering.

Shepherd laughed. "I already said it was cash or gold," he said. "Fifty-five is my bottom price. What about handguns? I can get you Zastava pistols from the same source. Easier to conceal than an AK-47."

"Don't really see the point of a handgun," said Kettering. "Seems to me that if you're going to be using a gun people need to see it. So the bigger the better." He grinned. "How about we call it fifty-two grand and I'll get you some gloves signed by John Conteh?"

Shepherd nodded. "You love to haggle, don't you? Okay."

Kettering held out his glass and the three other men followed suit. "Pleasure doing business with you," he said.

"The pleasure's all ours," said Sharpe. They clinked glasses and drank.

"You can get anything, can you?" asked Kettering.

"Pretty much," said Shepherd. "I sold a couple of tanks once."

Kettering laughed. "A tank I don't need, but I could do with bulletproof vests."

"That's easy enough," said Shepherd. "Let me come back to you with a price. What sort do you want?"

174

"What are the options?"

"Depends on what sort of protection you want. They go from cheaper ones that will stop a .22 and not much else, right up to vests with steel plates that'll stop a .45 at point-blank range."

"Yeah, the full Monty," said Kettering. "That's what we need."

"No problem," said Shepherd.

"And what about grenades?"

Shepherd stiffened and Sharpe's mouth opened in surprise.

"What?" said Sharpe.

"Grenades," said Thompson. He looked over his shoulder to check that no one could overhear their conversation. "Can you get us some?"

"What the hell do you want with grenades?" asked Sharpe.

"What's it to you?" snapped Thompson.

"James means it's a bit unusual, that's all," said Shepherd. "We don't get much call for grenades. They're a bit . . . specialist."

"But you can get them, right?" asked Kettering. "We'll pay good money."

"I'll talk to some people, see what I can do," said Shepherd. "And you're talking fragmentation grenades, right? You don't mean smoke grenades or flash-bangs?"

"Yeah, the real thing is what we want," said Kettering. "And about the guns. We're going to need a test fire."

"We can arrange that," said Shepherd.

"Up near us?" said Kettering. "I want to bring a couple of guys with us, just to show what we're buying."

"Just make sure they're people you can trust," said Shepherd. "And we'll need to arrange the venue. We'll pick you up and take you to wherever we do it."

"You don't trust us?" said Thompson.

"I don't trust anybody," said Shepherd. "If I get caught with a boot full of AK-47s then I'm banged up for ten years. So forgive me if I'm careful."

"I get it," said Kettering. "But no one is going to screw you over. We want those guns."

"How long after the test fire will you have the forty?" asked Thompson.

Shepherd looked at Sharpe. "A week?"

"A week to ten days," said Sharpe. "We can cover it from stock in the warehouse but I'll need to arrange a cover consignment."

"What's that?" asked Kettering.

"We put the guns in the base of a container, but we have to fill the container with a legitimate cargo. Fruit or veg is the best. Ideally we have the van in a convoy of legit trucks. Soon as we have a delivery date we'll let you know."

"And you'll deliver them to us in Birmingham?"

"We'll arrange a drop-off wherever you want, but again we won't tell you until the last moment. You check the guns, we check the cash, and Bob's your father's brother."

"So we've got a deal?" asked Kettering.

Shepherd nodded. "Looks like it."

176

Kettering beamed. He clinked his glass against Shepherd's again and finished his brandy. "Let's get back inside and watch the boxing," he said.

Shepherd waited until he was back in his Hampstead flat before phoning Hargrove. "It's on," he said. "We've agreed a price and they want a test fire."

"Well done," said Hargrove.

"The thing is, they want forty AK-47s and a stack of ammo. And hand grenades."

"Hand grenades?"

"Yeah. How do we want to play this?"

"Did they say what they want with grenades?"

"Said it wasn't our business, which is probably right. We're arms dealers so why the hell would we care what they're going to do with them?"

"Ray didn't say anything about grenades," said Hargrove. "And he didn't say anything about forty AK-47s. What are they planning, a war?"

"I don't think Ray's fully in the loop," said Shepherd. "If he was they'd have had him along tonight. They want assault rifles, bulletproof vests and grenades. I tried asking him why they wanted that much ordnance but they didn't say and I didn't want to push it because it was our first meeting."

"Did you get a read on them?"

"Kettering's not a nutter, that's for sure. I wouldn't have marked him down as a criminal. Looks more like an estate agent. Clean cut, bit of a Jack the Lad, maybe. Thompson's a bit harder but even so I wouldn't have thought he'd be the type to go on a murder spree."

"Could it be racial?"

Shepherd sighed. "I really don't know what's going on in their heads," he said. "At one point Thompson went over and had his photograph taken next to John Conteh. And one of the boxers they brought down from Birmingham was a Jamaican lad. If they're racists they're doing a bloody good job of hiding it."

"Could they be reselling?"

"It's possible, but at the prices I was quoting I doubt there'd be much profit left for them. It's the grenades that worry me. Guns, even assault rifles, can be used for defence. But there's nothing defensive about a grenade."

"I doubt we'll be getting to the point where we actually give them grenades," said Hargrove.

"That may be, but they're going to want a test fire before we get their money, and they're going to want to see a grenade."

"Do you have any thoughts on that front?"

Shepherd laughed. "I'm starting to realise why you wanted me on this op," he said.

"I wanted you because you're the best undercover agent around," said Hargrove. "But your inside track with the SAS would certainly be a help. If they're still happy to supply us with the guns would you ask if they could lend us a grenade or two?"

"I'll run it by them," said Shepherd. "Do you want to tell the superintendent that the case has moved up a notch?"

"I think we have to," said Hargrove. "We've gone from a couple of wideboys buying a few guns to something much more serious. I'll have a word with Fenby too. I want to know how the hell he managed to miss the fact that they're looking to equip a small army."

"I don't think it's Ray's fault," said Shepherd. "They were sounding us out, making sure we could be trusted, and the question of numbers came up when we were discussing price. They wanted a discount for volume."

"And you gave them a price for a grenade?"

"I said I'd put out some feelers. I figured it'd be best not to appear too keen."

He ended the call, then went through to the kitchen and switched on the kettle. All the champagne he'd drunk was playing havoc with his stomach so he popped a couple of Rennies into his mouth and chewed them as he made himself a cup of coffee. He carried it through to the sitting room and dropped down on to the sofa, then called the Major on his mobile.

"We're ready to go," said Shepherd.

"I've got half a dozen Yugos for you, plus ammunition," said the Major.

"I know this is short notice, but how are you fixed for grenades?"

"Bloody hell, Spider. Are these guys going to war?"

"Everyone keeps asking that," said Shepherd. "Can you help us out?"

"By grenades I assume you don't just mean flash-bangs."

"The real thing," said Shepherd. "What do you have on the base?"

"We mainly use the L109A1 but we have all the Nato stuff for familiarisation. And we've got a store of white phosphorus grenades."

"Anything that could have come from the former Yugoslavia?"

"We've got display models of the Yugoslavian M-75 and M-93."

"But not active grenades?"

"Not last time I checked. But I'll run through the inventory, see what we've got."

"Can I run something else by you? The buyers want to test fire the weapons before they buy. Hargrove is suggesting we do it out in the open. Can you think of somewhere?"

"Plenty of options around our old stamping ground, the Brecon Beacons. I can make sure we don't have any exercises on the day you do it. And the farmers out there are used to loud bangs."

"I'm a bit antsy about doing it out in the open," said Shepherd. "No back-up if things go wrong, nowhere to mount surveillance cameras or mics."

"You could wire up the odd sheep," said the Major. "Or if you want I could get a couple of our snipers in ghillie suits close by."

"I'm not sure that Hargrove wants a full-blown SAS operation. But I'll suggest it."

"Have you thought about suppressors?"

"For the Yugos?"

"Sure. We've been running tests on them and they work a treat. You still get a bang, of course, but you lose most of the crack. And if your targets are planning

180

mayhem in a public place then suppressors would be a big help. And from your point of view, it would cut down a lot of the noise when you're test firing. Just a thought."

"And a bloody good one, Boss. I'll run all this by Hargrove and let you know. How much notice will you need?"

"Providing I get it okayed in principle, a few hours at most. You take care, Spider."

Shepherd woke up early on Monday morning and went for a run around Hampstead Heath in his old army boots, the weighted rucksack on his back. He got back to his flat and showered and changed into a polo shirt and black jeans. He realised that he'd missed a call while he was in the shower — Charlotte Button. He called her back.

"Just checking in to see how things are progressing with Chaudhry and Malik," Button said.

"I'm seeing them this afternoon. I get the feeling that it's stalled a bit."

"It was never going to be a short-term operation," she said. "It will start moving eventually. It has to. They wouldn't put the two of them through all that training and then not use them."

"Unless there's a trust issue."

"Have they suggested that?"

"No, that's just me thinking out loud."

"We could think about pushing things forward," said Button.

"In what way?"

"They could start making a few suggestions themselves."

"I'd advise against that," said Shepherd. "They've been led every step of the way ever since they were recruited. I don't think now's the time for them to be coming up with ideas."

"I suppose you're right," said Button. "But it has gone very quiet. There's almost no chatter that we can find."

"That could be a sign that something big is being planned," said Shepherd. "Let's see how I get on with them this afternoon."

"Good," said Button. "And how are things going on with Sam Hargrove?"

Shepherd filled her in on what had happened at the boxing evening.

She listened without interruption until he mentioned the forty AK-47s. "Sorry, did you say fourteen or forty?"

"Forty," said Shepherd. "And they asked about grenades and bulletproof vests."

"What are their names?"

"Simon Kettering and Paul Thompson. The Brummie cops think they're responsible for a racist attack a while back."

"A murder?"

"A beating."

"Big jump from that to forty AK-47s. And the grenade thing's a worry. Sam made it sound as if it was a small arms buy."

"That's what we all thought. It was only over the brandy and the cigars that they brought out their shopping list. Sam's as surprised as we are."

"So what happens next?" asked Button.

"That's up to the Birmingham cops, I guess, but it looks like we set up a deal and then bust them."

"Good luck with it," said Button. "Just let me know where you are."

"No problem," said Shepherd.

He ended the call and looked at his watch. He'd arranged to meet Chaudhry and Malik at three o'clock so he had time to kill. That was the biggest drawback of the job that Button had given him. Babysitting the two men meant that most of the time he was just sitting around doing nothing but waiting for the phone to ring. He wasn't enjoying being a handler; he much preferred the adrenaline rush of being undercover. He switched on his TV and flicked through the channels, trying to find something interesting to watch. He gave up after five minutes and went over to the bookcase at the side of the fireplace. The books there had been selected by Damien Plant as the sort of books that would be owned be a freelance journalist, so mostly they were non-fiction, reference books and biographies. Tony Blair's autobiography was there, and as Plant was a diehard Conservative Shepherd figured that there had been an element of sarcasm in the choice, especially as a yellow sticker on the front cover showed that the price had been slashed to one pound. He took it over to the sofa, flopped down, and started to read.

★　★　★

Chaudhry fiddled with his tie for the hundredth time since he'd sat down at the table. He was in the Pizza Express down the road from the university and close to Trafalgar Square. The restaurant was on two levels and he actually preferred the basement level, which was larger and with more room between the two tables, but sitting at a table on the ground floor meant that he got a clear view of the entrance. He'd arranged to see Jamila at seven but had arrived fifteen minutes earlier and ordered a bottle of sparkling water, ice and lemon. Despite the water his throat felt dry and scratchy and it hurt when he swallowed. He could feel his hands sweating and he wiped them on his trousers, grateful that he'd liberally sprayed himself with deodorant before leaving the King's campus.

He'd done as his father had asked and made contact with Jamila on Facebook. She had accepted his friendship within an hour and he'd immediately gone to her page. There were several dozen photographs of her with her family, on holiday, and doing her volunteer work in Pakistan. Most of her friends seemed to be either girls or fellow students at UCL. Her hobbies were tennis and the theatre and she liked listening to Rihanna and Lady Gaga. In none of the photographs did she seem to have a boyfriend and her relationship status was single.

They'd messaged each other back and forth through Facebook and posted stuff on each other's walls, mainly music videos that they liked or YouTube videos of animals doing stupid things. Then one day she'd said

184

that she was having a boring week and he offered to take her for a meal and she'd accepted. So they still hadn't spoken, and he wasn't a hundred per cent certain that he would recognise her in a crowd. The pictures on her Facebook page gave off mixed messages. In Pakistan she was never without a headscarf and had her arms and legs covered, but there were pictures of her playing tennis on a grass court wearing very short shorts.

He swirled the ice cubes around his glass with his finger and when he looked up he realised that he'd been wrong to think that he wouldn't recognise her in a crowd. She was standing at the entrance, looking around, her chin up confidently, a slight smile on her face. Her skin was a rich caramel colour, her hair black and glossy, longer than it was in her pictures, but her eyes were her most striking feature: so brown they were almost black, with lashes that were so long they might have belonged to a cartoon character.

She was wearing a long coat and had a Louis Vuitton bag over her left shoulder, and as she turned in his direction the coat opened to reveal a tight skirt that ended just above the knee, the legs of a catwalk model and black high heels. As he looked up from the shoes he realised that she was looking at him and he stood up. His hand knocked against his glass and the water spilled over his trousers. He jumped back, cursing, and the glass fell on to the tiled floor, shattering into a dozen pieces. All the diners turned to look at the noise and Chaudhry felt his cheeks redden. He bent down to pick up the pieces of glass but a blonde waitress rushed over and said that she'd take care of it for him. As Chaudhry picked up his napkin and pressed it against the damp patch on his trousers, Jamila walked up to him.

"Oh dear, are you okay?" she asked, and Chaudhry was amazed to hear a Scottish accent until he remembered that she was from Glasgow.

"Sure. Yes. No problem." He carried on dabbing at his groin. "I'm such a klutz."

"Nice to meet you, Mr Klutz," she said. Her grin widened and she held out her hand. "I'm Jamila."

"Yes, of course you are," said Chaudhry. He held out his right hand and then realised that he was still holding his napkin. He apologised, transferred it to his left hand and shook hands with her. Her skin was soft and smooth and her fingernails were bright pink with gold tips. "Great to finally meet you," he said. "In person, I mean."

The waitress had put most of the pieces of broken glass on her tray. She stood up and smiled at Chaudhry. "Why don't I move you to a table downstairs?" she said. "Save you waiting while I finish cleaning up."

Chaudhry smiled at her gratefully. She took the two of them down the staircase to the lower floor and handed them over to a tall Australian waiter with a surfer's physique and sun-bleached hair. He took Jamila's coat, showed them to a table by the wall and gave them a couple of menus. Chaudhry ordered another bottle of water.

As the waiter walked away, Chaudhry apologised again. Jamila waved off his apology. "I'm forever knocking things over," she said. "I just hope I don't do it in the lab or thousands of people could die."

"Are you serious?"

She grinned. "No, they haven't let me near the dangerous stuff yet."

"I never liked microbiology," he said. "Everything is so . . ."

"Small?"

Chaudhry laughed. "Exactly. I prefer patients that I can talk to."

"But it's micro-organisms that'll be making a lot of them sick. Viruses and bacteria, they're the big killers."

"Well, cancer, heart attacks and strokes are the big killers, but I know what you mean," he said. He winced as he realised how he'd managed to be both arrogant and patronising in the same sentence. "Sorry," he said.

"Sorry?"

"I mean, you're right. It's an important field."

"It can be boring at times," she said. "My dad wanted me to be a doctor but I told him that I couldn't face spending the rest of my life around sick people."

Chaudhry chuckled. "That would pretty much rule out medicine," he said.

"I'm not even sure if I want to stay in science," she said. She shrugged. "Still, that's part of the reason for being at university, isn't it? To find yourself."

Chaudhry nodded but couldn't think of anything to say. He was finding it difficult to concentrate because every time he looked at her he got lost in her eyes.

"Do you drink?" asked Jamila, looking up from her menu.

He frowned, wondering if it was a trick question. He was a Muslim and Muslims didn't touch alcohol. "Not really," he said. He grimaced. "Actually, not at all."

"Never? Not even a taste?"

Chaudhry chuckled again. "It would be like eating pork," he said. "I wouldn't even want to try."

She put down the menu, looking uncomfortable.

"What's wrong?"

"Would you mind terribly if I had a glass of wine?"

"Of course not."

"You're sure?"

"Sure I'm sure." He held up his hands. "Just because I don't drink doesn't mean others shouldn't."

The Australian waiter returned with the bottle of sparkling water. He poured it for them and Jamila asked for a glass of white wine. As he headed off she smiled at Chaudhry and his stomach turned over. She did have the most amazing smile.

"So you don't drink because you're a Muslim?" she asked.

Chaudhry nodded. "Sure. The Koran says intoxication is forbidden."

"Raj, I'm not planning to get drunk."

"I know, but that's not what I meant." He felt his cheeks redden again. "I don't know . . . it's just part of me. No alcohol. Pray five times a day."

"And one day you'll make a pilgrimage to Mecca?"

"Of course."

"And you give a percentage of your earnings to charity?"

"I'm not actually earning yet. But when I am, yes, of course."

She leaned forward and his stomach turned again as she smiled. "I'm making you uncomfortable. All this talk about religion. I'm sorry."

"You're not. Really." That was a lie, he realised. But it wasn't the conversation that was making him uncomfortable, it was her striking beauty. "Your father. Does he drink?"

"He likes wine. But never more than two glasses."

"And he doesn't ask you to cover your head when you go out?"

Jamila laughed, quickly covering her mouth with her hand. "Of course not." She laughed again. "Just the thought of it." She shook her head. "My dad's not like that. He's been in the UK since he was ten. And my mum was born here. I've never seen her wear so much as a headscarf."

"What about when she goes back to Pakistan?"

"She's never been," said Jamila. Glasgow's her home. If you think I've got an accent, you should hear Mum. You couldn't get her to Pakistan if you paid her."

The waiter returned with Jamila's wine. Chaudhry caught him smiling at Jamila in a way that made him want to grab him by the throat and slam him against the wall. He shook his head, wondering how she'd managed to provoke such strong feelings in such a short space of time. He'd been in her company for barely ten minutes and he was already jealous when another man even looked at her.

"You've been to Pakistan, my dad says."

189

"Over the Christmas holiday," he said, nodding.

"On a health programme, right? That must have been really interesting."

Chaudhry's mouth had gone dry and he swallowed awkwardly. This was the first time he'd met her and he didn't want to start their relationship with a lie but he didn't have a choice. "It was hard work," he said. "My dad said you worked in an orphanage." He hoped that the change of subject wasn't too obvious but he was very uncomfortable lying to her and much preferred to be talking about her.

She nodded enthusiastically. "I did a gap year before I went to uni," she said. "I spent most of it in a city called Murree, in the Punjab. They'd had over twelve inches of rainfall and it was a real mess. A lot of people were killed, thousands of homes were destroyed and a lot of kids were abandoned so the number of orphans had gone through the roof. And food was in short supply; there were no medicines. It was horrible, Raj. It really made me appreciate what we have in this country. We moan about the NHS but at the end of the day at least you get to see a GP and if necessary you go to hospital for treatment." She smiled. "Why am I telling you that? You'll be a doctor soon."

"No, I know what you mean. I hate the poverty out there. My dad's always telling me how well Pakistan has done, how at independence in 1974 it inherited one jute factory, one textile mill and one university. But when I was there all I saw was the poverty."

"Where were you?"

"Karachi," said Chaudhry. At least that much was true. He and Malik had flown there from London before being transported to an al-Qaeda training camp close to the border with Afghanistan. "It was a small clinic in a deprived area. I was giving them vaccinations and offering basic healthcare advice." He felt his heart race as he lied, and his hands were damp with sweat. He wiped them on his trousers. He liked Jamila, really liked her, and he hated the fact that any relationship he had with her would be based on untruths. He felt a wave of shame and he looked round for their waiter. "I could do with a Coke," he said. "Where's our waiter gone?"

Jamila lifted her head and the Australian waiter rushed over, eager to please. She rewarded him with a beaming smile and nodded at Chaudhry. The waiter took Chaudhry's order and then they both chose their pizzas. Chaudhry was a little annoyed that Jamila asked the waiter for his opinion on what was good and even more annoyed when she took his advice and had the Padana with its goat's cheese, spinach, red and caramelised onions and garlic oil. It did sound good but Chaudhry couldn't force himself to follow the waiter's suggestion. His favourite was the Diavolo, but he figured that if there was any chance of a goodnight kiss then he'd be better avoiding the Tabasco, jalapeno peppers and hot spiced beef that gave it its kick, and so he went for a classic Margherita.

"Good choice, sir," said the waiter, with what Chaudhry took to be a sarcastic tone, and then he flashed Jamila another beaming smile before heading off to the kitchen.

"I didn't see any pictures of your volunteer work," said Jamila.

"Sorry?" said Chaudhry, confused.

"On your Facebook page. There weren't any photographs of you in Karachi. At the medical centre."

"I'm not a great one for taking pictures," said Chaudhry, hating himself for yet another lie. "And I was worked off my feet."

"Will you go back, do you think?" she asked.

"Probably not," said Chaudhry, and at least that was the truth.

"I'm definitely going back," said Jamila. She sipped her wine. "I thought of taking another year off and spending it at the orphanage but my dad says I should graduate first."

"Definitely," said Chaudhry quickly. Too quickly, he realised. "I mean, you'd find it much harder to get back into studying. Better to get your degree first and then take another year off before you start work."

"That's what my dad says."

The meal flew by. They ate their pizzas, Jamila ordered a second glass of wine, they shared a dessert, they had coffee, and all the time they talked and laughed as if they had known each other for years. She was the prettiest girl Chaudhry had ever seen, and he was all too well aware of how men's heads turned as they walked past their table. When the bill came she offered to split it with him but Chaudhry insisted that she allow him to pay. She agreed but made him promise that on their next date he would let her pay. His heart raced when she said that, and he couldn't stop grinning as they stood on the pavement looking for a taxi.

It turned out that he could have eaten the Diavolo pizza after all because he didn't get a kiss. But he did get a peck on the cheek and she squeezed his arm before she got into the back of a black cab. He stood rubbing his cheek as the taxi drove off. He'd had an amazing evening, and he knew that his father was right: she was the perfect girl for him. But he also knew that no matter how the relationship progressed it had started with him lying to her, not once but several times. He'd looked into her beautiful, sexy, wonderful eyes and he'd lied. His stomach lurched and before he could stop himself he was vomiting in the gutter.

Hargrove arrived at Thames House immaculately dressed as always. He was wearing a black pinstriped suit, a crisp white shirt and a blue and yellow striped tie, and was carrying a black leather briefcase, looking more like a stockbroker or merchant banker than a chief superintendent with the Metropolitan Police. Shepherd met him outside. He was also wearing a suit, but a black one that had probably cost less than Hargrove's trousers alone.

"Any idea what this is about, Spider?" asked Hargrove as they headed for the entrance.

"I know as much as you do," said Shepherd. Button had phoned him the previous evening and asked him to come in for a 10a.m. meeting with Hargrove and to walk him into the building.

"Is that because it's need-to-know or because she hasn't told you either?"

"The latter," said Shepherd.

Hargrove smiled thinly. "Of course you'd say that anyway, wouldn't you?"

"Charlie tends to play her cards close to her chest," said Shepherd. They walked into the reception area where Hargrove showed his warrant card and Shepherd signed him in. They walked through a metal detector and took a lift up to the third floor. Button was waiting for them in a windowless meeting room. She was sitting halfway down a large oak table with a pale-blue file in front of her.

She stood up, shook hands with Hargrove and waved him to a seat on the opposite side of the table. Shepherd hesitated as he wondered on which side of the table he should sit. His instincts were to sit next to Hargrove as they were working together on the arms case and Button had called the meeting, but he was still employed by MI5 and Button was his boss.

Button saw his indecision and nodded at the seat to Hargrove's left. "Why don't you sit yourself there? It'll be easier for me to show you what I've got."

Shepherd sat down next to Hargrove.

"Coffee?" asked Button.

Both men shook their heads.

"Okay, so I'll dive straight in. Basically there are some interesting developments in the Kettering and Thompson case that I need to run by you."

"That's a West Midlands case," said Hargrove quietly. "I didn't realise there was any MI5 involvement."

"Any case where terrorism is involved falls within our brief," said Button.

"Terrorism? We're talking about a group of Brummie villains purchasing weapons," said Hargrove.

Button nodded. "I'm afraid there seems to be more to it than that," she said. She flipped open the file on the table. Inside were a couple of dozen printed sheets topped by a photograph.

"We're all familiar with Norwegian right-wing extremist Anders Behring Breivik, of course. He detonated a car bomb in central Oslo killing eight people and went on to murder another sixty-nine at a youth camp."

Shepherd and Hargrove frowned. Button smiled at their confusion. "What Operation Excalibur seems to have missed is that three of the men they've been looking at met with Breivik just six months before the attacks."

The colour drained from Hargrove's face. "How could West Midlands Police not know this?" he said.

"They've been treating it as a purely criminal case," said Button. "I assume no one there thought of looking at the bigger picture."

"But why didn't a check on Kettering and Thompson throw up the link to the Norwegian?" asked Hargrove.

"Because that intel isn't on the Police National Computer," said Button.

"I know that," said Hargrove. "I ran the checks myself when we were first approached about the case. I don't understand this, Charlotte. A British group with links to a Norwegian mass murderer discuss acquiring high-powered weapons and alarm bells don't start ringing?"

"Well, they're ringing now, Sam. Loud and clear."

"That's what you think?" asked Shepherd. "You think this Brummie group is planning some sort of public attack?"

"All we know is that Kettering and Thompson met with the Norwegian in 2002 and were in email contact with him right up until the attacks. Six months ago Kettering, Thompson and another man flew to Olso and met with him again." She flicked through the papers in the file, then tapped one. "During interrogation Breivik claimed that he was a member of a new Christian military order. He called it the new *Pauperes commilitones Christi Templique Solomonici*. Effectively a new order of the Knights Templar. He told his interrogators that this group was formed in April 2002 by nine men — two from England, a Frenchman, a German, a Dutchman, a Greek, a Russian and a Serb. And himself. He says that there are now eighty of these knights and that they are preparing to seize political power in Western Europe with the aim of expelling all the Muslims."

She smiled thinly.

"How much of this is the fantasy of a deluded mind and how much is a serious terrorist threat has yet to be determined. I don't think we've uncovered anything that suggests a coup or revolution is on the cards. But the link with Breivik is a red flag. A very big red flag." She took out a surveillance photograph and slid it across the table to Hargrove. "This is the third man from the UK who was at that meeting. Roger McLean. I gather he doesn't appear on Operation Excalibur's watch list?"

Hargrove studied the picture and then handed it to Shepherd. McLean was a big man with a shaved head and a St George's Cross tattooed on his right forearm.

Shepherd shook his head. "They're not looking at him," he said.

"McLean's been around right-wing groups for more than twenty years. He was initially with the National Front, then switched to the British National Party, then just before he met Breivik he moved to the EDL. In 2003 he went off the grid."

"What exactly do you mean by that?" asked Hargrove.

"He didn't attend any party meetings of any of the groups, didn't go to any demonstrations, disappeared from the electoral roll, isn't registered with a GP, doesn't pay tax, doesn't, so far as we can see, have a bank account. But he does appear to be involved in several right-wing and anti-Islamic websites."

Button took back the photograph from Shepherd and handed Hargrove a printed screenshot of a website. "The Truth About The Muslim Menace".

"The nightmare scenario is that we have a group of British citizens who are set to emulate Breivik," said

Button. "We've had our psych people run profiles of Kettering and Thompson but we don't have enough information to decide whether or not they are capable of mounting a suicide attack. But we're told that they are the type who would go on a killing spree if they thought they had a reasonable chance of getting away with it." She sighed. "You can imagine the havoc a group with automatic weapons could cause in the city centre. The Bullring alone gets a hundred thousand visitors on an average day. It could all be over in a couple of minutes and the death toll would be horrendous. Hundreds, certainly. That's before we even start talking about grenades."

At the mention of grenades Hargrove turned to look at Shepherd, and Shepherd winced inwardly. Hargrove had realised that the intelligence on grenades could only have come from Shepherd.

"And with it being Birmingham, many of the victims would be Asian and Muslim," continued Button. "We've always considered that the high percentage of Muslims in the community meant that the West Midlands are less likely to suffer a terrorist attack. But the nature of these terrorists changes everything."

"We don't know that they are terrorists," said Hargrove. "They're saying that they want the guns for self-protection."

"Well, they would say that, wouldn't they?" said Button. "They're unlikely to go shopping for weapons on the basis that they're going on a killing spree." She took back the website screenshot and slid it into the file. "Birmingham is the UK's second biggest city and if it is in the firing line there are plenty of targets, from the Council House in Victoria Square to tower blocks, department stores, stations, hotels. And, as the city is slap bang in the middle of the country, there are plenty of escape routes. They could go on a killing spree and be on a motorway at seventy miles an hour before the police even get to the scene."

She shuffled her papers and smiled at Hargrove. "I realise that this puts you in something of an awkward position, Sam."

"That's putting it mildly," said Hargrove quietly. "You're going to take Operation Excalibur off West Midlands Police and they're going to blame me."

"Actually, that's not what I was going to suggest," said Button. "Your agent is in place and Dan here is on attachment to COG so if anything we'd be looking for the operation to be brought under the Met's jurisdiction. But I don't think that's necessary either. Basically we'd like you to continue running your undercover operation but to share any intelligence with us. I'd be happy to do that through Dan, but if you'd rather be the point of contact that would be perfectly acceptable."

"And would West Midlands Police be privy to the fact that we're sharing their intel?" asked Hargrove.

"Best not," said Button. "And frankly whether or not they knew that MI5 had a watching brief is immaterial to the way that they would handle the case."

Hargrove leaned forward. "That's not strictly speaking true, though, is it? They're treating it as if it

199

were a straight-forward criminal investigation but you believe there are terrorist implications."

"If West Midlands Police get a conviction for buying automatic weapons then Kettering, Thompson and the rest will go down for ten years. I think we'd regard that as a successful outcome. We'll just be monitoring to check that the investigation proceeds smoothly."

"And if I'm asked directly whether or not I'm passing intel on to the Security Services? What do I say?"

"I really don't see that happening," said Button. "But that would be one very good reason for using Dan as the conduit."

"Plausible deniability," said Hargrove.

"Exactly."

"And I'm assuming Ray Fenby doesn't get told?"

"I don't see any reason why he needs to know," said Button. "But there is one thing that perhaps we'd like to handle a little differently. West Midlands Police are treating this very much as a local crime issue. We would be very interested to see if there's any overseas connection. In particular, anything connecting Kettering and Thompson and the other members of this Knights Templar group — the German, the Frenchman, the Dutchman and the rest. We're running an investigation at this end following phone and email traffic, but if we can get Kettering or Thompson to reveal anything, that would be a bonus."

"I'll talk to Ray," said Hargrove. "But that's a tough one. Kettering and Thompson aren't stupid so he won't be able to push it."

200

"Understood," said Button. "But if you could perhaps ask him to keep his ears open for any Continental connection it'd be much appreciated."

Hargrove nodded but he looked uncomfortable.

"And again, it's important that Fenby isn't aware of our interest. I'd rather that stayed between the three of us."

Shepherd looked over at Hargrove and saw from the look on his face that the same thought had occurred to the chief superintendent. "Does that include Inspector Sharpe?" said Hargrove.

"I think we have to keep our involvement on a need-to-know basis," said Button. "And the fewer people that know, the better. The last thing we need is canteen talk leading to a blown operation."

Hargrove raised his eyebrows. "I can't see him opening his heart to the Birmingham cops over a cup of coffee," he said.

Button put up her hands. "Of course not," she said. "But I wouldn't want the Birmingham police to get all territorial and move in precipitously. So I'd rather that Razor wasn't aware of the new arrangement."

"Understood," said Hargrove, though Shepherd could tell that the chief superintendent wasn't happy.

"Now, regarding any European involvement, the fact that Spider's going to be suggesting that the arms are being brought in from Serbia might help," said Button. "Once we've planted the idea of weapons from Europe, we could perhaps suggest a test firing over there. Then if they are in contact with other groups it's not too much of a stretch for them to think of involving them."

"I worry that we might start overcomplicating matters," said Hargrove.

"It would be something of a coup if we could nail terrorists across Europe, especially if they have links with Breivik. Obviously Ray, Dan and Jimmy are the men on the ground and of course they have to play it by ear. It's just something to think about." She closed the file and pushed back her chair. "Well, thank you so much for coming in." She stood up. So did Hargrove and Shepherd.

Hargrove shook her hand. "Probably best if Dan is the conduit, as you suggest," he said.

Button nodded enthusiastically. "I think that'll be best," she said. "Do you mind if he stays here for a while? I've some admin business that I need to run by him."

"Not a problem," said Hargrove. He picked up his briefcase.

"I'll get someone to show you out," said Button. She took him to the door and handed the chief superintendent over to a young man in a blue blazer. As they headed for the lifts, Button went back into the meeting room and smiled apologetically at Shepherd. "For an undercover agent you're not very good at hiding your emotions," she said. "I can see from the look on your face that you're not happy about what just happened."

"I can't believe you did that," said Shepherd. "It made me look like I'd gone running to you, telling tales out of school."

Button sat down, frowning. "What?"

"Look at it from his point of view. He's running an undercover operation for the Birmingham cops and I'm brought in to help. A few days later he gets called into Thames House and told that Five is now pulling the strings. He puts two and two together and thinks that I told you that he's not up to it."

"Nonsense," said Button. "First of all, you and he have worked together and he knows you wouldn't pull a trick like that. But, more importantly, we haven't taken the operation from him."

"You just told him that all intel on the case now goes through me to you."

"With his full knowledge. It's not as if we're doing it behind his back."

"It still makes it a case of us and them. And telling him about the grenades." Shepherd gritted his teeth in frustration.

"What?"

Shepherd sighed. "That could only have come from me," he said. "So in that case I definitely was going behind his back." He shrugged. "Anyway, what's done is done. No use crying over spilled milk."

"It had to be done, you know that. This is turning into too big a case."

"It sounds like it," agreed Shepherd.

"How did the training go with Chaudhry and Malik? I gather you tied up half our watchers for a day."

"They needed bringing up to speed on the basics of counter-surveillance," said Shepherd. "Plus, the watchers wanted to do some training themselves so we ended up killing two birds with the proverbial stone."

"And you think they're capable of spotting a tail now?"

"Put it this way, they're a hell of a lot more prepared than they were. Any chatter on that front?"

"Nothing significant," she said, shaking her head. "If there is you'll be the first to hear about it." She sat back in her chair and tapped the file on the table. "This Birmingham case has given me an idea," she said. "I know I mentioned it before but I'm even more convinced now that we should be a bit more proactive with Chaudhry and Malik."

Shepherd frowned. "I said it wasn't a good idea then and I still think that."

"Hear me out," said Button. "You're up and running as an arms dealer. Khalid and his people are planning a terrorist attack for which they'll need equipment. If there was any way that we could put you in the mix, it'd make for a much better case and give us the inside track from the get-go."

"But Raj and Harvey are students. What reason could they have for knowing me?"

Button wrinkled her nose. "That we'd have to work on, but I'm sure there's a way. And if we have Khalid coming to you for weapons then we can wrap this up with no risk to the public."

"But one hell of a risk for Raj and Harvey," said Shepherd. "This is Khalid's show. He gives the orders and they do as they're told. Alarm bells are going to start ringing if they go from being foot soldiers to players."

"I'm not saying it'll be easy, the circumstances would have to be right and it'll take a lot of planning, but in a perfect world it'd make everything a lot easier."

"Yeah, well, the world's not perfect, not by a long chalk. And I don't want to put them in harm's way any more than we have to." He folded his arms. "These guys are just amateurs. It has to be kid gloves."

"Absolutely," said Button. "I'm not suggesting we do anything to put them at risk."

"With the greatest of respect, any form of proactive behaviour is going to do just that. These guys have already done far more than any member of the public can be expected to do. They gave us a top al-Qaeda team, the location of a training camp in Pakistan and they found Bin Laden. And they've risked their lives to do it. The least we can do is to watch their backs."

"Exactly," said Button. "It's precisely because they have taken risks that they've achieved so much. They could have just informed us about Khalid and his people and left it at that, but they were prepared to go to Pakistan and undergo al-Qaeda training, and that led directly to MI5's best-ever intelligence coup. Do you think we would have found Bin Laden if they hadn't taken risks? All I'm saying is that we need to keep this investigation moving forward and one way of doing that is to put you in play."

Shepherd could see that there was no point in arguing with her so he shrugged and said nothing.

"Look, Spider, no one is saying that we're going to rush into anything. Just give it some thought."

"Okay," he said. "But can we look at a way of getting me into the mix without involving Raj and Harvey? Five must have other al-Qaeda assets we can use as a pipeline."

Button nodded. "I'll ask around, see what's available." She stood up, bringing the meeting to an end. As he left the building Shepherd couldn't shake off the feeling that she'd lied to him.

He waited until he was outside Thames House before calling Hargrove on his mobile. "I just wanted to say that I had no idea that was going to happen," said Shepherd.

"Not a problem," said Hargrove. "Though I do feel as I've just been mugged at knifepoint."

"If I'd known I would have at least warned you."

"Spider, you work for MI5 now and Charlie's your boss. And I'm a big boy. I know the way things work."

"She's put us in a bastard position, though. If Superintendent Warner up in Birmingham finds out that we're going behind his back he's going to hit the roof."

"Hopefully that won't happen," said Hargrove. "And frankly she does have a point. If Kettering is planning a terrorist incident then with the best will in the world the West Midlands cops aren't geared up for dealing with it. If it was the Met then it would be a different story, but the chances are that if Warner does realise that Kettering is a terrorist rather than a vanilla criminal he's going to be picking up the phone to Five anyway. This way Charlie can hit the ground running if the call comes."

"Thanks," said Shepherd. "I was worried you might be annoyed."

"I'm not happy, but I'll get over it," said Hargrove. "My main worry is that Five will take all the credit for our hard work, but that wouldn't be the first time."

Hargrove ended the call and Shepherd rang Jimmy Sharpe. "Can you talk?" he asked.

"Till the cows come home," said Sharpe.

"Why can't anybody just answer that question with a straight yes or no?" said Shepherd. "Fancy a drink?"

"You read my mind," said Sharpe. "When and where?"

"I'll come to you," said Shepherd. "Just name a pub."

Chaudhry's mobile rang. He didn't recognise the number but he took the call. It was Khalid. Khalid routinely changed SIM cards and once a month he replaced his phone. The intelligence services now had the capability to track a phone and monitor its calls no matter what SIM card was being used and wherever possible Khalid would use a public phone instead.

"Have you been to evening prayers, brother?" asked Khalid.

"I have, brother," said Chaudhry. He and Malik had gone to the Dynevor Road mosque for the Maghrib prayers, which had to be performed just after sunset. It tended to be the busiest of the prayer sessions as those Muslims that had day jobs could conveniently drop by on their way home. The fourth of the five daily prayer sessions consisted of two rak'at prayed aloud, and the third in silence.

A teenager who had been praying in front of Chaudhry had neglected to turn off his mobile phone and during Chaudhry's silent rak'at the boy had received a text message. He had then taken out his phone and begun texting, much to Chaudhry's consternation. Chaudhry had been just about to say something when the imam had clipped the teenager's ear and told him to be more respectful. Chaudhry was becoming increasingly frustrated at the mosque; many of the men going there to pray seemed only to be going through the motions and he had smelled alcohol on the breath of several of the worshippers.

"Permit me to buy you and Harveer dinner," said Khalid. He never referred to Malik by his westernised name. Equally Raj was always addressed as brother or as Manraj. "There are two brothers who I would like you to meet."

"Of course," said Chaudhry.

"Half an hour from now, then, brother. At the Aziziye Halal. You know it?"

"Of course, brother."

The Aziziye Halal was a traditional Turkish restaurant on the ground floor of the Aziziye Mosque on Stoke Newington Road, next to a halal butcher where Chaudhry bought most of his meat. The mosque had started life as the Apollo Picture House in 1913 and had shown soft-core sex films during the seventies before being converted into a mosque in 1983. It was much larger than the Dynevor Road mosque, with room for two thousand worshippers, and it was far more salubrious, if for no other reason than the Dynevor Road mosque was underground and the Aziziye was on the upper floor with large windows. It was the Turkish community who had pressed for the cinema to be converted into a mosque, and generally it was only Turks who worshipped there. The Turks were as protective about their mosque as they were about the business they controlled in the area.

Malik was lying on the sofa reading a book on Japanese cooking.

"Khalid wants to see us," Chaudhry said. "At the Aziziye."

"The mosque?"

"The restaurant. Get ready."

"I hope he's paying."

"If he doesn't you can ask him for the receipt and get MI5 to pay." Chaudhry could see from the look on Malik's face that he thought he was serious. "Don't you bloody dare," laughed Chaudhry.

Twenty-five minutes later they were removing their shoes at the entrance to the restaurant. Khalid was inside, talking to a waiter. Standing with Khalid were two young Asians. Chaudhry recognised them from the mosque, though he had never spoken to them.

The waiter, dressed in a black shirt and black trousers, headed over to a stack of menus as Khalid turned and saw Chaudhry and Malik. He walked towards them and kissed them on both cheeks. He was wearing a blue and white striped dishdash and a white skullcap, holding a chain of wooden prayer beads, and smelled of garlic and cheap cologne. He waved over his two companions. "This is Lateef and Faisal," said Khalid.

"It's an honour, brother," said Lateef, shaking hands with Chaudhry then pulling him close into a hug. He patted him on the back with his left hand. "A real honour." He was an inch or two taller than Chaudhry with the looks of a Bollywood leading man; his hair was gelled and slicked back.

Faisal was short and stocky with darker skin and cheeks mottled with old acne scars. He stepped forward and hugged Malik. "Salaam, brother," he said.

The waiter returned with the menus and took them along to their cubicle. Most diners in the restaurant ate in small cubicles, divided up with chest-high partitions. They varied in size from small ones that accommodated just two people to family cubicles where more than a dozen could eat in comfort, sprawled on red patterned cushions around low tables.

The waiter held open the door of the cubicle and one by one they filed in and flopped down on the cushions. Khalid sat down at the head of the table. There was an LCD TV screen behind him showing advertisements for the restaurant. Khalid pointed at the TV and nodded at the waiter. The waiter switched it off and handed out menus. Khalid waved the menus away and ordered for them all.

Unlike many of the Turkish-run Muslim restaurants in the area, the Aziziye Halal didn't serve alcohol. The waiter brought a tray of fruit juices and water, and then disappeared to the kitchen. Khalid poured water into glasses for each of the men.

"So, Lateef and Faisal will soon be following the glorious path that you both trod," said Khalid. "I thought it might be a good idea for you to tell them what they can expect."

"Was it amazing, brother? Being with the mujahideen?" asked Lateef.

"They were not with the mujahideen," said Khalid. "They are mujahideen. That is what happens over there. You go as men who want to take part in jihad but you return as Islamic warriors, as mujahideen."

"The training, was it hard?" asked Faisal.

"It has to be hard," said Malik. "You don't know how weak you are until they get to work on you." He sipped his water. "I can play five-a-side all evening and never break a sweat," he said. "But after half an hour of physical training in the desert I thought I was going to die. We did obstacle courses and route marches; we walked in the hottest part of the day and we walked through the night. We ran, we crawled, we hid in trenches for hours. They teach you discipline like you wouldn't believe. I lost about five kilos while I was there."

Chaudhry nodded in agreement. "It opens your eyes to what they go through every day," he said. "Here we're soft and weak, and without training you wouldn't last a day out there."

"And they teach you to fire guns and stuff?" asked Faisal.

"Not just to fire them," said Chaudhry. "They show you how to strip and clean weapons, how to fix them, how to store them."

"AK-47s, right?" said Lateef.

"All sorts," said Chaudhry. "The AK-47 is the workhorse but they taught us about the Uzi and the guns that the Americans use — the M4 carbine and the M9 pistol."

"They make you strip and reassemble them blindfolded," said Malik. "You think you'll never get the hang of it but eventually you do."

"And what's it like, firing an AK-47?" asked Lateef.

"It's louder than you expect, and you smell the gunpowder for hours afterwards," said Chaudhry. "It doesn't kick as much as you'd think."

"But the Uzi kicks," said Malik. "The Uzi kicks like a living thing. It's like trying to hold on to a struggling cat."

A man with a long beard moved by their cubicle, followed by two women covered from head to foot in black burkas, their eyes shielded behind black mesh. There was no way of knowing whether they were his wives, his sisters or his elderly aunts.

The men fell silent until the new arrivals had made their way to their cubicle and seated themselves.

"Did you shoot anyone while you were out there?" asked Lateef.

"Brothers, this was a training camp," said Khalid softly. "You go to train to be mujahideen, not to fight. You are too valuable to risk in a desert gunfight."

212

Lateef lowered his voice. "We heard that sometimes they kill prisoners in the camps. For practice. Is that true?"

"I have heard that," said Chaudhry. "But it did not happen while we were there."

"Did you fire missiles, the sort that can bring down helicopters and planes?"

"We didn't fire them ourselves but we saw one being fired and we know what to do," said Chaudhry.

"That must have been awesome," said Faisal. He looked over at Khalid. "They should give us surface-to-air missiles here," he said. "Can you imagine what we could do? You can see the planes landing at Heathrow from miles away." He mimed firing a SAM missile launcher and made a whooshing noise.

Khalid was about to admonish him when the cubicle door opened and the waiter appeared with their food. He knelt down and put dishes on the table: stuffed vine leaves, filo pastry stuffed with feta cheese, fried meatballs served with chopped onions, salad and naan bread. When the waiter had left, Khalid leaned forward. "It is not about the weapons, brothers. Weapons are only the means to an end. Becoming a mujahideen is an attitude of mind. That is why you go to Pakistan. You go to become focused so that you can best serve Allah. A true mujahideen doesn't need a rocket or a gun to kill the infidel. But he needs the mental toughness to commit himself."

"They toughen you up over there, that's for sure," said Chaudhry. "They explain a lot too. You think you know everything about what it means to be a Muslim, but until you've seen what they go through . . ." He shrugged. "Our lives here are so easy. We forget that our brothers are being slain all over the world."

Faisal and Lateef nodded enthusiastically.

"What else did you learn, brothers?" asked Faisal.

"They taught us how to resist interrogation," said Malik.

"What do they do?" asked Lateef. "Do they torture you?"

"They rough you up a bit, but it's more psychological intimidation," said Malik.

"Did they waterboard you?" asked Faisal.

Malik laughed. "No, they didn't. It was more about showing you the tricks that the interrogators would use."

"Anyway, brothers, we're in England," said Khalid. "If ever you are arrested by the police you say nothing other than that you want a lawyer. That's all you say. The British police are not allowed to hurt you or trick you or use any pressure at all. And once you ask for a lawyer they can't ask you any more questions until the lawyer arrives." He sniggered. "The British are their own worst enemy."

"And bombs, did you learn about bombs?" asked Lateef.

Malik nodded. "We spent a week being taught about explosives and IEDs," he said. "They showed us how to make explosives from raw materials, how to make detonators and timers — everything. From small bombs you can put in a can of Coke right up to car bombs that can take out a whole building."

214

"Awesome," said Faisal.

"When are you guys going?" asked Chaudhry.

"Next week," said Faisal. "Wednesday."

"Both of you?"

The two men nodded. "We're going to a wedding," said Lateef, making quote-mark gestures around "wedding".

"How long?" asked Chaudhry.

"Three months, maybe longer."

"Excellent," said Chaudhry. "You won't regret it." He looked over at Khalid. "Are they going to the same camp we went to?"

Khalid shook his head. "A new one," he said. "Closer to the border." He waved at the food. "Let us eat while we talk, brothers. One thing I can tell you is that the food over there will not be as good as this, so enjoy it while you can."

Sharpe was standing at the bar, halfway through a pint of lager, when Shepherd walked in. He raised his glass in salute and ordered a Jameson's and soda from the blonde Polish barmaid. As soon as his drink arrived Shepherd took Sharpe over to a corner table, where they wouldn't be overheard.

"Charlie just stitched me up," said Shepherd as they sat down.

"In what way?"

"She told Hargrove that Five is going to be running Operation Excalibur."

Sharpe's eyebrows shot up. "I bet he was well pleased to hear that."

"Well, not running it, exactly. But I'm supposed to be filling her in on everything that happens. And she made a few suggestions as to how he should be handling things." He held up his hand. "And this is strictly between you and me. She made it clear that she doesn't want you to know."

"What?"

"She said that only Hargrove and I were to know what's going on. Hargrove briefs me and I pass the intel on to her."

"So why are you telling me if she specifically told you not to?"

Shepherd grinned. "Because she was playing silly buggers. She said that she'd rather you didn't know, which as far as I'm concerned isn't a direct order. If she ever finds out we had this conversation I'll just say that I misunderstood. Besides, what's she going to do, sack me?"

"Doubtful," said Sharpe. "Who else is going to get her tea whenever she wants it?"

"Screw you," said Shepherd. "I wanted to fill you in because you need to know that anything you come up with from now on is going to be fed straight to Five."

"I appreciate the heads-up," said Sharpe. He sipped his lager. "So you're now her man on the inside?"

Shepherd nodded. "I can't believe she did that to me, Razor. How's Hargrove going to trust me now? Why should he trust me? He knows that I'm going to be telling Button about every move he makes. And if he makes a mistake I'll be the one dropping him in it."

"He won't be making any mistakes," said Sharpe. "He knows what he's doing."

"That's not the point," said Shepherd. "The point is that at one fell swoop she's pretty much trashed my relationship with Hargrove. He says it's okay, but he would say that."

Sharpe chuckled. "Maybe that's what she wanted."

"What?"

"Maybe she got the hump because Hargrove wanted you on his team. He goes above her head to get you seconded to COG; she thinks that he's trying to steal you back so she plays her own little game to make Hargrove think that you're now her puppy dog."

"Piss off, Razor."

"Hey, don't shoot the messenger," said Sharpe. "Button's as smart as they come, you know that. She's going to protect her turf."

"I'm not her turf," said Shepherd.

"Yeah, you're more her bitch than her turf."

"Now you're really starting to piss me off."

"You work for her. You moved with her from SOCA to Five; you're part of her team. She sees Hargrove as a threat and Charlotte Button isn't a woman you can threaten."

"Hell's bells, Razor. Hargrove wanted me because he knows I can do the arms-dealer thing. He knows I've no interest in moving back to the Met."

"Yeah, well, maybe he's sort of hoping that you might."

Shepherd's eyes narrowed. "Did he say something?"

Sharpe shook his head. "Not in so many words."

"What words, then? Come on, Razor, spit it out."

Sharpe sipped his lager slowly, then put his glass down before answering. "Okay, he said it would be good to get the old team back together. He reckons that the pendulum is going to start swinging the other way and that we're going to be given the go-ahead to start taking down the big guys."

"So what are you saying? He asked for me so that he could persuade me to leave Five?"

"There you go, putting words into my mouth. No, of course he didn't come straight out and say that. But he definitely wanted you on this operation."

Shepherd sighed. "Why are people so bloody devious?" he muttered. "Aren't we supposed to be on the same side?"

"If Hargrove does want you in COG he can't come out and ask you, can he?"

"Why not?"

"Because then Button will accuse him of poaching her staff. He's got to wait for you to ask him and this could be a way of him testing the water." He sipped his lager. "Have you thought about it? Coming back to the cops?"

Shepherd snorted dismissively. "And know that every move I made was being second-guessed by box-tickers and accountants? And everything I did could be splashed across the newspapers at any point? I don't know why anyone would be a cop these days. Wouldn't want to be in SOCA again either."

"Like I said, Hargrove says it's going to change."

"Yeah, well, it's not up to him, is it? But it's not just the job, it's the attitude. If a cop makes a mistake he gets hung out to dry. If you're in CO19 and you fire your weapon you're on automatic suspension until the shooting is investigated. And effectively you're guilty until proven innocent. You make a decision in the heat of the moment because you think it's the right thing to do, but you're then judged by pricks who never leave their offices unless it's to get into the back of a chauffeur-driven car. Five is totally different, Razor. Everything I do is covered by the Official Secrets Act. No newspaper is going to splash my picture across the front page; no MP is going to call for my head because he wants to appease his constituents. Five looks after its own."

"Hargrove always had our backs," said Sharpe.

Shepherd nodded. "Yeah, he's old school. But he's just one brick in the wall. Say this operation goes tits up. Say we end up putting a round in one of those guys. Do you think Hargrove will be able to protect us?"

"You're not planning on shooting anybody, are you?" asked Sharpe. He grinned slyly.

"Just you, you soft bastard."

"You think you could take me?"

"One-handed," said Shepherd.

Shepherd was making himself a coffee when his John Whitehill phone rang. He had spent three hours drinking with Sharpe and while he was far from drunk he was still a little light-headed. It was Chaudhry.

"Hey, Raj, how're things?" he said, speaking slightly slower than usual to make sure that he didn't slur his words.

"I've something to tell you," said Chaudhry.

"Go ahead, I'm all ears," said Shepherd, pouring milk into his coffee.

"Can we meet?"

"Tonight?"

"I don't want to forget anything and I don't want to write it down," said Chaudhry. "My memory's not as good as yours."

"You're a medical student. You have to memorise millions of facts," said Shepherd.

"Which is why there's no room for anything else," said Chaudhry. "Look, I just met with Khalid. There's some stuff you need to know."

"I can see you, but I can't drive," said Shepherd.

"I'll come to you. I can see you on the Heath."

"Two guys on Hampstead Heath at night? Not sure that's a good idea."

Chaudhry laughed. "Don't worry, John, you're not my type. Look, I can cycle over and I'll be careful. No one's going to follow me on the bike."

Shepherd took a sip of his coffee. "Okay, come to the east side of the Heath. There's a petanque pitch there."

"A what?"

"That game where you toss balls. *Boules*, the French call it. It's near the bandstand, fairly close to the road. I'll get there first. If everything's okay I'll be wearing a baseball cap. If I'm not wearing a cap don't come near me. Just go back home and wait for me to contact you."

220

"You think someone might be following you?"

"No, but it's always a good idea to have a fallback position."

Shepherd ended the call. He finished his coffee, picked up his coat and a baseball cap off a hook by the door, and headed out.

He spent fifteen minutes strolling around the Heath making sure that he wasn't being followed. He did get two very nice smiles, one from a sixty-year-old man in a cashmere coat and a trilby, another from a teenager in a black leather motorcycle jacket.

He did a quick walk round the petanque pitch, then sat down on a bench and put on his cap. Chaudhry was on time, pushing his bicycle. He was wearing his duffel coat with the hood up. He leaned the bike against the bench and sat down.

"Are you okay, Raj?" asked Shepherd.

"I'm fine," said Chaudhry. He grinned at the baseball cap. "You really don't suit that," he said. He pulled his hood down. "You're about ten years too old for it."

Shepherd took it off. "Yeah, I was going to suggest holding a newspaper but as it's dark I thought that would just look plain silly. So what's up?"

Chaudhry folded his arms. "Khalid wanted me and Harvey to talk to a couple of young guys who are on their way to Pakistan. We had dinner."

"Nice," said Shepherd.

"They're off to a training camp next week. Not the one that we went to, a new one."

"Do you know where it is?"

"Closer to the border, he said. These guys are from the mosque. Khalid has recruited them the way he recruited me and Harvey. He did the same with us, introduced us to a couple of veterans before we went out to Pakistan. Now we're the veterans."

"That's how it works," said Shepherd. "Making you all feel part of the process, you against the world. It binds you together."

"They're both students at South Bank University. Sociology, would you believe? One is Lateef Panhwar. The other is his pal, Faisal. Didn't get his surname. They're both from Derby, up north. And they're flying out next Wednesday on PIA."

"That's terrific, Raj. Thanks."

"What will you do?"

"We'll see if anything's known about them. Then we'll arrange to have them followed in Pakistan, and hopefully nail down the location of the training camp."

"They're nutters, John. Serious nutters. They were talking about shooting down planes at Heathrow."

"Now that they're on our radar we'll be on their case twenty-four seven," said Shepherd.

"So I did good?"

"You did great, Raj. Really."

"What they're doing is so wrong," said Chaudhry. "People like Khalid, they're evil. They're twisting the Koran to make it sound like we should be killing non-believers and that our religion has to go into battle against all others. You know what jihad means, right?"

"Struggle," said Shepherd.

"Exactly. Struggle. Yet most of the younger brothers seem to think that it means a crusade. That we have to somehow destroy all other religions. But that's not what the Koran says."

"I think the majority of Muslims understand, don't they?"

"The older generation, maybe. But the young ones?" Chaudhry shook his head. "I'm not so sure. The Americans did themselves no favours when they invaded Afghanistan and Iraq. And whoever thought that Guantanamo Bay was a good idea should be taken out and shot. It produced a whole generation of Muslims who really do believe that America is evil."

"No argument here," said Shepherd. "But you've got to remember that Afghanistan and Iraq were a reaction to Nine-Eleven."

"And Nine-Eleven was a reaction to American support for Israel, everyone forgets that," said Chaudhry. He grimaced as if he had a bad taste in his mouth. "Bloody hell, now I sound like I'm defending al-Qaeda," he said. "That's not what I meant at all."

"Understanding someone's motivation doesn't mean that you agree with them," said Shepherd. "But your train of logic is spot on. Al-Qaeda resented what Israel was doing in the Middle East and blamed America for supporting them; al-Qaeda carried out the Nine-Eleven attacks; America retaliated by invading Afghanistan and Iraq. Muslims around the world saw that as an attack on their religion and that initiated all the terrorist attacks we've seen since — in Madrid, in London, in Algiers, in Yemen."

"And what the Americans did to Bin Laden is going to make it worse, right? It makes him the ultimate martyr."

"I would think so," said Shepherd. "Killing him was never going to stop al-Qaeda. It's not like a snake that you can kill by chopping off the head. It's more like a cancer where the more you attack the tumour, the more cancerous cells you release."

"So why don't the people at the top realise that?" asked Chaudhry. "If it's that obvious to you and me, why did Bush invade Iraq? Iraq, which wasn't even an al-Qaeda stronghold. In fact Saddam hated al-Qaeda more than the West did."

Shepherd shook his head. "I'm nothing to do with policy," he said. "I'm an Indian surrounded by chiefs." He smiled. "No offence."

Chaudhry wagged a finger at him. "You don't want to be confusing a Pakistani with an Indian," he said. "Even in jest."

"Not good?"

Chaudhry grinned. "Let's just say it could end in tears. Me, I'm a Brit first and a Pakistani second, so it's water off a duck's back. But even my dad gets upset if he's mistaken for an Indian, and he's as laid back as they come."

"I'll remember that."

Chaudhry sighed. "Anyway, the answer to my question — why did the US invade Iraq? — you know why, right? Bush Senior couldn't take Saddam down so his son did, the first chance he got. It was nothing to do with al-Qaeda and nothing to do with terrorism. And now look at the state the world's in." He sighed again. "We're screwed, aren't we? The West? No matter how this works out."

"What do you mean?" asked Shepherd.

"We stop Khalid and we stop Lateef and Faisal. We arrest everyone and they all go to prison. But there'll be others to take their place, won't there? They're already being recruited, right now. Kids and teenagers are being groomed to be the new shahid. Who's going to stop them?"

"Hopefully there'll be someone like you who'll do the right thing," said Shepherd.

Chaudhry sneered. "That's not much of a plan, is it?"

"Fair point," said Shepherd. "But that's the way it is, unfortunately. Back in 1984, before you were born, the IRA almost killed Margaret Thatcher, the prime minister. They blew up the hotel she was staying in, along with half her cabinet. She was pulled from the wreckage and the IRA released a statement saying that she was lucky and that she would have to continue to be lucky. But the IRA had to be lucky only once. That's the situation we're in now. We need to be lucky all the time."

"And like I said, that's not much of a plan."

"The security services are on full alert and they will be for the foreseeable future," said Shepherd. "There's a lot of surveillance going on; internet chatter and emails are monitored; GCHQ eavesdrop on phone calls. We've got CCTV, we've got all sorts of technological advantages that the terrorists don't have, and we've got right on our side."

"That gives you an advantage, does it? Having right on your side?"

"It means that there will always be people like you who want to do the right thing, Raj. No one is totally alone. Everyone has friends, relatives, workmates, neighbours. Providing there are people who are prepared to do the right thing, the terrorists will always be identified, sooner or later."

Two middle-aged women in matching raincoats, one with a spaniel, the other with a red setter, walked by. The woman with the spaniel glared at Shepherd with open hostility. He smiled at her and winked, and she wrinkled her nose in disgust and tugged hard at her dog's lead.

"I hope you're right," said Chaudhry.

"And what about you, Raj? After all this is over. What do you plan to do?"

Chaudhry frowned. "What do you mean?"

"MI5 can use guys like you."

"Brown-skinned Muslims, you mean?"

"I meant intelligent, self-motivated individuals who want the best for our country. You could go far, really. And not because of your ethnicity."

"My dad would . . ." Chaudhry laughed. "Actually, I don't know what my dad would say. But my mum, she'd freak out. She always wanted my brother to be a doctor and she went apeshit when he announced that he wanted to be an architect. The only thing that

226

calmed her down was me saying that I wanted to study medicine. If I were to change my mind now . . ."

"I think you'll make a great doctor," said Shepherd.

"I bet you say that to all your . . ." Chaudhry smiled. "What are we to you, John? How do you describe us?"

"You're an agent," said Shepherd.

"I thought you were the agent."

Shepherd shook his head. "I'm an officer. An MI5 officer. You're an agent. Or an asset."

"An asset? That's good to know." He smiled thinly. "I just wish this was over, John."

"I know. It will be soon."

"I just keep thinking that Khalid knows what we're doing."

"He doesn't."

"He's under surveillance, right?"

Shepherd nodded.

"Would he have been followed tonight? To the restaurant?"

"I would think so."

"I didn't see anyone," said Chaudhry.

"You wouldn't. The people we use are real professionals. And if we even suspected that he knew you were talking to us we'd pull you out immediately. But that's not on the cards, Raj. The fact that he wanted you to meet Lateef and Faisal shows that he trusts you. You're his golden boys."

Chaudhry shrugged. "I guess so."

"There's no guessing about it. He recruited you, he sent you to Pakistan for training, now he's getting ready for the big one. He's never going to suspect you because you're on the inside; he'll see any threat coming from the outside. That's why you and Malik are so important in all this. You're on the inside."

"You've been in my position before, right?"

"Lots of times."

"It's scary, isn't it? Lying all the time?"

Shepherd smiled. "It can be. But you get used to it."

"I don't want to get used to it," said Chaudhry. "I just want it to be over."

Shepherd opened his eyes and was disorientated for a few seconds until he remembered he was in his bedroom in Hereford. He'd driven up the previous morning, then taken Katra to watch Liam play rugby. Liam's team had won, and afterwards they'd taken him and half a dozen of his teammates for pizza. Shepherd shaved and showered and dressed in a polo shirt and black jeans before heading down to the kitchen. Katra was already up and by the time he'd picked up the newspaper from the hallway she had a cup of coffee ready for him.

"Breakfast?" she asked. She was wearing a baggy sweatshirt over cargo pants and had tied her brown hair back with a scrunchy.

"Egg and bacon would be great, Katra. I've got a busy day."

"Working on a Sunday?" she said, taking a frying pan from a cupboard.

"No rest for the wicked."

"Can I ask you something?" she said as she began to cook his breakfast.

"Of course," said Shepherd.

Katra had worked as his au pair for more than four years and he thought of her more as family than as an employee. Over the years she had lost most of her Slovenian accent though her love of soap operas meant that her pronunciation was a blend of north of England and the East End of London, with the occasional Australian twang thrown in for good measure.

"Now Liam's at boarding school and you're in London so often, I was just wondering if you really still needed me."

"Of course we need you," said Shepherd. "Liam's here between terms and at most half-terms too. And the house still needs looking after." He grinned. "Besides, who would cook breakfast for me? And I really don't want to be ironing my own shirts."

She laughed. "I like ironing," she said.

"Then you're not going anywhere. Plus, I don't know how long I'll be in London. My situation can change at short notice." He put down his newspaper. "Everything's okay, right? You are happy here?"

Katra turned round to look at him, the spatula in her hand. "Of course!" she said. "I have been happy ever since I started working for you."

"That's fine. You're happy, we're happy, everyone's happy."

"But what if you get married?"

Shepherd laughed. "Trust me, Katra, marriage isn't on the cards, not at the moment. And if I do meet someone it'll just mean twice as much ironing."

Katra nodded, reassured, and went back to cooking his breakfast.

An hour later and Shepherd was pulling up in front of the Stirling Lines barracks at RAF Credenhill, home to the SAS. He was driving an MI5 Range Rover that had been registered in the name of his Garry Edwards legend. He wound down his window. "Dan Shepherd, here to see Major Gannon," he told a young trooper.

The trooper consulted a list on a clipboard and nodded. "Can you show me photo ID, please, sir?" Shepherd took out his wallet and showed him his driving licence. The trooper looked at it carefully, handed it back and then wrote down the registration number of the car. "If you could park by the shooting range, Major Gannon is expecting you," he said, raising a boom barrier so that Shepherd could drive through.

The Major, dressed in a black Adidas tracksuit, was waiting for him in front of the shooting range. He grinned as Shepherd got out of the car. "Traded in the BMW?" he asked.

"Nah, this is a pool car. More in keeping with what an arms dealer would drive, apparently." Shepherd walked round to the rear and opened the tailgate.

"The guns are inside," said the Major, nodding at the double doors that led to the range. "I've got you three Yugos, but there're more if you need them. I thought there were six but three have been signed out."

"Three'll be fine," said Shepherd. He followed the Major through the doors into the range. He wrinkled his nose at the acrid smell of cordite.

At the far end of the range was a line of terrorist targets in front of a wall of sandbags. There was a table close to the entrance in front of a rack of ear protectors, and on the table was a wooden crate and a metal ammunition case.

"So I've been hearing stories about you from a couple of Navy Seals we've had embedded with us for a few weeks."

"Just make sure they're careful where they're pointing their weapons," said Shepherd.

"They do have a reputation for friendly fire, don't they?" agreed the Major. "Friendly fire ranks right up there with military intelligence in the tautology hit parade, doesn't it?"

"You know there are two thousand active Navy Seals? Hardly special forces, is it? I mean, how special can they be to let that many in?"

The Major grinned. "They're not exactly fans of you, either."

Shepherd's eyes narrowed. "They were telling tales out of school, were they?"

"What happens in Stirling Lines, stays in Stirling Lines," said the Major. "They were among friends; plus, they can't hold their liquor. Not like our lads."

"And what did they say?"

"Just that you were on the Bin Laden operation. Not that they knew who you were, not by name. Just that there was a Brit there and he was none too happy about the way it went down."

"They must have been well pissed if they talked to you about the Pakistan operation."

"What can I say? Part of the Sass initiation is to have your drinks spiked, you know that."

"Yeah, well, careless talk costs lives." He smiled ruefully. "I did give them a piece of my mind, that's true. No one told me that we were going out there to kill him. And I certainly wasn't there to shoot women and kids."

"It was messy?"

"It was a cock-up from start to finish," said Shepherd. "One of the choppers crashed. You know why?"

The Major shook his head. "But they do have a habit of crashing their choppers. The Iranian hostages. Somalia. All over Iraq and Afghanistan."

"This wasn't just pilot error, this was plain bloody incompetence. The compound was surrounded by a concrete wall, eighteen feet high. We were supposed to land inside the wall and that's the way they'd rehearsed it. For weeks. They'd built a mock-up of the compound in Bagram Air Base in Afghanistan. The plan was to fly over the compound and drop down on to the building. They'd rehearsed it a hundred times. But they screwed up. For the rehearsals they'd replaced the wall with a wire fence. I guess some prick decided that so long as it was the right size, all well and good. Except, of course, the downdraught could escape through the wire fence when they practised the manoeuvre. But as soon as we started descending towards the walls the downdraught blew straight back up and the pilot lost control. So they crashed because some idiot couldn't be bothered to build a wall."

The Major nodded. "Yeah, for the want of a nail. That's the big problem with the Yanks: everything's done for the lowest price. I wouldn't use an American weapon if you paid me."

"Yeah, well, let's make sure that this operation goes as it should."

"No problem," said the Major." He patted the crate. "I've put six clips in there, fully loaded."

"Excellent," said Shepherd. "And the suppressors?"

The Major nodded at a black holdall. "In there too. Do you want to check them?"

"No need," said Shepherd. "When do you need them back?"

"Whenever," said the Major. "They're off the books and the serial numbers won't cause us any trouble." He opened the ammunition box. It was filled with large polystyrene beads and the Major shoved in his hand and pulled out a spherical grenade. He brushed off a few stray beads and then gave it to Shepherd. It was painted a deep green with a thin yellow band across the top just below where the safety clip and fly-off lever were attached to the casing. Stencilled on the side were the yellow letters spelling out GREN HAND HE L109A1 and a lot number.

"You ever thrown one?" asked the Major.

Shepherd shook his head. "They were still using the L2A2 in my day."

"This is pretty much the same," said the Major. "Based on the Swiss HG85 but the boffins played around with the design so that the fragments can penetrate the latest body armour."

"Nice," said Shepherd.

"Yeah, funny the way that so much money is put into coming up with better ways of killing people," said the Major. "You'd think a grenade would just be a grenade, but someone somewhere thought it worth spending a few million quid on coming up with a better one." He took it back from Shepherd. "Bog-standard percussion fuse with a delay of three to four seconds. Effective killing radius is sixty feet unprotected, fifteen feet if you're wearing body armour and a Kevlar helmet, but frankly there wouldn't be much left of your arms and legs. Explosion produces about eighteen hundred fragments, any one of which could ruin your day."

"And you don't want it back?"

The Major put it back into the box. "It's non-traceable," he said. "The lot number won't lead anywhere, so if you do get caught with it just say you found it."

Shepherd laughed. "Yeah, that should do it."

"And you've no idea what these clowns want with grenades?"

"We've just got a shopping list, that's all. They're not very chatty about their motives but they're talking about forty Yugos and a stack of ammunition. Charlie reckons that they're tied in with the Norwegian mass murderer."

"White supremacists, then?"

"They didn't come over at all Ku Klux Klan when we met them," said Shepherd. "But they might have been on their best behaviour."

"So what do you think? They're going to start shooting blacks and Asians?"

"The Norwegian didn't, did he?" said Shepherd. "Most of his victims were white kids. He did what he did to draw attention to his manifesto. The only thing that made them targets was that they were at a left-wing camp. So, if anything, his target was political rather than racial."

"With any luck they'll head for Westminster and get all Guy Fawkes on the Houses of Parliament," said the Major.

"Chance'd be a fine thing," said Shepherd. "But that's not how it works with terrorists, is it? They always choose the weakest targets. And the guys we're dealing with are from the Midlands; there's no evidence they'll be heading down to London."

"So what's Charlie's plan? Nip them in the bud or let them run?"

"She's not letting me in on the bigger picture," said Shepherd. "She pinched the case from the Brummie cops, that much I do know."

"You think she's after the glory?"

"I don't know," said Shepherd. "But at the moment she's got me in the middle playing both ends. I'm reporting to Sam Hargrove, who reports to the top brass in Birmingham, then I get debriefed by Charlie. The shit's going to hit the fan if Charlie moves in over the heads of the cops."

"Hopefully none of the shit's going to head your way."

Shepherd shrugged. "I'm hoping that Sam will take the flak," he said.

"He's the guy you worked for when you were a cop, right?"

"Yeah, he's a straight shooter. One of the best. So I don't see that he'll hang me out to dry. But the Brummie cops are going to be spitting feathers when they find out that all the work they've done has been pinched by Five."

"It's a mucky business at best, isn't it?" said the Major. "It's so much more black and white in the military. Both sides wear uniforms and carry weapons and the best side wins."

"And the losers end up dead," said Shepherd. "Unlike the world of terrorism, where the losers end up as MPs."

The Major laughed. "Yeah, funny how the world changes," he said. "There's a whole generation already who've no real idea what a threat the IRA were. You ask most teenagers about the Brighton bombing and they wouldn't have a clue what you were talking about. But say what you want about the IRA, at least you knew what they wanted: the Brits out and a united Ireland. You might not agree with their methods, but you could understand what they wanted and why they did what they did."

"They murdered plenty of civilians," said Shepherd sourly.

The Major held up his hands. "Hey, you won't ever hear me defending the IRA," he said. "They killed enough of my friends over the years. What I'm saying is that at least you knew what was driving them. But this new lot of terrorists? Who the hell knows what their motivation is?"

"A life in paradise with seventy-two coal-eyed virgins if they kill the infidel," said Shepherd.

"Yeah, but they can't really believe that, can they?" said the Major. "Even if you believe in God you can't possibly believe that God, any god, would want to see innocents maimed and killed. Those guys who crashed the planes into the Twin Towers — what did they hope to achieve? And the British Muslims who blew up the tube. Does anyone know what they wanted?" He shook his head sorrowfully. "The world's going crazy, Spider. And an old fart like me just can't make any sense of it any more."

Spider laughed. "You've a fair few years left in you yet, boss," he said. "The mistake you're making is assuming that they think the way that we do. They don't. They're brainwashed, most of them. They're led into it, trained for it, then, if need be, they're pushed."

"But what are they trying to achieve? Death to all Christians? Because that's not going to happen. The Islamification of Europe? That's not going to happen either. And it's not about Iraq or Afghanistan because that happened long after the attack on the Twin Towers. And most of the troops have already been pulled out. There doesn't seem to be any objective; and if there's no objective, if it's just a religious war, then it's never going to end, is it?"

"It's all becoming a bit *Alice in Wonderland*," said Shepherd. "I can't believe that the London bombers really believed that their actions would change anything. Or that they were going straight to heaven. There's something else at work. Something self-destructive. Self-hatred, maybe, which spills over to hatred of the world. If you really want to worry about something, Major, think about what'll happen if they ever get a nuclear weapon. You know that the IRA would never have even contemplated using a nuclear bomb, but these morons will. That's what I find so scary." He laughed harshly. "I've got my psychological evaluation coming up so I'll see if the MI5 shrink has any ideas on what it all means." He patted the crate. "I'll get the guns back to you tonight."

"Good man," said the Major. "Just be careful, okay?"

"With the guns?"

The Major shook his head. "With the morons you'll be giving the guns to," he said. "Guns and civilians are always bad news."

Shepherd drove from the barracks to Hereford station and waited in the car for twenty minutes until the train from London pulled in. He waited until he saw Jimmy Sharpe emerge from the building before getting out.

Sharpe was dressed casually in a dark-green waterproof Barbour jacket and dark-brown corduroy trousers. He was holding a Marks & Spencer carrier bag. "Thought I'd bring some sandwiches," he said, holding up the bag.

"I can see you dressed for the country," said Shepherd. "What's with the Barbour?"

"Forecast said it might rain. And I thought this was how you country folk dressed for hunting, shooting and fishing, and we're going shooting, right?" Shepherd climbed into the Range Rover and started the engine. Sharpe got into the passenger seat. "Gear's good?" he asked as he tossed his carrier bag of sandwiches on to the back seat.

"Just what we needed," said Shepherd.

"Good to have mates in low places," said Sharpe, settling into his seat. He looked at his watch. "We got time for a pint, do you think?"

"I'm driving is what I think, Razor."

"Yeah, but I'm not."

"We can stop for a coffee on the way."

"In a pub?"

Shepherd smiled and shook his head. "You're incorrigible," he said.

Sharpe grinned with no trace of embarrassment. "It fits in with my legend. I'm an incorrigible arms dealer who takes a drink now and again." He rubbed his chin. "Do you think Hargrove will reimburse me for a first-class ticket?"

"From where?"

"I was in London. The train was packed and the chavs in standard class were doing my head in. So I sat in first class. But when I showed the conductor guy my warrant card he said he didn't give a toss who I worked for and made me pay the difference."

"Ah yes, there isn't the respect there used to be," said Shepherd, his voice loaded with sarcasm.

"What do you guys show? You know, when you want to identify yourself?"

Shepherd laughed. "The whole point of being in MI5 is that we don't identify ourselves."

"I thought it was MI6 that was the Secret Intelligence Service?"

"Yeah, well, Five is secretive too. It's pretty much like *Fight Club*. The first rule is that we don't talk about it. And we certainly don't flash our ID cards to get free rides on public transport."

"So how can you prove you're a spook?"

"What do you mean?"

"Say you're caught doing something you shouldn't and you get pulled by the cops. What do you use as a get-out-of-jail-free card?"

Shepherd chuckled. "First of all, I wouldn't get myself into a situation where the cops would be involved. But if something went wrong, and by some chance it did happen, then I'd stick to whatever cover story I had."

"And if they didn't believe you and you were arrested? They'd fingerprint and DNA you."

"Both of which would come back as unknown. But say they did keep me banged up, I'd be allowed my phone call and I'd call it in."

"Button, yeah?"

Shepherd shook his head. "There's a hotline we call that's answered by a duty officer. We explain the problem and the duty officer takes care of it. If it's the cops then it goes to the commissioner's office and he sorts it out."

"So you could get away with murder, could you?"

"Bloody hell, Razor, I'm not James Bond and there's no bloody licence to kill. And it's all hypothetical anyway. It's not as if I go around breaking the law."

Sharpe laughed and jerked his thumb at the boxes in the back of the Range Rover. "What's that back there? Chopped liver?"

Shepherd nodded. "Fair point. But if we do get pulled over by the traffic cops then I assume you'll flash them your warrant card before they start rooting around in the back."

"Yeah, that's one of the benefits of being back with the Met," said Sharpe. "At least everyone knows what a warrant card is. That SOCA ID was bloody useless." He folded his arms. "So where are we doing the show?"

"Out in the Brecon Beacons," said Shepherd. He tapped the TomTom unit on his dashboard. "Got the location programmed in already. There's a place we can drive off the road and not be seen. The nearest house is a mile away and the SAS sometimes do live-fire exercises out there so the locals are used to gunfire."

"And no back-up? That's a worry."

"Not a problem. We're not carrying cash so no one's going to get heavy for three guns and a hand grenade. Plus, you can take care of yourself, can't you? What do they call it? The Gorbals Kiss?"

Sharpe chuckled. "I'd never headbutt anybody, Spider. You know that."

"Anyway, Kettering and Thompson didn't look the heavy sort to me. Cerebral rather than physical. We'll be okay."

"And has Hargrove said anything about when we move in?"

"I know as much as you do," said Shepherd.

Sharpe slowly turned his head, a sly grin on his face. "Are you sure about that?"

"What, you think I've got some sort of inside track?"

"Heaven forbid," said Sharpe.

"What's wrong?"

"Nothing's wrong," Sharpe shrugged. "I'm just starting to feel like a third wheel on this job, that's all. Hargrove's gone very quiet ever since you came on hoard. He doesn't seem to be talking to me as much as he used to. Not just about this operation, either."

"You're paranoid," said Shepherd.

"Yeah? Well, just because I'm paranoid doesn't mean they're not out to get me."

"Razor, Hargrove has been talking to me because I've got access to the Sass. It's the only way we can get the weapons we need. Can you imagine the paperwork that we'd need to get assault rifles through the Met?"

"I guess," said Sharpe. He looked at his watch again. "How long before we're there?"

"Two hours, maybe."

"I'll catch forty winks," he said and settled back in his seat.

"I'll miss your sparkling conversation," said Shepherd.

Shepherd kept the Range Rover at just below the speed limit on the drive from Hereford to the Welsh border and through the national park to the town of Brecon. He stopped at a small pub on the outskirts, woke

Sharpe, and drank a cup of strong coffee while Sharpe drank a pint of lager. They sat at a table close to a walk-in stone fireplace and Shepherd waited until the barmaid was out of earshot before taking out a pay-as-you-go mobile and dialling Kettering's number. "We're about half an hour away," said Shepherd. "What about you?"

"Parked up already at the lay-by, like you said," said Kettering. "Traffic was light and we got here early. You've got the stuff?"

"Of course I've got the stuff. I wouldn't have driven all the way to sheep-shagging country for nothing, would I? We'll see you there." He ended the call and nodded at Sharpe. "All good. They're in the lay-by. We can let them wait a bit. Show them who's boss."

"Did you just say sheep-shagging? Doesn't Five have diversity-awareness courses?"

"I'm in character," said Shepherd. He finished his coffee and nodded at Sharpe's half-empty glass. "I'm having another coffee while you finish that."

Shepherd went over to the bar, ordered a second cup of coffee and then carried it back to the table.

"What do you think about Kettering and Thompson?" Sharpe asked as Shepherd sat down.

"In what way?"

"They're not Walter Mitty characters, are they? They're not fantasists."

"Fantasists don't normally buy dozens of automatic weapons," said Shepherd. "They might put photos of themselves holding replicas on Facebook but they don't usually follow through."

"So what's their game?" asked Sharpe. "What do you think they've got planned?"

"Who knows?"

"All that crap about defending themselves if there's another riot is crap. Grenades aren't defensive, and Kalashnikovs are overkill," said Sharpe. He took a long pull on his pint before continuing. "It's not about self-defence. They're planning something, something that's going to leave a lot of people dead."

"Maybe," said Shepherd. "But it's not going to get to that stage. They'll be busted long before they get a chance to use the guns."

"I hope so," said Sharpe. "But we could bust them today if we wanted. Conspiracy to buy automatic weapons. That'd get them ten years."

"Except they're not paying us today, are they? We need them to hand over the cash. What's bugging you? We've done this before. We do a show and tell, we arrange a handover and we hoover them up."

Sharpe shrugged. "This one just feels different, that's why. Kettering and Thompson aren't regular crims. They're not blaggers, they're not drug dealers, but they want enough guns to supply a small army. Don't you want to know why?"

"Not really," said Shepherd. "In the grand scheme of things the reason doesn't matter. They buy the guns, they go to jail and they don't pass go or collect two hundred pounds. And we move on."

"Yeah, maybe I'm over-thinking it." Sharpe drained his glass and patted his expanding waistline. "Okay, once more into the valley of death."

"There's confidence for you," said Shepherd. He stood up and Sharpe followed him out to the Range Rover.

After driving for fifteen minutes they arrived at the lay-by where Kettering had parked. There were four men sitting in Kettering's Jaguar. Shepherd flashed his lights and slowed down as he drove by. Kettering flashed back, pulled into the road and followed them.

It took Shepherd another ten minutes to drive to the destination on the TomTom. There was a fence running to their left with a barred gate leading to a track that wound round a gently sloping hill. Sharpe got out and opened the gate, waited for Shepherd and Kettering to drive through and closed it. Ahead of them, about a hundred feet or so in the air, a hawk was flying into the wind, its wings fluttering as it held its position over the ground. As Sharpe got back into the car the hawk plummeted down, its wings tucked in close to its body, and grabbed a small rodent in its claws.

Shepherd drove around the hill. The track petered out but the four-wheel drive kept the Range Rover moving easily across the field. The Jaguar had more trouble and slowed to a crawl.

Shepherd brought the Range Rover to a stop and climbed out. Sharpe laughed when he saw how much trouble Kettering was having driving over the rough ground. "He's not going to be happy about this," he said. "It'll play havoc with his suspension."

The Jaguar, its sides now splattered with mud, finally reached the Range Rover. It parked and four men got out. Kettering and Thompson were both wearing leather bomber jackets and jeans and had scarves round their necks. Kettering waved. "All good, Garry?"

"No problems," said Shepherd.

Kettering nodded at the two men who had been in the back of the Jaguar. "Friends of ours," he said. "Roger and Sean." The two men shook hands with Shepherd and Sharpe. Sean was broad-shouldered, with a military haircut and a Northern Irish accent that suggested Londonderry rather than Belfast. Shepherd had seen Roger McLean's photograph in Button's office — he was the right-wing activist who had met with the Norwegian mass murderer in 2002.

Sharpe walked over to the Jaguar. "Nice motor," he said.

"Yeah, can't beat a Jag," said Kettering.

"Be better with four-wheel drive, though," said Sharpe. He walked round the car, checked that there was no one hiding in the back, and nodded at Shepherd.

Thompson saw what he was doing and he grinned. "Don't trust us?" he said.

"Just don't want any surprises," said Sharpe.

"Better check the boot in case we've got a group of dwarves in there with shooters," said Kettering.

"We'll trust you," said Shepherd, opening the tailgate of the Range Rover. He used a screwdriver to lever off the top of the crate. Inside were three assault rifles, swathed in bubble wrap. He took one out and unwrapped it, then showed it to the four men. "You know much about guns?" he asked.

"A bit," said Kettering. He looked across at Thompson. "Handguns mainly, though." He nodded at Sean. "Sean here's the expert."

"Okay, well, this is a Zastava M70, manufactured in the former Yugoslavia. Barrel length 415 millimetres, gas-operated, air-cooled, 620 rounds a minute on fully automatic, muzzle velocity 720 metres per second with an effective range of 400 metres." He reached into the crate and pulled out a curved magazine. He held it up so that they could see it. "Thirty-round box magazine." He slotted in the magazine then chambered a round. "And there you are, good to go." He sighted down the gun at a rock in the distance. "Point and shoot. That's pretty much all there is to it."

"They're reliable, yeah?" said Thompson.

"Not much to go wrong with them," said Shepherd. "Trust me, it's a nice weapon. It's better than the crap the Chinese make and in my view it's more reliable than the Russian version. The one drawback, and it's a minor thing, is that you need to clean it thoroughly. If I were you I'd clean it every time you use it. The inside of the barrel isn't chromed so you have to stop rust setting in."

"Can you show us how to clean them?" Thompson asked Sean.

Sean nodded. "Sure. It's not difficult. But doing it will add years to its life."

"What happens if you don't clean it?" asked Kettering.

"It starts to rust and the inside gets pitted," said Sean. "That means there isn't such a tight fit for the round as it moves along the barrel so it doesn't go as straight. Take a new gun like this fresh out of the crate and at four hundred metres you should be able to put round after round in a target the size of a dinner plate. But if you don't clean it, after five hundred rounds or so you'd have trouble hitting a bus."

Shepherd and Sharpe nodded in agreement. Whoever Sean was, he knew his stuff.

"Got you," said Kettering. He held out his hands for the gun. Shepherd clicked the safety on and handed it to him.

Kettering smiled appreciatively as he held the gun. "And you're sure it's as good as the Kalashnikov?"

"It's better, I think. And I'm not just saying that because I'm bringing them in from Serbia. I could get the Russian version if I wanted. And I could get the Chinese version at a lower price." He gestured at the gun. "That's a good, reliable weapon. These are the fixed-stock versions but I can get you them with a folding stock."

"They'd be easier to hide, right?" said Thompson.

"Absolutely," said Shepherd. He unwrapped a second gun, slammed in a magazine and handed it to Thompson, after making sure that the safety was on. "With the folding stock you can hang them on a sling and hide them under a coat. Takes a second to snap the stock out."

Kettering nodded enthusiastically. "That sounds perfect," he said.

"How many are you going to be looking for?" asked Shepherd.

248

"Forty. Maybe more. It depends on your price."

Thompson was holding his gun awkwardly, as if he was scared that it was going to bite him. Shepherd smiled and pointed at the safety catch. "The safety has three positions," said Shepherd. "At the moment the safety is up, which means that the gun can't be fired. If you move it down one notch it's set for automatic firing which means it will keep firing so long as you keep the trigger pulled. You really don't want to be doing that because you'll empty the clip before you know it. Push the safety all the way down and you're in semi-automatic mode. That means one pull of the trigger fires one round."

"We can fire them, right?" said Kettering.

"That's why we're here," said Shepherd. He took a wooden target from the car. It was a wooden frame that folded down the middle. He assembled it, locked it into position and handed it to Sharpe. There was a cardboard tube next to the crate and Shepherd popped a plastic cap off one end and pulled out a roll of paper. It was a paper target that the SAS sometimes used, a cartoon of Bin Laden holding a Kalashnikov.

Kettering laughed when he saw the target. "I thought he was dead already."

"You believe that?" asked Thompson. "He was dead five years ago."

Kettering grinned at Shepherd. "Paul's a big conspiracy theorist."

"Bloody right I am," said Thompson. "You have to be blind not to see the way the world's going. Look, do you seriously think an old man sitting in a cave could have planned and carried out Nine-Eleven?"

"It's not something I've thought about," said Shepherd.

"How can you not?" said Thompson. "And how is it that, just as the Americans are pulling out of Iraq, they suddenly find out where he is? I mean, what are the odds?"

"Minuscule," said Sharpe. He flashed Shepherd a smile, clearly enjoying winding Thompson up.

"And then there's the whole dumping the body at sea. They go to all that trouble of finding him and then they go and drop him in the ocean first chance they get. That makes no sense at all. Unless it wasn't him they killed."

"What, you don't think it was him they shot?"

"Let me ask you this," said Thompson. "You know about Bin Laden, right? He had health problems. His kidneys. In fact he was in Dubai having treatment not long before the Nine-Eleven attacks. He had to have regular dialysis."

"Yeah, I heard that," said Sharpe.

"Now, did you see any of the photographs the Yanks released of the house where Bin Laden was staying in Pakistan? The house that he never left in how many years?"

"Yeah," said Sharpe. "They were all over the papers."

"What's your point?" asked Shepherd, who was rapidly tiring of the discussion.

"The point, Garry my old mate, is that in none of the pictures is there anything that looks remotely like dialysis equipment. So how does someone with kidney failure survive for years without an oil change? I had an uncle who died of kidney failure a few years back and he had to go in for dialysis three times a week, regular as clockwork." He tapped the side of his nose with his finger. "Trust me, that wasn't Bin Laden in that house."

"Are you done, mate?" asked Kettering.

"Check the internet," said Thompson. "Google it. It's all part of the global conspiracy."

"Is that why you want the guns?" asked Shepherd. "To fight back?"

"Enough, Paul," said Kettering, and this time there was a hard edge to his voice. "Let's get this done and we can get back in the warm."

Thompson looked away, avoiding Kettering's piercing stare. "Yeah, okay, it's getting cold, isn't it?" He flicked the safety down.

Shepherd reached over and pushed the barrel down so that it was pointing at the ground. "Not until I say so," said Shepherd. He flicked the safety back into the on position. "Okay, now out here in the open the sound of one of these guns firing will carry for five miles, maybe ten if the wind is blowing the right way. So I'm going to fit suppressors to cut down on the noise."

He unzipped a black holdall and took out a foot-long bulbous black metal tube and showed it to them. "This screws into the barrel and it reduces the noise by about half." He screwed the suppressor into the barrel of the gun that Kettering was holding.

"So it's a silencer?" said Kettering.

"We call them suppressors," said Shepherd. "It's only in the movies that they call them silencers. No gun can truly be silenced; you're always going to hear something."

He took a second suppressor from the holdall and attached it to Thompson's weapon.

"And they don't affect the accuracy?" asked Kettering.

"Not so you'd notice," said Shepherd. He looked at Sharpe. "Do you want to set up the target, yeah?"

"Okay, just make sure no one gets trigger happy while I'm doing it. How far?"

"A hundred metres should do it," said Shepherd.

Sean was looking at the suppressors and frowning. "Where did you get them from?" he asked.

"That's for me to know, mate," said Shepherd.

"That's pretty specialised kit."

"And we're pretty specialised suppliers," said Shepherd.

"You get them made here? Or overseas?"

"Sean, mate, that's need-to-know and you don't need to know."

Sharpe paced out a hundred steps and then stood the target up. He looked around, picked up a few large rocks and used them to weigh down the bottom of the target. He waved at Shepherd. "Okay!"

"Why don't you put an apple on your head and we'll do that William Tell thing?" shouted Shepherd.

"Yeah, and why don't I bend over and let you kiss my hairy Scottish arse?" shouted Sharpe as he walked back. "And tell them to keep those things pointing at the ground until I'm out of the way."

"Jeez, I shoot him in the leg once and trust just goes out of the window," said Shepherd.

"Are you serious?" asked Thompson.

"Of course he isn't," said Kettering.

"He has a point, though," said Shepherd. "Keep the safeties on, fingers out of the trigger guards and barrels down at the ground. We did have a prick down in London who let rip with a Mac-10 by mistake a few months back. Geordie guy. Could hardly understand a word he said but he looked like he knew about guns so we gave him a bit of leeway. Next thing we know he pulls the trigger on full automatic and twenty rounds go everywhere." He nodded at Sharpe. "Almost blew his nuts off."

"What about the Mac-10?" asked Kettering as he looked at the AK-47.

"Pray and spray," said Shepherd. "Very short barrel so the accuracy is shit. Gang bangers like them because they see them in the movies and because they're easy to hide. They use them a lot in drive-bys — they shove them through an open window and pull the trigger until the magazine's empty. But nine times out of ten you won't hit the target." He pointed at the AK-47. "That's a lot more accurate because you can put it to your shoulder and use the sights. If you need something a bit more compact you can get a folding stock. Of course, if you want Mac-10s I can get you Mac-10s. The customer's always right." He looked at Sean. "What do you think?"

Sean nodded in agreement. "Yeah, wouldn't touch a Mac-10 with a barge pole. The Yugo's way better."

Kettering laughed. "That's good to hear," he said. He turned to face the target. "So, safety off, right?"

"You got it," said Shepherd.

Kettering flicked the safety off, put the stock against his shoulder and looked through the sights.

"It's set for single fire," said Shepherd. "Don't want you to blow the target apart the first go."

Kettering aimed and pulled the trigger. There was a bang, muffled but loud, but the target seemed to be unscathed.

"You went high," said Shepherd. "Grip tighter with your left hand."

Kettering did as he was told and fired again. This time a small hole appeared dead centre of the chest.

"Nice," said Shepherd.

"Killed him stone dead," said Thompson.

"Not bad," agreed Sean, standing with his hands on his hips.

Kettering fired off the rest of the clip and most of them hit the target. The grouping wasn't impressive but Shepherd knew that the size of the AK-47's bullet meant that any shot to the chest at that range was pretty much guaranteed to be fatal.

When he'd finished, Shepherd checked that the weapon was safe before allowing Thompson to fire at the target. Thompson was far less proficient with the weapon and his first six shots all went wide.

"The bloody sights are off," said Thompson.

"Try sighting with your other eye," said Shepherd. "Generally one eye's better than the other. And just because you're right-handed doesn't mean you'll aim better with your right eye."

Thompson changed eyes and his next shot hit the target right between the eyes. Thompson whooped like an excited kid. "Now we're talking," he said, and he fired off another half-dozen shots; all but one went high.

"Squeeze the trigger, don't pull it," said Shepherd. "And you're anticipating the recoil."

"What does that mean?" asked Thompson, looking through the sights.

"You know it's going to kick so you pull against it but that just makes it worse. You need to be stable with a firm grip, and squeeze slowly."

"Okay, okay, I've got it," said Thompson and he fired off the rest of the clip. He got another shot into the head of the target, one to the chest and two to the groin. Shepherd realised it would take hours on the range to get the man anywhere near proficient with the weapon.

"How about letting Sean have a go?" asked Kettering.

"No problem," said Shepherd. He slotted in a fresh magazine and handed the weapon to Sean.

Sean brought the weapon up smoothly, sighted on the target and in the space of three seconds put six shots into the heart. He nodded appreciatively at Shepherd. "Nice," he said. He sighted again, took a couple of seconds to steady himself and put another six shots into the head of the target.

"Fucking show-off," said Roger. "Sign of a misspent youth, that is."

"Do you want a go?" asked Sean.

"I can't shoot for shit," said Roger. "I'm a lover, not a fighter."

They all laughed as Sean emptied the magazine into the target.

When he'd finished Shepherd took the weapon from him, pulled out the magazine, checked that the breech was clear and handed it to Sharpe, who put it back in the Range Rover.

"See, if you were firing Mac-10s you wouldn't get a single shot in the target from this range," Shepherd said to Kettering. "And they have a tendency to jam. It's horses for courses. But, like I said, the customer is always right."

"These suppressor things, how much are they?" asked Kettering.

"Negotiable," said Shepherd. "There isn't much call for them, frankly."

"What if we wanted one for each gun?"

"You want forty suppressors?" asked Sharpe.

"If the price is right, yeah," said Kettering.

Shepherd rubbed his chin. "That might take time," he said. "There's not a huge call for them so they're made to order. Usually a hundred."

"A hundred quid?" said Kettering.

"There's no production line and it's not as if they can be subcontracted out to China or India," said

Shepherd. "But if you order forty we can maybe do the lot for two grand. I'll have to check."

"Two grand is more like it," said Kettering. He looked at Sean. "What do you think?"

"It's specialist kit, no question about that," he said. "And it does the business. Cuts the noise right down."

"If you don't mind me asking, why do you need suppressors for all of them?" said Shepherd. He held out his hands and Kettering passed him the weapon.

Kettering shrugged as Shepherd pulled the magazine out and made the gun safe. "Just thought they'd be a good idea. Easier to . . ." He shrugged again.

"We just want them," said Thompson. "Not a problem, is it?"

Shepherd grinned and put the gun into the crate. "Nothing's a problem so long as you've got the readies."

"Can you deliver the suppressors when you deliver the guns?"

Shepherd looked across at Sharpe. "What do you think?"

Sharpe wrinkled his nose. "We might have to kick them up the arse, but yeah, we should be able to manage that."

Shepherd turned back to Kettering. "Seems like we've got a deal, right?"

"We're getting there," said Kettering. He looked around as if he was scared of being overheard, even though they were in the middle of nowhere. "What about the other things? The grenades?"

"Thought you'd never ask," said Shepherd. He nodded at Sharpe. "Grab the target and shove it in the car, yeah?"

"What did your last slave die of?" joked Sharpe, as he headed towards the target.

"Well, it wasn't overwork, I can tell you that," said Shepherd. He winked at Kettering. "You just can't get the staff these days." He took a grenade out of the ammunition box and showed it to Kettering. Kettering reached for it but Shepherd held up a warning hand. "No touching, mate," he said. "It's not a toy."

"I want to see it work," said Kettering.

Shepherd laughed. "They don't work," he said. "You pull the pin, you throw them and they go bang."

"Then I want to see this one go bang," said Kettering.

"Why?"

"Because I want to know that I'm buying the real thing."

"Oh, it's real," said Shepherd. "You pull the pin and release the lever and you've got a maximum of four seconds, which means you really want to be throwing it on a count of three."

"So let's do it," said Kettering.

"First of all, these make one hell of a bang," said Shepherd. "It'll be heard for miles. And second of all, it leaves shrapnel all over the place. It's not like picking up a few shell cases."

"What, you think someone might start looking around for evidence?"

"There'll be a hole about six feet wide and bits of metal for up to a hundred feet or so. I'm not saying you can't watch it go bang; what I'm saying is that as soon as it has, we're going to be wanting to get the hell out of Dodge."

"Not a problem," said Kettering. "I think we're pretty much done."

"Plus, you'll need to pay me two hundred quid."

"Two hundred?"

Shepherd held up the grenade. "These don't grow on trees. You break it, you pay for it. And once you pull the pin it'll be well and truly broken."

"You can add it to the bill, can't you?"

"Sure I can. But I really don't see the point. You can't check them all, can you?"

"The one will do," said Kettering. He held out his hand.

"You sure you want to do it?" said Shepherd. "The world looks an awful lot different when you're holding one of these things with the pin out."

"I'm a big boy," said Kettering. "What do I do?"

"The first thing you do is get the fuck away from us," said Sharpe, returning with the target under his arm. He threw it into the back of the Range Rover.

"He's not lying," said Shepherd. "Head away from us, well away from the cars. See over there where the ground slopes? Do it there. Pull the pin, then throw it as far as you can. Then you've got two choices. There isn't much cover out here so you can either run like fuck or hit the ground."

"Which is best?" asked Kettering.

Shepherd shrugged. "Six of one," he said.

"Are you serious?" asked Kettering. "You don't know the best way?"

"Truth be told, we don't get much call for grenades," said Shepherd. "You're lucky I had a contact who had this."

"But you can get more?" asked Kettering.

Shepherd exhaled through tight lips. "I'll be honest, it won't be easy. Grenades aren't like guns. Guns you can mess around with and nothing bad is going to happen. Even ammunition is inert unless you treat it really badly. But grenades you've got to treat with respect. Plus, you've got to know that they've been looked after. You can't mistreat them."

"Say I wanted a couple of dozen?"

"Bloody hell, mate, two dozen grenades? What the hell would you want with that many?"

Kettering laughed. "Just want to have them around for a rainy day. Sell me twenty-four for four grand."

Shepherd looked at Sharpe and Sharpe took the cue. "I guess we can do that," he said. "But transport's the thing. We'll have to talk to our guys."

"Looks like we've got a deal," said Shepherd. "I guess for four grand we can let you have this one for free."

"Is it made in Yugoslavia?" asked Kettering.

Shepherd shook his head. "Nope, but that's where we'll be getting them from. We know a supplier there. They're made by a Swiss company for the British but they sell them around the world. It's an L109A1 and the British Army have been using them since 2001. It's filled with RDX explosive and the steel shell does the damage. When it goes off it produces thousands of fragments that are designed to go through Kevlar body armour."

Kettering took a deep breath. "Okay, let's do it," he said.

Shepherd took Kettering's hand and showed him how to hold the grenade so that the lever was held in place. He pointed at the ring at the top of the lever. "When you're ready, pull out the pin. So long as you hold the lever in place, nothing has changed; you can stay like that for as long as you want. But as soon as you release that handle the grenade is live. A non-reversible chemical reaction starts that culminates in an explosion after three or four seconds. So here's the thing: once the handle is off there's nothing can stop it. There's no changing your mind."

"Understood."

"And don't freeze. It can be quite stressful and you might find your hand tightens up, so stay focused. Check the direction you're going to throw it, pull the pin, and throw. That counting to three is strictly for the movies. Pull, throw, count to three while you run and drop on three."

"And it can kill anything within a hundred feet, is that what you said?"

"I said the fragments will go that far, but they're only deadly within about sixty feet. Further than that and they're more like airgun pellets. They'll hurt but won't do much damage. The closer you are to the explosion, the more the damage. If it goes off while you're holding it there won't be much left of you, let's put it that way."

"Got you," said Kettering. He took another deep breath and nodded. "Okay." He laughed nervously. Beads of sweat had appeared on his forehead and Shepherd hoped that his hands weren't as sweaty because the last thing he wanted was a live grenade rolling on the ground.

"And as soon as it's gone off, we're in the cars and away," said Sharpe. "No hanging around." He slammed the Range Rover's tailgate shut.

"You'll call when you have a delivery date?" asked Kettering.

"Yeah, and we'll be dealing with you direct from now on," said Shepherd. "There's no need for Ian to be involved." Shepherd wanted Ray Fenby out of the loop so that there'd be less chance of Kettering and Thompson blaming him when the shit hit the fan. He pointed towards the slope. "Off you go, and whatever you do don't try to see it go off. If you can see it the shrapnel can rip through your eyes. Remember that."

"Good luck," said Roger. "Rather you than me. And, if you don't mind, I'll wait behind the Jag." He headed off towards the car.

"Piece of cake," said Kettering, and he walked away.

Shepherd looked over at Thompson. "If he blows himself up we can still sell the stuff to you?" he said.

"Sure, we don't really need him," said Thompson. Roger and Sean laughed out loud.

"I heard that!" shouted Kettering. He carried on walking and stopped about fifty yards away from them. "How's this?" he called.

Shepherd gave him a thumbs up. "Go for it," he called. "Just remember to throw it down the slope."

"Do we need to cover our ears or something?" asked Thompson.

"Not out in the open," said Shepherd. "In a confined space, maybe."

"And we won't get hurt?"

"Would I be standing here if there was even a chance of that?" said Shepherd.

"You'll be fine," agreed Sean. "Unless he fucks up and throws it the wrong way."

"Here we go!" yelled Kettering. He pulled out the pin, threw the grenade in a high arc down the slope, then turned and ran up the hill. After three paces he dropped face down on to the grass and a second later there was a dull thud that Shepherd felt in his stomach and through the soles of his feet. There was a cloud of white smoke at the bottom of the slope and a brown patch about five feet wide that smouldered though there was no fire. In a fraction of a second the small metal globe had been transformed into thousands of small deadly fragments.

Grenades were nasty weapons. Shepherd had never had to throw one in anger during his army days, and he was grateful for that. He'd shot men, and women, and on a few occasions he'd used a knife. He regretted none of the killings, but there was something basically unfair about a grenade. If you shot a man then there was a chance that he might fire first. In hand-to-hand fighting the more skilled fighter won. But there was no defence against a grenade. If you had one and the enemy didn't, and you threw it, then he was dead and you weren't.

Kettering was already up, jumping up and down and punching the air enthusiastically. "Did you see that!" he shouted.

Thompson stared at the rapidly dispersing cloud of smoke. "Fucking awesome!" He turned to look at Shepherd. "Was that fucking awesome or what?"

Shepherd nodded. "Yeah, awesome."

Kettering hurried up the slope. "That was amazing, Garry. My heart was pounding when I pulled the pin out, it really was." He shook his head. "I want to do it again."

"We need to go," said Shepherd. "The sound carries. No one's going to mistake a grenade for someone out shooting crows."

Kettering looked disappointed, like a child who'd been told his time at the funfair was over and that he had to go home.

"Cheer up, mate," said Sharpe. "Once you've bought them you can throw as many as you want."

"I might do that," said Kettering. "You know what would be cool? Throwing one in the canal. I bet there'd be one hell of a splash."

"So we have a deal?" asked Shepherd.

"Fuck, yeah," said Kettering. He held out his hand and Shepherd shook it.

"Cash on delivery," said Sharpe.

"Wouldn't have it any other way," said Kettering. "Give me forty-eight hours' notice."

"Fancy a drink to celebrate?"

"You know a place?"

"There's a decent pub a few miles from here. Don't know if they have bubbly but we can give it a go."

Kettering slapped him on the back. "Garry, lead the way. And you're buying."

The pub did have champagne. It was only Moët but it was cold and cost about a third of the price they'd pay in a London bar. Shepherd paid the barmaid and carried it and six glasses over to a table by a shoulder-high brick fireplace. They were the only customers inside, though half a dozen farm workers in overalls and heavy coats were standing outside drinking pints and smoking.

Shepherd popped the cork and poured the champagne. The men clinked glasses and drank.

"So what do you think?" asked Kettering. "A week? Ten days?"

"Thereabouts," said Shepherd.

"Excellent."

"Can I ask you something?" said Shepherd.

"Anything but algebra," said Kettering. "I was always crap at algebra."

"Why do you need so many guns? And the grenades?"

"Do you always ask your customers what they're going to do with the stuff they buy?" asked Kettering.

"It's not every day that I sell forty AK-47s." He shrugged. "If you don't want to tell me that's fine. I'm just interested, that's all."

"Best you don't know," said Thompson.

"He's right," said Sharpe. "Once we know, we're accessories before the fact."

"You a lawyer, James?" asked Kettering.

"I've known a few in my time," said Sharpe.

"You're not planning a race war or something, are you?" asked Shepherd.

Kettering stiffened and he stared at Shepherd with unblinking blue eyes. "What makes you say that, Garry?" he said quietly.

"Yeah, come on, that's a bit personal, innit?" said Sharpe.

Shepherd ignored his partner. He knew he was pushing it, but Button wanted to know what Kettering and Thompson were up to and the best way of getting that information was from the horse's mouth. "We met you through Ian, and Ian's as BNP as they come, isn't he? Kill the blacks, gas the Jews and burn the Pakis. England for whites only and all that. So when he first said that you and Paul wanted a meet, we naturally assumed . . ."

"That we were going out to shoot niggers and Pakis?"

Shepherd shrugged again. "You can see why," he said. "But then we saw you with Conteh at the boxing and we didn't know what to think."

"Leave me out of this," said Sharpe. "I couldn't care less what you're doing with the guns, so long as your money's good." He flashed Shepherd a warning look but Shepherd pretended not to notice.

"Let me get this straight," said Kettering. "You don't think I should have said hello to John Conteh, one of the biggest characters in the world of boxing, because he's black?"

"No, I'm not saying that," said Shepherd. "But Ian said you were, you know, in the EDL and all that."

"Yeah, I'm a patriot, Garry. We all should be. Family, friends and country, that's really all that matters in life. But being a patriot isn't about colour. It's about country. You heard Conteh speak that night; he's as Liverpool as they come and as British as you and me. I've plenty of black friends, Garry. And I've been with my share of black birds."

Thompson smirked. "I can vouch for that."

Sean and Roger nodded. "He is a sucker for that old black magic," said Roger.

"So none of that racist nonsense, okay?" said Kettering. "I know Ian's full of it and that's why we don't hang out with him too much. He's a good guy and that and we have a laugh but he's not one of us and never will be."

"Message received and understood," said Shepherd.

"Now don't get me wrong," said Kettering. "The ones that are flooding into this country, they're the ones that should be sent packing. I get as annoyed as anyone at these families from the arse end of nowhere who are given mansions to stay in and benefits and LCD TVs and all the trimmings. Them I would put up against a wall and shoot. But it's not them that's the problem. It's the bastards that are ruining our country that are the ones to blame." He drained his glass and Shepherd refilled it for him.

"Who are you talking about?" asked Shepherd. "The politicians?"

"You know who I mean, Garry," continued Kettering. "They want to control us all, they want us to be passive consumers, obedient taxpayers, working our whole lives to pay for their bloated lifestyles."

"What the hell are you talking about?" asked Sharpe. "You've lost me."

"You don't see it, do you? You really don't see what's happening to this country? To the whole of Europe? Do you think this recession was an accident?" Kettering shook his head. "It's all part of the great plan," he said. "They want to take our savings, our pensions, our assets, because then we have no choice other than to work for them." Sean and Roger nodded in agreement.

"Them?"

"The faceless bureaucrats who run our lives. The unelected elite. The men and women who control the money and make us dance to their tune. It's slavery, that's what it is."

"An international conspiracy? Is that what you're saying?" asked Sharpe, leaning forward.

"The biggest conspiracy that the world has ever known," said Kettering. "With the aim of producing a one-world government with a single currency ruled by a very small elite while everyone else spends their whole lives being controlled and told what to do." He waved his glass around. "It's happening already. That's what the EU is all about. The EU and the United Nations. They're just steps on the way to a world government. And the bastards that are running this country, Labour and Conservative alike, are helping them, working towards the destruction of Western civilisation. By mass immigration. By destroying the trade unions. By weakening the state education system to produce a population with IQs lower than that in most Third World countries. By ruining the healthcare system. By destroying our faith in the Church."

Kettering's eyes were wide and flecks of saliva sprayed from his mouth as he spoke.

"They want the population compliant, like cattle. And they've pretty much done it. They push us and prod us and control every second of our lives, from the cradle to the grave. Someone has to bring the people to their senses, to tell them that they have to stand up and fight before it's too late."

"Is that what the guns are for?" said Shepherd quietly.

Kettering didn't appear to have heard him. "We have to show the world what's really going on. We have to open people's eyes. Look at Nine-Eleven. No one gave the Muslims a second thought before the Twin Towers were attacked. They were getting on with their lives, not making a fuss. Bin Laden could see how that would be the end of his religion. If people don't fight for something they don't value it and they don't complain when it gets taken away from them. So he ignited a fire that has continued to burn. And when Bush and Blair invaded Afghanistan and Iraq they fanned the flames.

Now look just how strong and united the Muslims are. The world is scared of them. Look at how our own government bends over backwards to accommodate them. Well, it's time for the British people to stand up and inspire that same fear. It's time that the world respected us again."

"But how does killing civilians achieve that?"

"By making them think about their lives. By showing them how weak and defenceless they have become. That's what Anders Breivik achieved in Norway. And that's going to be repeated across Europe until the people rise up and defend their countries."

"Steady, Simon," said Thompson.

Kettering looked at Thompson as if seeing him for the first time. "We're among friends," he said.

"We don't know that," said Thompson. "Not for sure." He looked over at Shepherd and raised his glass. "No offence. I mean, we've known Sean and Roger for donkey's, but you two are the new kids on the block."

"None taken," said Shepherd. He smiled across at Kettering. "The Norwegian's the one that killed all those kids, right? Please don't tell me you're planning to kill kids."

"It was a socialist camp," said Kettering. "He knew what he was doing. He knew that by killing the way he did he'd get his whole country talking. The whole world." He drank more champagne. "Are you going to pull out of our deal? Is that what you're thinking?"

"Once the guns leave my hands it's not my problem," said Shepherd. "They can't be traced to me. I doubt that you'd tell the cops where you got them from and even if you did it'd be your word against mine." He shrugged. "Money's money, that's what I always say."

Kettering nodded, then leaned over and clinked his glass against Shepherd's.

"Doesn't it worry you, what's happening to our country?" asked Thompson.

"I don't give it much thought," said Shepherd. "I don't pay tax, I come and go as I please and I do pretty much as I like. I leave my money offshore, so even if the cops were to get on to me I could move overseas and they'd never get me. I'm bulletproof, mate."

"At the moment. But what will you do when they get rid of money and everyone is chipped?" said Thompson.

"Chipped?" repeated Sharpe.

"They'll do away with money and you'll have a chip under your skin that you use to buy everything, and the moment you step out of line your chip is wiped," said Thompson. "It'll be the ultimate controlling tool. If we get to that stage it's all over. The rich will get richer and richer and the poor will stay poor."

"I'm not poor, mate."

"Compared to the Russian oligarchs? Compared to Tony Blair and the Bushes and the rest of them? Compared to the bankers? They're the ones who are taking over, unless we do something."

"You're a great one for conspiracies, aren't you?" said Shepherd.

Thompson's eyes hardened. "You need to read more," he said. "You know what a false flag is?"

271

Shepherd did but he wanted Thompson to continue talking.

"It's when the government does something but blames it on someone else. Hitler did it when he burned down the Reichstag. The Yanks did it in the Tonkin accident when they claimed that the North Vietnamese attacked one of their destroyers. The biggest false flag of all time was Nine-Eleven."

"You think the Americans killed their own people?" asked Shepherd.

"It was Bin Laden who brought down the Twin Towers," said Thompson. "I'm not one of those morons who think they used explosives. Of course they used planes and of course it was Bin Laden behind it. But who was behind Bin Laden?"

Shepherd didn't say anything. He sipped his champagne.

"The Americans," said Thompson. "They trained him, they funded him and they told him what to do. And afterwards they killed him. Why? Because they wanted Iraq's oil and they wanted the world in fear, because a population living in fear is easier to control. You've read *1984*?"

Shepherd shook his head.

"You should," said Thompson. "George Orwell was way ahead of his time. Read *1984* and *Animal Farm* and you'll see exactly where the world is headed. It's one huge conspiracy, Garry. They wreck our economy, they keep us in fear, they destroy our national identity, they take away our faith, and then one day we wake up and we're all slaves. Unless we do something."

272

"I'm starting to wish I hadn't asked," said Shepherd, trying to lighten the moment. Kettering and Thompson were both staring at him intently.

"It's not a joke, Garry," said Kettering. "This isn't a race war; it's a fight for the survival of our species. Because once the elite has total control there'll be no going back. They'll control the food, the water, the money supply, the land, everything."

"So what do you guys do, when you've got the guns? Do you attack Downing Street? Do you take hostages? What's the plan?"

Kettering grinned and tapped the side of his nose. "That, Garry old lad, is on a need-to-know basis."

"And you don't need to know," added Roger.

"Amen to that," said Sean. He raised his glass and smiled thinly. "No offence."

"Well, that was just plain weird, wasn't it?" said Shepherd as he drove away from the pub and headed to Hereford. He beeped his horn at Kettering and Thompson, who were climbing into their Jaguar. They waved as he drove away. Sean and Roger were sitting in the back of the Jaguar, deep in conversation.

"What was weird was the way that you brought Ray into the frame," said Sharpe. "That wasn't right, you know that?"

"I needed to find out what they were planning to do," said Shepherd.

"Yeah, but mentioning Ray like that just makes them associate us with him even more. It made it sound like

Ray had been talking to us about them and they won't like that."

"It went okay," said Shepherd, accelerating past a mud-splattered tractor.

"We should tip Ray off and give him the option of pulling out."

"You're over-thinking it, Razor," said Shepherd. "It was a brief conversation and then we were straight on to the great conspiracy theory. They were so fired up about that they won't remember where it started."

Sharpe sighed and folded his arms. "Aye, maybe."

"The Roger guy, the bald one, is Roger McLean. Button reckons he met with that Norwegian who shot all the kids. He's anti-Islamic, big time. Button's going to be very interested to know that he turned up."

"And that Sean, what do you think? UDA?"

"Military-trained, that's for sure. He knew how to handle the Yugo. I'll run him by Charlie, see what she says. So what's your take on the Bin Laden thing?"

"The conspiracy?" Sharpe shrugged. "I can just about buy the Americans getting Bin Laden to attack the Twin Towers, but the whole global-conspiracy thing is a bit much. But it makes for a good story."

"What about the theory that the West demonised Bin Laden?"

"That's true enough," said Sharpe. "And they used him as an excuse to invade Afghanistan and Iraq. But that doesn't make it a conspiracy. A conspiracy needs some very clever people and it was George W. Bush, for God's sake. Didn't he have an IQ of 91?"

"I think that's an urban myth," said Shepherd. "But what they seem to be saying is that it's bigger than politicians. And it was the bankers that caused all the problems we have now, right? So I guess there are two options — either the bankers did it deliberately, in which case it is a conspiracy, or they were all just plain stupid. In which case why are they getting million-pound bonuses?"

"Yeah, well, my vote's for the latter," said Sharpe. He looked across at Shepherd. "What's your interest?"

Shepherd shrugged carelessly. "The Five case I'm on at the moment is about fundamentalist terrorism and there's an al-Qaeda angle. I just wonder how much of what al-Qaeda does is about Bin Laden and how much is just disaffected Muslims. I don't get the feeling that there's a master plan at work. But maybe there is. Maybe there's someone pulling all the strings on this, keeping our population in fear so that they won't notice that one by one their civil liberties are being taken away."

"I think it's much simpler than that," said Sharpe. "I think that there are a lot of unhappy people in the world and terrorism is just an excuse for them to vent their frustrations. A big chunk of the population is unhappy, unhappy enough to kill and maim civilians. And that's a pretty scary thing to admit."

"And what about those guys?" said Shepherd. "Kettering and Thompson."

"Them? They're as mad as bloody hatters. But with guys like Sean and Roger with them they could be dangerous. If they know more guys like Sean they could do a hell of a lot of damage with those guns."

"And the grenades," said Shepherd. "Let's not forget about the grenades."

They drove in silence for a few minutes, then Sharpe sighed and stretched out his legs. "I sometimes wonder if we should even bother fighting this whole Muslim thing," he said.

"What?"

Sharpe grimaced. "Well, first of all, they're going to win in the end, aren't they? They're ten per cent of the population now, give or take. But they're breeding way faster than us."

"Us?"

"You know what I mean. I've got two kids, which just maintains the status quo. You've got only the one and there's no sign of you having any more. But your average Muslim family breeds like rabbits. Six kids. Seven. Eight. And most of the guys have more than one wife. So they're breeding faster than us. And it won't be long before there are more of them than us and then they can vote in their own government and everything changes."

"You're crazy," said Shepherd. "Even crazier than usual."

"You can't argue with the maths," said Sharpe. "And if Turkey joins the EU then it'll happen even faster. How many Muslims are there in Turkey? A hundred million? How many do you think will head over to the UK for benefits and the NHS? I tell you, Spider, we'll be a Muslim country by the end of the century and probably a lot sooner."

"Yeah, well, neither of us will be around to see that."

"But that's my point," said Sharpe. "Maybe we should be trying to speed things up."

Shepherd shook his head. "Now you've lost me."

"Look, here's the thing," said Sharpe. "Would it be so bad if we became a Muslim country? Because if you look into it, it's not that bad for us guys. In fact, on balance, my life would be better."

"Now you're being ridiculous."

"Hear me out," he said. "Under Islamic law men get to run things again. No more women bosses, no more female home secretaries, no more Charlotte Buttons breaking our balls. No more foul-mouthed chavs screaming in the street. And I'm all for covering the faces of the ugly ones when they're out in public. The roads would be a lot safer as well, if they were prevented from driving. Women would do what women should be doing: staying at home and bringing up the kids. And we could have more than one wife too. Think how well that would work. You could have one as a cook, one as a cleaner, one for the bedroom, and one . . ." He struggled to find a reason for a fourth wife. "Anyway, you get my drift."

"You're mad," said Shepherd.

"Even the booze thing isn't a problem," continued Sharpe. "We had a group of Algerian cops over doing an undercover course at Bramshill. Drank like fishes. And the Turks are Muslims but they brew a good beer. The only downside that I can see is bacon."

"Bacon?"

"The pork thing. I love bacon butties and crackling and I wouldn't want to give that up. But the prayer thing isn't a problem. Look at those bastards who keep taking cigarette breaks — everything stops while they go out for a smoke. Well, I'd be happy enough to take five breaks a day for a lie-down."

"You don't lie down, you soft bastard. You kneel and pray."

"You know what I mean," said Sharpe. "I'm just saying that five prayers a day is no hardship. And giving ten per cent of your money to charity is a good thing. Especially if that meant lower taxes. And putting women back in the home means that unemployment would go right down, which is great for the economy."

"Please tell me this is a joke, Razor," said Shepherd. "You're starting to worry me."

"But the really great thing is the whole shariah law business. An eye for an eye. Now you tell me that the UK wouldn't benefit from a policy of removing the right hands of thieves. Or castrating rapists. And I'd definitely go for beheading some of the scumbags I've put away rather than them doing twelve years in a cushy jail before being sent home to their families."

"And stoning adulterers?"

Sharpe scowled. "I'm not saying that there aren't some negative aspects, but on balance I think there are advantages to shariah law. Plus, in every Muslim country I know of, the police are respected."

"Feared, you mean."

Sharpe shrugged. "Fear or respect, they don't spit in your face and get away with it like they do in this country."

"Come on, Razor. Corruption is rife in all those countries. You can buy your way out of their prisons, and the rich get away with murder."

"No system's perfect," said Sharpe. "I'm just saying that perhaps we shouldn't be fighting an Islamification that is going to happen eventually. Maybe we should start embracing it."

"Allahu akbar," said Shepherd.

"Indeed," said Sharpe. "Fancy a curry?"

"I thought a kebab would be more your thing after your Road to Damascus moment," said Shepherd.

"No, mate, a curry and a couple of Kingfishers is what I need." He grinned. "Mind you, have you noticed that you never see women serving in curry houses? There're no bolshy waitresses; it's always guys. I'm sure that's a Muslim thing."

"Razor, I swear to God, if you turn up for work in a man dress tomorrow I'm off this case." He grinned. "Okay, a curry it is. There're a couple of good places in the centre of Hereford. Soon as we've dropped the guns off at the barracks we'll swing by before we head back to London."

Shepherd waited until he was back in his Hampstead flat before phoning Charlotte Button.

"Kudos, Spider, that couldn't have gone better," she said.

"You got sound and video?"

"We got everything. Well done."

"Yeah, well, it was more by luck than judgement, I have to say. If they hadn't jumped at the chance of a drink I don't know how else we could have got them to the pub."

The pub they had gone to after the weapons demonstration had been fitted with hidden microphones and cameras and the farm workers outside had all been MI5 officers.

"All's well that ends well," she said. "And we now have Roger McLean in the frame and that's priceless. They've already arrived back in Birmingham and we have a team on him as we speak."

"What about Sean?"

"His name's not Sean, for a start. Aidan McEvoy. Ulster Defence Association hard man. The PSNI lost sight of him a year or so ago and assumed that he was in Ireland."

"Why would the UDA get involved with the likes of Kettering and Thompson?"

"We're working on that. Might just be personal. Might be that he's a hired hand. Of course it might also be that the UDA is connected to Breivik's Knights Templar group, in which case we have a major problem."

"The UDA has plenty of arms so if they're involved there'd be no need for them to be buying from me."

"That's what we're hoping," said Button. "A UDA lone wolf is bad enough; if the whole organisation was moving its attentions to the mainland we'd have a small war on our hands. But there's no point in crossing bridges. We've got McEvoy under observation now so we'll see where that leads us. But as far as today went, job well done." She ended the call.

Shepherd felt too tense to sleep. It was often that way after working undercover: the adrenaline was flowing and all his senses were on overdrive. During his undercover career he'd seen agents deal with the pressure in many different ways. Drink, drugs and gambling were easy crutches to turn to, but they'd never appealed to Shepherd. Running had always been his way of taking the edge off. Running cleared his mind, and aching muscles led more often than not to a dreamless sleep, but it was too late to go out running so he spent an hour doing sit-ups, crunches and press-ups before showering and heading to bed.

Chaudhry was sitting at the back of a lecture theatre typing notes into his laptop. There were more than a hundred students listening to the lecturer and most had laptops open in front of them, though a few were still taking notes the old-fashioned way, scribbling away on notepads. He felt his phone vibrate in his pocket as he received an SMS. He took out his phone. The message said "Now" and was followed by a mobile number he didn't recognise. It was Khalid. He changed his number every few days and changed his phone once a month. It was Friday and Chaudhry hadn't had any contact with Khalid for over a week. Chaudhry grimaced. The door was at the front of the lecture theatre and if he left now he'd have to walk past the lecturer, a forty-something surgeon with a tongue as sharp as his scalpel. Chaudhry looked at his watch. There were only another ten minutes until the lecture would be over so he decided to wait, though he packed away his laptop and put it into his backpack. As soon as the lecturer finished, Chaudhry picked up his bike helmet and backpack and hurried out into the corridor. There were too many students around so he went along to the cafeteria, where there were only a handful of people. He took out his mobile and called the number.

"What took you so long, brother?" asked Khalid.

"I'm at the university and I needed to find somewhere quiet," said Chaudhry.

"You can talk now?"

"Yes."

"Then listen to me, brother, and listen well. It is time."

Shepherd was walking out of Tesco Express when his mobile rang. It was Chaudhry.

"John, where are you?"

"Hampstead," said Shepherd. "What's wrong?"

"It's on," said Chaudhry. "Today. Today's the day."

Shepherd quickened his pace, heading for his flat. "What do they want you to do?"

"I don't know yet. Harvey and I are being picked up later today and that's when we'll be told. John, what do we do?"

Shepherd could hear the tension in the man's voice and he was breathing heavily.

"Just take it easy, Raj. Everything will be okay."

"This is it. This is when the killing starts. They want us to kill people. You have to do something."

"Raj, you need to be cool. No one's going to kill anybody. We've got your back. Let's just take this one step at a time. Now, who did you speak to?"

"It was Khalid."

"And did he say where you would be going?"

"He said nothing, John. Just to turn up outside an Indian restaurant and a van would collect us. Me and Harvey."

"Anyone else?"

"He didn't say."

"And the restaurant? Where is it?"

"Stoke Newington Church Street. At five o'clock. That's only four hours away." He was talking quickly again, the words tumbling into each other.

"It's going to be fine, Raj, I promise. Now, did he ask you to take anything with you?"

"No."

"What about clothing? Did he tell you what to wear?"

"Just casual stuff."

"Outdoor gear, indoor?"

"He didn't say."

"Did he say anything about bringing ID? Money?"

"He didn't say anything about that."

"Passport? Did he mention your passport? Or driving licence?"

"Nothing."

"Okay, now the phone we gave you. The one with the GPS. I need you to take that with you and to keep it switched on."

"He said no phone."

"You're sure?"

"Of course I'm sure. He was very specific about that. He said that Harvey and I were to leave our phones behind."

Shepherd tapped his phone against the side of his head as his mind raced, considering all his options.

"John, are you there?"

"Yes, Raj, I'm here."

"What do we do?"

"Are you okay to go?"

"I think so. But what do you think they want?"

"I don't know. I wish I did, but I don't," said Shepherd. "Okay, now listen to me carefully, Raj. I want you and Harvey to do exactly as you were told. I'll make sure that you're followed and that you're protected."

"You can do that? You're sure?"

"As soon as I've finished this call I'll get on to my bosses and arrange it. You and Harvey do as Khalid says and I'll make sure you're followed every step of the way."

"But what if they want us to kill, John? What if they give us guns or bombs?"

"Then we'll see that and we'll move in," said Shepherd. "Look, Raj, do you think you can take your phone with you? That would make it easier for us to follow you."

"But what if Khalid finds out? He'll know I disobeyed him."

"It's up to you, Raj. All I'm saying is that if you had the phone it would be easier for us to track you. But there's no pressure. It has to be your call."

284

Chaudhry laughed harshly. "No pressure? Are you serious? If they find out what I'm doing they'll . . ." He left the sentence unfinished.

"Raj, it's going to be okay."

"You promise?"

"I promise," said Shepherd. He ended the call with a sick feeling in the pit of his stomach because he knew that wasn't a promise that he could make. He phoned Charlotte Button and told her what had happened.

"Friday evening?" she said. "Worst possible time. Any idea of potential targets?"

"Raj had no idea. Unlikely to be a sporting venue, right? If they're being picked up at five I doubt they'll be in place by six. More likely seven."

"Seven o'clock in London? They could hit Soho, Leicester Square, the theatre district. Or it could be symbolic. Trafalgar Square. Downing Street. The London Eye."

"He wasn't specifically asked to bring ID so I can't see it'll be anywhere that would need identification," said Shepherd.

"Well, we can spend all day trying to second-guess them but that's not going to get us anywhere."

"They're being picked up outside an Indian restaurant on Stoke Newington Church Street. I've asked Raj to take his GPS phone with him so we can track him. He's reluctant, though, because Khalid specifically said no phones. What about Khalid? Are you going to have him tailed too?"

"Khalid shook his tail yesterday."

"How did that happen?"

"Khalid's hardcore al-Qaeda, Spider. Single-use SIM cards, disposable phones or callboxes, no computer of his own and only uses computers in Muslim-owned internet cafes, never conducts business at home but almost always face to face in public places."

"But he's under surveillance, right?"

"Most of the time, yes. But ninety-nine per cent of the time he does nothing. He sleeps, he goes to the mosque, he eats, he socialises. We've no idea what he says to the people he meets, which is why Chaudhry and Malik are so valuable. They're the only assets we have in his circle."

"But yesterday he lost his watchers?"

"It happens now and again. He goes into anti-surveillance mode and he's clearly been trained by experts. We could have a dozen men on him and he'd still lose them all."

"So he knows that he's being followed?"

"Our guys are experts too, Spider. I doubt that he knows that he's being followed; it's just that every time he goes active he employs all the anti-surveillance techniques at his disposal. Like I said, he's hardcore. I wish we knew what he was planning. We could be looking at anything, couldn't we? Guns. Bombs. Chemicals. We just don't know."

"There's nothing to suggest that it's a suicide attack," said Shepherd. "So I don't think it'll be bombs."

"They could be lying to Chaudhry and Malik," said Button. "It wouldn't be the first time."

"What do you need me to do?" asked Shepherd.

"Where are you?"

"Hampstead. Just dropping some stuff off."

"Soon as you've done that, come to Thames House," she said. "I'll get an operation room set up."

"I'd rather be closer to them."

"No can do," said Button. "You're not a professional follower. The last thing we need is you showing out. Soon as you can, okay?"

"I'm on my way," said Shepherd.

Chaudhry unlocked the door to his flat and wheeled in his bike. Malik was sprawled on the sofa eating his way through a bag of crisps and watching a quiz show on television. Chaudhry glared at him. "Why the hell is your phone off?" he said.

"Battery died," said Malik. "It's charging."

Chaudhry kicked the door shut and leaned his bike against the back of the sofa. "Khalid called," he said. "It's today."

"What?" Malik sat up, spilling crisps over the carpet. "What do you mean?"

"What do you think I mean?" said Chaudhry, tossing his helmet on to an armchair. He folded his arms and stood glaring down at Malik.

"Today? It's today?"

Chaudhry nodded. "It's today."

"What do they want us to do?" Malik asked.

"How am I supposed to know?" Chaudhry said, shrugging.

Malik stood up. Stray crisps fell to the carpet. "He didn't say anything?"

"Harvey, if he'd told me one word don't you think I'd have told you? He said be here, now. He said we'd be picked up. That's all he said." Chaudhry walked into the small kitchen and opened the fridge. "Why is there never anything to drink?" he said. "I bought three cans of Coke yesterday so where the hell are they?"

"This is fucked up," said Malik, coming up behind him. "Why didn't they tell us what's going on?"

Chaudhry slammed the fridge door. "Because the fewer people who know what we're doing, the less chance it gets out. Need to know."

"It's treating us like we don't matter, that's what's going on here." Malik screwed up his face and grunted. "Bastards, bastards, bastards."

"Relax," said Chaudhry. He switched on the kettle. "What happens, happens."

"Have you called John?"

"First thing I did."

"What if they . . ." Malik left the sentence unfinished.

"What?" said Chaudhry.

"What if they want us to . . . you know . . . shahid."

Chaudhry's mouth fell open. "Are you crazy? Where's that come from?"

"This doesn't feel right. This isn't what they said would happen. Maybe they've changed their minds. Maybe they want us to be martyrs."

"We talked about this. After all the training they've put us through they wouldn't throw us away like that. And remember what The Sheik said. They want us to be warriors, not shahid. Now stop talking nonsense."

288

He reached for a jar of Nescafe. "Do you want a coffee?"

"Do I want a coffee? We might be dead in a few hours and you're worrying about coffee?"

Chaudhry pointed a finger at Malik's face. "I told you, stop talking crap. Now do you want coffee or not?"

Malik nodded. "Okay, thanks," he whispered.

"It's going to be okay, Harvey. We always knew we'd get the call at some point." He spooned coffee granules into two mugs.

"I just worry that they might not be straight with us," said Malik. "We don't know what they're capable of, not really."

Chaudhry leaned against the fridge and folded his arms. "Khalid wants us in Church Street at five. We'll be collected and taken to wherever it is he wants us. What do you want to do? Call him and tell him we've had a change of heart?"

"We could do that," said Malik. "We absolutely could. We could just call it a day."

"We can't," said Chaudhry, shaking his head.

"We can. We've done enough. We just tell John that we want out. MI5 can't force us to go on like this. We gave them The Sheik. We showed them who's bad in the mosque. We can walk away with our heads held high." He gripped Chaudhry's shoulder so hard that Chaudhry winced. "Let's go, brother. Let's go before we're in any deeper."

"We can't do that," said Chaudhry. "We can't let John down. And what would Khalid do if we left now?"

"What do you mean?" asked Malik, letting go of his flatmate's shoulder.

"With everything we know about him and the organisation, how could he let us live?"

"We could run. Disappear."

"Harvey, how could we do that? To disappear we'd need money, we'd need documents, passports. The only people who could arrange that for us would be MI5. And if we run they're not going to help us, are they?"

"We've helped them already, haven't we? We gave them The Sheik. They owe us for that. In fact screw them. We can go to the Americans. They'd put us in their witness protection scheme. We'd have a whole new life in the States."

"Yeah, and who do we talk to? You want to phone the White House and talk to the President?" Chaudhry laughed harshly. "Sure, that'd work," he said sarcastically. "We don't even know for certain that they told the Americans about us."

"So we're trapped," said Malik.

"It's not a trap, it's an opportunity," said Chaudhry. The kettle finished boiling and he poured water into the mugs and stirred. "When we first went to MI5 we went because we knew that people would die if we didn't. We knew what Khalid and his people were planning to do, right?"

Malik nodded. Chaudhry splashed milk into both mugs and handed one to his friend.

"I've already spoken to John. He'll be watching us. They'll move in before anything happens and we'll be heroes." He raised his mug. "Trust me, Harvey. We'll be heroes, this will be over and we can get on with our lives." He clinked his mug against Malik's.

"I hope you're right," said Malik.

"We've got a live video feed from a van across the road," said Luke Lesporis, MI5's head of London surveillance. Lesporis had cut his surveillance teeth following drug dealers in south London, more often than not with dread-locks and a Bob Marley T-shirt. But his streetwalking days were almost a decade behind him. MI5 had hired him to head up their London surveillance team and he now had close-cropped hair and spent most of his time behind a desk in a Hugo Boss suit. He looked over at Charlotte Button and pushed his wire-framed designer spectacles up his nose and then pointed at one of the twelve LCD screens on the wall they were facing. Shepherd could see an Indian restaurant, and a traffic warden writing out a ticket. "The traffic warden's ours," said Lesporis. "We also have two motorcycle couriers and a black cab in the street and black cabs in the streets parallel. We've a Met helicopter on the way."

"Thank you, Luke," said Button. She was wearing a grey Prada suit and had hung the jacket on the back of her chair. A small gold crucifix nestled below her throat from a thin gold chain. They were in an operations room on the top floor of Thames House. There were no windows and the overhead lights were subdued to give them a better view of the LCD screens. There were half a dozen young men and women sitting at a bank of computer terminals, while Button and Shepherd were sitting in high-backed black leather chairs in front of a control console. Luke Lesporis was to their left, standing up and drinking occasionally from a plastic bottle. There was a large clock on the wall facing the door. It was twenty minutes to five.

"SAS?" asked Shepherd.

"They're on alert but we are confident we can handle this with the resources we have," said Button. "The Combined Firearms Response Team is ready to go and we've got six ARVs ready in north London. We've got three in position south of the river. We're drafting in teams from other forces and within the hour we should have at least a dozen more in place."

One of the lower screens was showing a map of London, centred on Stoke Newington.

Another screen flickered into life. This one showed a view from the roof of a building overlooking the street. Lesporis raised his hand and touched his Bluetooth earpiece. "We have a camera on the roof of a building opposite," he said.

"Tell them to make sure they're not seen," said Button.

Lesporis nodded and turned back to his computer.

Button smiled at Shepherd. "Coffee?"

"Coffee would be good," said Shepherd.

Button picked up one of the handsets in front of her and asked for a coffee and a tea. "And sandwiches," she said. "Whatever's going."

Two dark-haired young men in pinstriped suits walked in, both wearing Bluetooth earpieces. Button greeted them by name and they sat down at computer terminals and logged on.

"We've got two walkers on the ground — the traffic warden and a BT engineer — but this is going to be vehicle surveillance obviously," said Button. She picked up a Bluetooth earpiece and put it into her right ear.

"There's no chatter, no sense that anything big is happening?"

"It's quiet," said Button. "But it's been quiet for weeks. That can mean that nothing's happening or it can mean they've battened down the hatches in preparation for a big one."

A blonde woman in a grey suit raised her hand. "Helly telly coming online," she said.

"Thank you, Zoe," said Button. One of the top screens went live, giving them an overhead view from the Met's helicopter. "Ask them to give the target plenty of room," she said.

Zoe nodded and began talking into her Bluetooth headset.

"There's a police commander on the way but this is our operation," Button said to Shepherd.

"What do we do about Raj and Harvey?"

"In what way?"

"Hell's bells, Charlie, two of our men are in the middle of this. If the cops start shooting what's to say they won't be killed?"

"I can't lie to you, Spider. The primary aim is to safeguard the public. We'll do what we can to protect our assets but that has to be a secondary consideration."

Shepherd lowered his voice and leaned towards her. "Charlie, these guys trust us. You can't hang them out to dry."

"That's not what's happening here," she said. "At the moment we don't know where they're going or what they'll be doing. This is a surveillance operation. If we move to another level then hopefully we'll have eyes on them and be able to identify and protect our assets. One step at a time, okay?"

"Will you stop referring to Raj and Harvey as assets?" hissed Shepherd. "They're people. Human beings. They're not inanimate objects."

"They're assets. That's the technical term," said Button quickly. Her eyes narrowed. "I understand your depth of feeling," she said. "But keep in mind the big picture here. These people have been planning a major terrorist incident for several years so it's going to be big. Just how big we've yet to find out. Preventing that incident has to be our priority."

Shepherd opened his mouth to argue, but then abruptly changed his mind. As much as he hated to admit it, she was right. There would be no point in saving Raj and Harvey if dozens or hundreds of innocent civilians were killed. It was a simple matter of numbers. He nodded slowly. "I hear you," he said. "But I want to be here when the order is given."

"You will be," she said. "I don't want you going anywhere until this is over."

"We have two IC4 males on the street," said a balding middle-aged man in shirtsleeves.

294

Everyone looked at one of the centre screens. Chaudhry and Malik were walking down the road towards an Indian restaurant.

"Here we go," said Button. "Just so we're clear, Chaudhry is wearing the duffel coat, Harvey is wearing the green parka."

Both men had their hoods up so their faces were hidden.

Malik was rocking from side to side, transferring his weight from one leg to the other, like a junkie desperate for his next fix. They were standing in Stoke Newington Church Street, in front of the Indian restaurant. Malik had his hands in the pockets of his parka and had his head down, staring at the pavement as he rocked.

"Harvey, mate, you have to chill," whispered Chaudhry.

"Chill? We could die today, Raj. That's what could happen. I've never trusted Khalid. He's a cold-blooded bastard. Even when he smiles he doesn't smile with his eyes — have you noticed that?"

"No arguments here," said Chaudhry. "But getting all worked up isn't going to help anyone. John is on the case; he'll protect us."

"You don't know that," said Malik. "You don't know what he'll do."

"I trust him," said Chaudhry. "And you do too. We wouldn't have gone this far if it hadn't been for him. John's real, you know he is."

"I guess," said Malik.

"He's probably watching us now," said Chaudhry.

Malik looked up and started scanning the rooftops of the buildings on the other side of the road. "Do you think?"

"I'm sure of it," said Chaudhry. "He'll have people close by."

"Yeah, well, I hope they've got guns because if anything goes wrong I want them to put a bullet in Khalid's head."

Chaudhry laughed, but he stopped when he saw the white van heading down the road towards them. The driver and the passenger in the front seat were both Asian. "This could be them," he said. There were no side windows to the van, just the name of a plumbing firm.

Malik looked at the van. "Where's Khalid?"

"He said there'd be two men in the van. He didn't say he'd be there."

"Why not?" said Malik. "Why isn't he here?"

"I didn't ask and I doubt that he would have told me anyway."

Malik stared at the van as it got closer. "It's happening, isn't it? This is really happening." He looked back at Chaudhry. "I can't do this, Raj. I'm not up for it."

"You'll be fine, brother. I'll be with you every step of the way." He stepped forward and hugged Malik. "Trust me. Just trust me."

Malik nodded hesitantly. "Okay, I'll try," he said.

Chaudhry released his grip on Malik and looked into his eyes. "We're going to be heroes," he said. "Remember that."

Malik forced a smile just as the van pulled up at the kerb. "I just don't want to be joining the seventy-two coal-eyed virgins," he said. "Not today, anyway."

Chaudhry punched him gently on the shoulder.

"No virgin's going to give it up for you, brother; you're as ugly as sin."

The van stopped next to them and the passenger window slowly wound down.

"Salaam, brothers," said the man in the front passenger seat. He was wearing a white woollen skullcap and had a straggly beard. The beard worried Chaudhry because Khalid had always insisted that he and Malik were clean-shaven. It was important to blend in, he said, so no beards and no Muslim clothing.

"Who are you, brother?" asked Chaudhry. "I don't know you."

"I'm Harith. We are here to take you where you need to go."

"But I don't know you, brother. You could be anyone."

The driver nodded at Malik. "You know me, brother."

Malik leaned forward and put his hand on the door. "Afzal, brother, what are you doing here?" he asked the driver.

"I'm here on behalf of Khalid," said Afzal. "You're to get into the back of the van."

Malik looked at Chaudhry. "Afzal plays in my five-a-side league," he said.

"Where's Khalid?" asked Chaudhry.

"He's in the control room," said Afzal. "You're to get in the back." He looked at the cheap digital watch on his wrist. "We've got a schedule."

"What fucking control room, brother?" Chaudhry asked Afzal. "Nobody said anything about a control room. What's going on?"

"There're a lot of people involved," said Afzal. "He's running things so he's somewhere where he can't be found, organising. Now get in the back, brother. We're on a tight schedule."

Chaudhry and Malik walked round to the rear of the vehicle. Chaudhry pulled open the door. There were racks filled with tools and plumbing supplies on either side and plastic crates full of equipment in the middle. They both got inside. Malik sat on the floor while Chaudhry pulled the door closed. He checked that the door was secure and then sat down on one of the crates.

"Are we good, brothers?" asked Harith. "Are we ready to serve Allah?"

Malik nodded. "All good, brother," said Chaudhry. He pulled down the hood of his duffel coat.

"No mobile phones, right?" said Harith.

"No, we left them in the flat," said Chaudhry. "What's happening? What are we doing?"

"All will be explained to you at the right time," said Harith. The van moved away from the kerb and joined the traffic heading south, into the city.

"Right, everyone on their toes. Under no circumstances are we to lose this van," said Button. "Zoe, make sure the chopper stays high. I don't want them hearing it." On the screen the van had pulled back into the traffic and was moving south. "Luke, are you in contact with the bikes?"

"Tim is," said Lesporis.

One of the men in a pinstriped suit raised his hand.

"Right, Tim, let them know we've got the eye in the sky so they can hang back for a bit," said Button. "But on their toes. If the chopper loses the van I want the bikes straight back in. I need you to keep them up to date on the van's location every step of the way."

"Got it," said Tim.

"Luke, what about the cabs?"

Lesporis nodded. "Two running parallel and one behind." He pointed at the view from the helicopter. "One is four cars behind the target."

"Okay, let's get them all ahead of the target. And again, keep them informed, ready to move in if the chopper loses the van. Let's give them no chance of seeing our vehicles, right?"

A uniformed police commander appeared at the doorway, his hat tucked under his left arm. "Ms Button?" he asked, looking around the room.

"Commander Needham, welcome. There's a desk ready for you," said Button, pointing at a workstation and headset to her left. "The link to the Met is already up and your screen has access to the PNC once you've logged on."

The commander nodded and took off his jacket as he walked towards the workstation. "We have three armed response vehicles en route," he said.

"We need them well away from the target vehicle, and absolutely no blues and twos," said Button. "At least a hundred yards away at all times and under no circumstances can there be any visual contact. I can't stress that enough."

"Understood," said the commander, sitting down and adjusting the headset.

Button stared up at the screen showing the overhead view from the helicopter. "I need everyone to start considering possible targets," she said. "Any thoughts just shout them out — there's no need to be shy."

Chaudhry could feel his heart pounding as if it was about to burst out of his chest. He looked over at Malik. Malik's face was bathed with sweat and he was breathing heavily.

"Where are we going?" Chaudhry asked Harith. "You can at least tell us that."

"Soon, brother," said Harith. He handed a mobile phone to Chaudhry. It was a cheap Nokia. "You will be called on this and given instructions."

Chaudhry nodded. He ran his hand through his hair. "But what are we to do, brother? Why can't you tell us?"

"You are serving Allah, that is all you need to know," said Harith. "Put the phone in your pocket. When it rings, answer." He looked through the windscreen at the traffic ahead of them. "We will soon be there."

"Inshallah," said Chaudhry. God willing.

Shepherd looked up at the screen showing the map of central London. The position of the van containing Raj and Harvey was marked with a red flashing light. "The station," he said. "St Pancras."

Charlotte Button nodded in agreement. "I think you're right."

"Lots of people, high profile; they could do a lot of damage." He ran a hand through his hair. "We need to be looking for more of them," he said. "If they're attacking the station they might be going in mob-handed."

Commander Needham looked up from his console. He was holding a phone a few inches from his ear. "We might want to consider multiple targets," he said. "If this is in some way a repeat of Seven-Seven they could be planning to attack several places at the same time."

"What do you suggest, Commander?"

"I can talk to our CCTV centre and get our people looking for Muslims in vans." He smiled thinly. "God forbid we should be profiling, of course."

"Do it, please, Commander." The commander nodded and pulled on his headset. "Luke, you need to ask all our watchers to keep an eye out for other possible attackers. Vans, cars — if they follow the profile of this one then we're looking for two Asians in the front, more in the back. If they see anything they're to let us know immediately."

"Will do," said Lesporis.

Button looked across at Shepherd. "This could very easily go wrong," she said.

"You want to pull them over?" asked Shepherd.

"That's not going to help if there are others," she said.

"What about Khalid? Any news?"

"No sign of him," said Button.

"That's not good," said Shepherd.

"You're telling me."

Harith twisted around in his seat. "Two minutes and we will be there, brothers," he said. He pointed at one of the plastic crates. "Open that, brother," he said to Malik.

Malik leaned over and pulled the lid off the crate. Inside were two Timberland backpacks. One was black, the other blue. Chaudhry reached over to grab the black one and passed it to Malik, then he took the blue one for himself.

"Do not open them, brothers," said Harith.

Chaudhry rested the backpack on his knees. "What is it, brother? What's inside?"

"You do not need to know," said Harith. He gave a sheet of paper to Chaudhry. It was a map.

"This shows you where you are to go," he said. "Wait there and you will receive further instructions."

"Are we to become shahid?" asked Malik. He was sweating and his Adam's apple was bobbing up and down. He pushed down the hood of his parka and shook his hair from his eyes.

"If it is the will of Allah, who are you to argue?" said Harith.

"Why won't you tell us what's happening?" asked Malik.

Chaudhry put a hand on his friend's shoulder. "Hush, brother," he said. "This is what we trained for."

Harith nodded enthusiastically. "You must put your trust in Allah."

Malik opened his mouth to say something but Chaudhry squeezed his shoulder and shook his head.

The van came to a stop. "Allah be with you, brothers," said Harith.

"And with you, brother," said Chaudhry. "Allahu Akbar."

"Allahu Akbar," repeated Harith.

Malik opened the door and stepped out on to the pavement. Chaudhry followed him and slammed the door shut. A cold wind blew against their backs and they both pulled up the hoods of their coats as they watched the van drive away.

"Raj, what the hell are we going to do?" asked Malik.

Chaudhry hefted the backpack on to his shoulders and turned to face the building they were standing next to. St Pancras Station.

Button watched the van drive away from the station on the screen showing the feed from the police helicopter. "Tell the chopper to keep with the van," she said. "They're not to be stopped. Just keep an eye on them." She tapped her fingers on her lips as she stared at the map, which was now centred on the station. "Can we get a CCTV feed on the two of them?" shouted Button. "We need to see if they're being coerced."

"I'm on it," said a young man in a grey suit.

"And can we get video feeds from inside the station?" asked Button.

"I'll talk to the BTP's Major Incident Communication Centre," said the man, tapping on his computer.

Button looked over at Shepherd. "It has to be the Eurostar."

"I don't think they're after the Eurostar. Raj wasn't told to take his passport with him," said Shepherd.

"I have a feed now," said the man in the grey suit. "Screen five."

They all looked at the screen. Chaudhry and Malik were standing on the pavement, deep in conversation. They both had backpacks on.

"Shit," said Shepherd.

"Shit is right," agreed Button. "The question is, what are they up to? They might have fake passports ready to go abroad. But the security to get on the cross-Channel trains is as tough as at the airports so I don't see them getting bombs or guns on board. But they could do a lot of damage in the station. I just wish I knew what was in those backpacks." She called over to one of the men in front of the terminals. "Peter?" A middle-aged man in a sports jacket swivelled his chair to face her. "Is there any way we can get an explosives dog to the station, now?" asked Button.

"I'll try," he said.

"If we can run a dog through and get a reaction that will tell us something," said Button. "But on the QT, no confrontation."

304

"Got it," said the man, turning back to his computer keyboard.

"Can the dog tell the difference between explosives and ammunition?" asked Shepherd.

"I hope so," said Button.

"I have an ARV close to the station," said Commander Needham. "Do you want us to intervene?"

"Give me a moment, Commander," said Button.

"Understood, but be aware that our only chance of getting any sort of clear shot will be gone once they go inside."

"Duly noted," said Button tersely. She stared at the screen that showed Chaudhry and Malik standing at the Midland Road entrance. "What's your take on what's happening, Spider?"

"The backpacks are big enough for carbines, assuming they've got folding stocks," said Shepherd. "And bombs can be any size. The Seven-Seven bombers had backpacks and rucksacks." He shrugged. "I just don't know. There's no way of telling."

"The backpacks look bulky, don't they? Would carbines look like that? They look as if they're packed with something."

"Then that would mean explosives. And that would mean a suicide mission. That doesn't make sense. Raj and Harvey weren't being groomed to be martyrs."

"Unless they're being lied to. It wouldn't be the first time that men have been duped into becoming martyrs."

"Hell, Charlie. I don't know. I don't know what their mindset is. Certainly Raj and Harvey never believed that they'd be sent on a suicide mission."

"We have a clear shot," said the commander. "Do I have a green light?"

"Wait!" said Shepherd.

The commander looked at Button. "We can take them out now with zero collateral damage," he said. "We might not get another chance."

Button opened her mouth to speak but Shepherd held up his hand. "Just give me a minute," he said. "Let me think."

"The clock is ticking, Spider," said Button.

"Amen to that," said the commander. "If there are bombs in those backpacks we need to neutralise the threat now, before they go into the station," he said.

"Neutralise the threat?" repeated Shepherd. "Why don't you say what you mean? Shoot them. That's what you're suggesting, isn't it?"

"Easy, Spider," said Button. "We're just following protocol here. If they're carrying bombs and there's a chance that they are going to be detonated then we have to minimise civilian casualties. And the best way of doing that is to take them down sooner rather than later."

"I don't see triggers, do you? They've just got backpacks. There could be anything in them."

"Including bombs with timers."

"Let's just wait a little longer."

"We're running out of time," said Button.

Lesporis stood up. "Charlotte, we have another van approaching St Pancras. Two Muslim males in the front."

"What?" said Button, turning to look at the screen showing the map of London. A flashing light was moving east towards the station. "Do we have video?"

"Screen eight," said Lesporis. They looked at the screen. A white van was sitting at a set of traffic lights. "We have a bike behind them. That's where we're getting the video feed from."

"They're on Euston Road," said Button. "If they're going to St Pancras they'll be there in the next five minutes. How many are in the van?"

"We think three in the back but there are no windows so we can't be sure," said Lesporis.

"So there are more of them on the way?" said the commander.

"It seems so," said Button.

On the screen, Chaudhry was talking to Malik.

"I wish we had audio," said Button. She went over to stand behind Lesporis and put a hand on his shoulder. "Make sure our watchers stick with that van and find out where it goes."

"I'm on it," said Lesporis.

Chaudhry stopped and stared up at the sign above the station. A CCTV camera was looking down at them. Malik stood next to him.

"What are we going to do, Raj?" asked Malik.

"Let me think," said Chaudhry.

"Think? What the hell are you thinking about? What if we're carrying bombs? Those bastards could be preparing to blow us up right now."

Chaudhry turned to look at the van that had dropped them off. It was turning on to the main road.

"Raj? Come on, brother, get a grip, will you? What do we do?"

"He didn't say anything about a bomb. He just said we go into the station and we'll get further instructions." Chaudhry held up the map. "This is where we have to go."

"And you believe that? And where the hell is Khalid? For all we know he could be calling up mobile-phone detonators right now. We're dead men walking, brother."

"Just give me a minute, will you?" Chaudhry looked at Malik's backpack. It was bulky, as was the one on his back. He jiggled his. It made no sound. The pack was heavy, but not uncomfortably so. He tried to remember his time in the training camp in Pakistan. For several days they'd been shown how to make and use various types of explosives, and even how to construct a suicide-bomb waistcoat.

"They're not heavy enough," said Chaudhry.

"What do you mean?"

"If the target's a station then the bombs would have explosives and metal for fragmentation. Nuts, bolts, nails. Otherwise you just get a loud bang. Feel the weight. They're not packed with metal."

"So what do you think we're carrying? Packed lunches?"

"Poison? But that doesn't really make sense. Poison in a rucksack isn't going to hurt anybody. Guns, maybe.

308

Handguns. Perhaps that's it. Maybe we get into position and they call us and tell us to start shooting."

"I'm not shooting anybody. Look, let's just dump the backpacks and get the hell out of here."

"That's not an option, Harvey. Look, we're not carrying bombs. I'm sure of that. So we go inside and see what they want us to do next. We can stop at any time."

"So let's stop now."

"If we drop the bags and run, that'll be it. How do we know they'll catch Khalid?"

"That's not our problem, Raj."

"Yes, it is," hissed Chaudhry. "These people kill civilians. They're terrorists so that's what they want to do — terrorise. They kill and maim innocents because that way they spread terror. And if we don't stop Khalid maybe he'll kill your sister. Or my parents. Or our friends. These bastards don't care who dies, Harvey. They blow up tube trains and buses and even mosques. And if we don't stop them, who will?"

"I don't want to die, brother." Malik was close to tears.

"No one's going to die," said Chaudhry. "Not today. I promise."

The young man in the grey suit raised a hand. "BTP want to know how many feeds you want?"

"All of them," said Button.

"We can get them all but there are more than a hundred cameras inside and outside. They're asking if you want them to be selective."

"We need them all," said Button.

"I told them that but the point they're making is that if they send them as individual feeds we won't have enough screens here. They're suggesting they send us split-screen feeds with sixteen views per screen."

"That'll do," said Button.

The man put a hand to his Bluetooth headset and nodded as he listened to what he was being told. He put up his other hand and made a waving motion at Button. He muttered something into his headset and then nodded at Button. "What they're saying now is that you can have multiple feeds but you won't be able to home in on any particular frame."

"Just tell them to send the feeds now," said Button tersely.

The van that had been driving along Euston Road stopped outside the station. The video from the bike that was following the van shook for a few seconds and then stabilised.

Button turned to the commander. "Have you got a firearms team at the Euston Road entrance?"

The policeman nodded. "Already in place but still in their vehicle."

"Let's leave it that way for a while longer," said Button. She called over to a red-haired woman sitting at the far side of the room. "Marie, can you get me a floor plan of St Pancras showing all the entrances?"

"I'm on it," said Marie, tapping on her keyboard.

"The first feeds are coming through," said the young man.

310

"Thanks, Toby," said Button. She pointed at the wall of screens. "Let's clear the top row and put them all there."

"I've another ARV on the way," said the commander.

On one of the screens, three Asians got out of the back of the van on Euston Road. All were wearing backpacks.

A black screen flickered into life. It was filled with a map of the station, showing Euston Road to the left, Midland Road at the top and Pancras Road at the bottom.

Button walked over to the screen and tapped the top of the map. "This is where Chaudhry and Malik are," she said. "The Midland Road entrance." She moved her finger and tapped the left-hand side of the map. "This is where the second van is. I need everyone to start looking at the CCTV footage to see if we can spot anyone else. I'm as anti-profiling as anyone but we're looking for young male Asians with backpacks."

Shepherd got up and went to stand next to her.

"Chaudhry and Malik are about to enter the station," said the commander.

"We've got the van covered from the air, and it's no longer a threat," said Button, her eyes on the screen.

Each of the screens showing the CCTV footage from St Pancras was divided into sixteen viewpoints, four across and four down. One of the shots was a view of the main entrance. Shepherd could see Chaudhry and Malik standing together.

"If we move now we can take them down before they enter the station," said the commander. "But that window of opportunity is closing fast. If there are bombs in those backpacks . . ." He left the sentence unfinished.

Shepherd stared at the screen. Chaudhry was looking straight at the camera, almost as if he was looking right at Shepherd; then he smiled thinly.

"It's okay," said Shepherd. "There's no need to shoot."

"What do you mean?" said the commander.

"Spider?" said Button.

"It's okay, nothing's going to happen."

"How can you say that?" asked Button.

"His hood. The hood of his duffel coat. We agreed a signal: if he was in trouble he'd move his hood. His hood has been up since he got out of the van. He hasn't done anything to it so it's all good."

Button and the commander turned to look at the screen. Chaudhry was looking right at them. His face was strained and he was biting down on his lower lip. "He's stressed," said Button.

"Of course he's stressed. He's stressed because he knows we're following him and the cops have a habit of shooting innocent people." He smiled at the commander. "No offence," he said.

"We're not going to get another chance like this," said the commander. "Once they're inside we can't use the snipers so that means we'll have to go in, and then it's going to get very messy."

Shepherd ignored the policeman and stared intently at Button. "Charlie, this is a rehearsal."

"Are you sure, Spider? Are you absolutely sure?"

Shepherd pointed at the screen. "Raj and I have a prearranged signal. If there's a problem he'll pull down his hood. Or he'll bite his nails. If there was a problem that's what he'd do. He's not doing either. Harvey's hood is up too."

As they watched, Chaudhry turned and walked through the doors leading into the station.

"What if he's forgotten? What if in the heat of the moment he hasn't remembered?"

"He was looking at the camera," said Shepherd. "He was giving us a clear view of his face so that we can see it's him."

"There's a lot riding on this, Spider," said Button. "You have to be sure."

Shepherd swallowed, his mind whirling. He wasn't sure. There was no way that he could be. But if he admitted that to Button she'd give the order and the CO19 marksmen would start shooting.

"We have a window of about two seconds," said the commander.

"Spider?" asked Button.

"It's okay," he said.

Button nodded and looked at the commander. "Stand your men down," she said. "We won't be shooting anyone today."

The commander scowled at Button as if he thought she'd made the wrong decision, but he relayed the order to his team.

Button looked back at Shepherd and he could see the apprehension in her eyes. He knew exactly what she was thinking. If he was wrong both their lives were about to change for ever. And a lot of people were going to die.

Chaudhry and Malik walked together towards the Eurostar departure area. A train had just arrived and passengers were pouring out of the arrivals hall.

"What's going to happen?" asked Malik.

"I don't know," said Chaudhry.

"Are we going to France? Are we doing something on the Eurostar?"

"We can't, we don't have our passports."

"So why are we here?"

"I don't know, Harvey. Now just shut up, will you?" Malik flinched as if he'd been struck and Chaudhry felt suddenly guilty. "I'm sorry," whispered Chaudhry. "I don't know what's going on. But it's not about bombs, I'm sure about that."

"So what, then?"

"Wait and we'll find out."

A fearful look flashed across Malik's face. "Raj, what if it's radioactive? What if there's plutonium or something in the packs? It could be killing us now without us knowing."

"No one is going to kill us, Harvey. Remember what The Sheik said to us? We are Islamic warriors. Mujahideen. We are to fight and fight again, remember? We were never meant to be shahid. Only the stupid and ignorant kill themselves. That's not us."

"So why won't they tell us what's happening? Have a look at the phone, will you? Check it's working."

314

Chaudhry took the phone Harith had given him out of his pocket. He showed the screen to Malik. "See? When they call, it'll ring."

"Yeah? And maybe the phone is the trigger. Maybe when it rings the packs will explode or spew anthrax into the air."

"Harvey, will you look at the bloody phone? It's a phone, full stop. It's not connected to anything. It's not a detonator. Okay?"

Malik shuddered. "I can't take this much longer, brother. It's doing my head in, innit?"

Chaudhry wasn't listening to his friend. He was scanning the area, his eyes narrowed. "It's a rehearsal," he said quietly.

"What?"

"A dry run." He gestured with his chin. "Take a look around, Harvey."

Malik looked to his left. He saw two young Asians standing by a coffee shop. They both had backpacks similar to the ones that he and Chaudhry were carrying. Then he looked over at the entrance to the tube station just as two more Asians walked out. He saw they also had backpacks. Timberland backpacks. "Are they with us?" asked Malik. "I don't recognise them."

"You don't recognise them because they're not from our mosque," said Chaudhry. "Khalid has been recruiting from all over London. Maybe the country."

The two Asians who had come out of the tube station were deep in conversation. One of them was holding a mobile phone.

"I don't understand, brother. What are you saying?"

"Nothing's going to happen today. If it was going to happen it would have happened already."

"You mean it's a test, right?"

"I think so," said Chaudhry. "They wanted to check that we'd do as we're told."

As two more Asians walked from the direction of the Pancras Road taxi rank, Chaudhry's mobile rang and he jumped. The caller had withheld his number. Chaudhry took the call.

"Well done, brother," said Khalid. "You can make your own way home now. Someone will call to collect the backpacks and the phone. Allahu akbar." Khalid ended the call.

Chaudhry took a deep breath and exhaled slowly. "We go home," he said to Malik.

"It's over?"

"If anything it's just beginning," said Chaudhry

"They're walking towards the exit," said Button. "Did you see that? He took a call on his mobile and now they're heading towards the Midland Road taxi rank."

"Some of them are walking towards the tube," said the commander. "Maybe it's the tube they're after."

"No, they're all leaving," said Shepherd. He pointed at another CCTV feed. Two Asians with backpacks were walking towards the Euston Road exit. "And here, look." A tall Asian was walking slowly to the Pancras Road exit, while a fat Asian hurried after him. Both were carrying backpacks.

"He's right," said Button. "They all got phone calls and they're all leaving. It was a dry run. A rehearsal." Button patted Shepherd on the shoulder. "Well done, Spider. You called it right."

"And if I hadn't, Charlie? What then? Would have you killed them all?"

"If I was convinced that they were carrying bombs, and if I was convinced that they were going to use them, then of course."

Shepherd nodded slowly but didn't say anything.

Shepherd was just about to put the key into the lock of his front door when his John Whitehill phone rang. It was Chaudhry.

"John, it's okay," he said. "Were you watching? It was a test. It was just a test." His words were coming out so quickly that they were running into each other. "We were scared shitless, I can tell you. Harvey thought they were going to use anthrax or something. Then Khalid called and said we were to go home."

"I know," said Shepherd. "Just give me a minute." He let himself into the flat and closed the door behind him before switching off the burglar alarm. "Where are you?"

"Home," said Chaudhry.

"Is Harvey with you?"

"We're both here. It was a dry run. A rehearsal."

"I know," said Shepherd again. "We were watching you. I told you, MI5 has professionals. They watched you all the way from Stoke Newington and we had you on CCTV at the station."

"Did you see the others? There were other brothers there."

"We saw them," said Shepherd. "Did you recognise them?"

"Just one of them. The one who was driving the van we were in. Harvey had played football with him. But they all had the same backpacks. So you think we're going to attack the station? Is that what it was about? Next time they'll give us guns?"

"I don't know, Raj. It's possible. Did they say anything to you?"

"They just told us to go home and that they'd talk to us soon. Someone is going to collect the bags and the phone."

"I'll arrange a tail," said Shepherd.

"Do you think I should open the backpack, see what's inside?"

"Best not," said Shepherd. "It might be part of the test."

"So what do we do?"

"We wait and see what happens next," said Shepherd. "And well done, you handled yourself brilliantly. Tell Harvey from me, you guys did a great job."

"I just did what they said. I don't know what I would have done if they'd given me a gun."

"Let's meet tomorrow and we'll talk it through," said Shepherd. "And well done with the hood."

"The hood?"

"Letting me know that everything was okay by leaving your hood up."

318

Chaudhry didn't say anything for several seconds.

"You forgot, didn't you?" said Shepherd eventually.

"I'm sorry, John. I was just so caught up in what was happening."

Shepherd laughed softly.

"What?" asked Chaudhry. "What's so funny?"

"It doesn't matter," said Shepherd. "All's well that end's well."

"Did I do something wrong?"

"You did just fine," said Shepherd. "Let's meet tomorrow. We can talk about it then."

Ray Fenby used his remote to flick through the channels of his TV and sighed at the stream of dross that made up daytime television: endless repeats, banal talk shows and rolling news. There was nothing at all worth watching. He pushed himself up off the sofa and padded over to his poky kitchen in his bare feet. The worst thing about working undercover was that for most of the time he was doing absolutely nothing. Pretty much all of the people he came in contact with had jobs, in which case they were tied up all day, or they were criminals, in which case they were usually asleep.

Fenby's days were spent watching television, catnapping and waiting for the phone to ring. The fact that he was based in Birmingham just added to his misery because he had no friends or family in the city. At least when he'd been working in London he could drop round and have a beer with his mates. He opened the fridge. He'd run out of milk and there was nothing there that he wanted to eat, but there were half a dozen cans of Carlsberg Special. He sighed and wondered whether it was a good idea to start drinking at three o'clock in the afternoon, finally deciding that it probably wasn't but that he was old enough to make bad decisions. He took out a can, popped it open and took it back to his sofa. He flopped down and drank.

His doorbell rang and he frowned. His flat was on the third floor with a door-entry system at the main entrance, and he hadn't buzzed anyone in. He figured it was either Jehovah's Witnesses or a cold caller wanting him to change his electricity supplier so he ignored it. His bell rang again, more insistently and for longer this time. He put the Carlsberg can on the floor and went to his front door. He looked through the peephole. It was Kettering. And Thompson. Fenby frowned. Kettering and Thompson had never been round to his flat before, though they had dropped him off outside the building. He took a deep breath and mentally switched himself into Ian Parton mode before opening the door. He forced a smile.

"Hey, guys, what's up?"

"We're on the way to the pub and thought we'd swing by and see if you wanted a pint," said Kettering.

"Yeah, sure, I'll get my coat," said Fenby.

He moved down the hall to get his jacket, but as he did so Kettering and Thompson followed him. As he turned round to look at them, a third man stepped into the hallway. He had close-cropped hair and a strong chin with a dimple in the centre. He was wearing a long dark-brown leather coat and as he reached up to scratch his head Fenby caught a glimpse of a heavy gold identity bracelet.

"This is Mickey. He's an old mate from London," said Kettering.

Mickey nodded at Fenby but didn't say anything. He clasped his hands over his groin and studied Fenby with cold blue eyes.

"Haven't got any bubbly, have you?" asked Kettering.

"Afraid not," said Fenby. "Just lager."

"Not really thirsty anyway," said Kettering. He took out a leather cigar case, tapped out a cigar and lit it. He blew smoke slowly up at the ceiling and smiled. "Can't beat a Cuban," he said.

Fenby wasn't sure what to say. Something was wrong, he was certain of that, but he couldn't for the life of him work out what it was.

"How about we sit down and have a chat?" said Kettering.

The three men bundled Fenby into his sitting room and pushed him down on the sofa. Kettering sat down in an armchair while Mickey stood by the door, glaring at Fenby. Thompson went over to a bookcase by the window and began flicking through the books there.

"So how are things?" asked Kettering.

"Good. All good," Fenby said, nodding.

"Spoken to James and Garry at all?"

Fenby frowned and shook his head. "No. Why?"

"Just wondering." Kettering grinned. "How long have you known them?"

"Is there a problem, Simon?"

Kettering's smile hardened. "Why don't you tell me?"

"I'm confused, mate," said Fenby. "Has something happened?"

"I think it has," said Kettering. He looked across at Thompson. "What do you think, Paul? Has something happened?"

Thompson nodded. "It looks like it," he said.

Fenby's heart was racing. He was outnumbered three to one and it looked like he had a major problem on his hands. "Guys, come on, what is this, a wind-up?"

"How long have you known Gracie?" asked Kettering.

Fenby's throat had gone dry and when he swallowed he almost gagged. "A few years. I don't know. I mean, we're not bosom buddies. I met him in a pub. We got talking, like you do. And he's sold stuff to friends of mine."

"Edwards too, yeah?"

"I know James better than Garry. But like I said, I'm not in his pocket. We've had a few beers, watched a few games, had a few nights on the town, but he doesn't have me around for Christmas dinner."

Kettering nodded slowly. "What team does he support?"

"What?"

"His team. What's his team?"

"Rangers. He's Scottish and doesn't bother much about the English teams. But he'd take Liverpool over Man U."

"Married?"

"He's never mentioned it."

"Where's he live?"

"I'm not sure. Croydon, maybe."

"What car does he drive?"

"We've always been drinking so we've been in cabs. Look, Simon, what's going on?"

"Just answer the questions, old lad. You're doing fine," said Kettering. "Where was the last time you saw him?"

"Couple of months ago."

"I said where, not when."

"A pub."

"Where, exactly?"

"Central London. The east end."

"On his own?"

"There was a group of us."

"What was he drinking?"

"Champagne. He's big on the old bubbly, like you guys."

"Who else was there?"

Sweat beaded on Fenby's forehead as he felt Kettering forcing him into a corner. He was having to lie but without being able to base his lies on anything solid; and without a foundation of truth the tower of lies he was building threatened to come crashing down around him. He had to do something to break the line of questioning. He stood up. "I need to take a leak, guys," he said.

"Sit the fuck down," said Thompson.

Fenby tried to smile, hands out, showing his palms, forcing his body language to be as open as possible. "Guys, come on, this is me. Let me take a leak."

Kettering looked over at Mickey and nodded. Mickey reached into his jacket and pulled out a revolver.

"For fuck's sake, guys, what's going on?"

"Sit down," said Kettering. "Or I swear to God Mickey'll put a bullet in your nuts."

Fenby stared at the weapon. It looked real enough. It was a big gun and he figured it would make a lot of noise if it went off. His bedsit was one of a dozen in the building and a lot of the occupants were unemployed, which meant there was a good chance that someone would call the police. That wouldn't help him, of course, but it might make them think twice about pulling the trigger. "You're going to shoot me? The cops'll be all over you. Even in Birmingham they dial three nines when they hear gunshots."

Just as Fenby finished speaking Mickey stepped forward and whipped the gun across his face, smashing several of his top teeth and ripping open his lip. Fenby fell back on to the sofa, blood pouring down his face.

"Get him a towel," said Kettering and Thompson went through to the bathroom.

Tears trickled down Fenby's face, mingling with the blood that was streaming from his torn lip. His jaw felt as if it was on fire but he also felt light-headed, as if he was seconds away from passing out. He blinked his eyes and realised that both of his hands were shaking. He folded them, but his upper body was still wracked with tremors. Thompson came out of the bathroom and threw a towel at Fenby, who grabbed it and held it to his face. Pain lanced through his jaw and he swallowed blood.

Kettering got up from the armchair. He walked over, sat down on the arm of the sofa and leaned towards Fenby. "Here's the thing, mate," he said. "Mickey here saw your pal Gracie at the boxing thing I was at in London. He didn't say anything at the time because he was on another table but he recognised Gracie. Except he wasn't Gracie when Mickey saw him. His name was . . ." He looked over at Mickey. "What was his name?"

"Alistair something or other," said Mickey. "He was putting together a cannabis deal. Tons of it, coming in from Morocco. This was about a year ago."

"And tell him what happened," said Kettering.

"Ship was boarded when it arrived in Southampton. Three tons of cannabis got seized by Customs and half a dozen guys got sent down. But Alistair wasn't touched. No one could understand why, because he was involved from the start."

Fenby shrugged. "That's news to me."

"Yeah, well, it does make you think, doesn't it?" said Kettering. "So I asked Mickey here to make a few enquiries. And you know what? No one in London has heard of your mates. James Gracie, Garry Edwards. No one's heard a dicky bird."

"They're fucking arms dealers," muttered Fenby. "They don't advertise."

"We weren't looking in the Yellow Pages," said Kettering. "We asked people who asked people and no one knows anything about them. They don't exist, mate. They're on nobody's radar."

"Except yours, Ian," said Thompson.

"Yeah, except yours," said Kettering, staring at Fenby.

"He was an undercover cop, that's what I was told," said Mickey.

"Bollocks," said Fenby. "I know guys he's sold guns to. If he was a cop he couldn't sell guns, could he?"

"He showed us guns, didn't he?" said Thompson. "That doesn't prove a thing."

"It's entrapment," said Fenby.

"That's a big word for a football hooligan," said Mickey.

"Fuck you," said Fenby. He took the towel away from his mouth and stared at it. It was wet with blood. "I need to get to hospital."

Kettering looked across at Thompson and gestured with his chin. Thompson went into the kitchen.

"Where's he going?" asked Fenby. Blood was trickling down his chin so he pressed the towel against it, wincing with the pain.

"He's going to have a look around, Ian. A good look."

"Why?"

"Because we think you're a fucking slag copper, that's why," said Mickey. "Same as your mate."

Fenby stared at Kettering. "Simon, they took you out and showed you the guns. They gave you a hand

326

grenade to throw, you said. A fucking hand grenade. The cops don't do that."

"They do if they really want to stitch you up," said Kettering. He took another long pull on his cigar. "They could be waiting for us to get the money so that they can seize that. Plus, they might be trying to see who else they can pull in. Your mates asked a hell of a lot of questions in the pub after their little demonstration. For all I know they were wired and it's all on tape. So if you are a cop, Ian, and if you're in on this, save yourself a lot of pain and just tell me now."

"Do I look like a fucking narc?" asked Fenby.

"Who knows what a narc looks like?"

"How long have you known me?"

"That's not the point, is it? The question is, are you an undercover cop or not?"

There was a crash from the bedroom, the sound of a drawer hitting the floor.

"If there's anything in this flat that says who you really are, then you're fucked," said Kettering.

"Totally fucked," said Mickey. "I'm going to see to that."

Fenby stared sullenly at the two men as he dabbed at his smashed lips.

Chaudhry was walking up the stairs, about to leave the mosque in Dynevor Road with Malik, when he saw Khalid coming down.

Khalid beamed. "Salaam, brothers," he said. "Is everything good?"

"You tell us," said Chaudhry.

"You sound upset, brother," said Khalid. He put a hand on his shoulder. "Wait for me in the coffee shop round the corner until I have prayed," he whispered. His breath was rancid and Chaudhry fought the urge to retch.

Khalid leaned close to Malik, kissed him on both cheeks and then went down the stairs.

"What did he say?" asked Malik.

"He wants us to wait for him," said Chaudhry.

"That's it? We wait? Like dogs? What about the fact that we sat in all last night and he never called?"

"Hush, brother," said Chaudhry. Half a dozen young Pakistanis came thudding down the stairs. One of them was wearing a coat over candy-striped pyjamas and was chewing gum. Chaudhry shook his head contemptuously.

They went out into the street. Fajr prayers had to be completed before sunrise so the road was still illuminated by street lights and there were delivery trucks parked in front of many of the businesses. Chaudhry took Malik along to the coffee shop. It was a popular place for Muslims to take their morning coffee after prayers and was always busy at that time of the day. They found a corner table and Chaudhry ordered two coffees from the Turkish girl behind the counter. She was pretty and he watched her slim figure as she busied herself at the coffee-maker. She glanced over her shoulder and caught him looking and he felt his cheeks redden.

"You're Raj, aren't you?" she said with a smile, as she put the two cups down in front of him.

"Yeah. Do I know you?"

"I'm the girl that keeps serving you coffee," she said. "I heard your friends call you Raj."

"Yeah, that's me."

"I'm Sena." She smiled again and went on to the next customer.

Chaudhry took the coffees over to the table. "I think she fancies me," he said as he sat down.

"Who?"

"The girl behind the counter. Sena."

"You've got a girlfriend."

"Who?"

"You know who. That bird your dad fixed you up with. What was her name?"

"Jamila? She's not a girlfriend."

"Got on like a house on fire, you said. Brains and beauty."

"It's early days," said Chaudhry. "And she's from a good Muslim family so it's going to go very slowly."

"Whereas Turkish girls are easy, is that what you're saying?"

Chaudhry laughed. "No, I'm just saying that she told me her name and I think that she fancies me." He sipped his coffee. "The Jamila thing is a bloody minefield," he said. "It's like every second thing I say to her is a lie."

"What, you don't fancy her?"

"I fancy her, sure, but because of what we're doing I'm going to have to keep lying to her. I want to tell her the truth but I can't. I don't want our relationship to be based on lies but it is."

"So put her on the back burner until this is over," said Malik. "Like you said, she's a Muslim; she's not going to rush into anything." He looked at his watch. "What's taking Khalid so long?"

"You know he likes to pray twice as long as anyone else," said Chaudhry. "It's his thing."

"And treating everyone like mushrooms," said Malik. "That's really his thing. He likes controlling people. That's what this is about. He wants us to be at his beck and call."

They had waited in all evening expecting Khalid to phone, but he hadn't. At just before eight o'clock a man they didn't recognise had turned up and asked for the backpacks and phone and taken them away. Both backpacks had been locked with small padlocks but they had been able to peep inside and it looked as if they contained only old telephone directories. Chaudhry had asked the man when Khalid would call but he had just shaken his head and said nothing.

They had almost finished their coffee when Khalid appeared in the doorway. He looked around, then waved at them to join him on the pavement.

"Too many ears," he explained. "These days the mosque leaks like a sieve. We can trust nobody." He gestured with his chin. "Walk with me."

He headed off along the pavement and Chaudhry and Malik joined him, Chaudhry on Khalid's left, Malik on his right. "You seem tense, brothers," said Khalid.

"Tense?" repeated Malik. "Of course we're tense. What were you playing at? Was it a test, is that it?"

330

Khalid's eyes narrowed. "Are you questioning me, brother?"

"If I was questioning you I would have done it when you told us to get into the van," said Malik. "We did everything you asked of us. And then you told us to go home. So I ask you again, brother, was it a test?"

Khalid nodded slowly. "Yes. You were being tested."

"So we're not trusted? After everything we have been through you still don't trust us?"

"It's not a matter of trust," said Khalid.

"Are you sure? Because trust shouldn't be an issue, brother. We have met The Sheik, remember? Have you, brother?"

"No," said Khalid. "I was never granted that honour."

"That's what I thought," said Malik. "We had tea with The Sheik. He told us how valuable we were to him, how we were a resource that would be used with care, that our mission would be as important as that of the martyrs of Nine-Eleven."

"You are angry," said Khalid. "I understand." They looked right and left and crossed a side street.

"Harvey, chill, brother," said Chaudhry. "We're just a bit concerned that nobody told us what was happening," he said to Khalid.

"I understand," said Khalid.

"You understand?" Malik glared at Khalid. "Do not patronise me, brother. Was it your idea to test us?"

"Harvey, mate, give him a break, will you?" said Chaudhry.

"We were told to run a rehearsal," said Khalid quietly. "It was a question of testing the logistics."

"The logistics?" repeated Malik.

"We needed to make sure that we could get everyone in the right place at the right time. We had to arrange vehicles and drivers. We had to check that phones worked and that we could get everyone to work to a schedule." Two Pakistanis walked towards them and Khalid stopped speaking until they had gone by. "You are very important to our organisation, brothers," he said. "We have a lot riding on you so we have to be sure that everything works. We must leave nothing to chance."

"And the test, was it successful?" asked Malik.

Khalid shrugged. "Mostly."

"Mostly?" said Chaudhry. "What do you mean, mostly?"

"One brother didn't turn up," said Khalid.

"What happened?"

"We don't know," said Khalid. "But we will find out."

"Do you think he's a spy?" asked Malik, and Chaudhry tensed.

Khalid turned to look at Malik. "Why would you ask that, brother?" he said quietly. He stopped suddenly, catching the two men unawares.

Malik looked over at Chaudhry, a look of panic in his eyes.

"We were talking about it earlier," said Chaudhry. "We thought that you didn't trust us, that you suspected there might be a spy in the organisation."

332

Khalid continued to stare balefully at Malik. "That's what the police are doing, isn't it?" said Chaudhry. "They put spies in the mosques and they pay informers to betray our brothers."

"It is not the police," said Khalid, still looking at Malik. "It is MI5, the security service." He started walking again and the wind tugged at his dishdash. Chaudhry and Malik matched his pace. "The brother who let us down is not a spy, I am sure of that. But he has shown that he cannot be relied upon so we will have to deal with him." He laughed softly. "But a spy? No."

"So when do we do it for real?" asked Chaudhry.

"You are eager," said Khalid. "That's good. But we have to wait until the moment is right."

"And the backpacks?" said Malik. "Why did we have to have backpacks?"

"That was to test the logistics," said Khalid. "Why do the backpacks concern you?"

"You know why the backpacks worry us," said Chaudhry.

"Brothers, the backpacks were a test of our logistics. To see if we could get a dozen pieces of equipment to a dozen brothers and get them to a specific location at a specific time." He smiled. "You thought you were carrying explosives, didn't you?" he said.

"We didn't know what to think," said Chaudhry.

Khalid nodded slowly. "You thought that there might be explosives in the packs, but still you went. That showed commitment, brothers. And don't think that commitment wasn't noticed and appreciated."

"You wanted to see if we were prepared to become shahid?" said Chaudhry.

"Was there any doubt about that, brother?"

Chaudhry sighed. "I had hoped that I had already proved my loyalty," he said. He nodded at Malik. "Harvey too."

"The two of you are too valuable to become shahid," Khalid said. "A lot of time, trouble and money has gone into training you and it would be a waste to make you martyrs. The operation we are planning will involve guns, not explosives. And provided you follow your instructions you will kill more kaffirs than died in the Twin Towers and you will live to fight another day."

"That's what he said? You're sure?" asked Shepherd. "He said explosives weren't going to be used?"

Chaudhry nodded. "Word for word, pretty much."

"Guns," said Malik. "He said we'd be using guns."

They were sitting in a coffee shop in Camden, close to the market. Chaudhry and Malik had spent twenty minutes walking among the market stalls before Shepherd had called Chaudhry and assured him that they weren't being followed. They sat in a corner away from the windows.

"No explosives but lots of casualties?" said Shepherd.

"More than died in Nine-Eleven," said Chaudhry. "That's what he said."

Shepherd raised his eyebrows. "With guns? Did he say what type?"

Malik shook his head. "He said there would be lots of casualties and that we would get away."

Shepherd sipped his coffee. It was important intelligence that he'd have to pass to Button as soon as possible. There had been about a dozen men at St Pancras, but how could a dozen men kill three thousand civilians with guns?

"How far do we take this, John?" asked Chaudhry.

"What do you mean?"

"We went to the station with backpacks. What if there had been bombs in those packs and they'd been detonated remotely?"

"That was never going to happen, Raj. Like Khalid said, you're too valuable to waste on a suicide attack."

"We don't know that for sure," said Chaudhry. "Suppose they target the Prime Minister? Or the US President? You don't think they'd worry about sacrificing me or Harvey if they had a target like that?"

"They've never talked about using you for an assassination," said Shepherd. "And none of your training has been for that."

"We were taught sniping in Pakistan," said Malik.

"You're over-thinking it," said Shepherd. "Trust me, you're worrying about nothing. Everything that happened at St Pancras points to a large-scale operation using a dozen or so men. And even a dozen men with suicide bombs wouldn't kill more than a hundred or so people." He shrugged. "That sounds blasé and I don't mean it that way, but it's a matter of effectiveness. The four bombers in London on 7th July 2005 killed fifty-two people and injured seven hundred, and while that's horrific it's still not the thousands that Khalid is talking about. Suicide bombs are terrible things but a bomb in a crowded station is effective only within twenty feet or so; there are simply too many bodies around absorbing the shrapnel. You get horrific injuries close to the source of the explosion but beyond fifty feet it's survivable and at a hundred feet you'd be unlucky to get a scratch. What Khalid is talking about is something much, much bigger."

"So what's the plan, John?" asked Chaudhry. "What do we do?"

"We wait and see what Khalid does next. I'll talk to our technical people and we'll see about increasing our electronic surveillance. Now we know he won't let you take your phones with you we'll have to come up with something else."

"Tracking devices in our shoes?" said Malik. "Real secret-agent stuff?"

"Something like that," said Shepherd. "The stuff they have these days is incredibly small. It's not like it was in the old days when you used to have a metal box taped to your crotch and a microphone stuck to your chest."

Malik looked at his watch. "Do you mind if I push off, John?" he asked. "I've got a five-a-side match later."

"Sure," said Shepherd. "I think we're done. Good job."

Malik got up to leave. "I'll stay and finish my coffee, brother," said Chaudhry. Malik nodded and left. Chaudhry stirred sugar into his coffee. "So how long have you been working with MI5?"

"Fifteen years, give or take," lied Shepherd. He'd already agreed with Button not to reveal his police or SAS background to Chaudhry and Malik. She'd decided that they'd react best to him if they thought he was career MI5 and believed he was fairly senior in the organisation, rather than an SAS trooper turned undercover cop who had been with the Security Service for less than two years.

"How did you deal with the stress? The constant lying?"

"I compartmentalise the job," said Shepherd. "You can't be on all day every day. So you make sure you have time on your own, or with your family, when you can be yourself."

"But I can't do that, John, can I? I have to lie even when I'm with my parents. My dad, he'd probably be proud of me, but my mum would hit the roof. And even if they were cool with what I was doing I can't tell them, can I? I can't tell anyone that I helped kill The Sheik. Or that I'm working against terrorists who are planning to kill thousands of civilians. I have to lie to my family, to my friends, to my fellow students. There are only two people that I can be honest with: you and Harvey."

"I understand," said Shepherd.

"Understanding is all well and good, but I need to know how to deal with it," said Chaudhry.

It was a good point, Shepherd knew, but he wasn't sure how to respond to it. Chaudhry was right, undercover work was stressful. Most operatives couldn't do it for more than a few years. Divorces, breakdowns and career burnouts were common, which is why his bosses at the Met, SOCA and MI5 insisted on six-monthly psychological evaluations for all its undercover people. But Chaudhry and Malik didn't have the luxury of a psychologist; all they had was Shepherd, and all he could offer them was the benefit of his experience.

"Do you feel guilty about lying, is that it?" asked Shepherd.

"With my family, of course. They ask me how my studies are going and I say great and they ask me what I do in my free time and then I'm a bit evasive, and I really had to lie about the whole Pakistan training-camp thing. But that's not where the stress comes from. It's when I'm talking to Khalid and the others that it gets to me. My heart starts beating like it's going to burst and sometimes I can feel my legs trembling. My mouth goes dry, which means I sometimes stumble over my words. If they see that they're going to know that something is wrong."

Shepherd nodded sympathetically. "You have to try to believe in what you're saying," he said. "You're like an actor playing a part, and you have to convince yourself that you are what you're pretending to be. That conviction will then flow out of you. But to be honest, Raj, you're worrying too much. You're not pretending to be someone else; you're yourself. It's only your beliefs that you're misrepresenting. All you need to do is to convince Khalid and the rest that you're an Islamic fundamentalist who has embraced jihad. All the hard work has been done. You went to Pakistan, you went right into the lion's den, you went through with the rehearsal at St Pancras. You've already proved yourself."

"But sometimes Khalid looks at me like he doesn't believe me."

"What do you mean, specifically?"

Chaudhry shrugged. "It's difficult to explain. He stares at me, like he's looking through me. He frowns sometimes, like he's thinking that something's not right. He does the same with Harvey."

"That's your guilty conscience kicking in. You know you're lying and you know that lying is wrong, and because you're basically a moral person you expect to be punished for what you're doing. I'm not saying you want to be caught out, but part of you expects it to happen. Only sociopaths can lie without any sort of guilt."

Chaudhry grinned. "That's what my dad always used to say when I was a kid. He didn't care what I'd done, provided I told the truth."

"That's what all parents tell their children," said Shepherd. "Not that they always mean it."

"My dad did," said Chaudhry. "Even if I did something stupid, provided I owned up to it and provided I said I was sorry and tried to make it right, he wouldn't punish me. Mind you, Dad didn't have to punish me, it was enough to know that I'd disappointed him."

"He sounds like a good guy."

"He is," said Chaudhry. "He's never laid a finger on me, my whole life. A lot of Asian parents reckon that if you spare the rod you spoil the child, but my mum and dad have been great." He smiled ruefully. "I wish I could tell him what I'm doing."

"You can't," said Shepherd. "You know that, right?"

"Oh, I had it drummed into me by Ms Button. But the fact that he doesn't know means that I have to lie to him, and you don't know how much I hate that."

"No, I understand. I have a son, and I hate having to lie to him. But when you work for MI5 it comes with the job."

Chaudhry tilted his head on one side. "You said you weren't married."

Shepherd's stomach lurched. He'd made the worst possible mistake that an undercover agent could make: he'd slipped out of character. He'd been so relaxed in Chaudhry's company that he'd answered as Dan Shepherd and not as John Whitehill. He forced himself to appear relaxed, and smiled as if he didn't have a care in the world, but he could feel his heart pounding. "She died, a few years ago," he said.

"Sorry," said Chaudhry.

"Yeah, my life's a bit complicated to say the least," said Shepherd. "Thing is, it always sounds strange to say widower, but I guess that's what I am. Easier to say I'm not married."

"And you're a single parent?"

Shepherd nodded. "He's at boarding school, so it works out well." He felt strange giving out personal information, which was something he almost never did when he was working. But having Chaudhry talk about telling the truth had struck a chord. Shepherd didn't enjoy lying, even though over the years he had become an expert in the art of telling untruths.

"I bet he misses you."

"I think he's having too much fun at the moment," said Shepherd.

"But he knows you work for MI5?"

"To be honest, no."

"And you're okay lying to him?"

"It's not like that," said Shepherd. "I very rarely look him in the eye and lie to him. On the very rare occasions I do then it's because there's a very good reason."

"And don't you forget sometimes? Forget what you said before? That's my nightmare, that I'll give myself away by forgetting something."

"I'm lucky," said Shepherd. "I've got a photographic memory. I pretty much remember everything I see and hear."

"Eidetic they call it, right?" said Chaudhry. "Kid I went to school had it. But the funny thing was that he wasn't that great at exams."

"Same with me," said Shepherd. "Just because you can remember stuff doesn't mean you can write great essays. But it's a big help when you're undercover."

"I worry that I'm thinking too much before answering. Especially with Khalid. It's as if I have to run everything through a filter, checking that I'm saying the right thing. It's so bloody stressful."

Shepherd empathised. It was exactly how he worked when he was undercover. It was vital that he never said anything that wasn't known by his character, so everything that came out of his mouth had to be analysed and approved. Often he would go into an operation fully briefed on most of the people he would come across, but that didn't mean his character had access to the same information. He had to be constantly aware of who he'd met and who he hadn't, and what he had said to them. He understood exactly what Chaudhry meant about it being stressful, because he had to do all that without any sign of hesitation. Hesitation could easily be taken as evasiveness so it was important that conversations flowed. Humour was good, banter back and forth could slow down a conversation and give him time to think, but sometimes jokes weren't appropriate. Props were good, especially drinks. If a question blindsided him a sip of his whisky would give him time to get his thoughts straight. And as much as he disliked smoking, a cigarette was a perfect way of getting a few seconds of thinking time.

"The trick is to rehearse stories in your head," said Shepherd. "Get so familiar with them that you can tell them without thinking. That way if you're in a situation that makes you uncomfortable you can relax and tell the story because in your mind you've told it a hundred times before. And it helps if it's a funny story. If you get people laughing that takes their mind off you. Makes them less suspicious, anyway."

"Khalid doesn't have much of a sense of humour," said Chaudhry. "And he's not one for anecdotes."

"Then try asking him questions. Play stupid. Most people think they're smarter than everyone else and you can play to that. You don't need to act like a simpleton but asking for help and for information will make him feel superior. You have to be careful that you don't come over as if you're pumping him for information. Don't ask for facts, or for hard information. Tell him you're feeling anxious and ask him how he deals with that. Ask him how he stays so focused. Give him the opportunity to talk about himself; that's what people love to do most."

Chaudhry laughed. "You make it sound like seduction," he said. "That's exactly how you go about winning over a woman, right? Make her laugh, ask her about herself."

"That's not far off the mark," said Shepherd. "In a way it is all about seduction. You need them to like you and trust you, so you say and do whatever you have to, to achieve that."

"And then when they trust you, you fuck them. It's exactly the same." Chaudhry nodded thoughtfully. "Yeah, I can do that."

"You've got to be careful, though," said Shepherd. "You've heard of Stockholm Syndrome? Where hostages start to build empathy with their captors?"

"Sure."

"Well, it can happen when you're undercover. You're putting so much effort into getting them to trust you that there's a danger of you starting to get drawn into the relationship."

"I doubt that's going to happen with Khalid," said Chaudhry. "He's a nasty piece of work. He really does hate us, you know."

For a moment Shepherd wondered what Chaudhry meant by "us" and then he realised that he was talking about the British.

"What I can't understand about people like him is that they're happy enough to live here and take advantage of what this country has to offer, yet they put all this effort into trying to destroy it," said Chaudhry. "He gets full benefits, you know. He managed to persuade his GP to say that he's got a bad back so he gets disability payments and everything."

"Is he really in pain?"

"Is he hell," said Chaudhry. "But he faked it. They gave him a scan and sent him to a specialist who found nothing, but what can they do? If he says he has constant back pain they have to believe him, so now he gets a couple of hundred quid a week from the state. They pay his rent, he doesn't pay council tax, and he was saying that he never pays his electricity or water bills because they can't cut him off since he's disabled. I tell you, John, this country is going to the dogs." He sipped his coffee and sighed. "I'm sorry. I didn't mean to sound off. It's just that I hate what's happening to England. And it's people like Khalid that are trying to ruin it for everyone else. He wants sharia law here. He wants women to cover themselves. He wants us to become a Muslim country. I just don't get it. If he's that unhappy with things here why doesn't he just go and live in Pakistan, or Saudi Arabia?" He smiled at Shepherd. "Have you ever been to Pakistan?"

Shepherd shook his head.

"It's a cesspit, mainly," said Chaudhry. "Don't get me wrong, the people are great and I've got family out there, but it's corrupt, it's dangerous, and the rich hold the power of life and death over the poor. If you're rich or connected to the army you can get away with murder, literally. It's a country where the rich are getting richer and the poor are getting poorer. That's why practically everyone in Pakistan wants to come and live in England. I don't understand why anyone would prefer that way of life to the way we live here." He shrugged. "Rant over," he said.

"Not a problem," said Shepherd. "Better you let off steam with me rather than let Khalid know how you feel." He looked at his watch.

"Have you got to go?" asked Chaudhry.

"I'm fine," said Shepherd. "I can stay as long as you want. That's what I'm here for, Raj. To help you in any way I can."

"Can I ask you something?"

"Sure."

"Is your name really John?" asked Chaudhry, his voice a low whisper as if he was afraid to ask the question.

Shepherd smiled as he stared at Chaudhry, but his mind was racing. Protocol was to stick with his MI5 alias under any circumstances, and to never, ever, admit that he was anyone other than John Whitehill. But the fact that Chaudhry had asked the question meant that he already suspected that Whitehill was an alias, and if he believed that and Shepherd still lied then it would destroy any trust they had. "No," said Shepherd. "It isn't."

Chaudhry closed his eyes and sighed. "I knew it," he said. He opened his eyes again. "But I appreciate your honesty. You could have lied but you didn't. I respect that."

"Don't take this the wrong way, Raj," said Shepherd. "It's the way that MI5 works. It has to be that way. If you don't know my real name then you can't let it slip out by mistake. Also, it protects me. The John Whitehill name is specific to this operation so if it gets used by anyone we know where they picked it up."

Chaudhry frowned. "I don't understand."

"Suppose we hear the name Whitehill mentioned on a phone tap out in Pakistan. That's an immediate red flag for us and we'd know that we have a problem in London. But if my real name was being used it might have come up in a dozen operations, so we wouldn't know where the problem was."

"I guess that makes sense."

"And suppose you knew my real name as well as my cover name, it would just add to the pressure you're under. Yet another lie you have to tell." He leaned towards Chaudhry. "If you want I'll tell you my real name," he said. "You've earned the right to know who I am. But it's in your best interests not to know. And if you ever need to contact MI5, the John Whitehill name is the key to instant access to me or, if I'm not available, to another case officer who will be apprised of your situation immediately. If you were to call up and ask for me by my real name they'd deny all knowledge of me."

"So you're under as much pressure as we are, aren't you?" said Chaudhry. "We have to lie to everyone around us and you have to pretend to be someone you're not."

"It's not the same thing, not really," said Shepherd. "Look, Raj, many's the time I've sat opposite a handler just like you're sitting opposite me."

"Is that what you are?" asked Chaudhry. "My handler?"

"That's the jargon," said Shepherd.

"It makes me sound like an animal."

Shepherd smiled. "It's not meant that way," he said. "It's more a question of 'handle with care'. But the point I'm making is that I'm usually the one being handled. And I know how difficult it is to be undercover. I know how lonely it can be. I know how you feel isolated and vulnerable. And I know that I'm your lifeline." Chaudhry lowered his eyes and stared at the table. "Raj, look at me," said Shepherd. Chaudhry did as he was told. "I understand exactly what you're going through and I'll do whatever I can to make it easier for you. I'll be watching your back every step of the way. And I promise you that I won't lie to you, okay?"

Chaudhry nodded slowly. "Thanks," he said.

Shepherd caught a black cab back to Hampstead. As he was letting himself into the flat one of the three mobiles he was carrying began to ring. He took it out. It was his Nokia, the Garry Edwards phone. The caller was withholding his number but he took the call anyway. There were only two people who had the number: Ray Fenby and Simon Kettering.

"Garry, how the hell are you?" It was Kettering.

"All good," said Shepherd. "What's up?"

"Got someone who'd like a chinwag with you, if you're up for it," said Kettering. "Friend of mine from Germany is interested in the same sort of kit you're getting for me."

"Sweet," said Shepherd.

"Big numbers too. Figured you and he ought to get together."

"No problem," said Shepherd. "Where are you?"

"Let's do it down your way," said Kettering. "Just wanted to check that you were interested. I'll fix up a time. Tomorrow good for you?"

"Sunday? You not going to church?"

"Ha bloody ha," said Kettering. "Are you around or not?"

"I'll clear my diary," said Shepherd.

He ended the call and sat down on the sofa, tapping the mobile against the side of his head, his forehead creased into a frown. A European connection was exactly what Button had been hoping for. The last thing that Shepherd had expected was to have it handed to him on a plate.

Kamran Khalid never felt at home in London, but he never felt as if he was out of place either. He wore a long grey shirt over light-green baggy pants and had a white skullcap on his head, and the man he was with wore similar clothing, but in the English capital in the third millennium there was nothing at all unusual about the way he was dressed. Nor was there anything unusual about his ethnicity — as they walked across the bridge from Stratford town centre the majority of people around him had Asian or Arabic heritage and in the space of five minutes he had heard half a dozen languages spoken, none of them English. London had become one of the most ethnically mixed cities on the planet, which is why it was the perfect place for a terrorist to hide. The police weren't permitted to stop and question anybody solely on the basis of their appearance, not even to ask if the person had the necessary permission to be in the country. Khalid did have the correct paperwork. Better than that, he had a British passport. And the man who was with him, an Arab, had a Dubai passport and the correct visa to allow him entry into the United Kingdom. The passport was a fake, but it was a good one. The visa was real, though, obtained by the simple means of paying a thousand-dollar bribe to a corrupt HKBA official.

They were heading towards Westfield shopping mall in East London, close to the site of the 2012 Olympics. With three hundred shops, seventy restaurants and almost two million square feet of retail space, it was the largest urban shopping mall in Europe.

The two men spoke in Arabic, but they kept their voices low and whenever anyone of Arabic appearance was near they kept silent. Both men had spent three hours carrying out anti-surveillance procedures before meeting, including switching cabs and using the public transport system, and they were confident that they were not being followed.

"It is busy, brother," said the Arab. His real name was Abu al Khayr, which means "one who does good". From the standpoint of the men and women plotting terrorist atrocities in the West his name was appropriate because he was an al-Qaeda paymaster. He travelled the world and funnelled the organisation's money to where it would do the most harm. He appeared on FBI, CIA and MI5 databases under several names but he had never been fingerprinted and none of the security services knew his true role within al-Qaeda.

"It's always busy," said Khalid. "Busiest at weekends but even on a quiet day there will be tens of thousands of people here." They took the escalators to the top floor and bought coffees at Pret A Manger, then sat at a table by the window so they could watch the crowds pass by.

"So tell me about security," said Abu al Khayr.

Khalid chuckled softly. He nodded towards an obese woman with badly permed hair who was standing next to a gangly Asian by the escalators. Both wore black suits and had identification cards strapped to their forearms in clear plastic holders. They were deep in conversation. "That is your security," he said. "They are usually in pairs and are more involved with giving directions than they are with monitoring what is happening. There are other security guards wearing peaked hats but they are not armed and they do not appear to be well trained. They have radios but that is all."

As they watched the pair, a woman in a full burka with two toddlers stopped to ask the Asian a question. The Asian pointed down towards Marks & Spencer.

"There are a lot of sisters here," said Abu al Khayr.

"This is London. There are sisters wherever you go," said Khalid. "It cannot be helped. One in five Londoners is now a Muslim. We can instruct our brothers to be careful but even so there are certain to be Muslim casualties."

Abu al Khayr nodded. "Martyrs," he said. "There will be a place in Heaven for them." He looked up at a small black plastic dome in the ceiling, a few inches across. "There is CCTV everywhere," he said, a statement and not a question.

"Every square foot is covered by CCTV cameras, every walkway, every shop, every restaurant, every entrance and exit. There is nowhere that is not covered. But that is their problem — there are too many to be monitored in real time. Once they are aware of an incident they can look at it, and they have all footage stored on hard drives, but in terms of monitoring real-time security they are virtually useless. By the time they realise what is going on, it will be too late. And at that point the more footage they get the better. Every time the world sees the video of the planes smashing into the World Trade Center it reminds them of our victory. So we want the world to see what happens here."

They sat in silence as they drank their coffee, both deep in thought.

"So tell me what you think we should do," said Abu al Khayr eventually.

Khalid finished his coffee. "Let me show you," he said.

The two men left Pret A Manger and went down one level. "This is the first floor," said Khalid. "On this level there are only two ways out, and one is through the Marks & Spencer store. From there they can get outside, so we will need a brother there to stop people leaving. But it is also our way out." He pointed down the mall towards the John Lewis store. "To the right of John Lewis there is a single door leading to car park A. That gives us direct access to the mall." He pointed up to the second floor. "There is no escape from upstairs. There are restaurants, the bowling alley and the cinema. But the top two floors are always less busy than the ground floor and the lower ground, so it is there we will strike first."

They took the escalators down to the ground floor. Khalid took Abu al Khayr through the crowds to a set of glass doors that led to the bridge leading across the railway lines to Stratford Regional Station and the town centre. It was the way they had come into the mall. "This is the exit to the station," he said. "There are five doors, a single at each side and three double doors between them. Do you see the handles?"

Each door had a long vertical chrome pole as a handle. Abu al Khayr nodded.

"All we need is a chain and a padlock," said Khalid. "It will take a matter of seconds and all of the doors will be locked shut. Once done no one can get out, and no one can get in."

"The glass is reinforced?"

"It is. It will resist a sledgehammer."

"And how many exits are there in total?"

"On the ground floor there are six. All have the same type of doors and all can be chained shut within seconds."

There was a constant stream of shoppers entering and leaving the mall. "Won't people try to stop them locking the doors?" asked Abu al Khayr.

"This entrance is the busiest," said Khalid. "We will have a brother wearing a security uniform." He grinned. "We already have two brothers on the security staff and hope to have more within the next few days. The owners are very keen to demonstrate their commitment to diversity."

"They make it so easy," said Abu al Khayr.

"Always," said Khalid. "They see it as a strength but it is their biggest weakness. And one that we shall take full advantage of."

They began walking through the mall. It was packed with shoppers and they were constantly being bumped into or having to step aside to avoid strollers and wheelchairs.

"How many people are here?" asked Abu al Khayr.

"On a busy day, more than forty thousand. On a quiet day, maybe half that."

"That's a lot of people," said Abu al Khayr. "As big as a football stadium."

"Exactly," said Khalid. "And think how many passengers there are on a plane. A few hundred. Here we have tens of thousands of people and not a single check on who comes and goes." Three Asian youths in baggy jeans and baseball caps pushed by them, swearing and laughing. "Do you think anyone has searched them for a knife?" asked Khalid. "Or a gun?" He shook his head. "There are no checks at all. Not one."

They reached the halfway point of the mall. Shops branched off to the left and at the end were four double doors that led to more shops outside the main mall. Khalid put his mouth close to Abu al Khayr's ear. "One man could lock the doors and start shooting. In the panic they would have only one way to run." He looked up and gestured at the levels above them. From where they were standing they could see shoppers on the first and second floors and beyond them the glass ceiling and the clouds high in the sky. "Just look around you. Look at the crowds. Think of them panicking and falling over each other, like stampeding cattle. And from above come the bullets of our brothers."

Abu al Khayr nodded enthusiastically. Khalid started walking again and Abu al Khayr hurried after him. They walked towards the John Lewis store.

"This is the most complicated area," said Khalid. "Ahead there are two double doors that lead to John Lewis. To the left are six doors leading to the outdoor shops, and to the right are six doors leading to Stratford International Station." Abu al Khayr looked around. There were shoppers walking in all directions and it was as crowded as a Moroccan souk. "You notice how the ground floor of John Lewis is on the other side of the doors?" said Khalid. "Once the mall doors are locked our brothers will be able to exit through the store. They can enter on the first floor, use the internal stairs and leave at ground-floor level. They can do the same at Marks & Spencer at the other end."

"I understand," said Abu al Khayr. "They can mingle with the shoppers and escape."

Khalid heard Arabic voices behind him and he looked over his shoulder. An old man with a long straggly grey beard was admonishing two young boys who could have been his great-grandchildren. Next to him was a woman in a full burka sitting in a wheelchair. All that could be seen were her eyes but from them alone it was clear she was as old as the man. An Arab man in a baggy grey suit was pushing the wheelchair, probably the woman's son. The man caught Khalid's glance and he smiled and nodded. Khalid smiled back. He and Abu al Khayr walked away from the Arab family and headed down an escalator to the lower ground level.

There was another exit midway down the mall, at the end of a line of shops leading off a bustling food court. There were three double doors which could be locked with a single padlocked chain.

The final two exits were at the far end of the mall — two double doors leading to the car park and five leading outside to the tube station.

The two men walked outside and sat down on a bench from where they could watch the shoppers pouring into the mall.

"We will need a minimum of fourteen brothers," said Khalid. "That will give us one at each entrance. If they simultaneously lock all the doors then no one can get in, or out. But the more brothers we can get the better. I would prefer twenty."

"Do we have that many?"

Khalid nodded. "We can bring brothers in from Europe. I have spoken to mosques in France and Germany and they have brothers ready and willing to help."

Abu al Khayr grinned. "So we can do it?"

"We can and we will," said Khalid. He took a printed guide to the mall from his shirt pocket and unfolded it. On one side was a floor plan showing the four levels. "Getting access could not be easier," he said. "The brothers can arrive by tube, by train and by car. I suggest all the weapons are brought in by car. There are two car parks, A and B." He tapped them on the map. "Access to car park B, the bigger of the two, is from the lower ground floor only, here and here. Car park A connects to the mall on the lower ground floor, the ground and the first floor. Brothers arriving from the train and tube can collect their weapons and equipment from the car parks on the lower ground floor, then take up their positions. I think two vehicles, parked close to the entrances to the malls. Then we should have a vehicle in each of the three lower levels of car park A, again as close to the mall entrances as possible. That's five vehicles and we need two brothers in each, a driver and an organiser. The brothers with the guns must stay hidden in the back. If we can use sisters in the front, that would be better. Just a husband and wife doing their shopping together."

"There are sisters we can use, but not many are trained in the use of weapons," said Abu al Khayr.

"No need," said Khalid. "They only have to be in the vans. In fact they can drive away before the shooting starts."

"And the police? What happens when the police arrive?"

Khalid grinned. "We will launch the attack at six o'clock," he said. "Most of the police work during the day. It will take them time to call in reinforcements. The first armed response unit will take at least ten minutes and what can one car do? They will see that the doors are locked and they will have to wait for superior officers to arrive. And in the evening that will take time."

"They won't enter the mall?"

"Not with the doors locked, and not when they realise there are armed men inside. They are constrained by health and safety rules. All they will do is keep the area clear until they are able to assess the situation. By the time they've done that it will all be over."

"What about the SAS?"

Khalid shrugged. "They are based in Hereford and even if they leave immediately and fly to London in helicopters they will be too late. This won't be like

Mumbai, where the brothers had to move from room to room looking for targets. We will have all the targets here that we need. The only limiting factor will be the amount of ammunition that our brothers can carry."

"And how many casualties do you anticipate?" asked Abu al Khayr.

"In the first ten minutes I would expect there to be at least a thousand dead and many more injured. If we can continue for half an hour, the total could reach four thousand."

"It defies belief," said Abu al Khayr.

Khalid chuckled softly. "You can believe it, brother," he said. "Hundreds will die in the first few seconds because no one will have time to react. Then there will be panic but there will be no way out. Most will hide in shops but they will be trapped there. The mall is so crowded that every bullet will find a target. Our brothers can continue to shoot until their ammunition is expended."

"And then? What happens then?"

"Then they leave. This will not be a suicide mission, brother. If carried out properly we will kill thousands and our brothers will escape to kill again."

Abu al Khayr nodded as he studied the map. "Yes," he said enthusiastically. "I can see how it will work."

"Inshallah," said Khalid. God willing.

Shepherd headed down the road to Hampstead tube station. A vendor was giving away copies of a glossy magazine at the entrance to the station and Shepherd took the opportunity to stop and have a quick look

358

around. He waited on the northbound platform until two trains had gone through, then he walked across to the southbound platform and caught a train to Charing Cross. To the casual observer he was simply sitting and reading his magazine on the train, but in fact he was taking careful note of everyone who got on or off.

When he did get off the train he walked slowly down the platform and was one of the last passengers to step on to the escalator. He walked through the station as if he was going to buy a ticket but then changed direction abruptly and headed instead for the taxi rank. He took a black cab to Thames House, confident that no one had followed him.

Charlotte Button was waiting for him in a meeting room on the third floor. Several dozen photographs taken from CCTV footage at St Pancras station were pinned to a board that took up most of one of the walls. "How did it go?" she asked him as he sat down at the long highly polished table in the centre of the room.

"He's a bit squirrelly, but that's to be expected," said Shepherd.

"Not too squirrelly, I hope."

"He'll be fine. But I was wondering if it would help for the two of them to have a chat with Caroline Stockmann." Stockmann was an MI5 psychologist who was responsible for Shepherd's six-monthly psychological evaluations.

Button turned her back on the photographs and folded her arms. "What makes you say that?"

"It's no biggie, it's just that the pressure is mounting and Caroline is always good at getting to the heart of any problems I might have."

"Caroline evaluates you twice a year to check that you're up to undercover work," said Button. "If it ever gets to the point that you're showing signs of being overstressed then we can move you into another area of work. That's not an option for Chaudhry and Malik. This isn't their job; it's their lives. Even if they are under pressure there's not much we can do other than offer as much support as we can. It's not as if we can pull them out and put in someone else, is it? We've got to work with what we've got."

"I agree. I just thought it might help them, that's all."

"Do you think I should talk to them?"

"I'm not sure that'll help," said Shepherd. "To be honest, relaxation techniques are what they need. Yoga or meditation. They're fairly tightly wound at the moment."

"Which is good," said Button. "Considering what they've been through and what they're now involved in, they should be stressed. If they suddenly start looking as if they haven't got a care in the world then their al-Qaeda handlers are going to think that something's wrong." She sat down opposite him and linked her fingers. "We're on the home stretch, Spider. St Pancras was a dry run and the real thing is likely to be in days rather than weeks."

Shepherd nodded. She was right. There would be no point in doing a full rehearsal and then putting everything on the back burner.

Button pointed at the photographs. "From our point of view the St Pancras rehearsal was a gift from above, it really was. We've identified eighty-seven possibles from the CCTV footage, based on ethnic status, age and possession of a backpack."

"Ethnic profiling?" said Shepherd.

"We've no choice," said Button. "There were thousands of people at the station and most of them had luggage of one form or another. Now we know that Chaudhry and Malik were given backpacks by Khalid it's a fair enough assumption that anyone else involved also had a backpack. What we've done is trawl through the CCTV footage looking for Asians with backpacks. We've done male and female even though previous attacks in the UK have always involved men. If we'd widened it to include all ethnic groups there would have been thousands and we don't have time for that."

"And you think they had eighty-odd people there?"

"Of course not. What we've got to do now is compare them with our watch list and disregard those who are just innocent travellers."

"What about the passengers who arrived from France? Can't you check with the Border Agency?"

"Unfortunately it's not as simple as that. Passports are checked in France before passengers board but they're not checked at this end. And they're not photographed. But we have CCTV footage of passengers disembarking at St Pancras so we can check that footage against the footage inside the station. We're using a facial recognition system at the moment but it's not great so we might end up doing it manually."

She stood up and walked back to the photograph display. Seven photographs had been put to the right-hand side, separate from the rest. The top two were of Chaudhry and Malik.

"We've already identified four from our watch list," said Button. "They all came up from the tube station at different times and from different trains." She tapped a photograph directly below Malik's. "This one was one of the leaders of Muslims Against Crusades and we have some very nice footage of him burning poppies on Remembrance Day in 2009." She tapped a second photograph, and a third. "These two are from Leeds. Bangladeshi origin but born in the UK. They were both students there up until three years ago. For a while they were full-blown fundamentalists wearing skullcaps and dishdashas to lectures and growing their beards long, then they went off the radar. We know they visited Pakistan last year for six months, and as you can see from the CCTV photographs they are now cleanshaven and wearing western clothing, which is as big a red flag as you'll ever get. They've obviously been told to alter their appearance to blend in."

She pointed at one of the two remaining photographs. "This one wasn't on our watch list but we got a match from the Police National Computer. His father and elder brother set fire to his younger sister five years ago. Third-degree burns over most of her body and she'll never walk again. The father and brother were sent down for ten years. He was also charged but the CPS didn't think there was a good enough case to make against him."

"Honour killing?"

"Not much honour in it, but yes, they wanted her dead because she was going out with a Sikh boy. She was seventeen. She survived only because a neighbour saw what was going on and dialled 999. Although when the ambulance arrived the entire family turned on the paramedics and said that it was Allah's will that she died. Anyway, this guy is from Bradford and had no legitimate reason to be at St Pancras that we know of; plus, he was in Pakistan last year, supposedly to attend a wedding but we've checked flight manifests and he was out of the country for three months."

"Must have been one hell of a wedding."

Button ran a finger along the last photograph. "This one's a little unusual in that he's Egyptian and not Pakistani. Riffat Pasha. At least that was the name he used when he claimed political asylum a few years back. He popped back up on the radar when he started posting on a Fundamentalist website, one of those 'kill all infidels and we'll go to Heaven' rant sites. He's working in a hotel in Mayfair as a kitchen porter."

"Why hasn't he been deported?"

"Because there's a whole industry geared up to keeping him here. He's had a child with a Portuguese woman so if we did try to throw him out of the country his human rights would kick in. Besides, he hasn't actually done anything yet, other than post inflammatory statements."

"Are you thinking his hotel could be the target?"

"It would make sense. We're getting someone to take a look at their staff list to see if anyone else there is on our watch list." She sat down again. "Once we've identified all the members of the cell we can put them under surveillance."

"What about nipping it in the bud and pulling them in now? The rehearsal has to be evidence of conspiracy, hasn't it?"

"We've gone in too soon before and it always ends in tears," said Button. "The cases collapse and the suspects get public sympathy and compensation. We need to catch them in the act, or at least with weapons or explosives."

"I wish I had your confidence," said Shepherd.

"Spider, we'll have them under constant surveillance and as soon as it looks like they're ready to go we'll move in. We'll have all the phone taps we need and we'll be monitoring emails; we're also looking to get trackers fixed to the vehicles. We've identified four vans dropping off Asians with backpacks, the one Chaudhry and Malik were in and three others. We're running checks on the vans now, but they were all sold within the last two weeks so we're not holding out much hope that we'll be able to trace the new owners. However, we'll put an all-points alert out on them so fingers crossed we'll spot the vans somewhere."

"Unless they trash the vans and get new ones for the operation."

"There's no need for them to do that," said Button. "So far as they're concerned the rehearsal went perfectly. I understand your concerns, but we need to let this run a while longer."

"You're the boss, Charlie," said Shepherd.

"Don't worry, I know where the buck stops," she said.

"There's something else I need to talk to you about."

"I'm all ears."

"Kettering just phoned to say that he wants to hook me up with a German guy."

Button's eyes widened. "That's brilliant, Spider."

"Is it, though? He says he wants to link me up with him in London tomorrow and that we could be talking about a big arms sale. But my Spidey sense is tingling."

"What's the problem?"

Shepherd grimaced. "I'm not sure," he said. "But it doesn't feel right. It came out of the blue and now it's rush, rush, rush. And the timing is off. It would make more sense for them to wait until we've delivered the first order."

"What does Fenby say?"

"His phone's off," said Shepherd. "Went straight through to voicemail. I left a message for him to call me."

Button toyed with a small gold stud earring as she looked at him thoughtfully. "You realise it would move the investigation up a notch," she said. "If we could link Kettering and Thompson to terrorist groups in Europe."

"I know, I know. I wish I could be more enthusiastic. But . . ." He raised his hands and then let them fall back on to the table. "It just doesn't feel right."

Button stopped playing with her earring and nodded slowly. "Then we go with your instincts," she said.

"I just don't want to screw it up because of a hunch."

"What about Sam? Have you spoken to him?"

Shepherd shook his head. "He's not going to be able to advise me, and if I do go sticking my head into the lion's den I don't want the Brummie cops watching my back."

"So you're thinking of meeting them? Even though you have doubts?"

Shepherd rubbed his chin. "If I don't Kettering's going to know there's something wrong, isn't he? I might be able to play for time, but if I refuse to meet the German then there's every chance he'll pull out of our deal, which means everything goes tits up." He sat back and sighed. "I don't have a choice, do I? It's a rock and a hard place."

"We can minimise the risks," said Button.

"I'll have to talk to Razor. Kettering wants him there too."

"But he can't tell Sam. You realise that, don't you?"

Shepherd smiled ruefully. "I hope you can see the irony of that," he said. "You tell Sam Hargrove to keep Razor in the dark, and now you want Razor to lie to Sam."

"Point taken," said Button. "What would you rather do? Is it better to tell Sam and have him lie to the Birmingham cops, or keep him in the dark?"

"If it all goes wrong he's going to find out anyway."

"So you want me to fill him in? I'm happy enough to do that. Though it might well mean that MI5 takes over the entire operation."

"To be honest, it looks like we're heading that way whatever happens," said Shepherd. He ran his hands through his hair. "Okay, Razor and I go to the meeting. Five provides the back-up. You fill Sam in."

"Where and when are you going to see them?"

Shepherd shrugged "He's going to let me know first thing tomorrow."

"And what do you want in the way of support?" asked Button.

"Armed back-up, close but not obtrusive. And I'll go to see Amar and fix myself up with a GPS tracker and audio."

"Whatever you need," said Button.

"Guns is what we'll need, Charlie."

"You want to be armed?"

"It'll fit in with our legends. We're underground arms dealers. No reason we couldn't be carrying."

Button grimaced. "I don't see that we can authorise Razor to carry a weapon."

"But it's not a problem for me, right?"

"It's a lot of paperwork, but I'll make it happen," said Button. "But, please, try not to shoot anyone."

"I'll do my best," said Shepherd.

Abu al Khayr tapped on the steering wheel as he looked up and down the street. It was early evening, the pavements were crowded and there was a steady stream of people pouring out of the tube station. "What if he doesn't come?" he asked.

Khalid was sitting in the passenger seat, toying with a subha, a string of Muslim prayer beads. There were one hundred wooden beads on the string, one as big as a pea and the rest about a third of the size. Some of the beads were made of a wood that was as black as polished coal, and others were a dark brown, close to the colour of Khalid's own skin. The small beads were there so that he could keep track of the ninety-nine times that he repeated the name of Allah whenever he prayed. He wasn't praying as he sat in the van; he fingered the beads merely from habit. The beads had been a gift from his father on the day that he had turned eighteen, and he had carried them every day since. "He'll come," said Khalid. "He thinks we're going to eat. He never turns down free food."

"And you think he's a traitor?"

Khalid continued to let the beads slip through his fingers one at a time. "I'm not sure. But traitor or not, we have to do what we have to do."

Abu al Khayr nodded. "You are right, brother. We can't afford any weak links, not at this stage."

Khalid looked at the digital clock in the dashboard. It was seven o'clock.

"There he is," said Abu al Khayr. He nodded at the entrance to the tube.

Khalid smiled when he saw the three men crossing the road towards the van. The man in the middle was Tariq Jamot, a regular at the Dynevor Road mosque. He worked for a tyre and exhaust centre and his fondness for fast food meant that he was a good fifty pounds overweight and had earned the nickname Fat Boy. The men either side of him were taller and leaner. All were second-generation Pakistanis, though only Jamot was London-born; his companions had grown up in Leeds. Fat Boy trusted the men he was with; there was no question of that. They often prayed together and they had attended the extra lessons that the mullah held in the mosque late into the night after last prayers. That was where they had been selected for further training and offered the chance to go to Pakistan. All had accepted the offer and all had returned committed to jihad and prepared to give their lives for the faith. Except that when the call had come, Fat Boy had been found wanting. The two men with Fat Boy had both arrived at St Pancras, ready and willing to do whatever had been asked of them. Fat Boy had received the call but had stayed at home, claiming that he was unwell.

Khalid waved through the open window and the three men waved back.

"Lamb to the slaughter," murmured Abu al Khayr.

"Hush, brother," said Khalid, still fingering the beads. "And smile."

Abu al Khayr smiled and revved the engine as the three men got into the van through the side door and took their seats, Fat Boy still in the middle.

"I have booked a table at a restaurant owned by a friend of mine," said Khalid, twisting round in his seat. "He makes the best chapli kebabs in London."

"My favourite," said Fat Boy, rubbing his hands together.

Khalid smiled. He knew that.

The five men chatted and joked as Abu al Khayr drove to the restaurant in Seven Sisters, a couple of miles north of Stoke Newington. The traffic was heavy but even so they pulled up in an alley at the rear of the restaurant after just fifteen minutes.

The three men in the back climbed out and Khalid joined them. "I'll find somewhere to park," said Abu al Khayr, and he drove off.

"Right, brothers, in we go," said Khalid.

He pushed open a wooden door that led into a small yard where there were a couple of mopeds with boxes on the back labelled with the restaurant's name and phone number. There was a wooden shed to the right, packed with cases of canned food and cleaning equipment. Khalid walked to the back of the building and knocked on the door there. A lock clicked and the door was opened by a cook in a stained white apron. He nodded at Khalid and the four men trooped inside. They were in a kitchen lined with stainless-steel work surfaces, two grease-covered ranges covered by dirty extractor hoods and three old refrigerators. One of the fridges shuddered as its compressor went off. Hanging from hooks were metal spatulas, spoons and knives.

"Are they shut?" asked Fat Boy. "Why's no one cooking?"

"They opened specially for us," said Khalid. He gestured with his chin and the cook locked the back door.

A pair of double doors swung open and two men appeared, dark-skinned and with matching heavy moustaches. One of them was carrying a wooden chair and the other was holding a carrier bag. The one with the chair set it down, then he hugged Khalid and kissed him on both cheeks. The second man followed suit.

"Which one is it?" asked the man who had brought in the chair.

370

Khalid turned and pointed at Fat Boy. "Him."

Fat Boy stiffened, but before he could move his two companions each grabbed an arm. He struggled so they held him tightly. "What?" said Fat Boy. "What do you want? What's happening?"

Khalid looked at him coldly. "It's time to pay the price for your cowardice," he said.

Fat Boy opened his mouth to scream but the cook stepped forward and shoved a cloth into his mouth, then tied it roughly at the back of his neck. Fat Boy tried to push himself backwards but his shoes couldn't get any traction on the tiled floor.

Khalid set the chair down in the middle of the kitchen and motioned for the two men to get Fat Boy to sit. Fat Boy struggled but he was out of condition and the men holding him were fitter and stronger. His instructors in Pakistan had told him that he needed to lose weight and exercise more and for a few weeks he'd followed their advice but as soon as he'd returned to London he'd fallen back into his bad habits. It was a question of discipline, Khalid knew. To carry out jihad one had to be focused, committed and driven. A jihad fighter needed to be physically and mentally fit, and Fat Boy was neither. With hindsight it had been a mistake to send him to Pakistan, but it was felt that his technical expertise would be useful. And that much was true. He had taken naturally to bomb-making and at one point his instructors had considered sending him to Iraq to help with the struggle against the occupying powers.

The man with the carrier bag knelt down by Fat Boy's side. He took out a roll of duct tape and used it to bind Fat Boy's ankles to the legs of the chair. Once the legs were securely bound he used the tape to fasten Fat Boy's wrists together.

Fat Boy's eyes were wide with fear and his nostrils flared with each panicked breath that he took.

The man finished tying him securely to the chair and stood up. He reached into his carrier bag and took out two black-and-white-checked keffiyeh scarves. He handed one each to Fat Boy's companions and they wound them round their heads so that other than their eyes their faces were completely covered.

Fat Boy had stopped struggling but he was making a soft moaning noise behind the gag.

Khalid took out his mobile phone. It was important to record what was about to happen, as a warning to others.

"You know why this is happening, and it is your own fault," said Khalid.

Tears were streaming down Fat Boy's face.

"This is your own doing and no one else's," continued Khalid. "We trusted you. We trained you. We helped you to meet your full potential, to become a soldier of jihad, to fight for your people and for Allah. We asked only one thing of you, that you follow our instructions. But when the call came, what did you do? You let us down. You were found wanting. We gave you simple instructions and you failed to follow them and that means that we can never trust you again."

Fat Boy shook his head and tried to speak but the gag reduced the sound to a garbled moan.

"There is nothing you can say to us," said Khalid. "You said you were sick but you still went to work on the day after we needed you. And sickness is no excuse. We need total loyalty. And we demand it. And when we do not get it, we react accordingly."

The man with the carrier bag took out a clear polythene bag and handed it to one of Fat Boy's companions. To the other he gave the roll of duct tape.

Khalid switched on the phone's video camera and began to film. Fat Boy moved his head from side to side but there was no way he could stop the polythene bag being pulled down over his head.

The cook leaned against one of the work surfaces and folded his arms. He grinned as he watched Fat Boy struggle. "Allahu Akbar," he whispered. God is great. "Allahu Akbar."

"Allahu Akbar," repeated Khalid as he took a step forward, holding the phone in front of him. "Allahu Akbar."

The rest of the men in the kitchen began to take up the chant as the man with duct tape slowly wound it round Fat Boy's neck, sealing the bag. The inside of the polythene bag began to cloud over but they could all see the look of panic in his eyes.

The duct tape wound tighter and tighter and the bag began to pulse in and out in time with Fat Boy's ragged breathing.

The chant grew louder and louder, echoing off the kitchen walls. "Allahu Akbar! Allahu Akbar!"

Khalid took another step forward so that Fat Boy's terrified face filled the screen. Condensation was forming on the inside of the polythene bag and his chest was heaving.

"Allahu Akbar! Allahu Akbar!"

A damp patch spread around Fat Boy's groin as his bladder emptied. His whole body began to tremble, as if he was being electrocuted.

"Allahu Akbar! Allahu Akbar!"

The chef was screaming the words at Fat Boy, his hands clenched into fists, his eyes burning with hatred.

Fat Boy shuddered, and then went still. He wasn't dead yet, Khalid knew. It was too soon for that. But he was now unconscious and death would follow within minutes.

The men stopped chanting and Khalid stopped recording. He gestured at Fat Boy. "And that, brothers, is what happens to anyone who betrays us," he said. "Let it be known that once you commit yourselves to jihad, there is no going back. One way or another you go to meet your maker. You can go as a martyr and receive your reward in Paradise; or you can go like this piece of cowardly shit, terrified and pissing in your pants." He slipped his phone back into his pocket. "As soon as he is dead we can dump his body, then we can go and eat."

Shepherd looked across at Sharpe. "You ready?" he asked.

They were sitting in a Range Rover in the car park of the Seattle Hotel, close to Brighton Marina. Kettering and Thompson had arranged to meet them in the hotel bar. Shepherd had told Kettering that he would have preferred the meeting to have been in London but Kettering had said that the German was insisting on Brighton.

Sharpe grinned. "I was born ready," he said.

"I'm serious, Razor," said Shepherd. "This could very easily turn to shit."

"It won't be the first time," said Sharpe. He gestured at Shepherd's leather jacket, which concealed a Glock in a nylon shoulder holster. "Don't see why I can't have a gun."

"Because you're a cop, and this isn't a police operation."

"Well, it is, sort of," said Sharpe.

"Yeah, well, even if it was they wouldn't give you a gun, would they?" said Shepherd. "Those days are long gone. Now you'd have to be in one of the specialist units and you'd have to have your paperwork current, and even then they wouldn't let you carry in plain clothes."

"But you can just get a gun and shove it under your jacket?"

"That's the power of Five," said Shepherd.

"Let's just hope a cop doesn't spot it," said Sharpe. "They shoot unarmed Brazilian electricians so they'd have a field day with you."

"No one's going to spot it," said Shepherd. "It's my fallback position, that's all. The meet's in a hotel bar and I doubt that anyone's going to be pulling out a gun. Besides, you've got a vest so what are you complaining about?"

"And what if they shoot me in the head?"

"No one's going to shoot anyone," said Shepherd. He looked at his watch. "Okay, let's go."

He climbed out of the Range Rover and zipped up his jacket. It would make it harder to pull out the gun but it meant that it would stay well hidden. He took his mobile phone from his pocket and checked that it was on and working. It was a Nokia, and while it was a functioning phone it was also a tracking device and a permanent transmitter. Amar Singh was one of MI5's best technicians and the phone was his own personal design. Everything that was said within a ten-foot range of the phone would be transmitted to Singh and Button in Thames House. There were two armed MI5 officers in the hotel and two more in a coffee shop close to the marina. They were also listening to the output from the phone that Shepherd was carrying. They had already agreed a warning phrase. If Shepherd were to say the words "I can't stay too long" then that meant they were to move in with weapons drawn.

Shepherd locked the car and he and Sharpe headed towards the front of the hotel.

"That's them, outside," said Sharpe.

Shepherd realised that he was right. Kettering and Thompson were standing to the right of the hotel entrance, smoking cigars. Kettering was talking earnestly and Thompson was nodding. Both men were wearing long overcoats and Kettering had a bright-red scarf round his neck.

376

Thompson spotted them first and he said something to Kettering. Kettering turned and waved.

"Garry, James, great to see you," he said.

"No problem," said Shepherd, shaking hands with them both.

The two men shook hands with Sharpe. "Are we going inside?" he asked.

Kettering held up what was left of his cigar. "Can't smoke in there," he said. "And it's busy. Walls have ears and all that. We've got somewhere more private fixed up." He slapped Sharpe on the back. "Hope you've got your sea legs."

"What are you talking about?" asked Shepherd. "You said the bar."

"Like I said, the bar's busy," said Kettering. He started walking towards the marina. Sharpe followed him down the path but Shepherd stood where he was.

"Where are you going?" he called, more for the benefit of the MI5 team than for his own information. Kettering was clearly heading to the boats.

Kettering turned round, took a long pull on his cigar and blew a cloud of bluish smoke before answering. "The German who wants to meet you has a boat moored here. That's not a problem, is it?"

Shepherd grinned. "It's fine by me," he said.

"Good man," said Thompson, putting his arm round Shepherd and guiding him towards the marina. "We've got some bubbly and smoked salmon on board."

"Who else is on the boat?" asked Shepherd, again for the benefit of those listening.

"Just Klaus," said Thompson.

Ahead of them were several dozen large yachts and motor cruisers. "Which one?" said Shepherd.

"The cruiser, the one with the blue stripe," said Thompson. "The *Laura Lee*."

"Doesn't sound very German," said Shepherd.

"He's chartered it," said Thompson. He flicked the butt of his cigar into the water.

Shepherd looked at the boat. It was big, close to a hundred feet long, with a large seating area at the stern and a glass-sided bridge that sloped back sharply. There was a man standing in the bridge looking at them. Short, stocky and wearing a captain's hat. "Is that him?"

"That's the captain," said Thompson.

"Who else is on board?"

"Why?" asked Thompson. "What's wrong?"

"Nothing's wrong. I just like to know who I'm dealing with and you seem to be making it up as we go along. First you say you want to meet in the hotel bar, now we're on a boat and it's not just your German buddy. For all I know you've got Captain Bligh and the Pirates of the fucking Caribbean on board."

"There's the captain and that's it," said Thompson. "And I don't know what you're so worried about. What is it? You think we're going to mug you?"

Kettering and Sharpe had reached the boat and they turned and waited for the other two to join them. There was a short gangplank leading from the jetty to the stern and Sharpe walked over it unsteadily, followed by Kettering.

As Shepherd got closer he looked up at the bridge. The captain flashed him a salute. Shepherd stopped and looked at Thompson. "Who's the captain?"

"The guy that drives the boat. It's worth a million bucks. He comes with the charter. The owner doesn't want amateurs crashing his pride and joy, now does he?"

"His name," said Shepherd. "I meant who is he? Do you know him?"

Thompson shrugged. "Greig something or other. He works for the German." He patted Shepherd on the back. "Come on, Garry, chill. Think of how much money you're going to make out of this." Shepherd walked over the gangplank and joined the others.

There was a large sitting area with cream leather seats running round the edge. Sliding doors led through to the main cabin, which was larger than the flat Shepherd was using in Hampstead. The floor was gleaming teak, there was a large LCD screen on one wall and in one corner there was a well-stocked bar. Marble and chrome stairs led up to the bridge and beyond the stairs was a stainless-steel galley.

"It's one hell of a boat," said Sharpe, stepping into the cabin and looking around.

Kettering took off his overcoat and tossed it on to a leather armchair. "Make yourselves at home, guys," he said.

Thompson slipped off his coat and dropped it on top of Kettering's. He sat down on a leather sofa and adjusted the creases of his trousers. "Take a pew, James," he said.

A long glass table on two carved marble bases was surrounded by eight high-backed black leather chairs. Sharpe pulled one out and turned it to face Thompson before sitting down.

"Where's this German, then?" asked Shepherd.

"Klaus!" shouted Kettering. "Where the hell are you?"

A wooden door slid open and a barrel-chested man appeared. He was wearing a brown leather jacket over a tight-fitting pale-blue V-neck and white jeans. He had a thick gold identity bracelet on his right wrist and a wristwatch with a dial so large that Shepherd could see the numbers on it from across the cabin. His hair was close-cropped, giving him the look of an American marine, and he smiled showing slab-like teeth.

"This is Klaus," said Kettering.

Klaus held out his hand and shook with Shepherd. He had a strong grip but Shepherd's was just as firm. "Good to meet you," said Klaus.

"You don't sound very German," said Shepherd.

"I went to school in England," said Klaus. "And my mother is English." He shook hands with Sharpe, then headed for the stairs. "I'll tell the captain to get going," he said.

Shepherd realised that the engines were running. "What's going on?" he asked Kettering.

"We're going for a spin," said Kettering.

"Like fuck we are," said Shepherd. "You wanted a chat in private, fine. You want to drink bubbly on your boat, all well and good. But I'm fucked if I'm going out to sea."

"It's not the sea, mate," said Thompson. "It's only the Channel. People swim across it."

"What are you scared of, Garry?" asked Kettering.

"I'm not scared. I just don't like being pissed around. I'm more than happy to talk business with Klaus, and if he wants a demonstration I can arrange that. But I don't have time to go messing about on boats."

"We can talk just as easily here, right?" said Sharpe, stretching out his legs. He looked around. "Where's the bubbly? Let's crack open a bottle and get down to business."

"Guys, come on now, this is a great boat," said Thompson. "Let's just take her out for an hour or so. We can fish."

"Fish?"

"It's got rods and everything," said Thompson.

Shepherd looked over at Sharpe. Sharpe was smiling but Shepherd could see the tension in his eyes. Something was wrong. Something was definitely wrong. "I'd really rather stay moored up," said Shepherd.

Klaus came back down the stairs. He headed out on to the rear deck and began untying the ropes that kept the boat moored to the jetty.

"Relax, Garry," said Thompson.

"I just don't like surprises," said Shepherd.

Thompson stood up and patted him on the back. "A few glasses of bubbly will soon get you relaxed," he said. "Come on, sit down."

"Guys, no one said we were going out to sea. I'm not happy about this."

Kettering reached inside his jacket and took out his leather cigar case. He opened it to reveal four thick cigars and he offered one to Shepherd.

"I don't want a fucking cigar," said Shepherd.

"You need to relax, Garry. Get some sea air in your lungs."

"Make up your fucking mind, will you? Do you want me smoking or breathing in sea air? This is fucked up, Simon. This isn't how professionals do business." He looked over at Sharpe again, trying to get a read on what his partner was thinking. If they were going to pull out they had to do it now, while they were still in port. And if he was going to call for help it would have to be done within the next minute or two.

Sharpe was still smiling but his eyes had narrowed. Then he gave a small shrug and clasped his hands behind his neck. He was leaving the decision up to Shepherd.

Klaus came back into the cabin. "Okay?" he said.

Shepherd nodded. "I guess so," he said reluctantly.

"Great," said Thompson. "I'll get the bubbly."

He went into the galley and opened a large stainless-steel fridge. Shepherd sat down on a beige leather bench seat under a long window. The engines roared and the boat reversed away from the jetty. Thompson pulled out a bottle of Bollinger and grabbed five glasses off a tray as Kettering lit a cigar.

Shepherd was trying to get a read on Kettering and Thompson but was failing. They seemed relaxed enough and their bonhomie appeared genuine. It could be that they just wanted to go out on the boat, and they were right that there would be no chance of them being overheard out at sea. Though of course they weren't taking into consideration the fact that Shepherd's phone was broadcasting everything that was being said back to Thames House and to the back-up teams in the hotel and in the coffee shop. Shepherd had no idea what the MI5 teams were doing but he assumed that they had now left both places.

Thompson popped the cork too enthusiastically and champagne sprayed over the floor before he started pouring it into the glasses. Klaus took a glass and gave it to Sharpe, then took one for himself, while Thompson gave glasses to Shepherd and Kettering before filling his own.

Kettering stood up and held his glass high. "To the future," he said. "And to the men who will shape it."

They all stood up, raised their glasses in salute and then drank. It was good champagne, Shepherd knew, but he couldn't taste it. His mind was racing, still trying to work out what was going on. If Klaus was a German then Shepherd was a Dutchman.

Kettering looked out of the rear windows at the marina in the distance. "When will we be in international waters, do you think? Twelve miles, isn't it?"

"We're not going out twelve bloody miles, I hope," said Shepherd.

Klaus was staring at Sharpe with a sly smile on his face. Sharpe hadn't noticed but the way the man was staring gave Shepherd an uncomfortable feeling. The atmosphere had changed now that they were out at sea.

Thompson was holding the empty champagne bottle, his feet planted shoulder-width apart. He caught Shepherd's look and smiled but his eyes stayed hard.

"You really don't remember me, do you?" asked Klaus, still staring at Sharpe, his voice a low growl.

Everything appeared to slow down as Shepherd's adrenal glands kicked into overdrive. He swallowed and even that seemed to happen in slow motion, and he realised that the dull thud he could hear was the sound of his own heart. Thompson was hefting the bottle as if he was about to throw it; Kettering was holding his cigar in one hand and his champagne glass in the other, blowing a cloud of smoke up at the ceiling; Sharpe was turning to look at Klaus, frowning; Klaus's grin was turning into a snarl.

Shepherd reached for the zipper of his bomber jacket, trying to make the move look casual. Time started to move at its normal speed again and he forced a smile. "Lads, I can't stay too long," he said.

"You fucking slag!" Klaus shouted at Sharpe. "There's only one thing worse than a grass and that's a fucking undercover cop." He reached behind his back and pulled out a revolver. Sharpe stepped towards Klaus, pulling back his fist but Thompson smashed the champagne bottle against the side of his head and he dropped to the floor like a stone.

Klaus swung the gun round to point it at Shepherd and Shepherd raised his hands. He still had the glass of champagne in his right hand. "What the fuck's going on?" he asked.

"Your pal's a cop," said Klaus.

"Like fuck he is," said Shepherd. "I've known him for donkey's. He's no grass."

"I said cop," said Klaus. "He works for the Met. Came across him a year or so ago. He was involved with a group of guys bringing in cannabis from Morocco. Customs grabbed the lot but when the dust cleared there was no sign of him. And he wasn't James Gracie back then. Alistair something or other. I was always on the fringes so I never spoke to him, but it was him all right, no question."

"Well, that's fucking news to me," said Shepherd, keeping his hands in the air. He nodded his chin at the glass he was holding. "I want to put my hands down, is that okay?"

"No, it's not fucking okay," said Thompson. He strode over and took the champagne off him, then pushed him down on to the bench seat. "Put your hands behind your head and cross your ankles."

"What?"

"You heard him," said Klaus. "Sit the fuck down, put your hands behind your head and cross your fucking ankles."

Shepherd looked at Kettering. "Simon, mate, there's no reason to be like this. If he's bad, it's fuck-all to do with me."

"Just do as you're told," said Kettering.

Shepherd slowly put his hands behind his neck and crossed his legs at the ankles.

"See the thing is, mate, we know you're a cop too."

"Give me a break," said Shepherd.

"Your name's Dan Shepherd," said Kettering. He gestured at Sharpe with his cigar. "And that's Jimmy Sharpe."

Shepherd felt suddenly calm. There was no point in lying now that they knew who he was. He stared at Kettering. Kettering held his look as he took a long pull on his cigar.

"Your mate told us everything. Eventually."

"You're making a big mistake, Simon," said Shepherd quietly.

"We'll see about that," said Kettering. He leaned over the table and put his cigar on to a large crystal ashtray.

"You haven't bought the guns yet. Conspiracy is as good as it gets, and you could probably play the entrapment card. Get a good lawyer and you'll walk, more than likely."

"What about the dead cop?" said Kettering.

"What dead cop?"

"The cop we killed back in Brum," said Kettering.

Shepherd's jaw tensed. "What are you talking about?"

"You're good," Kettering said. "I'd hate to play poker with you." He looked across at Thompson. "Playing it straight, right to the end." He turned back to Shepherd, his eyes cold. "There's no going back for us now. Whatever we do we're finished in the UK. You've got us on tape, I bet, and even if you haven't there's more than enough evidence to put us away for — what? Ten? Fifteen? Twenty?"

"Killing a cop means you'll never get out," said Shepherd.

"Yeah, well, if you'll forgive the pun, that ship has already sailed," said Kettering. He gestured at the seat Shepherd was sitting on. "Lift that up," he said. "There's a storage space underneath."

Shepherd slowly took his hands from behind his head, uncrossed his legs and stood up. He gingerly lifted the bench seat. In the space below there was a body wrapped in polythene, bound with grey duct tape. He cursed and let the seat fall back. "You didn't have to do that," he said.

"Well, I sort of did," said Kettering. "And I need you to get the body out because we'll be dropping it over the side shortly."

Shepherd turned to face Kettering, his hands bunching into fists. "Why kill him? He was just a cop doing his job. That's all any of us are doing. It's not personal. You're breaking the law and it's our job to stop you. You don't kill someone for doing their job."

Kettering scowled at Shepherd and opened his mouth to speak. But then he changed his mind and nodded at Klaus. "Fucking shoot him, will you? He's giving me a headache."

Klaus smiled thinly and pulled the trigger. The sound of the gunshot was deafening in the confined space and the bullet hit Shepherd just below the heart. He fell backwards, his arms flailing.

Amar Singh looked across at Charlotte Button. "They shot him," he said. "The bastards have bloody well shot him."

Button ignored him. She clicked on her mic and spoke to the leader of the armed teams. "What's happening there, Bill?"

"We're waiting for a police launch. It's on its way."

"You heard the shot?"

"We heard it."

"Soon as you can," she said.

She bit down on her lower lip as she considered her options. A helicopter was a possibility but it would take time and even then the police helicopters weren't armed. She could call in the Met but getting an armed response unit out to sea would be a logistical nightmare.

Singh was looking at her fearfully and she managed a small smile.

"What are we going to do?" he asked.

"At the moment I'm just praying that they didn't shoot him in the head," she said. "And that if he was shot in the chest your bulletproof vest held up."

Shepherd lay on his back, his chest on fire. The Kevlar vest under his shirt had stopped the bullet but it had still hurt like hell. His mind raced. If he played dead there was a good chance that Klaus would fire again and this time Shepherd might not be so lucky. His gun was in its shoulder holster but to get at it he was going to have to unzip his bomber jacket. The armed teams would have heard the shot and they would be on their way but it would take them time to get a boat and motor over to the *Laura Lee*. He was going to have to take care of it himself. His arms were out to the sides so if he made a move for his gun Klaus would see it and have all the time in the world to put another bullet into him.

"Is he dead?" Kettering's voice.

"I don't know."

"Shoot him again."

Shepherd heard footsteps. He held his breath, playing dead. If Klaus shot him again it would probably be another chest shot. Civilians tended to avoid head shots, partly because it was a smaller target than the chest but mainly because shooting someone in the face was more personal. Shepherd half opened his eyes. Klaus was walking towards him, the gun at his side.

"He's not breathing," said Klaus.

"Shoot him again. Better safe than sorry."

Shepherd felt his lungs burning but he continued to hold his breath. He was going to get only one chance and he had to choose his moment.

"He's dead," said Klaus. "I shot him in the heart." Shepherd heard a dull thud, which he hoped was the sound of the gun being put on the glass table.

"Looks like he's gone," said Thompson.

"Then let's toss him over the side with the others," said Kettering. "And hurry up. He probably had his people at the marina so we need to get the bodies over the side and ourselves over to France. Wrap all three of them in chains and drop them over the side. The water's plenty deep enough so no one will ever find them here."

Shepherd heard footsteps. Then he heard a grunt as someone bent down over him. He opened his eyes. It was Klaus, looming over him. Shepherd reached up and clawed his fingers down Klaus's face, searching for the eyes. He felt his fingers slide into the eye sockets and he pushed hard. Klaus screamed and fell back.

Shepherd knew he had only seconds to react and that every decision he made was crucial. There were three men in the cabin and another on the bridge. He'd seen one gun and hopefully that was now on a table but that didn't mean there weren't more on the boat.

He lay where he was and pulled down the zipper of his bomber jacket with his left hand while he groped inside with his right. His fingers were wet with Klaus's blood but the Glock had a non-slip grip. There was no safety to worry about either, and there was already a cartridge in the chamber.

Klaus was groaning, his hands clasped over his face, blood trickling down through his fingers.

Still lying on his back, Shepherd grabbed the Glock and pulled it from its holster. All he could see was Klaus, rocking back on his heels and wailing like a banshee. He pulled his leg back, put his foot in the centre of Klaus's chest and kicked him hard. Klaus fell backwards.

Shepherd brought his left hand up to support his right wrist, his finger tightening on the trigger as he looked for a target.

He found Kettering in his sights, standing by the table, his eyes wide and confused. Kettering cursed and looked to his right. Shepherd realised what he was looking at: Klaus's gun on the table.

"Don't move!" shouted Shepherd, but Kettering was already reaching for the gun. "Freeze!" Shepherd yelled.

Kettering grabbed the gun and began to swing it round. He said something but Shepherd couldn't hear him above the sound of Klaus's screams. Shepherd fired once, hitting Kettering six inches below his Adam's apple. Kettering stiffened and the gun dropped from his fingers, clattering back on to the glass table.

Shepherd got to his feet, sweeping the cabin with his Glock.

Thompson was standing by the stairs leading up to the bridge. "Don't shoot," he said.

"Keep your hands where I can see them," said Shepherd. Kettering sank to his knees, blood gushing over his shirt, his mouth working soundlessly.

Thompson moved towards the table but Shepherd fired close to the man's foot. "The next one goes into your chest," he said. Thompson straightened up and raised his hands.

"Does the captain have a gun?" Shepherd asked. Thompson shook his head. "If you're lying I'll shoot you first," said Shepherd.

Kettering fell forward and thudded face down on to the deck.

"He doesn't," said Thompson. "I swear."

Shepherd gestured with the gun. "Up the stairs. Try anything, even look at me wrong, and I'll put a bullet in you."

Thompson went slowly up the stairs to the bridge. Shepherd stayed well back in case Thompson tried to kick out but Thompson just did as he was told. The captain smiled when he saw Thompson but his face fell when he saw Shepherd and the gun in his hand.

"I need you to take us back to the marina," said Shepherd. "I don't have time to mess about so if you fuck around I'll shoot you in the leg. Do you understand me?"

The captain nodded and immediately started turning the boat to starboard.

"Take us back to the jetty," said Shepherd.

"I'm just looking after the boat," said the captain. "This is nothing to do with me."

"Just take us back. You can talk to the cops there," said Shepherd. He waved the gun at Thompson. "Back downstairs," he said.

He followed Thompson down the stairs into the cabin. "Down on your knees and put your hands behind your neck," he said. "While you're at it, cross your ankles. See how you like it." Thompson obeyed sullenly.

Shepherd looked over at Sharpe. "Razor!" he shouted.

Sharpe groaned.

"Can you get up?"

Sharpe groaned again.

Shepherd kept the gun aimed at Thompson's face as he fished his mobile out of his jacket. He tapped out Charlotte Button's number with his thumb. The boat continued to make a sweeping turn to the right. Klaus stopped moaning. He crawled into a foetal ball and sobbed quietly. Shepherd knew that he'd done a lot of damage with his fingers and that Klaus would be losing at least one of his eyes.

The phone rang and Button answered. "Thank God," she said. "Are you okay?"

"All good," he said. "One dead, two under control and one who's going to need medical attention. We're heading back to shore."

"There's a police boat heading your way. You're sure you're okay?"

"I'm fine," he said. He looked over at Sharpe, who was starting to come round, moving his head and moaning. "Razor's going to have a sore head for a few days."

"Well done, Spider. I have to confess that my heart was in my mouth for a while there."

"I was worried myself," admitted Shepherd. "I'm just glad he didn't go for a head shot. And tell Amar I owe him a drink. His vest was a lifesaver."

He ended the call and went over to Sharpe, keeping his gun trained on Thompson. Sharpe struggled to sit up. He put his hand against his temple and it came away bloody. He groaned loudly and looked up at Shepherd. "Who am I?" he said.

"Are you serious?" said Shepherd.

Sharpe grinned. "Had you going," he said, getting unsteadily to his feet. He looked down at Kettering. Blood was pooling around him on the polished wooden decking. "Was it him that hit me?"

Shepherd gestured at Thompson. "It was him."

Klaus sobbed and his whole body shuddered.

"What's his problem?" asked Sharpe. "Did you shoot him?"

"Clawed his eyes out," said Shepherd. "He started it."

Sharpe walked slowly to the galley, picked up a tea towel and pressed it against his wound. He looked out of a window and pointed. "There's a launch heading this way with four guys in it. I hope they're on our side."

"They are," said Shepherd. "Are you okay to cover Thompson while I go up to the bridge?"

"Now you trust me with a gun?"

Shepherd chuckled and handed the Glock to Sharpe. He picked up the gun that Klaus had been using. It was a 9mm Beretta and he checked that it was loaded and that the safety was off. "I figure you'd have trouble with the stairs," he said. "If he gets off his knees, shoot him."

"Will do," said Sharpe.

Shepherd went up the stairs to the bridge. He was fairly sure that Thompson hadn't been lying about the captain being unarmed but he felt more comfortable with the Beretta in his hand. He needn't have worried. The captain had both hands on the wheel and they were heading straight for the marina. In the distance Shepherd saw a small launch. There were four men in

394

casual clothes standing at the prow and as the wind whipped at their jackets he caught glimpses of guns in shoulder holsters.

"I had no idea what was going on," said the captain. "You've got to believe me."

"Tell that to the cops," said Shepherd. "I need you to cut the power." He pointed at the launch. "Those guys are going to board us."

The captain did as he was told and the boat slowed.

"I didn't do anything. I just drive the boat."

"What did they tell you was going to happen to me and my friend?"

The captain swallowed but didn't reply.

"You knew they were going to kill us, right?"

"I'm just the captain."

"And you knew there was a body down there?"

The captain nodded.

"Well, that's the body of a cop, mate. So maybe you should just keep quiet until you've got a lawyer."

Chaudhry was walking down the Strand to King's College when he first suspected that he was being followed. It wasn't any of the signs that he'd been taught to watch out for, it was much more subtle than that. It was a feeling, a sense that he was being looked at that actually made the hairs stand up on the back of his neck. It happened first as he walked out of Charing Cross tube station and the feeling was so strong that he turned and looked behind him, but he didn't see anyone who was obviously tailing him.

Chaudhry usually cycled to college but it had been raining when he left the flat so he'd taken an umbrella and made the journey by tube instead. The rain had died down by the time he arrived at Charing Cross and it was barely spotting so he'd left his umbrella in his backpack and made do with pulling up the hood of his duffel coat.

He shivered again as he passed McDonald's, then he remembered what he'd been taught about doubling back so he did a quick U-turn and headed back to the entrance. As he reached McDonald's door he made eye contact with an Asian man in his twenties wearing a dark-blue Puffa jacket and brown cargo pants. The man's eyes widened and his mouth opened a fraction but then he clamped it shut, looked away and thrust his hands into his pockets.

Chaudhry forced himself to show no reaction. He went inside, joined the queue and bought himself an Egg McMuffin and a coffee and sat down at a table by the window. He pushed down the hood of his duffel coat and pulled his tablet computer out of his backpack. As he took a sip of coffee and switched on the tablet the man in the blue Puffa jacket walked back on the other side of the road, talking into his mobile phone.

Chaudhry's stomach was churning and he didn't feel like eating but he forced himself to take a bite of his McMuffin, then chewed slowly as he pretended to read. The man in the blue Puffa jacket didn't return. When he'd finished the coffee and the McMuffin he cleared his tray and headed out of the door. He stood on the

396

pavement and looked around casually as he pulled up his hood again. The street was busy but there was no sign of the Asian man. He was starting to wonder if he'd imagined it. The hairs were no longer standing up on the back of his neck. Perhaps the guy had just been startled by eye contact with a stranger; maybe Chaudhry was being oversensitive.

He started walking towards the college, resisting the urge to look over his shoulder. Part of him wanted to do another double-back but he knew that would be too obvious. He checked reflections in the shop windows but the angles were wrong and he couldn't get a clear view directly behind him.

It wasn't until he'd reached the entrance to King's that he had the opportunity to glance to his right, but he could do it casually for only a second or two and there were simply too many people to register them all.

He walked inside, showing his student ID, and then took out his mobile phone. Standing with his back to the wall he pretended to make a call. Through the window he watched businessmen and shoppers walk to and fro, all of them moving purposefully, getting from A to B as quickly as possible. Jobs to get to, shopping to be done, appointments to be kept. Then he saw him. His hands still in his Puffa jacket, walking slowly and looking around as if trying to work out what went on inside the building. Chaudhry turned away and went up to the canteen, his heart pounding, the silent phone pressed tightly against his ear.

Shepherd had just returned from a run on the Heath when his John Whitehill BlackBerry rang. It was Chaudhry. "Yes, Raj, what's up?" he said, tossing his weighted rucksack on to a kitchen chair.

"I think I'm being followed," said Chaudhry.

Shepherd was about to open the fridge door and grab himself a bottle of chilled water but he stopped, his hand outstretched. "Tell me what happened," he said.

Chaudhry explained what had happened in the Strand and at the college. "What should I do?" he asked.

"First, you need to take it easy," said Shepherd. He could hear the stress in the man's voice, the clipped words and the ragged breathing. "You're safe where you are, so even if there is a tail nothing can happen while you're at King's. What about Harvey?"

"I don't know. He'd already gone when I left the flat."

"I'll talk to him," said Shepherd. "Have you got lectures all day?"

"Pretty much."

"So what time would you normally leave?"

"Five-ish. What are you going to do?"

Shepherd sat down and took off his boots. "I'm going to sort this out, Raj, don't worry. Stay where you are and just carry on as normal. I'll put together a team to watch over you when you go home tonight, then we'll know for sure."

"But what if they . . ." He didn't finish the sentence.

"What, Raj? Spit it out."

"I don't want to end up dead," said Chaudhry. "What if this is al-Qaeda? What if they know what I'm doing? Maybe it's time to call it a day."

"Raj, you're getting ahead of yourself. You need to relax. If there's a tail that's all it is, a tail. If they wanted to take you they'd have done it as you left the flat. Or lured you somewhere quiet. If you are being followed then you're not in any danger."

"What do you mean 'if'? Don't you believe me?"

"You're under quite a lot of stress at the moment, Raj; you might be a bit oversensitive, that's what I'm saying. But by this evening we'll know for sure. Until then you need to carry on as usual."

"I'm shitting myself here," said Chaudhry.

"I know you are, Raj. But there's no point in counting chickens. I'm on the case so you'll be followed every step of the way from college to your flat and if there's any hint of a problem we'll pull you out."

"You swear?" asked Chaudhry.

"Raj, mate, there's no way I'll put you in harm's way. I promise. Now get on with being a student and keep your phone on. I'll fill you in once I've got everything sorted. And don't leave the campus, for any reason, until you hear from me."

Shepherd ended the call. He dialled Malik's number but it went straight through to voicemail. Shepherd didn't leave a message. He shaved, showered and put on a blue polo shirt and black jeans, then tried Malik's number again. It went through to voicemail again and this time Shepherd left a message asking him to call back.

Malik returned the call as Shepherd was in the back of a black cab heading towards Thames House.

"Where are you, Harvey?"

"University," said Malik. "What's wrong?"

"Probably nothing," said Shepherd. "But Raj thinks someone might have been following him this morning."

"Oh fuck," said Malik.

"It might be nothing — it's easy to start jumping at shadows when you're under pressure," said Shepherd. "I'm going to get some of our people to follow Raj home and then we'll know one way or another. What about you, Harvey? Did you notice anything today?"

"No, but I wasn't looking for it. What should I do?"

"Can you stay where you are until later this evening?"

"I was planning to hit the library anyway, so yes."

"How about you stick to that? Stay put until you hear from me this evening. If we find that Raj does have a tail we'll put a counter-surveillance team on you as well."

"This is bad, isn't it, John? We could be fucked."

"Or it could be nothing. We'll take it one step at a time. But if you see anything that worries you over the next few hours, you call me straight away."

"Bloody right I will," said Malik.

"Harvey, it's going to be just fine," said Shepherd. "I give you my word that nothing bad's going to happen."

He ended the call as the taxi pulled up in front of Thames House, wishing that he felt as confident as he sounded.

"So, you a spy, then?" asked the taxi driver.

400

Shepherd had been deep in thought so he missed the question. "Sorry, what?"

The driver jerked his thumb at the building. "MI5. You a spy?"

Shepherd took out his wallet and handed the driver a twenty-pound note. "I could tell you but then I'd have to kill you," he said.

"They all say that," said the driver. "Everyone I drop here pretends to be James bloody Bond."

"He was MI6," said Shepherd. He nodded at the note. "Keep the change," he said. "And can I have a receipt?"

The driver laughed. "See, that James Bond, you never see him asking for receipts, do you?"

There was no name on the door, just a number, but Shepherd knew that it was the office of Luke Lesporis and he knocked twice before opening it. Lesporis looked up, pushing his wire-framed designer spectacles up his nose as Shepherd came in.

"You sounded rushed on the phone, Spider, what's up?" The jacket of his Hugo Boss suit was draped over the back of his chair and he'd rolled up the sleeves of his shirt.

"Remember the two guys I took to Reading, the ones you helped arrange the training exercise for?"

"Sure, Raj Chaudhry and Harvey Malik, right? The guys we followed to St Pancras."

"Yeah. I need to run counter-surveillance on Raj. He's a student at King's College in the Strand. That's where he is now."

"What's the story?" asked Lesporis, picking up a pen.

"He thinks someone followed him from the tube station. Asian man, blue Puffa jacket, brown cargo pants."

"Professional, you think?" asked Lesporis as he scribbled on a yellow legal pad.

"I'm tempted to say no because Raj is a complete amateur. But he might just have been lucky. He did a backtrack and almost stumbled over the guy."

"How long have we got?"

Shepherd looked at the clock on the wall. It was just before ten. "He's got lectures all morning. We could send him home at lunchtime, or I could get him to stay in the building all day. Whatever works best for you."

"The latter," said Lesporis. "I'm really pushed today. We've got three ongoing operations and I've just had to put together a rush job on a Saudi diplomat who's arriving at Heathrow in an hour with a million euros in a suitcase."

"If it makes it any easier he's going to be travelling home on the tube so we won't need vehicles."

"Home being the flat we started at last time?"

"That's it. But this time there's no chance of a vehicle; he'll take the tube to Manor House and walk to the flat."

"Easy-peasy," said Lesporis. "Tell you what, I'll pitch in myself. It'll be good to be on the pavements again."

"Could do with a check throughout the evening, though. See if there's anyone hanging around outside the building."

"That's easy enough. I can put a BT technician in the street and run a PCSO by now and again. I'll have a guy waiting at the Stoke Newington end so one other and me should be enough in the Strand. Do you need pictures?"

"That would be great, Luke. There's a snag, though. If Raj is being followed then I'll need Harvey checked out too."

"Where's he?"

"He's at the London Metropolitan University — Holloway Road, Islington. He's in the business school today and I've told him to stay there all day. I know it's all short notice but if Raj is hot then there's a chance that Harvey is too."

Lesporis nodded thoughtfully. "Not a problem," he said. "If Raj is tailed from the Strand I'll know pretty quickly, so once we've identified the tail I can peel off and head up to Islington. I'll get in place and the others can join me as and when. Do you have any idea who might be after him?"

"He said Asian so my worry is al-Qaeda."

"They have some real pros, but they also have a fair number of amateurs," said Lesporis.

"The guy Raj thinks was following him was almost on top of him, so not a pro. But it's not the one he saw that I'm worried about; it's the ones he didn't see."

"Understood," said Lesporis, scribbling a note on his pad. He smiled, showing perfect teeth. "Consider it done. I'll give you a call as soon as I know anything."

"You're a star, Luke. Thanks."

Shepherd's mobile rang. It was Button. "A little bird tells me that you're in the house," she said.

"I'm in with Luke, fixing up some counter-surveillance on Raj and Harvey."

"Problem?"

"I'm not sure. We'll know in a few hours."

"Can you pop up to my office on your way out?"

"I'll be right up. Luke and I are done," said Shepherd.

Button was sipping a cup of tea when Shepherd walked into her office. She flashed him a smile and asked if he wanted anything but he shook his head and sat down. "I just wanted a chat about what happened on the boat," she said.

"All good," he said.

"You were shot, Spider."

"I was wearing a vest."

"Thank God."

"Actually, God had very little to do with it," said Shepherd.

"You nearly died."

"I've been shot before, Charlie."

"I'm just saying you were in a very violent situation and I wanted to check you were okay."

"Physically or mentally?"

She smiled. "You know what I'm going to suggest."

"A sit-down with Caroline Stockmann?"

"I think it's called for. I'll get her to give you a call and fix it up." She ran a hand through her hair. "It's a pity that it went the way it did," she said.

"You're telling me."

"I meant in terms of the investigation. We really needed to know what Kettering and Thompson were planning."

"Thompson will talk," said Shepherd. "With Kettering out of the picture he'll sing like the proverbial."

"The problem is that Kettering was the top dog. And the fact that he's dead means his European contacts will go to ground. We'll sew up the UK end, that's a given, but my feeling is that they were part of a bigger plan and that plan is probably going to go ahead no matter what happened here."

"I think you'll find that Thompson knows a lot about what was going on," said Shepherd. "He was the one always mouthing off about the global conspiracy. He'd be the one pushing for coordinated action with the Europeans, I'm sure of it."

"We'll certainly give it a go," said Button. "I tell you, it's hard enough dealing with the Islamic fundamentalists but when we have home-grown right-wingers threatening terrorist outrages as well we're going to be stretched resource-wise."

"I don't know. Penetrating groups like Kettering's is a lot easier than trying to get into the Islamic cells."

"No argument there," said Button. "If it wasn't for Chaudhry and Malik we wouldn't have achieved a fraction of what we've managed so far."

"I just hope it doesn't come back to bite them," said Shepherd.

"What do you mean?"

"Charlie, they gave up Bin Laden. And by dropping that bloody map the Americans have put their lives on the line."

"Is that what the counter-surveillance is about?"

Shepherd shrugged. "Raj thinks he's being followed. He might just be jumping at shadows. We'll know by tonight."

"Keep me in the picture."

"Soon as I know, you'll know," said Shepherd.

Malik looked at his watch. It was four o'clock in the afternoon and his last lecture had just finished. He went to the library, which was almost empty, and sat down at a table by the window. He pulled a bottle of water from his backpack and took a sip. He had three essays to write but couldn't drum up the enthusiasm for starting any of them so he opened up his laptop and started browsing through YouTube, listening through headphones so as not to disturb the other library-users.

He started off looking at music videos but soon got bored with that. He searched for "suicide bombers" and began looking through the videos, mainly news footage of attacks in Iraq, Israel and Pakistan. There were some comedy videos too, though Malik failed to see why anyone thought it was acceptable to make fun of terrorists.

A girl sat down opposite him and he hurriedly closed the YouTube window, even though she couldn't see the screen.

"Sorry," she said. "You don't mind if I sit here, do you?" She was in her twenties with shoulder-length black curly hair and a wide smile.

Her skin wasn't quite as dark as Malik's and though she had a definite accent he couldn't place where she was from.

"Sure, yeah, no problem," he said. He'd been so busy watching videos that he hadn't noticed how the library had filled up and now most of the tables were occupied. "I'm only skiving really."

She leaned over the table towards him, her voice a low whisper. "Yeah, me too," she said. "I left my key in the flat and my flatmate won't be back until eight so I thought I'd just hang out here."

"Yeah, it's one of the few places left in London where you can sit for free," he said.

She gestured at his laptop. "Were you watching a movie?"

"Just browsing through YouTube," he said. "Nothing special."

"What's your name?"

"Harvey. Well, it's Harveer but everyone calls me Harvey."

"Harveer? Is that Indian?"

"Pakistani," said Malik.

"Oh, I'm sorry."

"It's no big deal. What about you? Where are you from?"

She grinned mischievously. "Guess."

"Guess?" He sat back and linked his fingers. He studied her olive skin, her dark-brown eyes and her jet-black curly hair. Not Asian, he was fairly sure of that. Her skin was too light. Her English was good and there was a trace of an American accent, which probably meant that she'd gone to an international school somewhere. She wasn't oriental and she wasn't dark enough to be from the Philippines or Indonesia.

Her smile widened. "Do you want a clue?"

"I'm thinking Lebanese," he said. "Or one of the Gulf states."

She raised one eyebrow. "Well done," she said. "Qatar. No one ever gets where I'm from."

"I've never been," he said. "What's it like?"

"Hot in the summer. Dusty. Nice restaurants. That's pretty much it. I prefer London."

"Who doesn't?" he said.

"And you study here, right?"

Malik nodded. "I'm doing an MBA in Business Studies."

"And what was your degree?"

"Computing." He pulled a face. "Hated it, but my dad's a programmer so he pushed me into it."

"So you're going to work in the City?"

Malik frowned. "The City?"

"That's what guys with MBAs do, isn't it? Work for a bank or a broker. Become a master of the universe."

Malik shook his head. "I'm going to open a sushi restaurant. The best sushi restaurant in London. Top end. I'm going to fly in the best fish from around the world and employ only top Japanese chefs."

"I love sushi," she said.

"Then you can come to the opening night."

408

"You're really going to do it? It must cost a fortune to set up a restaurant."

"I'm working on the finances," said Malik. "But it's going to happen." He leaned forward. "So you know my name, what's yours?"

"Nadia," she said. "Hey, are you good with computers?"

"I studied them for three years," said Malik. "What's the problem?"

"My laptop keeps freezing but I don't know why. Maybe you could have a look at it some time."

"Sure." He nodded at her bag. "Have you got it with you?"

"It's at home. Can I call you?"

"You want my number?"

She smiled prettily. "That's normally how it works, Harvey." She took out her mobile phone and looked at him expectantly. He grinned and gave her his number. He hadn't been thrilled at the idea of spending the evening in the library, but it was turning out to be the best place he could have been. "What are you smiling at?" she asked.

"Just pleased to meet you," he said. "I hadn't planned to be here but I'm glad I came."

She smiled and nodded. "I was thinking exactly the same thing," she said.

Chaudhry left King's at just after five o'clock. He walked along to the tube station at Charing Cross with the hood of his duffel coat up, resisting the urge to look over his shoulder. He went down to the platform, took out his Galaxy tablet and began reading, just as he did most days when he was on the tube. John's instructions had been clear. No looking around, no backtracking, no looking for a tail. And no looking for the counter-surveillance people either. When the train arrived he managed to find a seat in the middle of the carriage. And he kept his eyes on his tablet.

He stuck to his instructions, and the only time he looked left or right was when he had to cross a road and even then he made a conscious effort to avoid eye contact with anyone nearby. When he got home he got himself a can of Coke from the fridge. He was halfway through it when his phone rang. He looked at the screen. It said "Dentist", which meant it was John Whitehill calling.

"How's the weather?" asked Whitehill.

For a moment Chaudhry was confused, but then he remembered the procedure. "It's fine," he said. "I was imagining it, right? Just me being oversensitive."

"I'm afraid not. You were being followed."

Chaudhry's stomach turned over. "Shit," he said.

"Two Asians. One in a blue Puffa jacket, just like you said. He was waiting for you outside the university and got on the tube with you. He was in the next carriage. The other guy was waiting for you at Manor House."

Chaudhry could feel his heart pounding. "Shit, shit, shit," he said. "I'm screwed, right?"

"There's no need to panic, Raj. You're at home and we've got your flat under surveillance. Nothing can happen to you while you're there. I've got two men with guns in a car round the corner and they can be with you in seconds."

"Where's Harvey? He should be home by now. You said you talked to him, right?"

"Raj, take it easy. Harvey's on his way home. All the signs are that he's not being followed, but we won't know for sure until he gets back to the flat. When he does get back, make sure you stay in for the night. No popping out for a takeaway."

"I'll be hiding under the bed, mate," said Chaudhry.

Shepherd laughed. "There's no need for that," he said. "Look, it's probably nothing. Maybe someone that Khalid has sent to check that you're on the straight and narrow. Make sure you're not out drinking or letting the side down."

"What about the mosque?" asked Chaudhry. "Do you think it's safe? I mean, I can pray at home, it's no biggie, but I'd prefer to go to the mosque."

"Let's wait and see what we can find out about your tails," said Shepherd.

"Seriously, I'm shitting myself here."

"I understand, Raj. But if there was any question of them intending to harm you it would have happened already. Surveillance is just that. Watching. And like I said, so long as you stay put nothing can happen to you."

"And you're not lying about the men with guns? You've got armed cops nearby?"

"I told you I'd never lie to you, Raj. But they're not cops. They work for MI5. Different rules. They don't wear uniforms and they don't make a song and dance

411

about doing what has to be done. In the very unlikely event of anyone trying to do you any harm they'll be straight round and they'll take care of it."

"Thanks, John," said Chaudhry. He grinned. "It's funny, I know that's not your real name but I can't think of you as anything other than John."

"John's fine. A rose by any other name and all that."

"Well, whatever your name is, I'm glad you've got my back." He ended the call and switched on the TV. He had studying to do but he couldn't concentrate so he lay on the sofa and watched the news and then a very unfunny situation comedy about three Americans sharing a flat in New York that seemed to be about five times the size of the one that he and Malik lived in. He got up and opened the fridge but there was nothing in it that he wanted to eat. He found a packet of pistachio nuts in a cupboard and began to eat them, piling the broken shells on a copy of *The Economist*.

It was just before eight when Chaudhry heard the sound of a key in his lock. He bolted off the sofa and dashed to the kitchen. He grabbed a breadknife from the sink and stood in the kitchen doorway, his heart pounding. The door opened slowly.

"Harvey, is that you?"

"Who the bloody hell are you expecting? Ninja assassins?"

The door opened wide and Harvey walked in, shaking his head. Chaudhry ducked back into the kitchen and returned the knife to the sink.

Malik closed the door and tossed his bag on to the floor.

412

"Lock it, will you, mate?" said Chaudhry. "And put the bolt across. Do you want a coffee?"

"Yeah, coffee'd be good," said Malik. He locked the door. "Has John called?"

"A while back. He said he'd call again once they'd followed you."

"There was no one following me," said Malik, dropping down on to the sofa and reaching into the bag of nuts.

"You shouldn't have been looking," snapped Chaudhry. "Didn't you listen? We had to come home and not do any checks at all. There were people doing that."

Malik swung his feet up on to the coffee table. "Chill, brother," he said. "I did what John said. But I was the only one who got on the bus and no one got off with me. So I can't see that anyone could have been following me." He looked around. "Where's the remote?"

"Why are you so bloody cool about this?" said Chaudhry. "There was someone following me. Don't you get what that means?"

"John said it was probably nothing." He shelled a nut and popped it into his mouth.

Chaudhry walked towards him, his eyes blazing. "Are you retarded? He said that because he doesn't want us to worry. You know what he told me? He said there are guys with guns waiting round the corner, ready to step in if we get in trouble. Does that sound like nothing, you soft bastard?"

Malik stopped chewing, his forehead creased into deep frown lines.

"I'm serious, mate. Guys with guns. We could be in deep shit here. Of course John doesn't want us panicking, but that doesn't mean we should sit around like all's well with the world."

Chaudhry's mobile rang and both men froze. It was on the coffee table by Malik's feet. It continued to ring — "Poker Face" by Lady Gaga — so Malik picked it up, then he grinned.

"It's your dentist," he said.

Chaudhry's face hardened. "That's John."

Malik turned the screen towards him. "It says it's your dentist. Relax, will you?"

Chaudhry took the phone from him and pressed the green button.

"How's the weather?" asked Whitehill.

"As well as can be expected," said Chaudhry. "Harvey's just got home."

"I know, that's why I'm calling. There's good news and bad news."

"Okay," said Chaudhry hesitantly.

"The good news is that Harvey was clear. There was no one on his tail."

"And what's the bad news?"

"The two men who followed you are sitting outside in a van."

Shepherd checked his rear-view mirror but Malik's Golf was nowhere to be seen. He slowed to sixty. "I've lost eyeball," he said into his radio mic.

"Delta One, I have them," said the driver of the surveillance vehicle closest to the VW. "We're just coming up to junction three. All clear."

Delta One was in a white Transit van with the name of a building company on the side. There were another two MI5 vehicles following Malik and Chaudhry. Delta Two was a middle-aged lady in a Mini and Delta Three was a young man in a suit at the wheel of a Ford Mondeo. All were highly trained in counter-surveillance and took it in turns to get close to the VW and check for anyone following.

Shepherd was in his Volvo and had been ahead of them since they had joined the M1. Prior to getting on the motorway Malik had carried out two simple anti-surveillance measures. He'd gone completely round a roundabout and exited without indicating, and he'd made a left turn after indicating right. Both times the VW had been closely followed by one of the MI5 surveillance team.

By the time the VW had joined the M1, the surveillance team were sure that there was no one following, but they had continued to keep the car under observation while Malik changed his speed according to Shepherd's instructions: a spell at 80 mph was followed by five minutes at 50 mph. When they had reached junction two he indicated that he was going to leave the motorway but at the last moment changed lanes and continued heading north.

"Let's go on to junction four, just to be on the safe side," said Shepherd.

"Delta One, junction four," echoed Delta One.

"Delta Two, junction four."

"Delta Three, junction four."

They carried on up the M1 to the fourth exit. It was starting to rain as Shepherd arrived at the Gateway Services and he switched on his wipers. He parked well away from the main buildings. Five minutes later Malik's Golf arrived and parked four bays to the left of Shepherd's Volvo. The rain was falling heavier, pitter-pattering on the roof of the car. Shepherd switched off the engine.

The three MI5 vehicles parked at various points around the car park. In the rear of the van there were two men in work clothes with holstered Glocks.

Shepherd climbed out of his Volvo, turned up the collar of his jacket and hurried over to Malik's Golf. He got in the back and wiped the rain from his face. "Great weather for ducks," he said.

"What does that mean anyway?" said Malik. "I don't see ducks looking particularly happy when it rains."

Chaudhry punched his friend lightly on the shoulder. "Chill," he said.

"Chill? We've had to drive to the arse end of nowhere again. Why couldn't we meet in London?"

"Because we don't want to risk being seen. This way we can wipe your arse and know that no one sees us."

"Wipe our arse?" asked Malik. "What do you mean?"

"It's how the surveillance boys refer to anti-surveillance," said Shepherd. He grinned. "Don't worry, your arses are clean."

"So what's the story?" asked Chaudhry.

Shepherd took an envelope out of his jacket. "The van was outside your flat for most of the evening." He took out a photograph and showed it to Chaudhry. It was of a white van parked in a side street. There were two Asian men sitting in the front. "These are the guys," he said. "They stayed there until the lights went out. Then they drove to Willesden. They're driving up to Scotland now. We're tailing them to find out where they go. The good news is that they don't seem to be pros. We didn't see any sign of counter-surveillance activity. We've run a trace on the van and it's registered to a trading company in Glasgow."

"Why would they send someone from Glasgow?" asked Malik, taking the photograph from Chaudhry.

Shepherd ignored the question. He took two more photographs from the envelope, head-and-shoulders shots that looked as if they had come from a passport application. "Recognise them?" he asked Chaudhry.

Chaudhry pointed at one of the pictures. "That's the guy I saw," he said. "How bad is this, John? If it was serious they wouldn't have gone back to Scotland, would they?"

"They're both British-born. Brothers. Their parents are from Pakistan." Shepherd tapped the photograph of the older of the two men. "Salman Hussain," he said. "He's not on any watch lists and he's not on the PNC, which is why we think they're not pros."

"PNC?" repeated Malik. "What's that?"

"Police National Computer," said Shepherd. "It means he's never been in trouble with the police."

He held up the other photograph. "This is his younger brother, Asad Hussain. Also not known to the police or the security services."

Chaudhry frowned. "Asad? Asad and Salman?"

"You know them?"

Chaudhry ran a hand through his hair. "Bloody idiots," he said. "Stupid bloody idiots."

"Who are they?" asked Shepherd.

Chaudhry sighed and slumped back in his seat. "My dad's trying to marry me off to this girl, the daughter of a friend of his. Jamila Hussain. She's a student at UCL. I've been out for dinner with her a few times." He gestured at the photographs. "These idiots are her brothers. They're obviously getting all protective over her, checking out that I'm suitable."

"By following you?"

"Checking that I don't have a girlfriend and that I'm not in the pub every night. Making sure that I'm a good Muslim and that I wouldn't sully their virginal sister."

"And probably making sure that you're not white," said Malik. He grinned at Shepherd. "No offence."

"None taken," said Shepherd. He looked at Chaudhry. "You're sure, Raj?"

Chaudhry nodded. "I haven't met them but she mentioned them a few times. Asad and Salman. Salman's pretty fundamentalist but his dad keeps him in check. Asad's more easy-going but they're both very protective about Jamila. She said she had a real

418

problem convincing them that she'd be okay in London on her own. In their eyes it's worse than Sodom and Gomorrah." He smiled apologetically. "I'm sorry about that," he said. "Wasting everybody's time."

Shepherd put the photographs back in the envelope. "Hey, don't worry about it," he said. "I'm just glad it had a happy ending. And it shows that the training we did worked just fine. You spotted the tail and we checked it out and no one's the wiser."

"Are you telling me this has all been a waste of time?" asked Malik.

"Better safe than sorry," said Shepherd. "Think of it as another training exercise."

"And you'll pay for my petrol, right?"

Shepherd took his wallet out of his pocket. "No problem, Harvey."

Malik and Chaudhry were sitting on the sofa watching TV when Malik's mobile rang. He looked at the screen but didn't recognise the number. He frowned over at Chaudhry. "Dunno who it is." he said. "Do you think it's Khalid?"

"Tell you what, brother, why not press the green button and you'll find out?"

Malik took the call.

"Harvey?" It was a girl.

"Yes?"

"It's Nadia."

"Nadia?"

"You've forgotten me already? Oh dear."

Malik grimaced. The girl in the library. "Sorry, yes, Nadia, yeah, of course. Hey. How are you?"

"I'm fine," she said. "But my laptop's given up the ghost. I couldn't ask a huge favour . . .?"

"Sure, you want me to have a look at it?"

"Would you, Harvey? That would be great. I've got an essay here that's got to be in tomorrow and the thing won't even boot up. You couldn't come round here now, could you?"

"Where are you?"

"Finsbury Park. Is that close to you?"

"Just down the road," he said. "Text me your address and I'll come right round."

He ended the call and grinned at Chaudhry.

"Not Khalid, then?"

"Some bird I met in the library. Nadia. Fit like you wouldn't believe me."

"What does she want?"

"Why do you think she wants anything, brother?"

"Because she's a fit bird and she's ringing you. I'm putting two and two together."

"She wants help with her laptop." Malik picked up a thick pullover and put it on.

"Who's going to take care of her dog?"

Malik frowned. "What dog?"

"Her guide dog. She's blind, right?"

Malik scowled. "Screw you, brother."

Chaudhry laughed. "Well, that'll be the only screwing you'll get."

"I'm fixing her laptop. End of."

"You told her to switch it off and on again?"

Malik laughed. "That'll be the first thing I try." He headed for the kitchen balcony to get his bike. "See you when I see you."

"You'll be back for Isha'a?"

"I don't know brother," Malik called from the kitchen. "Maybe. Depends how it goes."

"We need to be seen at the mosque every day, brother. It's important."

"I know. I was there this morning." He grinned. "But don't wait up, yeah?"

"You should take a biscuit for the dog," said Chaudhry. He was still laughing as Malik wheeled his bike from the kitchen and out through the front door.

Malik looked up at the building where Nadia lived. She was in apartment 4G, which probably meant she was on the fourth floor, so he didn't think there was much chance of taking his bike up with him. Outside an office he found a run of black railings with a painted metal notice warning that bikes would be removed but the office was in darkness so he figured he'd be okay. He pulled a plastic-covered chain from his pocket and padlocked the rear wheel and frame to the railings. He went back to the main entrance and pressed her bell on the entryphone. It rang out and she answered.

"Hello?"

"It's Harvey, computer repairs a speciality."

"Come on in, Harvey. Take the lift to the fourth floor."

The lock buzzed and Malik pushed the door open. The lift was small and seemed to take for ever to reach the fourth floor. He walked along to Nadia's door and knocked. He waited, switching his weight from foot to foot, and was just about to knock again when the door opened.

She smiled up at him. "My knight in shining armour," she said.

"I am here to serve," he joked. She opened the door wide and he stepped across the threshold. She was wearing a blue sweatshirt with the word LONDON across the front in alternating red, white and blue letters, and a dark-blue skirt. She'd tied her hair back with a scrunchy and for the first time he noticed the wrinkles at the corners of her eyes and around her neck. He realised that she wasn't as young as he'd first thought. In her thirties, maybe. But still pretty. "So where's the laptop?"

She closed the door. "No need to rush," she said. "We can have a chat first."

There was a small kitchen to the right, and a door to the left that he assumed led to the bedroom. There was a two-seater sofa in green leather facing a flatscreen TV on the wall. He took off his jacket and sat down on the sofa. "Sure," he said. "Chatting is one of my favourite things."

The bedroom door opened and a man walked out. He was Asian, wearing a Chelsea football shirt and holding a gun. Malik started to get up but the man moved quickly and pushed him back down, prodding him in the chest with the barrel of the gun.

"What is this?" asked Malik, his voice a frightened squeak. "What's going on?"

"Like I said, Harvey, we're going to have a chat. You, me and my two friends."

A second man came out of the bedroom. Another Asian. This one was holding a knife and a coil of wire.

Malik looked at Nadia fearfully. "I haven't done anything," he said.

"I hope that's true," said Nadia.

Chaudhry's alarm woke him at six-thirty, which gave him plenty of time to shower and eat breakfast before heading to the mosque for Fajr, the first prayers of the day. He went to the mosque for Fajr most days. Malik tended to oversleep and more often than not performed his prayers on a mat in the bedroom, positioned so that it pointed to Mecca.

After he'd showered and pulled on a clean shirt and jeans, Chaudhry popped two slices of bread into the toaster and then knocked on Malik's door before pushing it open. "Rise and shine, Harvey," he said. He flicked on the light. Malik's bed was empty. Chaudhry grinned. "You naughty, naughty boy," he whispered to himself.

His mobile phone began to ring and he hurried back into the kitchen. He picked it up, expecting to talk to his friend, but it was a number he didn't recognise. It was Khalid.

"Good morning, brother," said Khalid. "Today is a joyous day because today is the day we carry out Allah's work."

"That's great news, brother," said Chaudhry. His heart began to pound and he took a deep breath to steady himself.

"I need you and Harveer to be ready to go at five o'clock, brother," said Khalid. "The same place as last time. You will be collected."

"We will be there," said Chaudhry.

"Today we shall teach the kaffir a lesson they will never forget," said Khalid. "Inshallah."

"Inshallah," repeated Chaudhry. God willing.

Shepherd was dragged from a dreamless sleep by his ringing BlackBerry. He rolled over in his bed and grabbed for the phone. It was Chaudhry. "Hey, Raj, what's up?"

"It's today," said Chaudhry. "We're to be picked up at five o'clock."

Shepherd sat up, suddenly wide awake. "What happened?"

"Khalid just phoned. Pretty much the same as last time. We're to be picked up outside the restaurant again."

"And no indication of what they're planning?"

"Same as before," said Chaudhry. "But there's a problem. Harvey's not here."

"Where is he?"

"He went to see some girl last night and didn't come back."

"Have you called him?"

"His mobile's off. It goes straight through to voicemail."

"Hell's bells. Does he often do that?"

"It's a first. I don't know what's going on."

"What about Khalid?" asked Shepherd. "Did you tell him that Harvey was AWOL?"

"I couldn't," said Chaudhry. "He'd hit the roof. Look, can you get access to text messages?"

"Why?"

"She phoned him last night. Then she sent him a text with her address."

Shepherd already had Malik's number. "What company does he use?" he asked.

"T-Mobile, I think."

"All right, Raj, I'm on it. This girl, do you know anything about her?"

"Just that she's called Nadia and that she's fit. What do I do?"

"We've got your back, Raj. Just turn up and we'll follow you, same as before."

"But this time it's for real, right?"

"I guess so. It's very unlikely they'd test you twice."

"Can't you just arrest them now?"

"We need to get everybody in the act," said Shepherd. "I'll let you know about Harvey. But if he gets in touch with you first, let me know."

Shepherd ended the call. He went into his kitchen and switched on the kettle, then phoned Charlotte Button. He relayed what Chaudhry had told him.

"I'll get everyone in gear," said Button.

"I need to access a phone," said Shepherd. "Malik is AWOL."

"Is that a problem?"

"He's away with a girl. I just need to talk to him and get him back on track."

"The best person to talk to is Rob Waterman. He's our go-to guy with the phone companies. Give me a couple of minutes and I'll text you his home number. I'll see you in Thames House."

The line went dead. The kettle still hadn't boiled so Shepherd left the phone by the sink and went through to the bathroom and showered and shaved. When he got back to the kitchen with a towel wrapped round his waist there was a text message on his office mobile phone. He made himself a coffee with a splash of milk and then phoned Rob Waterman, who was surprisingly cheerful despite the early hour.

"No need to apologise. I'm an early riser and I've been up since four," said Waterman. "Charlotte has already called to tip me the wink. Give me the number and if you have the company that would save me a step."

Shepherd gave him the information and Waterman said he'd phone back. Shepherd changed into blue jeans and a black polo shirt and was just pulling on socks when Waterman called back.

"Already?" asked Shepherd.

"These days it's as easy as pushing a few buttons," said Waterman. "The text message was just an address followed by a name, Nadia, and a smiley face. Do you have a pen?"

"Don't need one," said Shepherd.

Waterman gave him the address of a flat in Finsbury Park. "Couple of things you need to know," he said.

"The phone is off now but the last time it was on it looks as if it was in the apartment. It was certainly in the immediate vicinity. That doesn't mean it's still there, of course."

"And the other thing?"

"The phone that sent the text message has been very busy. It's a pay-as-you-go sim card and it's been operative for only twenty-four hours, but in that time it's made several calls to Dubai, Palestine and Pakistan. Short calls, never more than a minute."

"Any significance in the numbers?" asked Shepherd.

"My guys are checking that now, but I wouldn't hold your breath. I'm guessing disposable sim cards all round."

"Any other calls or texts made within the UK?"

"No texts. Several calls, all under a minute and all to other pay-as-you-go mobiles. Three phones in all, but that's including the number you gave me."

"What about a location?"

"It's off too but was last on at the same Finsbury Park address. In the area, anyway."

"You're a marvel, Rob, thanks," said Shepherd. "Do me a favour and keep an eye on both phones and give me a call as soon as they go live again."

Waterman promised he would and Shepherd ended the call. He sipped his coffee and put two slices of toast into the toaster, figuring it was going to be a long day and he'd best stock up with fuel. He ran through his options, then phoned Amar Singh. Singh was also wide awake. He had young children so lie-ins were generally reserved for the weekend.

"What's up, Spider?" asked Singh.

"It's a bit embarrassing, but I need someone who looks Asian," said Shepherd.

"And what, I'm the only Asian you know?"

"The only one I can trust this with, yeah," said Shepherd.

Chaudhry stopped combing his hair and stared at his reflection in the mirror above the sink, wondering if it was possible to see a lie in a man's eyes. He'd read a couple of books on body language and he knew that there were signs that gave away when a lie was being told. If he was going to get through the day he'd have to conceal all those signs. He took a deep breath and exhaled slowly. "It's going to be fine," he said to himself. "Everything is going to work out just fine. By tonight, it'll all be over." He took another deep breath, then gave his hair a final comb. As he walked into the kitchen to make himself a cup of tea he began to tremble uncontrollably and he put both hands against the fridge to steady himself. He took slow deep breaths, trying to quell the rising sense of dread that was threatening to overwhelm him. "A few hours," he muttered to himself. "All you have to do is keep it together for a few more hours. You can do it, Raj."

He switched on the kettle, then picked up his phone. He scrolled through his contacts list until he found Jamila's number. He had a sudden urge to hear her voice and he pressed the green button. When she answered it was obvious that she had been sleeping and he apologised for waking her.

"That's all right, I had to answer the phone anyway," she joked.

"I forgot it was so early," he said. "Sorry. Just wanted to wish you a happy day, that's all."

"Are you okay, Raj?"

"I'm fine."

"You sound a bit stressed."

"I've got a test later today. I was up all night studying for it."

"Busy, busy boy."

"That's the life of a med student," he said.

"Too busy to see me?"

Chaudhry laughed. "Of course not. Can we do something at the weekend?"

"Let me check my diary." She paused and Chaudhry felt his pulse quicken. "I'm joking," she said. "Of course we can. What do you fancy doing?"

"We could go down to Brighton. Walk along the beach."

"Perfect," she said. "Sunday's best for me."

"Sunday's great," said Chaudhry. "I'll check train times and get back to you."

"I can drive us," she said. "I'll pick you up."

Chaudhry felt another wave of panic start to overwhelm him and he gripped the phone so tightly that his knuckles whitened. "Jamila?"

"Yes?"

He took a deep breath. "I really like you, you know."

"I like you too. Raj, are you sure everything's okay?"

"I'll be okay when this test is out of the way."

"Well, good luck with it," she said. "I'll be keeping my fingers crossed for you."

"Thanks," he said. "I feel better knowing that."

Shepherd drove to Finsbury Park and found a metered parking space round the corner from the flat where Malik had gone to meet the girl. Fifteen minutes later Singh arrived in a white Mercedes four-door coupé. He had to park on the other side of the road and Shepherd walked over and got in next to him. Singh was wearing a black suit that was clearly a brand name and a blue silk shirt.

"This is nice," said Shepherd, looking round the car. It still had its new-car smell and there wasn't a mark on any of the surfaces.

"I wanted the CLK but the wife said we needed doors for the kids," said Singh. "I said the kids could take the bus but for some reason she didn't agree." He shook hands with Shepherd. "Good to see you, Spider."

"Thanks for coming, Amar," said Shepherd. "You didn't have to dress up."

"This old thing?" laughed Singh, running a hand down his jacket. "It's MI5 and they notice good tailoring. In SOCA they couldn't care less — it's all tax inspectors and Customs officers, cheap suits and scuffed shoes." He nodded at the zipped-up jacket that Shepherd was wearing. "That's pretty stylish," he said. "So I'm guessing you didn't choose it yourself."

"Damien picked it out for me," said Shepherd. "It's what all the best arms dealers are wearing, I'm told, and it does a decent job of concealing my Glock."

430

"You're carrying? You didn't say that I was going to be dodging bullets." He gestured at his suit. "I don't want this damaged; I'm still paying for it."

"I don't think it's going to come to that, Amar," said Shepherd.

Singh switched off the engine. "So what do you need?"

"I've got a guy who went round to see a girl last night. Her name's Nadia. His phone's off and so is hers. I need him back home now but I can hardly go knocking on the door claiming to be a friend of his."

"Because he's Asian?"

"Partly. But if it makes you feel any better it's because, like you, he's young and good-looking." He looked at his watch. It was just after nine-thirty. "We need to get a move on. We'll go into the building, you go up to the door and have a listen. See what's happening. Then knock. Assuming she opens it, ask if Harvey's there."

"Harvey?"

"Short for Harveer. Harveer Malik. Studying for his master's in Business Administration at the London Metropolitan University. You can say you're on his course; it's not too much of a stretch. If he's not there ask her when she last saw him. Try to get a look around if you can."

"And how do I know where he was?"

"You were with him in Stoke Newington when she sent him a text last night. Her name's Nadia."

Singh nodded. "Okay," he said. "And you don't think I need to borrow your gun?"

"I'll be close by," said Shepherd.

The two men climbed out of the Mercedes and walked round the corner. The building was a purpose-built apartment block that looked as if it was council-run. There was a main entrance with two glass doors and beyond it a tiled reception area with two sets of metal lift doors. There was an entryphone system but no CCTV camera. The flat they wanted was on the fourth floor. Singh pressed the button for one of the flats on the sixth floor, but there was no response. He tried another flat and this time a woman with a heavy East European accent asked who it was.

"Postman, can you buzz me in, please, darling?" said Singh, and within seconds the lock buzzed.

Shepherd pushed the door open and as they got into one of the lifts he pressed the button for the fifth floor. When they got out they walked down one floor.

"It's 4G," said Shepherd. There was a fire door leading to a corridor with doors to the flats on either side. "I'll stay here."

"And I shout if I need you?"

"I'll be watching you, Amar. If there's a problem I'll be with you in seconds."

Shepherd unzipped his jacket as Singh opened the fire door and walked down the corridor. The flat was on the left. Singh took out a ceramic contact microphone from his pocket. There were white earphones connected to it, giving the equipment the look of an iPod. He popped the earphones into his ears and gently pressed the microphone against the door. There was a small dial on one side that allowed him to change the frequency being listened for and a dial on the other side. Singh jiggled both dials as he listened intently. At first he thought the flat was unoccupied but then he heard a voice. A man. His frown deepened as he realised that it wasn't English.

He stood stock-still with the microphone pressed against the wood. After almost a minute he heard a woman's voice but again he didn't recognise the language.

He put away the microphone as he walked back to the fire door. He didn't say anything until the fire door had closed behind him. "There's something not right," he said.

"Tell me."

"There's a woman in there but she's not speaking English. Not Urdu and not Hindi either. Your guy, where's he from?"

"British Pakistani," said Shepherd.

"So Urdu, right?"

"I'm not sure. I've never heard him speak anything other than English."

"Well, whatever they're speaking it's not Urdu. It didn't sound like general conversation either. More like she was giving orders or instructions. But that's just a feeling because I didn't understand a word." He ran a hand over his hair. "There was something else too. The guy groaned."

"Groaned?"

"That's what it sounded like." He shook his head. "Like I said, it feels wrong. Anyway, there's definitely someone in there but I'm not sure that knocking's the right thing to do."

Shepherd looked at his watch. "We don't have time for anything fancy," he said.

"You don't think we need back-up?"

"In a perfect world, yes, but this is a far from perfect situation," said Shepherd. He reached into his jacket and slid the Glock from its holster.

"Spider, I'm not trained for this. I'm an equipment geek."

"You're an MI5 officer, Amar. And a bloody good one."

"Wearing a fifteen-hundred-pound suit," he said. "Don't suppose you'll let me go home and change?"

"This is what we do," said Shepherd. "You knock and give them your best smile and ask for Harvey. See how they play it. They might well not open the door. Was there a viewer, a peephole thing?"

Singh shook his head. "No."

"That's something," said Shepherd. "They'll have to open the door to check you out."

"Okay. And if they open the door, what then?"

"If there's a problem in there there's every chance they'll just close the door in your face. I'll step in."

"And do what?"

"Stop them closing the door, for a start. Then we'll play it by ear."

"And what do I do?" asked Singh.

"Which side were the hinges on?"

Singh frowned. "The left, I think. The door handle's on the right."

"Then I'll stand on the right. When you see me move, you move to the left." He patted Singh on the shoulder. "You'll be fine, Amar."

They went back down the corridor, walking on tiptoe.

Nadia looked at her watch, then back at Malik. "Why are you making this so difficult, Harvey?" she asked. "Do you know how long you've been sitting in that chair? Almost twelve hours. Just tell me who you've told and the pain will stop. We're not hurting you for the fun of it. We just want the information, that's all."

Malik closed his eyes and shook his head slowly. They had used a dishcloth to gag him when he'd started screaming and his hands were tied behind the chair. He'd lost all sense of time. She'd said twelve hours but she could just as easily have said twelve days. They'd started with threats, then they'd beaten him, then they'd broken two of his fingers and then they'd gone to work on his right foot with a pair of pliers. She knew that he was hiding something from her. Malik didn't know how she knew but she knew. It was as if she was able to look into his very soul.

She bent down and softly stroked his cheek. "We don't want to hurt you like this, Harvey. No one wants to hurt you. But you have to tell us who you told about The Sheik. You did tell someone, didn't you, Harvey? Just nod. You don't have to say anything. Just nod."

Malik's cheeks were wet from crying but his tears had finished hours ago. He was exhausted, mentally and physically, but he knew that the moment he admitted anything it would all be over. They would kill him, he knew that for sure. He and Raj had been taken to meet Bin Laden and they had told MI5 and MI5 had told the Americans. They were directly responsible for the death of Bin Laden and if he admitted that then he was sure they would kill him. The one chance he had was to just keep denying that he'd done anything wrong.

His instructors at the al-Qaeda camp in Pakistan had taught him the basics of interrogation. Real secrets had to be buried deep and it helped to visualise them locked away in a safe or a vault. Then the safe was to be put in a deep dark place. That's what Malik had done. The truth was in an old-fashioned safe with a rotary dial and each time they tortured him he focused on the safe. And he kept repeating to himself that so long as the safe stayed locked they wouldn't kill him.

What the instructors hadn't done was prepare him for the pain. In Pakistan he'd been slapped and punched and been made to stand for hours with a sack over his head, but that was nothing compared to what Nadia and her two companions had done to him.

The one with the gun had hit him on the knees with so much force that he was sure the left one had cracked. Later he'd brought the butt of the gun down on Malik's right hand, breaking his fingers. Then he'd used the pliers. And all the time he'd been smiling as if he enjoyed every second of the torture.

The other man, the one with the knife, had been more precise with the pain that he'd inflicted. He had worked the knife into Malik's hands with the precision of a surgeon. That was when they'd gagged him. The man would torture him for a few minutes then they would wait for him to stop crying before removing the gag and asking him if he was ready to talk.

He'd pretended to be confused, that he didn't understand what they were asking. That was the first line of defence, the instructors had said. Play dumb. And if that didn't work, say nothing. Then, if the pain became unbearable, lie. Lies had to be checked, which meant that the interrogation would have to stop.

The problem for Malik was there was no lie he could tell Nadia that would stop the punishment. She had only one question for him. Who did he tell?

At first he'd denied that he'd gone to Pakistan, but Nadia knew which camp he'd been in and who had trained him. Then he'd denied that he'd been taken to see The Sheik, but Nadia knew when he'd been and who had taken him to the compound in Abbottabad. She knew everything, Malik realised. And that meant she had been sent by al-Qaeda.

At just after midnight the man had stopped using the knife; he had produced a pair of pliers and gone to work on his toes. Malik kept passing out, and each time that happened they would wait until he woke up. The waking up was the worst time, because for a few seconds he'd imagine that it was all a dream and then the horror would pour over him like a cold shower, the realisation that the torture was real and that there was nothing he could do to stop it. Well, there was one thing he could do, of course. He could tell the truth. He could tell them that he was an MI5 informer, that he'd told MI5 where Bin Laden was hiding. If he told her that then the torture would stop. Everything would stop.

The more the men had tortured him, the gentler Nadia had become. She would stroke his cheek, call him sweetheart, tell him that she hated seeing him in pain. "Just tell me the truth," she'd said to him a hundred times or more. "Tell me the truth and I'll make them stop." But Malik couldn't tell her the truth because he knew without a shadow of a doubt that if he did they would kill him.

As dawn broke he was unconscious most of the time and the carpet around his feet was wet with his blood. That was when Nadia had started asking him about Chaudhry. She knew that he had been in Pakistan with him. She knew that Chaudhry had gone with him to the compound in Abbottabad. She began to ask more questions about Chaudhry. Who his friends were. Where he went, who he spent time with. How often he went to see his parents. Malik began to hope that Nadia was starting to believe that he hadn't betrayed The Sheik and was looking for someone else to blame. Chaudhry. Malik tried to concentrate, tried to work out some sort of strategy that might result in him staying alive. If he could make them think that Chaudhry was the traitor maybe they would let him live. And if he could get away he would be able to get help; he would call MI5 and they would pull both of them out and keep them safe. As the minutes went by and they continued to hurt him and make him bleed he clung to the hope that he might somehow be able to fool them.

438

"How long have you known Raj?" she asked.

"Since we were kids."

"Do you trust him?"

"Yes."

"Do you think he would betray The Sheik?"

"No. I don't know. Maybe."

"What about you, Harvey? Did you betray The Sheik?"

"No. I swear. As Allah is my judge."

"Allah is not your judge today, Harvey. I am. And I do not believe you."

Then the gag was pushed into his mouth and the man with the pliers began to work on his toes again and he screamed into the dishcloth.

When Malik came to, the man with the pliers was standing in front of him. There was blood on the serrated tips and what looked like pieces of flesh. The man was looking at Nadia and Nadia was staring at the door. Then there was a ringing sound. A doorbell.

Nadia waved at the man with the pliers to go into the kitchen. He knelt down and picked up his knife, then hurried over to the kitchen door. The doorbell rang again. The man in the Chelsea shirt aimed his gun at the door and whispered something at Nadia. She shook her head and pointed at the bedroom.

There was a knock on the door, three rapid taps.

The man in the Chelsea shirt disappeared into the bedroom and closed the door.

Nadia bent down and put her mouth next to Malik's ear. "Make a sound, any sound at all, and I will slit your throat myself," she said. She patted him gently on the cheek, then walked slowly over to the door. "Who is it?" she asked.

Malik heard a man's voice but it was muffled and he couldn't hear what was said. The doorbell rang again, three short rings followed by a longer one.

Nadia slipped the chain lock on and opened the door a fraction. "Who is it?" she asked. "What do you want?"

"I'm here to get Harvey," said a voice.

Singh hadn't expected the girl to be so pretty, but he could see that she was nervous.

"This is my apartment. There's no Harvey here," she said. "You must have the wrong address."

She tried to close the door but Singh put up his hand and held it open. "Harvey said he was coming here. You're Nadia, right?"

She frowned. "Who told you that?"

"Harvey did," said Singh. "He said he was coming to see you. Said he might stay overnight and that if he did I was to pick him up here."

"He gave you this address?"

Singh nodded and grinned. "How else would I know to come and ring your bell? Now stop messing about, Nadia. If Harvey's still in bed then tell him to get his trousers on, will you?"

Shepherd listened, his gun pointing up at the ceiling. Singh was ad-libbing brilliantly, making it very difficult for her to close the door in his face. If anything he was doing too good a job because if Nadia did have Harvey captive in the flat there was a strong possibility that she

440

might decide to do something about the man at her door.

"Nadia, I know what it's like, family honour and all that, but if Harvey's there he needs to get out here now, and if he isn't you need to tell me where he is because his phone's off." He winked. "Come on, honey, I don't care what the two of you got up to."

Nadia looked over her shoulder, then nodded. "He's in the bedroom," she said. She reached for the chain.

Singh looked across at Shepherd and as he did so Nadia's hand froze. She'd seen the look, Shepherd realised. And now everything had changed.

He pushed Singh to the left, stepped back and kicked out hard with his right leg. His foot hit the door just under the handle and he pushed forward with all his weight. The chain ripped out from its mounting and the door crashed open, banging into the woman. She staggered back into the room as Shepherd stepped across the threshold, bringing his left hand up to support his right as he swung the Glock around. He moved slowly and evenly, any jerking and his shots would be sure to be off target. There were four people in the room. The woman, still staggering backwards. An Asian man standing by the kitchen, holding a bloody knife. Malik, tied to a chair, a strip of cloth around his mouth, his eyes wide and fearful, his right foot hacked and bleeding, blood on his shirt. The door to the bedroom was open and Shepherd glimpsed another Asian man, this one holding a gun. Four souls, three targets, one gun, one knife. Shepherd's training kicked in without any conscious effort. The man with the gun was the imminent threat. Shepherd brought the gun to bear on the man's chest. He was in his twenties, tall and lanky with deep-set eyes, wearing grubby cargo pants and a Chelsea football shirt that was flecked with blood. Malik's blood.

Shepherd didn't shout a warning. He didn't have to. Everyone in the room knew exactly what was happening. If the man with the gun had dropped it and raised his hands then Shepherd would have switched his attention to the man with the knife, but that didn't happen. The man's finger was tightening on the trigger and even though Shepherd could see that the man's aim was off he still fired, just once. The bullet hit the man a couple of inches below the heart. The sound was deafening and instantly the stench of cordite assaulted Shepherd's nose and made his eyes begin to water. The man fell back into the bedroom, a look of surprise on his face, his mouth forming a perfect circle. The gun dropped to the man's side and then slipped from his fingers and fell on the carpet.

Shepherd stepped forward with his left leg as he swung the gun towards the man by the kitchen. He was aware of the woman's arms flailing as she tried to regain her balance but she had no weapon so she wasn't a threat.

The man with the knife was overweight, his hair greasy and unkempt. He had taken off his shirt and was wearing a string vest pulled out over baggy jeans. Clumps of hair sprouted from his armpits and chest hair was poking through the holes in the vest. The man was moving towards Shepherd, the knife raised high, his lips drawn back in a snarl. Again Shepherd said nothing. There was no need. He wasn't a police officer; no one from Professional Standards was going to be investigating the shooting; there'd be no suspension, no court case, no comebacks. All the man had to do was drop the knife and raise his hands, but he didn't. He started to run towards Shepherd, growling like a cornered dog. Shepherd shot him in the face. Blood, brain and skull fragments sprayed over the wall and the man fell forward, slamming on to the floor with such force that Shepherd felt the vibration through the soles of his feet.

Shepherd smoothly turned the gun towards the woman, his finger tightening on the Glock's trigger. She had regained her balance and was already putting her hands behind her neck. Nightingale stared at her and she met his gaze with no trace of fear in her eyes. She knelt down on the floor, her eyes fixed on his. Shepherd kept the gun pointing at her face as she went down, knowing that the slightest increase in pressure on the trigger would send a bullet into her skull. There was a hint of a smile on her face as if she expected him to shoot her. Shepherd was breathing slowly and evenly, totally relaxed.

The woman looked up at him, the movement tightening her neck.

"Amar, get in here," said Shepherd.

Singh stepped into the room and closed the door.

Shepherd gestured at the woman with his gun. "Very slowly now, lie face down and keep your hands behind your neck."

The woman did as she was told.

"Untie Harvey," Shepherd said to Singh. "But give me that roll of duct tape first."

Singh picked the roll of tape off the table and handed it to Shepherd. Shepherd holstered the Glock, then straddled the woman's legs and used the tape to bind her wrists. He ripped off another length of tape and put it across her mouth.

Singh went over to untie Malik as Shepherd put his ear against the door. He couldn't hear anything in the corridor.

"Try this," said Singh, and he tossed over the ceramic microphone. Shepherd slotted in the earphones and pressed the microphone against the door. Still nothing.

"What happens now?" asked Singh, who was on his knees behind Malik, working at the wires around his wrists. "Do the cops come?"

"Not necessarily," said Shepherd. "It sounded loud in here but in another apartment it'll just be two loud bangs and they won't know where they came from. If they do dial three nines the cops will ask a lot of questions that the caller won't be able to answer. It might not even get reported."

Singh nodded at the body in the bedroom doorway, the man who had been holding the gun. "But you have to call it in?"

"To Charlie, yes. Not to the cops. If we're lucky it can be dealt with in-house."

He went over to the window and pushed open the blinds so that he could squint down into the street below. The apartment looked out on to the side road where they'd parked their cars but if he pressed his head against the wall he could just make out the main road. Traffic was flowing freely. If the police did arrive then there would be an armed response vehicle and their first action would be to set up a perimeter around the building.

Shepherd went over and squatted down in front of Malik as Singh finished untying him. "Harvey, mate, can you stand up?"

Malik stared back at him but didn't react.

"Is he okay?" asked Singh.

"He's in shock," said Shepherd. "Get a blanket round him and make him some tea. With lots of sugar." He put his head closer to Malik's. "It's going to be okay, Harvey. You're safe now." Malik continued to stare at him with blank eyes.

Singh returned from the bedroom with a quilt and he wrapped it round Malik before heading to the kitchen.

Shepherd took out his phone and leaned over the woman. He prodded the back of her neck with the barrel of his Glock and she tensed. "You have no idea how hard I'm fighting the urge to put a bullet in your head," he whispered. He tapped the gun against her head and then straightened up and called Charlotte

Button. She answered on the third ring. "We've got a problem," he said.

The four men in white paper suits with blue surgical caps and blue shoe protectors looked like a police Scene of Crime unit but they were all employed by MI5. They had rolled the two corpses into black body bags and were preparing to take them downstairs to their waiting van.

"What's going to happen to them?" Shepherd asked Button.

"We'll have a medic remove the bullets and mess around with the wounds, then we'll deliver them to a medical school that we use."

"Are you serious?"

"Best way of getting rid of a body is to let a group of students dissect it," said Button.

A doctor had already checked out Malik and insisted that he be taken down on a stretcher. Malik's foot was badly disfigured and two of his fingers had been broken. It looked as if his kneecap had been shattered too. When the paramedics carried him out he was still in shock but he managed a weak smile when Shepherd patted him on the shoulder.

Shepherd nodded at the woman, who was lying face down on the carpet with her wrists bound. "And what about her?"

Button grimaced. "She's more of a problem. We can't let her near a lawyer, or anyone else who might spread the word."

The four men took the bodies out of the flat and along to the lift.

"What if anyone sees them?" asked Shepherd.

"We've got a HAZMAT van downstairs and an ambulance, and if anyone asks it's a virulent TB case. But no one will ask. We've got four of our people down there in police uniforms. Everything's under control."

The doctor reappeared in the doorway. He was a fifty-something grey-haired man in a rumpled blue suit. He was carrying a medical bag. The paramedics followed him. One was holding a collapsible stretcher.

"How is he?" asked Button.

"His vitals are fine, but he's going to be in shock for a while. I've given him antibiotics and something for the pain but what he really needs is rest. A lot of rest."

Button pointed at the woman on the floor. "Can you put her out for the next hour?"

"No problem," said the doctor. He knelt down beside the bound woman and opened his bag. He rummaged around and took out a hypodermic, then injected the contents into her left buttock.

Shepherd looked at his watch. It was almost midday. "What do we do, Charlie?"

"Chaudhry can go on his own. Once we know what the target is, we move in."

"What if they want to know where Harvey is?"

"He's out with a girl and he's uncontactable. I don't see that as a problem, do you?"

Shepherd shrugged. "I don't know. I guess they'll realise it was short notice. But what about Raj? What do we tell him?"

"Nothing," said Button. "He mustn't know what's happened to Harvey."

"Why not?"

"Because he'll want to be with his friend. Or it'll put the wind up him. Either way it's best that he doesn't know."

"Charlie, we owe him the truth."

Button's eyes flashed. "No," she said firmly. "We owe him our protection. This is the end phase and he has to go into it with a clear head."

"So we lie to him?"

"If that's what it takes, yes." She put a hand on his shoulder and looked into his eyes. "It's for his own safety. You can see that, can't you?"

"Sure, of course. But I don't like the idea of lying to him, not after everything he's done for us."

"In a few hours this will all be over, Spider. And when it is you can tell him everything. But, until then, Harvey stays under wraps and Raj isn't to know."

"She's under," said the doctor, picking up his case. "Make sure her airway stays clear."

"Take her down, then," Button said to the paramedics.

"What's going to happen to her?" asked Shepherd.

"We'll take her to Thames House for questioning," said Button. "A lot depends on who she is and who else wants her."

"The Americans?"

"We'll see," said Button. "The important thing right now is that she's isolated."

The two paramedics rolled her on to the stretcher, lifted her up and carried her out.

"I'll see you back at the ranch," the doctor said to Button and she smiled.

"Thanks again, Will. You're a godsend."

"So where do you want me?" asked Shepherd.

"Thames House, same as last time," said Button. "But first you're going to have to check on Raj."

"And what do I tell him about Harvey?"

"Tell him that as soon as we know where Harvey is, he'll know."

Shepherd sighed. "I really hate having to lie to him."

"It comes with the job, Spider."

"Have you ever lied to me, Charlie?"

She shook her head. "No. But then I've never had to."

Abney Park Cemetery was more than just a piece of ground where corpses were buried, though there were some very famous people rotting in the ground, including William and Catherine Booth, the founders of the Salvation Army. It was a local nature reserve and park as well, a place where lovers walked arm in arm and spinsters exercised their dogs. It was also a pretty good place for a clandestine meeting with its twisted pathways, tangled vegetation and ivy-covered monuments and gravestones. Shepherd had made a point of never meeting Chaudhry and Malik on their home turf but today was different. There were only hours to go and Chaudhry needed hand-holding like he'd never needed it before.

The park was a short walk from the flat and Chaudhry reached it first. He waited just inside the gate, his duffel coat buttoned up to the neck and the hood up. Shepherd arrived in his Volvo and managed to find a parking space close to the entrance. As he walked in he saw Chaudhry but ignored him and walked towards the centre of the graveyard down a tree-lined path. Left and right were gravestones so old that time had obliterated most of the carved lettering, though various shapes were still discernible: urns draped in flowers, crosses, angels, wreaths. As the path turned to the right and they were no longer visible from the entrance, Shepherd slowed and Chaudhry fell into step next to him.

"I thought you said we should never meet in Stokie," said Chaudhry.

"Yeah, well, the best laid plans of mice and men and all that," said Shepherd. "As a rule the handler should stay well away from the agent's turf, but the rule book's been torn up today."

"Harvey's phone is still off. What do I do?"

"You go ahead without him."

"Did you get the text message from his phone?"

It was a good question, Shepherd knew. A good question and an obvious one and if he answered truthfully it would be followed by a host of other good and obvious questions. Did Shepherd go to the address? Did he go inside? Was Harvey there? Was the girl? At some point he was going to have to start lying and the big question was: when?

"Yeah, it was a flat in Finsbury Park."

"And?"

Not a question, just an invitation to supply more information. Shepherd sighed and then cursed under his breath.

"What's wrong?" asked Chaudhry.

They walked past a stone angel, its hands clasped in prayer. It wasn't lying that Shepherd found difficult. He was a good liar, and he knew exactly what he had to do. He had to look Chaudhry in the eye and tell him that he had been round to the flat and it had been empty. There had been no sign of Malik and no sign of the girl. The police were looking for them now and as soon as Shepherd knew where Malik was, Chaudhry would know too. It was a simple lie, easy to tell and easy to back up.

"I went to the flat," said Shepherd. "He was there."

"What?"

"The girl he'd gone to see was with two other guys and they were torturing him."

Chaudhry stopped and turned to face Shepherd. He put his hands on Shepherd's shoulders and moved his face so that it was just inches from Shepherd's. "Are you serious?" he hissed.

Shepherd nodded. "Yes. He's in hospital. He's in a bad way but he'll be okay."

"Why didn't you tell me right away? Which hospital?"

"I don't know. I didn't ask. But he's going to be fine."

Chaudhry let go of Shepherd's shoulders, walked away and then stopped. He whirled round and pointed a finger at Shepherd's face. "You're playing me. Handling me — that's what you called it."

"No, Raj. If I was handling you I'd have lied and said that everything was okay. But I told you I would never lie to you and I'm sticking to that."

Chaudhry put his hands up to his head and covered his ears as if he didn't want to listen to anything that Shepherd had to say. "I don't believe this," he said. "This can't be happening." He walked away and again turned back after a couple of steps. "Who?" he said. "Who tortured him?"

"We haven't identified them yet. The woman is presumably the one who sent him the text. They're all Asians."

"Do you think Khalid is behind this?"

"Probably not. If he was why would he take just Harvey? And why would he call you this morning and tell you both to get ready?"

"So who, then?"

Shepherd held up his hands. "I don't know, Raj. If I did I'd tell you."

Chaudhry frowned and began pacing up and down. "Is it about The Sheik? Is it al-Qaeda? If it was al-Qaeda why did they take Harvey and not me?" He stopped pacing. There was a wild look in his eyes and his hands were shaking. Shepherd recognised the symptoms. Shock. Stress. Fear. "Maybe they are coming for me. Maybe when they come to pick me up they'll torture me." He walked back to Shepherd and stared at him. "You've got to pull me out now. And my family. We need protection. What do you call it? Witness protection?"

"No one's saying you need protection, Raj."

"The fact that Harvey's in hospital suggests that I do," said Chaudhry. "If Harvey had been protected he wouldn't have been tortured would he?"

"We've got the people who were hurting him."

"Hurting him? They were going to kill him. And then they would have gone after me."

"Raj, they're out of the picture." Shepherd wasn't going to lie to Chaudhry but he didn't think it would be a good idea to tell him that he'd personally shot and killed the two men.

"But what if there are more of them? What if they weren't alone?" Chaudhry began pacing again. Shepherd watched and waited for him to calm down. Adrenaline would be coursing through his system and it would take time for it to work its way out.

"You've got to get me and Harvey out of this," said Chaudhry.

"Harvey's out already," said Shepherd. "He's been taken care of. The woman is being questioned so we'll find out who she is and who sent her."

"And what about me?"

"That's what I want to talk about, Raj. That's why I'm here."

Chaudhry stood and glared at him. "Talk? I think we're way past talking." The shaking of his hands had intensified and he looked down at them as if seeing them for the first time. "For fuck's sake, look at me."

"It's stress. It'll pass."

"Don't patronise me!" hissed Chaudhry. "I'm a med student. I'll be a doctor soon. I know why I'm shaking. I'm shaking because my best friend is in hospital and it could have been me. I'm shaking because unless I do something I could end up dead."

"You're not going to end up dead, Raj." Shepherd took a step towards Chaudhry but Chaudhry put up his hands to ward him off.

"You can't say that," said Chaudhry. "You don't know." He put his hands over his face and swore vehemently.

Shepherd said nothing. He had to wait for the anger to subside.

Chaudhry turned his back on Shepherd and started walking down the path. Shepherd walked after him. For two or three minutes there was only the sound of their shoes squelching on wet leaves.

"I need to see him," said Chaudhry eventually.

"Sure," said Shepherd.

"Today."

"Not a problem."

Chaudhry turned to look at him. "That's your technique, is it? Agree with everything I say? That's your way of handling me?"

"It's not about handling you. I think you should see Harvey. I think he'd want to see you."

454

Chaudhry started walking again, his arms folded, his head down. Every now and again he would shake his head as if trying to clear his thoughts.

They reached the old church in the centre of the graveyard. Abney Park Chapel had been an impressive building in its time, built when churches were meant to stand for centuries. The walls were made of blocks of grey granite and the roof tiles were slate. The chapel had been closed for years and most of the lead flashings had been stolen. Vandals had also damaged many of the slates, with the result that water had seeped inside and caused so much damage that the chapel would almost certainly never again be opened for worship, especially as the percentage of Christians in the area was declining year by year.

Chaudhry stopped and looked up at the spire. "How many people have died because of religion?" he asked quietly.

"A lot," said Shepherd. "A hell of a lot."

"Why is that? What it is about religion that makes people go out and kill?"

Shepherd shrugged. "That's something else that's above my pay grade," he said.

Chaudhry's shoulders began to shudder and for a moment Shepherd thought that he was crying. Then he heard a throaty chuckle that grew into a full-blown belly laugh. Chaudhry turned round, laughing and shaking his head. "Pay grade," he said. "You're a funny man, John." He pulled his hood down and rubbed his eyes.

"Just trying to lighten the moment, Raj."

Chaudhry wiped a tear from the corner of his eye. "You really are a piece of work," he said. "You know, I still can't think of you as anything other than John Whitehill, freelance journalist. You did a good job with that." He sighed. "Okay," he said. "I'm ready. Talk."

Shepherd nodded. "I need you to be there at five. I need you to get into the van so that we can follow you."

"They'll want to know why Harvey's not there."

"You can just say his phone's off and that you couldn't reach him."

"And what if they don't believe me? Or what if they know something's wrong? What if it's a trap?"

"It's not a trap."

"You don't know that, John. Not for sure." He bit down on his lower lip, then shook his head. "I can't get into that van on my own," he said. "I'm sorry, I just can't."

Shepherd said nothing for several seconds, then he took a deep breath and exhaled. "Okay," he said. "Maybe there's a way round this."

"Here he comes," said Charlotte Button, pointing at one of the twelve LCD screens on the wall. Chaudhry was walking along the pavement towards the restaurant where the van was due to collect him. He had the hood of his duffel coat up, his head down, his hands in his pockets. He walked slowly and purposefully.

Button looked at the clock on the wall. It was five minutes before five. They were in the operations room on the top floor of Thames House and more than a dozen officers were bent over computer screens and talking into Bluetooth headsets. Commander Needham was at his desk, talking animatedly into a headset. He turned, gave Button a thumbsup and held up four fingers. Four more ARV units on the way. She smiled back at him and mouthed "Thank you."

"Luke, what do we have in place?" she asked.

Luke Lesporis looked up from his terminal. "Two black cabs in Stoke Newington Church Street; two bikes in parallel streets; two delivery vans, each facing a different direction. I've got an outer perimeter with two more bikes and four black cabs all within half a mile. The other vans we identified at St Pancras are all covered too."

An LCD flickered into life and they had an overhead view of the street. Then the screen went black and all they could see were greenish figures and red spots marking car engines. "We have helly telly," said a blonde woman in a dark-blue suit.

"Thanks, Zoe. Tell them we don't need infrared," said Button. "And to keep high — no tipping them off."

"Will do," said the woman.

"Luke, please tell me that we have eyes on Khalid."

"He's in a terraced house in Tower Hamlets with three other men," said Lesporis. "Spent a lot of time washing his arse this morning but we had a dozen men on him so we stayed with him."

"Has anybody heard from Shepherd?" asked Button. She sighed when there was no reaction. "Well, somebody try his mobile again. And keep trying."

Chaudhry had reached the Indian restaurant and stood with his back to it, looking down the street.

"The van's on its way," said Lesporis. "The same one as last time. The plumber's van."

"Right, everyone, here we go," said Button. "We need to stay on top of this. All the signs are that this is the real thing."

Commander Needham raised a hand. "Two more ARVs en route," he said. Button thanked him. She had a strong feeling that they were going to be needed.

The van pulled up at the kerb. Harith was in the front passenger seat, bundled up in a thick cloth coat and with a white wool scarf wound twice round his neck. "Salaam, brother," he said. "Where's Harveer?"

"He's not feeling so good," said Chaudhry.

"What do you mean?" said Afzal, leaning across from the driver's seat. "Is he not coming?"

"No, he's coming, but he was just on the toilet. He's got the shits."

"Nerves," said Harith. "Probably nerves."

"No, he's picked up a bug." He looked down the pavement. "Here he comes now."

A figure in a green parka was hurrying towards the rear of the van, the fur-lined hood up, his hands deep in the jacket pockets.

"Get in the back, brother," said Afzal. "And make sure that Harveer doesn't throw up. This is my uncle's van and there'll be hell to pay if I return it stinking of vomit."

"I'll watch over him, brother," said Chaudhry.

"Make sure you do," said Harith, winding up the window.

458

Chaudhry went to the rear of the van and opened the door.

"What the hell is going on?" asked Charlotte Button as she saw the man in the green parka walk up to Chaudhry. Chaudhry got into the van and the man in the parka followed him. "Who is that?" she said, pointing at the LCD screen. "Is that Malik? Malik's still in hospital, right?"

Nobody answered and other than the police commander everyone in the room avoided eye contact with her.

"Will somebody please find out if Harveer Malik is still in hospital? If he is then we need to know who is wearing his parka." The words had barely left her mouth before she realised that there was only one person who could possibly have stepped in to take Malik's place. "Has anyone managed to get through to Dan Shepherd?" She was faced with a dozen or so shaking heads. "I think we now know why," she said.

Shepherd sneaked a look at his watch. They had been in the back of the van for just over half an hour and without windows he had no idea in which direction they were heading. When they first got into the van they had headed south but there had been a number of turns and a round-about and now with no indication of the speed of the van he couldn't even calculate how far they were from Stoke

Newington, never mind in which direction they were going.

He was sitting on the floor at the rear of the van, facing the double doors. He was about the same height and build as Malik and provided he stayed in that position, with his hood up, the driver and front passenger couldn't see his face. He'd found a pair of wool gloves in Chaudhry's flat and he was wearing them to conceal his hands.

Chaudhry kept talking to Harith to keep his attention away from Shepherd, mainly asking questions about what was going to happen. Harith kept telling him to wait, that all would soon be explained.

During a lull in their conversation Afzal looked over his shoulder. "Harvey, brother, are you okay? You're quiet."

Shepherd grunted and shrugged.

"He'll be okay. He's just got a tummy bug," said Chaudhry, leaning forward to get between the driver and Shepherd. "So where's Khalid?"

"The control room," said Afzal.

Harith held up a mobile. "He called me on this just half an hour ago," he said. "This time it's for real, brothers. This time we change England for ever. From today onwards they will treat us Muslims with the respect that we deserve." He looked at his wristwatch. "It is time," he said.

"Time?" repeated Chaudhry.

"Brothers, it's time for you to learn what it is that you are to do," said Harith. "Today will be a glorious day. Today the British government will learn what it means to betray its Muslim population. Today is the day we strike back. Today we teach them to respect us. And to fear us." He reached into his jacket and pulled out a sheet of paper. "We are going to Westfield shopping mall. There will be more than a dozen brothers there. This is where you need to go."

He handed the paper to Chaudhry. The sheet was folded in half and Chaudhry opened it, then leaned over and tapped Shepherd's shoulder with it. Shepherd took it and stared at the hand-drawn map. It was marked "First Floor". There were two crosses by doors that led to a car park.

"We will drop you at the car park. In the crate next to you are two backpacks. They contain your weapons, ammunition, a chain and a lock. There are also ski masks so that you can cover your face. At exactly six o'clock you are to run the chain through the handles of the doors and use the lock to fasten it."

Shepherd slowly pulled down the zip of his parka. Underneath he was wearing his leather jacket. The Glock was in his shoulder holster, snug under his left arm.

"All the doors will be locked and there will be brothers on every level, at every entrance and exit. Then you are to begin shooting. In the backpacks are guns and pre-loaded clips. You are to shoot as many kaffirs as you can, avoiding brothers and sisters wherever possible. Do you understand?"

Chaudhry nodded. So did Shepherd.

"You will be on the first floor. You are to go straight inside and chain the door shut. And then begin shooting. After ten minutes you are to make your way to Marks & Spencer. You can use the internal escalator to reach the ground floor. It has its own exit, separate from the mall. As you move through the store you can drop your weapons and remove your masks and disappear into the crowds. Once outside you can make your way to the tube. There are Oyster cards in the backpacks."

Chaudhry smiled. "It is a good plan, brother."

"Are you all right, Harveer?" asked Harith.

Shepherd waved his gloved hand and grunted.

"You should look at the map."

"I told him not to order the prawn vindaloo," said Chaudhry. "Never a good idea to go with the prawns. Get a bad one and you're as sick as a dog."

"But you can do this, brother? You're not going to let us down, are you?" Shepherd didn't react. "Harvey?" said Harith.

"He'll be fine," said Chaudhry.

Harith stared at the hood of the parka. "Harveer?"

Shepherd grunted again and waved his hand.

Harith's eyes narrowed. He reached inside his coat and pulled out a gun.

"Gun!" shouted Chaudhry, and he lunged forward, trying to grab it.

Shepherd grabbed for his own Glock as Chaudhry seized Harith's wrist. Afzal looked over at Harith, his mouth wide open. Harith lashed out with his left hand and smacked Chaudhry across the nose. Blood spurted down Chaudhry's chin but he refused to let go of Harith's wrist.

"What are you doing?" shouted Afzal. "What's happening?"

Shepherd pulled the Glock from its holster and slipped his finger on to the trigger.

Harith pulled the gun towards himself and screamed at Chaudhry to let go even though they both knew that as soon as Chaudhry released his grip Harith would fire.

Chaudhry managed to get his left hand on the gun and he wrenched it up, but as it jerked it went off and a bullet ripped through the thin sheet-metal roof of the van. The shock made Chaudhry release his grip on the gun and Harith roared and brought the gun down, aiming it at Chaudhry's face.

Shepherd leaned back and fired two quick shots that both hit Harith in the face. The bullets erupted out of the back of the man's skull with enough force to smash the windshield. Blood and brain matter splattered across the dashboard.

Chaudhry sat back on his crate, gasping for breath.

Shepherd pointed the gun at Afzal's head. "Pull over," he said. "Pull over now or I'll put a bullet in your head. Your choice."

"Okay, okay," said Afzal, trembling. "I'm doing it."

He indicated to the left, ignored the blare of a horn from behind them and stopped at the kerb. Shepherd handed the Glock to Chaudhry. "Keep that pointed at his head. If he moves, shoot him."

Chaudhry nodded nervously as Shepherd pulled out his mobile phone.

"What just happened?" shouted Button, frowning at the LCD screen showing the view from the police helicopter. "Why did they stop?"

On screen they saw a motorcycle dispatch rider pass the van and a few seconds later Lesporis twisted round in his seat.

"The front passenger has been shot. There's blood all over the windscreen," he said.

"I have an ARV thirty seconds away," said Commander Needham.

"Hold off on that, Commander," said Button. Her mobile phone rang and she picked it up. It was Shepherd calling. She took the call and held the phone to her ear. "What the hell is going on, Spider?"

"The target is Westfield shopping mall, the one in Stratford. They're using guns, not explosives. The attack is due to happen at six p.m. They'll seal all the exits and start shooting. The plan is for the attackers to escape through the department stores because they have exits leading to the outside."

"Give me a minute, Spider." Button stood up. "I need everybody's attention, right now." She looked over at the clock on the wall. It was twelve minutes to six. "We are looking at multiple armed attackers at Westfield shopping mall, Stratford." She pointed at Commander Needham. "We need all your ARVs there now, and any others you can raise." She looked over at Lesporis. "Luke, maintain surveillance on the other vans. As soon as you can confirm that they are heading to the mall, we need them intercepted and neutralised."

Button pointed at Zoe. "Get the Met helicopter over the mall, now." Zoe nodded and started talking into her headset.

A tall man in a black leather jacket looked over at Button, waiting for instructions. She only knew him as Terry and he was her SAS liaison. The SAS had a team outside the house where Khalid was holed up, ready to move in and do whatever was necessary. The SAS weren't hampered by the same rules and regulations that governed the police so the house clearance wouldn't turn into a siege situation.

"Hang fire, Terry," she said. "Let's wait until we have them all."

Terry nodded. "Ready when you are, ma'am," he said. He was holding a pack of chewing gum and he slid a piece into his mouth.

Button put her mobile back to her ear. "What's your situation, Spider?"

"All good," said Shepherd. "The passenger took a bullet; the driver's under control. I need to get to the mall."

"Negative on that. We'll take it from here."

"Charlie, I saw all their faces on the photos at Thames House. I'm the only one that can ID them. Get a bike here and I can be there in minutes. The cops aren't going to know who to take out. It could get very messy."

"We can take out the vans before they get there."

"And what about the ones who aren't in the vans? What about the ones going by tube? Or bus? I need to be there, Charlie. Get me that bike."

Button looked over the clock again. The seconds were ticking away.

"What's happening?" asked Chaudhry. He turned to look at Shepherd and as he did so Afzal slid his hands off the steering wheel.

Shepherd pointed at the driver. "Raj, keep the gun at his head. Afzal, you do anything other than grip that wheel and he'll put a bullet in you, I swear."

"Okay, okay," said Afzal. His face was bathed in sweat and his hands were trembling.

"I'm serious, Raj. He moves, you shoot him."

Chaudhry nodded. "I will do," he said. His voice was shaking and he took a deep breath. "I will," he said, louder and more confident. "What are you going to do?"

"I'm going to the mall." He pulled the lid off the plastic crate containing the backpacks and pulled one out. He unzipped it and looked inside. There were two Glock pistols, several dozen filled magazines and two boxes of extra ammunition.

"I'm coming with you," said Chaudhry, keeping his eyes on the driver.

"You can't," said Shepherd.

"I've been trained," said Chaudhry. "I can shoot."

Shepherd slung the backpack over his shoulder. "Raj, trust me. There are armed cops from all over London heading towards that shopping mall. The last thing you want to be is an Asian with a gun. Best will in the world, you might as well have a bull's-eye on your chest."

466

"The world is fucked up, John."

"Yeah, isn't it just?" He heard the roar of a motorcycle engine and, in the distance, the sound of a siren. "Now listen to me, Raj. In a few minutes the cops will be here. Armed cops. They know you're one of the good guys and they know you're in the van, but accidents can happen so as soon as they get here you slide the gun to the back of the van and you do exactly as they tell you. They have a procedure to follow and it doesn't involve them minding their manners. Just grit your teeth and it'll soon be over."

"I hear you."

A motorcycle pulled up behind the van.

"I've got to go, mate," said Shepherd, taking off the wool gloves. He held out his hand. "And my name's Dan," he whispered so that Afzal couldn't hear him. "Dan Shepherd." Chaudhry reached out with his left hand and awkwardly shook with Shepherd, all the time keeping the gun aimed at Afzal's head. "You did good today, Raj. Really good. But your part's over now."

"I'll see you again, right?"

Shepherd nodded. "You can count on it."

He climbed out of the back of the van. A group of housewives were staring wide-eyed at the van. One of them was pushing a toddler in a stroller. "Ladies, you need to get away from the van for your own safety," he said. The siren was louder now. The women hurried away.

The dispatch rider was dressed all in black, his face hidden behind a tinted visor. He nodded at Shepherd and revved the powerful engine. Shepherd climbed on to the pillion. The engine roared and the bike sped off.

"Right, everybody, status reports, please, and let's keep them short," said Charlotte Button. "Commander?" She looked over at Commander Needham.

"I have three ARVs heading to Westfield now," said the commander. "The first one is ETA nine minutes. The second will be there in eleven and we're looking at twelve minutes for the third. I've asked two to go to the main entrance and one to the other end of the mall. All on the ground floor. That's where we assume most of the shoppers will be."

Button nodded. "That's three confirmed but more on the way?"

"I'm working on that now," he said. "The timing is dire."

"I'm sure that's deliberate," said Button. "What about the vans?"

"We are close to the three that we've been tailing and can take them out on your word," said the commander.

Three of the screens on the wall were now showing floor plans of Westfield shopping mall. Entrances were marked with flashing red squares.

"Let's see if we can tell what the drop-off points are going to be," Button said. She pointed at the screens. "We're looking at fourteen entrances and exits in all. Several are reached by the car parks so if we can ascertain that any of the vans are heading to particular car parks we take them out and then we'll know that those entrances are going to be safe." She called over to Lesporis. "Luke, we do have comms with Spider?"

"Working on it," said Lesporis.

"Soon as you can," she said. "And tell your watchers that as soon as they know where their targets are going to pull in they must let us know. And Zoe, that goes for the helicopter. The sooner we know where exactly they're headed, the sooner we can take them out."

Zoe flashed Button a thumbs-up as she continued to talk into her headset.

"Commander, we need regular police in the area because assuming the armed response teams start firing there's going to be panic. We'll need to get people moving in the right direction."

"Can I suggest an evacuation of the mall and the surrounding shops?" said the commander.

Button looked over at him. She knew that the commander was covering his back, making sure that everyone realised that the decision to allow the terrorists to continue was her decision and hers alone. "As soon as we know that we can neutralise all the shooters, we'll clear the area," she said. "If we evacuate now we might tip them into shooting before the six o'clock deadline. But your suggestion is noted."

Button looked at the clock. Ten minutes to six.

Lesporis raised a hand. "Charlie, Tango Two is heading for car park A, at the John Lewis end. Nowhere else it can be going."

Button turned to the commander. "Take out Tango Two, Commander."

Commander Needham nodded and pressed a number on his console.

Lesporis raised his hand again. "We have Spider on comms," he said. Button reached for a headset and put it on.

The motorcyclist was a true professional, barely using his brakes as he wove in and out of the traffic. They had already gone through two red lights, taking one at full speed and the other much more slowly with the bike's hazard lights flashing. With no official markings or siren they were leaving angry looks and blaring horns in their wake.

The driver had had to remove the full-face helmet and pass it back to Shepherd because HQ wanted to talk to him and he needed the microphone and earphone built into it. It was now only the driver's glasses that kept some of the wind out of his eyes as the bike continued powering east.

"Spider, can you hear me?" Button's voice was coming through the earphone.

"Yes, I hear you." There was no mic switch so Shepherd assumed it was voice-activated.

"What's your ETA?"

"At the rate we're going four minutes, maybe five."

"You're armed?"

"I have the guns that Khalid supplied, plus a few dozen clips."

"Where were Chaudhry and Malik supposed to go?"

"They were dropping us at one of the car park entrances that would put us on the first floor. We were

470

to chain the doors, start shooting and then escape via Marks & Spencer."

"Spider, it looks as if most of the vans are heading to the car parks. We're taking them down now so the imminent threat is from the terrorists arriving by the tube and by bus. The likelihood is that they will be heading for the main entrances on the ground floor and the lower ground floor."

"Which is where I should be?"

"Exactly. The first ARVs to reach the mall will head for the main entrance too and move in that way."

Shepherd looked at his watch. It was eight minutes to six. "Charlie, you have to give them my description. Blue jeans, black polo shirt, brown leather jacket. I'm wearing Harvey's green parka but I'll dump that as soon as I get off the bike. The last thing I need is to get caught in friendly fire."

"It'll be done," said Button. "We have ARVs en route but most of them are going to be getting there after six so you're going to be on your own for a few minutes."

Shepherd's stomach lurched as a bus pulled out in front of them. The motorcyclist had seen the vehicle and accelerated at the same time as he leaned over to the right. Shepherd leaned in sync and they missed the bus by inches. "How's Raj?" asked Shepherd.

"Raj?"

"Raj Chaudhry. I left him at the van with a gun."

"The van has just been secured. We're taking him to see Malik. Spider, one other thing. We're going to start evacuating the mall within the next couple of minutes. We're on to the mall people now and we're going to start emptying the first and second floors through the department stores."

"What about just sounding the fire alarm?"

"If the terrorists lock the ground-floor doors we'll just be sending people towards the guns," she said. "Best you and the ARVs get there first."

Shepherd looked over the shoulder of the motorcyclist. Ahead of them was Westfield mall. "Almost there, Charlie."

"Good luck, Spider."

Button looked up at the screen showing the view from the police helicopter. She could see the motorbike arriving at the main entrance to the mall. "Commander, how are we doing with the ARVs?"

"Two minutes until the first one arrives," he said. "Two minutes after that we should have a vehicle at car park B."

"And the vans in transit?"

"Two have been stopped without shots being fired. We should have the third within the next minute or so."

Button looked over at Zoe. "What's happening with the evacuation?" she asked.

"I'm having problems getting someone there to approve it," said Zoe. "No one seems to know who's responsible for authorising it."

"Head of security, presumably."

"He's saying that unless he knows the nature of the threat he's not prepared to evacuate the building. I'm contacting the owners of the mall as we speak." She held up her hand and began talking into her headset.

472

Button caught the commander's eye. "Do you have any uniforms close by?" she asked.

"Two TSG vans already, more on the way," he said. "No blues and twos and they're staying in the vans until needed."

"I think we need them in now, Commander," she said. "Tell them to go straight up to the top floor and get people moving through the department stores."

Zoe waved at Button and Button nodded for her to speak. "It's okay. The CEO is on to the head of security now. He'll get the security teams to begin moving people out."

"Through the stores, not through the main entrances," said Button. She looked back at the commander. "We still need your people in there, Commander. We need to start getting people out. But discreetly. No panic."

"They're on their way," said Commander Needham. "They've been told to say that there's going to be a power cut."

Button looked at the screen showing the overhead view of the mall. Shepherd was standing by the bike, opening his backpack. It was five minutes to six.

Shepherd rested the backpack on the pillion of the motorbike and handed the helmet to the driver. "Thanks," said Shepherd.

The driver slid the helmet on as Shepherd unzipped the backpack. The guns were both Glocks, similar to the MI5-issued one that he'd left with Chaudhry. He pulled one out, ejected the magazine, checked that it was full and then slotted it back into place.

"Anything I can do?" asked the driver.

"Are you firearms trained?" asked Shepherd. He slid the Glock into his shoulder holster.

"Afraid not. Strictly surveillance."

"Then thanks but no thanks," said Shepherd. He took off Malik's parka and gave it to the driver. "You can hang on to that for me, if you don't mind." He shouldered the backpack and began running towards the main entrance.

Zoe waved over at Charlotte Button. "The security guards on the upper floor are now directing people out of the mall and into the department stores."

"Excellent," said Button. She looked over at the clock. Four minutes to six.

"We've just intercepted the fourth van," said the commander. "It was heading for car park B. Four men in custody; no shots fired."

"And the ARVs?"

"First one will arrive in about one minute. Second one two minutes later."

"Make sure they have a full description of Spider and explain that he is armed. I don't want any friendly fire incidents."

"They've been informed," said the commander.

Button looked up at the screen showing the overhead view from the helicopter. Spider was running towards the main entrance.

Heads turned as Shepherd ran through the crowds. He scanned the faces, his trick memory comparing them with the photographs he'd seen at Thames House. He slowed to a jog as he reached the entrance. The glass doors were wide open as shoppers poured in. He walked into the mall and checked his watch. There were three minutes to go before six o'clock. That meant that the terrorists were almost certainly already in place. He looked around, breathing slowly and evenly.

Two security guards were standing to his left. They were Asians, wearing black suits and with their identification cards in clear plastic cases strapped to their arms. One was in his forties, dark-skinned and wearing tinted glasses. The other was younger, with lighter skin, and carrying something in his hands. Shepherd moved to the side to get a better look. The man was holding a length of chain and a padlock. The older man looked at his watch. There was a black Timberland backpack at his feet. The two men were standing with their backs to the wall, watching the shoppers walking into the mall. Two middle-aged Chinese women went over and asked them for directions and the younger security guard pointed up to the first floor.

Shepherd walked over, his hand slipping inside his jacket. "How's it going, guys?" he asked.

"Can we help you, sir?" asked the older guard.

Shepherd stood facing them, using his body to conceal the Glock as he pulled it out. "I need the two of you to stand facing each other right now," said

Shepherd. "If you don't I'll shoot you." The younger guard opened his mouth to speak but Shepherd jabbed the gun in his stomach. "Don't say anything. Just do it. I don't have time to fuck around." The men turned to face each other. Shepherd patted them down but didn't find a gun. He kicked the backpack to the side. It was heavy. He took the chain and padlock with his left hand and gestured with the gun. "Put your arms round each other, like you were hugging." The men hesitated and Shepherd jabbed the younger guard again with the barrel of the gun. "Do it or I swear I'll shoot you both."

The two men put their arms round each other. Shepherd kept hold of one end of the chain and let the rest fall to the floor. He draped it over the neck of the younger guard, then, using his left hand, he wrapped the chain round their waists and round their necks; finally he pushed it between them and pulled it hard to tighten it. He fastened the chain with the padlock and pushed the men to the floor. The guards said nothing as they glared defiantly up at Shepherd. He holstered his Glock, picked up the backpack and began to run to the entrance at the far end of the mall. Several shoppers saw what was going on but hurried by, not wanting to get involved. London was a city where passers-by who intervened in violent situations tended to end up in hospital. Or worse.

The mall was so crowded that Shepherd couldn't manage more than a jog and he was constantly having to change direction. People he banged into cursed and shouted at him but he was so focused on checking faces that what they said barely registered. He was looking for two things: faces from the Thames House surveillance photographs and Asians with backpacks.

He took a quick look at his watch. A minute and a half to go. He barged between a group of teenagers. One of them lashed out with his foot and caught Shepherd's calf but Shepherd barely felt it. He slowed to a walk, scanning faces. Walking in through the glass doors were two Asians in Puffa jackets, both carrying backpacks. Shepherd's hand went to his gun. One of the Asians said something and the other laughed. They were too relaxed to be a threat, Shepherd realised. One of them went over to a display of store guides; he took one and unfolded it. The two men looked around, trying to get their bearings. Shepherd took a deep breath, knowing that he had come close to shooting two innocent shoppers.

He moved closer to the doors. A police ARV arrived and it screeched to a halt. The doors opened and three armed officers got out, all holding MP5s. A tall Asian man in a long raincoat walking from the train station whirled round to look at the police car. He had a backpack and he took it off and began to fumble inside it. He turned so that his back was to the approaching policemen. Shepherd caught a glimpse of a pistol. He pulled out his Glock and fired twice, catching the man in the centre of his chest.

The armed police all jumped as if they'd been stung and then crouched low as they covered the area with their MP5s. Shepherd threw down the backpack that he'd taken from the security guards and turned and ran from the doors. He didn't have time to explain to the police that he was on their side. People were screaming all around him and some were running out into the street.

He slotted the Glock back in its holster as he ran towards the escalators that led to the lower ground floor. He stopped and looked down over the balcony. No one on the lower ground floor had reacted to the screaming or to the shooting.

He couldn't see the doors that led to the outside, but he heard shouts of "Armed police" at the entrance behind him. He hurried on.

As he rode down the escalator he looked left and right, scanning faces, checking for bags. He was almost at the bottom when he saw an Asian man with a backpack facing a shop window and looking at his watch. As the man turned round Shepherd recognised him. He was one of the men from Leeds who had arrived at St Pancras on the tube. The man started to walk away from the shop and Shepherd ran up behind him. He pulled out his Glock and slammed it against the side of the man's head and he slumped to the ground without a sound. Two middle-aged women screamed and backed away from Shepherd as he holstered his gun. Shepherd looked down at the unconscious man. He'd be out for a while, certainly until the police had arrived in force.

Most of the shoppers in the vicinity seemed unconcerned about what had happened and continued to walk by, looking down at the prone figure but not stopping to help. Even the two screaming women soon fell silent and hurried away.

Shepherd did a full three-sixty turn but didn't see anyone else that he recognised so he jogged over to the entrance that led to the tube station. He stopped when he saw that an Asian man in a green anorak with the hood up was walking purposefully towards the entrance. Shepherd had seen the man's face before, in Thames House. It was the Egyptian, Riffat Pasha. Pasha was carrying a backpack in his right hand as he looked at his watch. He looked scared, as if he might be having second thoughts about what he was about to do.

Shepherd ran towards him, pulling out his Glock. Pasha saw him, saw the gun, and then began to grope inside his backpack. Shepherd stopped, steadied himself and took aim. As Pasha's hand appeared from the backpack holding a gun, Shepherd fired twice, both shots to the chest. Pasha fell backwards and hit the ground hard. Shoppers screamed in terror and began running out of the mall.

"He's got a gun!" screamed a woman with close-cropped hair and a nose ring.

Shepherd looked at her in amazement. "I think they know that," he said.

The woman pointed at Shepherd. "He's got a gun!" she screamed again at the top of her voice. She backed away, then turned and ran towards the entrance.

Blood was pooling around Pasha. His legs shuddered and then went still.

"Armed police! Drop your weapon!"

The shout came from above him. Shepherd looked up. Two cops on the floor above were aiming their MP5s at him. A third armed officer was on the escalator, keeping his weapon trained on Shepherd as he moved smoothly down to the lower ground floor.

"Armed police! Armed police!" More shouts, this time from the entrance to his left. Two more armed officers.

Shepherd bent down and placed the Glock on the floor, then straightened up and put his hands behind his neck. He slowly knelt down and waited as the armed police ran towards him. "Please don't shoot me," he muttered to himself. "I really don't like being shot."

Khalid beamed and looked across at Abu al Khayr. "It is after six o'clock, brother," he said. "It has started."

The two men were alone in the sitting room of a terraced house in Tower Hamlets, home to an Afghan refugee and his family. The man was a diehard Taliban soldier but had claimed to have been a government official who had been forced out of his village under threat of death. In fact al-Qaeda had funded his travel from Afghanistan to the UK and had guided him through the asylum process. Along with him had come his wife and four children. All had been in the country for three years and his council-funded home was often used as a safe house and as a place to store weapons and materials. A false wall behind the water tank in the attic had concealed more than a dozen of the handguns that were being used in the attack on the shopping mall.

The man had taken his wife and children to see a movie and was under instructions not to return before

480

nine that evening. But there were two other men in the house; both worshipped at a mosque in west London and were trusted associates of Khalid's.

Khalid was sitting on a sofa with a floral pattern and Abu al Khayr was settled in a matching armchair. On a pine coffee table between them were eight cheap Nokia phones lined up in a row. On the wall above the fireplace was an LCD television tuned to Sky News. Khalid knew from experience that the station was almost always the first to cover a breaking news story.

"How long before we know?" asked Abu al Khayr.

On the television a blonde woman with unnaturally smooth skin and hair that looked like a blonde plastic helmet was talking earnestly about a car crash on a motorway in the north of England.

"The first reports should be out within minutes," said Khalid. "Someone will call the station because they pay for tip-offs. They will check with the police and then they will announce it. But it will take another half an hour or so before they have pictures." He rubbed his beard. "But as we speak the kaffirs are being killed in their hundreds. It is a glorious day, brother, a day that will live for eternity."

"It is a pity that we could not be there to witness it," said Abu al Khayr. "It would be quite something to see."

"There will be CCTV footage of everything and the media will show it," said Khalid. "The whole world will bear witness to our triumph."

"Allahu akbar," said Abu al Khayr.

"Allahu akbar," echoed Khalid.

They heard a dull thud from the hallway.

"What was that?" asked Abu al Khayr.

Khalid pulled a face. He stood up and as he did so he saw a movement through the lace curtains at the window that overlooked the street. Three men, all dressed in black, their faces concealed. He turned to say something to Abu al Khayr but at that instant something smashed through the window and rolled across the carpet. It was a small metal cylinder and Khalid immediately recognised it for what it was. He closed his eyes and clamped his hands over his ears. The flash-bang was deafening even with his ears covered and he staggered back.

The door to the sitting room was kicked open and a black figure burst into the room, cradling an MP5. The gun kicked twice and Abu al Khayr slumped back with two holes in his chest pumping blood.

Two more soldiers moved into the room and fanned left and right, bent low as their guns swept the room.

Khalid's ears were still ringing from the explosion but he raised his hands high. "I am a British citizen!" he shouted. "I demand to see a lawyer!"

"That's not going to happen," said the soldier.

"I have my rights!" shouted Khalid. "I am a citizen and I am unarmed. I do not have a weapon."

The soldier used his left hand to pull out a Zastava M88 pistol from the holster on his hip. He tossed it at Khalid and it bounced off the man's chest and clattered to the floor. Khalid stared at it in horror.

"You do now," said the soldier. He brought his left hand up to support the MP5 and pulled the trigger twice. The first shot hit Khalid in the chest, just above the heart, and the blood hadn't even begun to flow from the wound before the second shot hit him in the face. Khalid fell backwards and hit the coffee table hard before rolling off it and ending up on the carpet. Mobile phones were scattered around his body.

Major Allan Gannon pulled down the mask that had been covering his face and he clicked on his radio. "Tell her ladyship that we have neutralised the situation, Terry," he said into his radio mic. "No survivors." He clicked off the mic. "What the lady wants, the lady gets," muttered the Major. He stepped over Khalid's body, picked up the M88 in his gloved hand and pressed it into Khalid's lifeless palm.

The doctor finished examining Malik's mangled foot and replaced the dressing.

"Will I be able to play the piano again, Doc?" asked Malik. The doctor smiled but didn't reply.

"Well, it's good to see that you haven't lost your sense of humour," said Button.

The doctor took a final look at Malik's chart and then left. They were in a private room in Cromwell Hospital in South Kensington. Malik had been booked in under an assumed name.

"What happens now?" asked Malik.

"You stay here until you're well enough to leave," said Button. "Then it's up to you."

"I suppose it could have been a lot worse," said Malik. He nodded at Shepherd. "If John hadn't turned up." He shuddered at the thought of what would have happened if the torturing had continued.

"Yeah, well, maybe next time you'll be more careful," said Chaudhry. "I mean, the fact that a pretty girl seemed interested in you really should have tipped you off that you were being set up."

"Yeah, well, twenty-twenty hindsight is a wonderful thing. Who was she anyway?" Malik asked Button. "She isn't a student, right?"

"Her name is Alena Kraishan. She was born in Palestine but has spent time in Iraq and the Gulf states under other names."

"Is she in al-Qaeda?"

"She works for pretty much any Islamic terrorist group that pays her," said Button.

"How old is she?" asked Malik.

"Thirty-one," said Button.

"She looked good for thirty-one," said Malik. He shook his head. "Bloody typical. First time a really fit bird fancies me and it turns out she just wants to kill me."

"Harvey, focus, will you?" said Chaudhry. He looked at Button. "She knew that we'd betrayed Bin Laden," he said. "We're screwed."

"Not necessarily," said Button. "The fact that she was interrogating Harvey suggests that she wasn't sure. If she knew for a fact that you were working for us she would have killed him there and then."

"It sounded like she knew everything," said Malik.

"That's what a good interrogator does," said Button.

"She was going to kill me," said Malik.

"But she didn't. And now we have her in custody."

"But as soon as she gets to a phone she'll tell them what happened," said Chaudhry.

Button shook her head emphatically. "That's not going to happen. She's being held in Belmarsh Prison. In isolation. No phone. No lawyer. No nothing."

"Can you do that?" asked Chaudhry.

"We're MI5," said Button. "We can pretty much do anything we want. She's being held under the name she used to enter the country. But the Americans have her under two other names, one of which was involved in a plot to blow up the American Embassy in Islamabad. They're asking for extradition and they're going to get it. D Notices have already been issued so there won't be a word in the press. She'll be gone within a week and the Americans won't be letting her near a phone."

"Guantanamo Bay?" asked Malik. "Do you think they'll send her there?"

"I don't know for sure what they have planned," said Button. "But a little bird did tell me that the Americans are keen to rebuild bridges with the Pakistan government and one way of doing that might be to give her to them. The Pakistanis would love to question her about terrorist groups active in Pakistan and when they've finished interrogating her they'll throw away the key. She's never going to be a threat to you again." She looked over at Chaudhry. "To either of you."

"And the two men with her?" asked Malik.

"It's going to be a package deal," said Button. "And we'll be keeping a close eye on you both for the foreseeable future." She nodded at Shepherd. "John here will be available whenever you need him. And you can have as much security as you need."

Chaudhry smiled at Shepherd. "What do you think, John?" he asked.

"I think you're both in the clear, but you might think about a change of identity. And relocation."

"Do you think that's necessary?"

"For your peace of mind, maybe. But no, I don't think they'll send anyone else. And if they do, you know what to look for."

Chaudhry grinned. "Yeah, pretty girls who want their laptops repaired."

"Hey, she was very convincing," said Malik.

"I'm not sure that you're going to have to do anything drastic," said Button. "We've already started a disinformation campaign to muddy the waters."

"What do you mean?" asked Malik.

"We've got the Pakistanis saying that one of Bin Laden's wives betrayed him. She's in custody and they're putting it about that she was getting jealous of one of the other wives."

"A woman scorned?" said Chaudhry.

"It's perfectly possible," said Button. "She was in the compound when the Seals went in. Plus, the Americans are now suggesting that they were helped by the courier that died in the attack. It's all grist to the mill."

"So you think it's over?" asked Chaudhry.

"You'll still have as much protection as you need, but yes, I don't think either of you needs to worry overmuch. But if you want a change of identity we can absolutely do that for you. Also, I've spoken to my bosses and there's quite a bit of money coming your way. By way of compensation for what you went through and as thanks for everything you did."

"What about the reward for Bin Laden?" asked Chaudhry.

"We're talking to the Americans," said Button. "I'm quietly confident that at least some of that money will be coming your way."

"Too bloody right," said Chaudhry. "It's the least they can do. If it wasn't for us they'd never have known where Bin Laden was."

"So when do we get the money?" asked Malik.

Chaudhry laughed. "Bloody hell, Harvey. At least wait until you're out of bed."

"I'm just asking. I want to get started on my restaurant."

"I think you'll find you've got more than enough money to do that," said Button.

Malik grinned and flashed a thumbs-up at Chaudhry.

"What about Khalid?" Chaudhry asked Button.

"He died resisting arrest," she said.

"Which was convenient," said Shepherd.

Button raised one eyebrow. "Meaning what?"

Shepherd shrugged. "Just that it keeps things neat and tidy. With him being a British citizen it would have been a bit harder to send him off to Pakistan."

"Indeed it would have been," said Button coldly.

"So picking a fight with armed cops was convenient, that's all I'm saying." He tilted his head to one side. "Was it CO19? Or did the SAS go in?"

"The latter," said Button. "But I'd really be happier not discussing operational matters here."

"I can quite understand that," said Shepherd. He patted Chaudhry on the back. "What about you, Raj? Not thinking of going into the restaurant business with Harvey?"

Chaudhry smiled and shook his head. "I'm going to be a doctor. And I'm going to be Dr Manraj Chaudhry. I'm proud of what I've done and I don't want to hide."

"You should think about working for us," said Button. "You could do very well in MI5."

"Miss Button, that's not going to happen," he said. "Not in a million years. I've done my bit. I'll leave the job of fighting terrorists up to you."

ISIS publish a wide range of books in large print, from fiction to biography. Any suggestions for books you would like to see in large print or audio are always welcome. Please send to the Editorial Department at:

ISIS Publishing Limited
7 Centremead
Osney Mead
Oxford OX2 0ES

A full list of titles is available free of charge from:

Ulverscroft Large Print Books Limited

(UK)
The Green
Bradgate Road, Anstey
Leicester LE7 7FU
Tel: (0116) 236 4325

(Australia)
P.O. Box 314
St Leonards
NSW 1590
Tel: (02) 9436 2622

(USA)
P.O. Box 1230
West Seneca
N.Y. 14224-1230
Tel: (716) 674 4270

(Canada)
P.O. Box 80038
Burlington
Ontario L7L 6B1
Tel: (905) 637 8734

(New Zealand)
P.O. Box 456
Feilding
Tel: (06) 323 6828

Details of **ISIS** complete and unabridged audio books are also available from these offices. Alternatively, contact your local library for details of their collection of **ISIS** large print and unabridged audio books.